# Sylvie's Chance

# Sylvie's Chance

A novel
by Carolyn Dale

Cairn Shadow Press
2020

This is a work of fiction. Names, characters, places, and incidents are products of the author's imagination or are used fictitiously and are not to be construed as real. Any resemblances to actual persons, living or dead, is entirely coincidental.



Cover painting by Gerald McShane
Photograph: Louisa Magill Epperson Taylor, c. 1866

ISBN: 978-1-7341352-2-0
Library of Congress Control Number: 2020916419

Cairn Shadow Press
*Sylvie's Chance*
First Printing October 7, 2020

Contact: www.cairnshadow.com; www.carolyndale.com

Printed in the United States of America
Cairn Shadow Press
Bellingham, Wash. 98225

# Contents

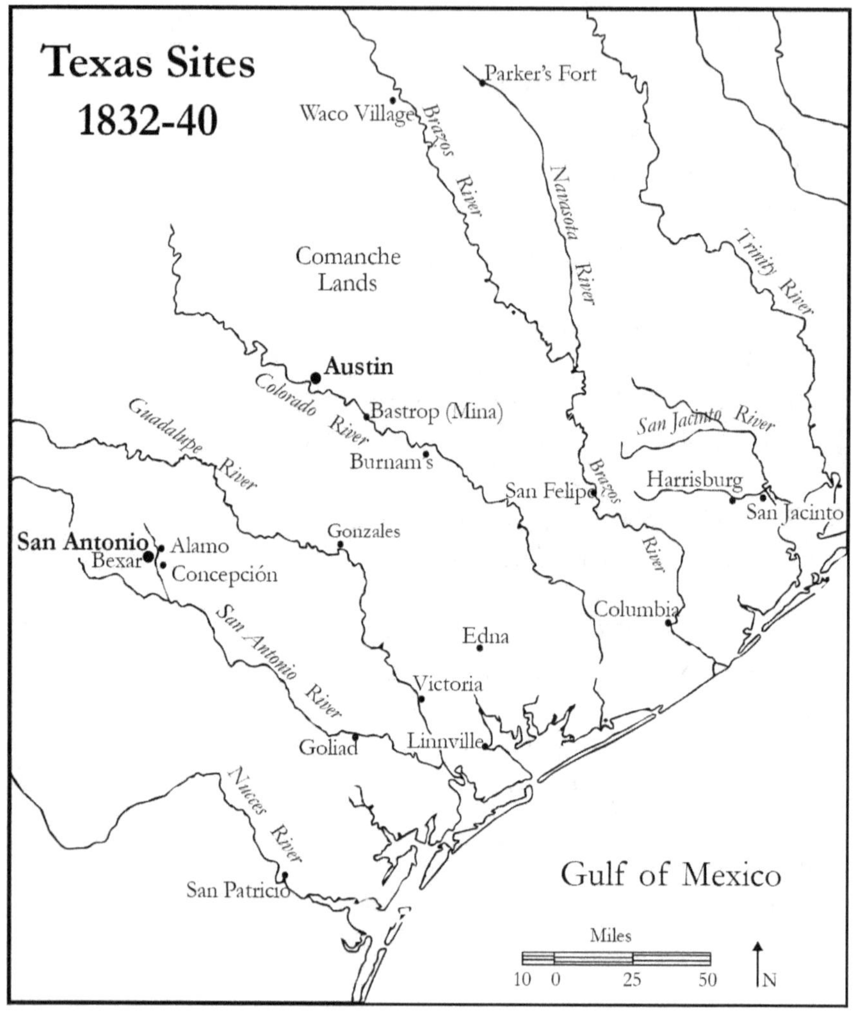



**Towns and rivers play key roles in the story of *Sylvie's Chance***

Colonies founded by Stephen Austin and other *empresarios* in Mexico's province of Coahuila y Tejas appear as settings for this novel. Much of the area became the Republic of Texas after the war for independence in 1836, and its capital, Austin, was named by 1840.

# Cast of Characters

## The French community of Cahokia, Illinois

### The Pensoneau family and relations

**Sylvie** – Marie Sylvaine is the daughter of Etienne Pensoneau and his third wife, Elizabeth Clark; she is orphaned by the age of four. Her half-siblings Laurent and Jeanne are a generation older.

**Laurent** – Son of Etienne Pensoneau and his first wife (both deceased), he is married to **Fernande,** and their eldest son is **Etienne.** They have two other boys and a young daughter, **Celeste**. After Laurent dies, Fernande remarries.

**Jeanne** – Daughter of Etienne Pensoneau and his first wife (both deceased), she becomes legal guardian for Sylvie when Laurent dies. She is married to **Nicolas,** and among their children are:

• **Marguerite**, the eldest, who marries **Vital Jarrot.**

• **Isabelle**, who wishes to marry **Edward**, her first cousin once removed; she is close to Sylvie's age, and the two are good friends.

**Amy** – Formerly a slave, her status was changed to indentured servant by Sylvie's father. When she gains freedom, she wishes to join family and friends in New Orleans.

**Matthieu** – A slave once owned by Sylvie's father, he was sold by Laurent and Jeanne along with the gristmill where he worked. Due to his age, Matthieu remains enslaved under Illinois laws.

**David Kerr** – Sylvie's half-brother from her mother's first marriage, he lives in Missouri and marries there. Their mother married James Kerr's older brother, John, and following his death, married Etienne Pensoneau. Elizabeth died when Sylvie was four and David was about seven years old.

**Aunt Lizette LeCompte Pensoneau** – Widow of Louison, the older brother of Etienne Pensoneau, she is the daughter of **Old**

**Mme. LeCompte,** who is more than one hundred years old. Lizette is the mother of ten children, including:

- **Paschal**, a trader and translator, who marries Shikina, a Kickapoo Indian, and joins her band when they are forced west of the Mississippi River.
- **Edward**, who manages the family's farmlands and is in love with his first cousin once-removed, **Isabelle**.
- **Narcisse**, a lawyer, who speculates in land and develops a new town; he marries a distant relative, Félicité Pensoneau.
- **Louisa**, a close friend of Sylvie's, marries **Octave Borne** and moves to New Orleans.

## The Jarrot family

**Madame Julie** – Wealthy widow of Nicolas Jarrot, she is a noted hostess among the French communities; she has five daughters and two sons:

- **François,** a physician who served in the Black Hawk War and contracted consumption.
- **Vital**, a lawyer and adjutant colonel in the war, who marries Jeanne's daughter **Marguerite** and pursues politics with his friend **Abraham Lincoln**. He is a trader, land agent, and entrepreneur in a number of ventures.

# American Colonies in Texas

## The Kerr family and relations

**James "Jim" Kerr** – Sylvie's uncle by her mother's first marriage, he is one of Stephen Austin's original colonists in Texas, and later administers the DeWitt colony. He marries **Sarah Fulton**, and the two have a son, **Charles**. Jim's daughter **Minny** is the only surviving child from his first marriage.

**Aunt Peggy** – Margaret Kerr Brown is Jim's sister; she lives on a farm in Troy, Missouri, and her husband has been a trader in Texas.

**Nancy Brown** – A settler in Gonzales, and widow of John "Waco" Brown, she runs her home as a boarding house with her one surviving child, **Duff**.

**Peter Kerr** – Distantly related to James Kerr, he is awarded the contract for a mail route after his first business ventures in Texas fail. He eventually settles in Bastrop (formerly Mina) and goes into the cattle business.

**Anise** and **Shade** – A couple whose oldest son is **Jack;** other children are **Nelson, Caroline** and **Edwina**. They and others in the extended family, **Annette** and **Rosanah**, were brought as slaves to Texas from James Kerr's home in Missouri.

**The Magill family**

**Andrew** – Elder son of **Samuel** and **Nancy Magill** of Kentucky, he arrives in Texas in 1834 and joins Stephen Austin's colony at Mina (later Bastrop) in 1835. He serves as an early Texas Ranger and fights in battles for Texan independence from Mexico. His sister stays in Kentucky when his parents come to Texas along with his younger brother **James.**

**Logan Vandeveer** – A cousin to Andrew Magill, and an early settler in Mina (Bastrop), he and his brother begin a cattle business. He marries **Lucinda Mays.**

**Rachel Berry Flint** – A distant cousin to William Magill, she lives in Gonzales and is widowed a second time when her husband is killed at the Alamo in 1836. She has children from both marriages and flees with her family toward the San Jacinto River after the town is burned down.

# Acknowledgments

Many people generously shared their time and expertise over the dozen years I spent researching this novel. I remain very grateful to them, and to the others who have helped immensely with the book's editing and design.

Le Centre de Référence de l'Amérique Française, Quebec, Canada, welcomed me to its archives, and Peter Gagné, archivist, helped to locate and translate unpublished records compiled by Cyprien Tonguay of early Pensoneau genealogy in La Cahokie, Illinois. This started my long voyage of discovery about my ancestors.

Staff at the Bastrop County Historical Society and Museum, Bastrop, Texas, readily opened their files on William H. Magill, my grandfather five generations back, and identified the current location of his home in the 1830s. The owners of the Orgain Mansion, who maintain the house, welcomed my husband and me and invited us to tour and photograph it.

James L. Haley, exhibit curator at Joseph & Susanna Dickinson Hannig Museum, Austin, shared helpful insights and resources on women's lives in early Gonzales, Texas. Robert Garcia, volunteer at Mission Conceptión National Historic Park, San Antonio, gave a vivid recounting of the battle in 1835 and his ancestors' role in it, as well as in the siege of Bexar. I am also indebted to him for the book *San Antonio and its Beginnings*.

Three online resources have been especially valuable for detailed accounts and documents of the 1830s in Texas: the Texas Historical Association Handbook Online, the Sons of DeWitt Colony Website, and the Texas General Land Office database. All of these provided essential background reading. A fuller list of helpful sources appears at the end of this book.

For encouragement, support, critiques, and suggestions, I am especially indebted to my first readers: Tim Pilgrim, Anna Eblen, Kathy Sheehan, Bonnie Henning, Penny Page, Roz Spitzer, and Sarah

Brownsberger. Special thanks go to Glen Larum for perusing several versions, and to Karen Brown, for her invaluable copy editing. Jan Dale Koutsky assisted with art, design, and graphics, for which I am very grateful.

This story would not have emerged without the research and documents pertaining to Magill and Pensoneau family histories compiled by Ella Jordan Dale, Barbara Dale Thompson, Eugene "Bud" Dale, and their heirs. The family photo of Louisa Magill from 1866, which appears on the cover of this book, both haunted and intrigued me while I was growing up. I kept wondering, *What was her story?* And as I delved into historical research, I discovered her parents' tale, which is depicted in this novel. No photo exists of Marie Rebecca Pensoneau Magill, the basis for the fictional heroine Sylvie, since she died before the age of photography. Instead, I imagine this photo of her daughter Louisa suggests what she looked like.

Truly, without the support and involvement of generations of my family, this book would not exist. The inspiration itself arises from their longtime interest in history and geneaology, and from the great storytelling I was fortunate to hear over many years. With special thanks to my grandmothers, great-grandmothers, and their grandmothers.

— Gratefully, Carolyn Dale, August 2020

# Prologue

**April 1836**
**West of the Brazos River, Mexico**

Sylvie Pensoneau had been foraging wild greens for the past few days, finding cress along the stream and wild onions and garlic farther back in the woods, so she knew where to start hunting for deer. But it was early April, and while her conscience pleaded that this was not the right season, her reason spoke up sternly: she had to provide for her fellow refugees and keep the group alive—all the little ones plus their mother who had just given birth back in the cabin.

The place belonged to Mrs. Carter, an elderly woman who had taken them in off the road, desperate as they were with hunger and drenched from continuous rains. She had helped with the childbirth and was letting them stay for a few days. Sylvie had coaxed the friendlier of Mrs. Carter's two dogs to join her on outings, and now they were following a faint animal trail uphill and across an open, grassy meadow.

On the far side, thin trees grew so tightly that they cut the light and air; within the copse, leaf buds still held tight and dry leaves crackled underfoot. This was the right kind of place for pheasant, turkey, or deer. She would have to spot a young buck, though, rather than kill a doe in springtime.

The dog knew to stay still as they waited, listening, among the trees. When it did emit a low rumble, she shushed it. When it gave short barks, Sylvie suddenly saw the Indian, a young man about her age, who stood nearby, watching her. He wore a blanket over one shoulder and cradled a rifle across his chest. She knew it would be primed and ready, though the way he regarded her seemed more curious than threatened—or threatening. He wore buckskin leggings with wide, decorated side panels and beaded knee bands.

The dog backed up, growling and glaring from side to side, and Sylvie realized she was already surrounded. The other Indians would soon step forward, depending on what this one decided. Her sight tunneled to a dark corridor with the sky at the end amid unfurling leaves, the last she might ever see. Her thudding heartbeat blocked all other sound. When her vision cleared after a few moments, she looked back toward the man.

He was tall, with a long nose and lean cheeks. His black hair was pulled to the back, and he wore a headband that was finely beaded and embroidered, its elaborate floral vines outlined in black. The cluster of feathers attached at the side pointed downward, and now she realized that though he looked nothing like local Indians—Karankawa, Apache, Waco—he also did not look like the greatly feared Comanche.

In fact, he resembled Indians from Sylvie's childhood along the Mississippi River in southern Illinois, a world away from these woods stretching along the road that connected American colonies in Mexico. Her family had a legacy of dealing with several tribes over past generations, reaching back to the early fur trade in French Canada. He could be a Delaware, one of the consummate traders along routes stretching this far west. She had not pointed her rifle at him, and now she lowered it, holding it loosely across her waist.

His glance traveled from her braids, weather-tanned skin, and worn calico dress down to her moccasins, whose elaborately beaded floral design, resembling the one on his headband, gleamed in the low light. She was nineteen, but she was small in stature for an adult. Her dark eyes and black hair would suggest French heritage—or, more likely, Spanish, around here.

*"Bonjour,"* Sylvie said.

His eyes flickered with understanding, but he did not speak.

Three other Indian men emerged, and then she saw, indistinctly through the trees, a train of pack mules and a boy holding light halters of several horses. Another man, shorter, approached her. He wore a finely beaded wide shoulder strap, or bandolier, attached to a bag that fit snugly on the side of his shirt; the designs and fringe on both could only be Delaware work.

*"Bonjour,"* he replied. *"Vous êtes Française?"*

She nodded, and he inquired what she was doing in these woods and where the rest of her people were.

When she asked if he was Delaware and he nodded, Sylvie decided she might trust him with the truth. She could not recall any Delaware fighting against American settlers in this province of Mexico, Coahuila y Tejas. Continuing in French, she explained she was hunting game for herself and friends who were fleeing the war between colonists and the Mexican army; they were hungry and had no means.

"You are filling the roads, all you refugees. We have seen hundreds of people, women and children. Your army flees also and does not fight." The men shook their heads.

Sylvie sighed, for there was no way to counter such a sad and desperate assessment. The main army for the Texas colonists and settlers who were fighting for independence from Mexico had been massacred at Goliad, and the other forces—quickly assembled militia groups of farmers and ranchers—were moving east, keeping ahead of Mexican troops.

She had been in the town of Gonzales when it was burned down and had set out with the others in the middle of the night to flee toward safety in Louisiana. That was weeks ago, and a hundred miles since—on foot or driving the creaking oxcart. She knew the Delawares' trading networks ran from the Eastern seaboard through Illinois and Missouri and now extended to the edge of the Great Plains, so she asked about this group's route.

The man replied that they had been to Santa Fe and were now returning to Missouri. "We are traveling off the main roads to stay away from this war."

"Do you know the Kickapoo in Missouri? Do you know any French traders with them?" Sylvie asked. When he nodded, she rushed on. "My cousin, my kinsman, is a translator and trader for them. His name is Paschal Pensoneau, and he is married to the daughter of a chief; her name is Shikina. When that band had to move west of the Mississippi River, Paschal went with them."

"I know of him; we have done business in the past. He is the main translator for the Delaware on the Missouri, at a place the *Anglais* call Westport."

Relief flooded over Sylvie. Not only was she establishing rapport with these traders, but she also had gained some family news. Years had gone by without her hearing how Paschal was faring

"Are you going there, to Westport?" she asked. The man nodded, watching Sylvie closely.

"And do you have food to trade? Will you do some trading with me now?" Sylvie waited while he considered her question.

"What do you have to exchange?" He was looking at her rifle, but she rested that against a tree and stooped to take off her moccasins. As she held them out, the beadwork glittered in a narrow shaft of sunlight. She could tell he was interested. They were nearly new, for she had barely worn them since the day Paschal had given them as a gift, back home in Illinois.

"If you accept these, you can take them to my cousin. He will know they are from me; my name is Sylvie—Marie Sylvaine. Tell him that you helped me by giving us food after we were driven from our homes by this war. I am certain he will be quite generous with you in return."

The man remained silent, and Sylvie added, "These moccasins have substantial trade value, as you can see."

Finally, he nodded. "We have some food to spare. You are how many?"

"Five children, four adults, and a newborn baby."

The man shook his head in dismay that women and children would be left in such straits. He signaled, and two others approached. After conferring in low voices, they began smiling, and Sylvie imagined they were discussing how they might turn this transaction into a substantially favorable exchange later with Paschal.

The first man went back to the pack train and after a few moments arrived with game birds and several pouches. Sylvie allowed herself some deep breaths.

*"Les dindes,"* the man said, handing her two gutted turkeys tied by their feet. "And dried venison, pemmican, flour, maize. Do you want tobacco?"

"No, no one uses tobacco."

"It is money; you can trade it with soldiers, and then maybe some *Anglais* will help you. The food is only for women and children. None of this can go to either army—not to Texan forces, nor to Mexican. We have to remain neutral as we pass through this territory, and we cannot be seen as taking sides."

"I understand."

The men now avoided looking her in the eye, and her skin pricked at their pity. It was humiliating that the Texan army had been slaughtered and the militia troops were retreating, that uprooted settlers, women and children by the hundreds, were trailing them along the primitive roads. She knew the same had been done to Indian villages when entire tribes were forced off their lands and made to trudge for months to new, unfamiliar places. That history gave these men a clear view of her current plight.

"The boy will go with you a ways," the older Delaware told her. "Do not imagine that you two are alone, or that you can lead him into a trap. No one else will see us, however."

*"D'accord,"* Sylvie agreed. This group must have had as many as twenty mules; some carried large bundles of fur and hides, most likely buffalo and beaver. She could see a few horses farther back among the trees from where the boy was emerging to escort her.

"Goodbye, cousin of Paschal Pensoneau," the man said. "He is a good trader. He advanced us money, gunpowder, and supplies for this trip, against the furs and silver we are bringing back. These trade moccasins will count nicely—in our favor, of course."

"It will work out well," Sylvie agreed. And yet she wondered how Paschal would react to news of her being encountered alone, scrawny and travel worn, in the woods of eastern Texas. The last time she had seen him at his mother's house in Cahokia, he had teased her about going to the American colonies in Mexico. Surely he would recognize the moccasins and wonder about her ventures over the past several years.

The boy followed Sylvie downhill, across the meadow and past the creek, and left her within sight of the cabin. She turned to shake hands and thank him, and they wished each other good luck as they said farewell: *"Adieu et bonne chance."*

She began to breathe regularly and said a few cheerful things to the dog, imagining the others' amazement and delight when she returned with the food. She moved easily across grassy areas but in others felt the sting of rocks and a few spines of nopal cactus growing low to the ground. Many of the refugees were traveling barefoot, and now she would as well.

"Westport, Westport." She repeated the place where Paschal lived, embedding it in memory. The dog padded next to her, wagging its tail at the smell of meat. These goods would sustain her group for a time, perhaps even renew some vitality and hope. But if their lives as refugees outlasted the supplies, what else could she find to do?

# Part 1

Summer 1832 — Spring 1833

∼

The French communities of
Cahokia, Illinois; Ste. Geneviève, Missouri;
and New Orleans, Louisiana


Voyage on the Gulf of Mexico

Chapter 1

**August 1832 – Nearly four years earlier**
**Cahokia, Illinois**

Sylvie felt closest to her parents when she looked out over the Mississippi River from the high bluffs on the Illinois side. Her mother and father had died before she was four years old, and she remembered her mother as a soft voice singing in English, her father as a dark figure in a brocade vest that scratched her cheek as she sat on his lap, his voice rumbling from deep inside, emerging in French.

On this August morning already growing warm, she gazed down at the deep-flowing green current, feeling certain they had loved this river and all the rivers that had brought them and their forebears from early Québec to Montreal, then west along the waterways for furs, then south to the little outpost of Cahokia, below on the banks, which had grown to be the heart of the French trading system for the entire Mississippi River Valley.

That was long ago, and today Sylvie had resolved to start setting a course for her own future. Feeling keenly that she was only fifteen years old, plus an orphan, it was reassuring to sense her ancestors' presence, to draw on it as a touchstone for her day's mission. First, though, she sat on her favorite flat gray rock and unpacked a bit of breakfast.

She'd risen at the farmhouse before anyone else was awake and packed chunks of bread and cheese, a flask with cold coffee from the night before, and an apple and carrot for the horse, which she'd saddled on her own. She'd managed to ride a ways on the main road and cross into the verge's bushes and trees without meeting any neighbors who would ask where she was going, setting off so early. She planned to ride into Cahokia to pay a visit, and it was not seemly for a girl to make the twenty-mile round trip alone. She didn't fear Indian attacks—

the war against Black Hawk's bands of Sac and Fox had ended earlier in the summer—but she was wary of the strangers who now traveled the roads, the arriving Americans who spoke German, Dutch, and strange varieties of English from Scotland and Ireland.

The horse whickered companionably and bumped its nose against her knee. It was switching its tail against the rising mosquitoes, and the coarse hairs stung Sylvie's shins below her brown calico skirt sprigged with red. She brushed off crumbs and took another drink of coffee before getting up to resume their trip.

The loud bark of an air horn drifted up from the river, and peering beyond the treetops, she could see the new steam-powered ferry *Ibex* pulling away from the quay near Cahokia, a black plume of smoke puffing from its funnel as it cut across the current, en route to the town of St. Louis on the western bank. Sunlight silvered the edges of its arrowhead wake. As that noise faded, faint breeze carried the sound of distant voices chanting. Farther south, she could make out crewmen hauling the heavy ropes of a keel boat, working their way slowly north along the towpath toward the port.

St. Louis itself stood gleaming in the sunlight, both its high wooden palisades girding the long, straight streets—nearly twenty, now—and its symmetrical blocks of white stone houses. The city's dozen church spires wavered through layered air on their reach toward heaven, forming a mirage that kept wrinkling as updrafts of heat off the western plains mixed with humidity from the river. It was a good time for its residents to pray, Sylvie thought grimly as she turned to repack the saddlebag. As the Missouri militiamen had started coming back from the war that summer, cholera trailed their footsteps, and an epidemic now was sweeping the town, killing hundreds of people each week.

For some time, the French farming towns across the river had felt safe, and then one day a man who was ill had come into Belleville. Refused a room at the hotel, he had gone into the courthouse—and ended up dying there, the disease killed so quickly. That event began the changes spiraling in Sylvie's life, for her older half-brother Laurent, who was raising her, had gone into Belleville—their father had built that courthouse—and returned home only to take to his bed and die of cholera two days later. Sylvie shook her head, knowing she would stop to weep for a time if she followed these thoughts any further, and she took up the reins to lead the horse through the hemp and wild grapevine back toward the road.

Some time later, she arrived safely at the center of Cahokia; she was small and light, the way was downhill, and the horse enjoyed a canter while the day was still cool. Passing Holy Family Church, with its walls of upright timbers and its pretty, round window over the entrance, she stopped before the Jarrot House and tied the horse to a rail on the street. She was paying an unexpected visit, and she started following the path through the gardens toward the solid brick house, whose pillars at the front supported a balcony that led from a ballroom on the second floor.

Soon she caught sight of Madame Julie Jarrot and two of her grown daughters seated under an arbor and engrossed in a game of cards.

When Madame Julie glanced up, she set down her hand and told her daughters that they would take a moment to talk with the young Pensoneau girl. The Jarrot family was grieved by Laurent's untimely death, and as a longtime friend, Madame Julie would naturally want to help poor Sylvie if she could. She had not seen her since the funeral and the wake that had followed.

"How lovely to see you, and what a surprise," Madame Julie said, speaking French, as Sylvie drew near the table.

"It's so nice to see all of you!" Sylvie bent to kiss Madame Julie on both cheeks, which were pink over high cheekbones. With her fine, aquiline nose and wide, full-lipped smile, she was still considered lovely, deep in middle age and widowed for a dozen years. Sylvie stepped about the table to greet both daughters, bobbing past the ruffles and puffy sleeves of their dresses, which were cut low at the neck and gathered loosely below the bust. Her braids swung, colliding with their shoulders, and her skirt wafted dust from the road.

"Who is with you?" Madame Julie asked. "Surely you didn't ride all this way alone, *ma chère petite*."

"But I did; I am visiting on my own today."

At Sylvie's bright smile, Madame Julie held back any critical response. Laurent's widow, Fernande, still needed to supervise Sylvie like a parent, so was today's unlikely trip a sign that the household continued in disarray, so beset by grief?

"Please sit down and have something cool to drink." Madame Julie smiled warmly and patted a chair.

Sylvie declined and thanked her, shifting from foot to foot. "I am hoping to speak with Vital, please, if he is at home."

Madame Julie replied that he was in the office upstairs in the house, working on accounts and paperwork. "You're welcome to go in—it's down the hall past the ballroom."

As Sylvie bobbed a brief curtsy, Madame Julie asked her to be as quiet as possible because her elder son, François, was not feeling well and was resting in his room. As Sylvie  continued toward the house, Madame Julie exchanged a look with her daughters.

"*Mon dieu*," the elder one murmured. "What happens now for that poor girl?"

"I expect she'll go to live with Jeanne at some point. She is the elder half-sister, and the father's will from years ago designated her as Sylvie's guardian, if anything happened to Laurent."

"Jeanne's household is already so large, with the five children, and she's so strict!"

"True, but Sylvie gets along well with the two eldest girls, they are so close in age. The will appoints a guardian for Sylvie until she marries or turns twenty-one. So there's not much choice." Madame Julie smiled slightly with the satisfaction of knowing these details of the other family's affairs. Jeanne and her husband and children lived just a few houses away.

"*Oh, la, la*," the daughters murmured; they sighed and lightly clucked their tongues. Madame Julie absently sifted through her little pile of winnings, silver bits cut from Spanish coins. The sun was getting warm even in the shade, and her glass of lemon water felt sticky.

"*Maman*, it's your turn." Both daughters were fanning their face with their cards.

Inside the house, Sylvie crossed the cool front hallway toward the staircase to the second floor, which she had visited only a few times. The Jarrot family often hosted dinners and dances, and over the years, Sylvie had stayed downstairs with the other children. They had passed dozens of evenings playing games, sampling food off the buffet tables or hiding underneath to sip filched wine, sneaking out to the slave quarters to hear the music, and generally engaging in mischief. Vital, a dozen years older than Sylvie, had taken part in this play for years, but François, as the elder son, had become the man of the house at a young age after the father had died.

Sylvie started tiptoeing up the stairs. Partway up, on the landing where the stairway turned, sunlight from a tall window draped shadows over wood wainscoting and mauve wallpaper with little white flowers. Reaching the second floor, she stopped at the door to the ballroom, where she would dance once she turned sixteen. A few times, she had peeked around the older girls' full skirts to watch the musicians and the lively stomping and swaying, though she hadn't yet entered the room as a young woman who could be courted. But all that would change in the spring, when she made her entrance to society through this very doorway.

No one was around. She stepped onto the wooden floor shining in honey stripes from light slanting through the French doors that led out to the balcony. She took a few tentative steps and then twirled as her memory delivered a cacophony of flute, violin, and accordion, stamping feet, and lusty singing. The room looked so odd, empty, especially with the two fireplaces coming just halfway up the walls. One balcony door was propped open, and the clinking of glasses and murmur of voices floated in from outside.

She began breathing normally and danced more steps along the bright stripes on the pine flooring. She lifted her braids, visualizing her hair piled high. Her gown would be silk, seeded with pearls, flounced with satin ribbons. She grasped her skirt, which reached just below her knees, and began humming. Oh, with whom would she dance? That question merited several minutes of dreamy scenarios. There were so many young men, yet so few years of dancing—sometimes merely months—before a girl's marriage was set, the mothers decided things so efficiently.

The toe of her soft leather shoe struck a knot rising above the pine board worn down around it, and Sylvie stumbled and slowed. She lightly clasped her hands before her chest and hoped she hadn't made noise. Life was sad just now, as a surge of grief for Laurent washed over her. The surprise it brought was that she had been without it for several hours. Grief was like that, coming and going in waves, then pausing into respites that were lengthening as time passed. This golden light in the ballroom was particularly fine and warm, as diffuse as a gentle spirit. She twirled slowly, her hopeful visions feeling almost as bittersweet as memory, as though she were looking into this room from some unknowable future.

After all, she had no mother to help with her dresses, oversee her hair, lend her jewelry, or manage her suitors; no father to look on fondly yet sternly from the side of the room. She didn't have Laurent anymore, to sit at the head of the dining table as marriage scenarios played out. She mustered some loyalty and tried to imagine Fernande, or even Jeanne, acting as the doting female for her entrance into society. But it didn't quite work, and she sighed, probably a little too loudly. Then she recalled she didn't want to marry anyway, not until she was at least twenty, and she took a final twirl, her skirt whirling high above her knees.

Sylvie decided to leave the ballroom by the far doorway, which must lead to the hallway where the office was located. At least that was what she remembered from when she was very young and François had let a few children come along when he needed to get more coins for the men playing cards downstairs. He had knelt over a little red chest full of gleaming silver and gold pieces. Now she wondered if a room farther down the hallway, with its door closed, was where he lay ill and asleep.

François had been in battles against Black Hawk, and the rigors of marching and camping in the woods had brought on a relapse of the lung illness the *Anglais* called consumption. He'd served as medic for the company of volunteers from Cahokia, and three men had been killed in fighting after they'd been ambushed in Kellogg's Woods. They were the town's only losses.

Sylvie found it odd that the elder Jarrot brother would serve so humbly and risk his life and health, while the younger brother, Vital, was given easier duties and a higher rank. He had served as a colonel and adjutant to John Reynolds, the governor of Illinois who had declared the war and then commanded the volunteer militia. Sylvie understood that Vital kept military records and handled correspondence. He had come back to Cahokia only recently from working at the capital with the governor.

As her eyes adjusted to the dimness, Sylvie listened closely. Where was Vital to be found? Past the partly open door at the first room, she spied the corner of a huge armoire. That might hold Madame Julie's famous dresses, the one from Paris made of cloth of gold that the daughters had worn for their weddings, or others among her bejeweled silks and satins. Sylvie could practically feel precious fabric sliding on her fingertips as she stepped through the doorway and studied the darkly shining wooden wardrobe with its beautiful inlays of light-colored strips. If she took just a few steps—two or three—and swung the door open just a touch more, for someone had failed to latch it . . . She peered into the armoire and reached a hand toward a burgundy velvet brocade.

*"Bonjour, petite, qu'est-ce qu'on fait?"*

Sylvie whipped around to see Vital at a desk, papers in hand, watching her.

"Sylvie, what are you doing? *Maman* is at home, in the front garden with my sisters." He looked serious, and Sylvie noticed that her friend of many years now had wrinkles by the outer edges of his eyes.

"Yes, I saw them, and she said I should come up." Sylvie's face grew hot as she tried to think past her embarrassment. Vital laughed and got up, and they exchanged cheek kisses. Though of medium height, he had to stoop, she was so petite. His face was brown from sun and less round than she remembered, and his dark hair drew a sharper point at the front.

When Sylvie asked if he had a few moments to talk with her, he motioned to a chair by the desk, and she glanced over the stacks of papers and account books.

"Are these records you're keeping for the war?" she asked.

"That and more. There's so much to get caught up, with the farm and the lands. The manager and overseer are very good, but only family members can make certain decisions. This business isn't very interesting for you, though. How are things at home? You are all still grieving, surely."

"Yes, it's been difficult." Despite her resolve to remain poised, Sylvie wiped quickly at the corners her eyes.

"I am sorry I wasn't back here for Laurent's funeral; I regret missing it and not being able to offer condolences. He was a fine man, and he's left not only you, but Fernande and their four children. Can you stay at home for a time and help her?"

"Yes, at least until fall, when I should go back to the convent school. But I actually came today because I have a question for you, and it bears on where I may live in the future. You keep military records, and I'd like to find out about one of my relations, my mother's son, David, from her marriage before her husband died and she married my father."

"I remember him, of course." Vital had been about sixteen when Sylvie's parents died, so he would recall how Sylvie and David, who was about five years older, had lived with their parents as a family, all together in their own large brick house in Illinoistown, now called East St. Louis.

Vital continued, "After your parents died, David went to live with an aunt and uncle on your mother's side, in Missouri, isn't that right?"

"Yes, he's been living on a farm near Troy, north of St. Louis. And I've visited him and our Aunt Peggy several times over the years. But this spring I heard he volunteered with the Missouri militia to fight Black Hawk. I believe he was in the war, and he should be back now. But I haven't heard from him, nor from my aunt. So I'm wondering if you have any records that might tell if he's all right."

"David Kerr," Vital said thoughtfully. "My work is mainly for the Illinois troops, but I am certain I would have noticed his name, given the family connection, if it appeared on lists of killed or wounded. I can check more, though, and let you know if I find anything."

"Thank you; I will appreciate any help you can give me." She paused to take a deep breath. "I am thinking of going to live with them—with David and Aunt Peggy."

"You'd go away to Missouri, and live among Americans? I would miss you a great deal—we all would—if you stayed away very long."

"But we're all Americans now, aren't we?" Sylvie smiled mischievously.

"I mean the *Anglais*, and, forgive the question, but that family is Protestant, *non?*"

*"Beh, oui."* Sylvie felt warmed that he cared where she might live and whether she might stay away long.

Vital crossed his arms, leaned back, and narrowed his eyes a bit, watching her. "You are supposed to live with Jeanne, now, as your older half-sister from your father's first marriage. She becomes your guardian; at least that's what I've been hearing from *Maman.*"

"Oh Vital, I cannot go to live at her house. She is so strict—mass twice a day, and she hardly lets her children speak without permission, and no one can say what they honestly think. And … she doesn't really love me." Sylvie's voice quavered and she cleared her throat.

"Oh, I am sure—"

"No, you should have seen her at the funeral, all laced up in her black dress, draped with veils when we're near to swooning with the heat. And we'd barely tossed the first clumps of earth onto Laurent's casket before she was telling everybody exactly what my life was going to be like. When I'm sixteen in the spring, Jeanne will want me to marry quickly, to clear the way for her own daughters."

Vital grimaced sympathetically, but Sylvie caught a glint of amusement as well. "And that would be a grim fate? Be patient, Sylvie. You will hear news soon from your aunt, or from David himself. The mail in Missouri has been very slow because of the epidemic. But tell me, do you know the company David served in, or his commanding officer?"

"He enlisted with the Clark County militia, under a Mr. Richardson. That's the last I heard."

Vital turned slightly to look down at the ledger books for a few moments. "There are some reasons why people won't want to talk about that company and what happened at the end of the war. But you might as well hear it from me. The volunteers who served under General Henry were in the battle at the end, at Bad Axe River. Right in the thick of things. But hardly any soldiers or militia were killed there."

"So why is that so bad?"

"Dozens of Indians were killed, and not just warriors and young men. Children and women and old people were shot. Some drowned trying to swim away, and others were killed while fleeing. There were incidents of scalping—not just by Indians but also by our side. It wasn't the kind of courageous battle that soldiers like to talk about."

"But not everyone would do those horrible things, surely, like killing women and children or taking scalps."

"No, clearly not. Messages I saw that were going to the generals said many of the militiamen were upset and remorseful, that they didn't realize children were trying to hide in the brush. But the Indians had wanted to surrender and weren't taken seriously. And some of the militia were calling for revenge for those attacks on settlers that happened earlier."

As they sat quietly, Sylvie began to imagine the scene and then struggled to suppress the images that arose. She did not want to place her half-brother within such horrors, though she was certain he would have behaved decently. But why had she not heard from him or her aunt, after her letters?

"Maybe when men come back from war, from battles like that, they're different from before," she said. "Do you think so? What if he is back, but he's changed?"

"I think that could be the case. Do I seem any different to you?"

"Yes, you seem a little older."

"I wasn't even in a battle myself." Vital smiled and shook his head. "This was a short war with many officers. So many ambitious men, for such a small war. Or it should have been, anyway—smaller and over sooner. There's been so much death and suffering for the Indians, as well."

Vital's voice grew low with feeling, and he paused. The Jarrot family still had extensive trading ties with a range of Indian tribes from the decades Vital's father, an immigrant from France, had devoted to building his fur trade. Vital kept in touch with different bands and families, some of whom visited the house as friends.

As he spoke of the suffering of women and children, and the villages that were destroyed, Sylvie thought of the wider impacts of the war and realized she should already have inquired about François and his health. "And your own brother, returning so ill," she commented. "How is he feeling today? Your mother said he was up here, resting."

"He's about the same. He'll recover, though, as he's young and strong. It's a question of time, eating good foods like butter and cream, and getting clean air and sunshine." François, as a physician, had instructed his family on the best treatments for his ailment. "Would you like me to see if he's awake so you can say hello?"

"No, don't disturb him. I've taken enough of your time, and I should be going. Thank you for talking with me."

"I'm glad you've brought your questions to me. I hope you'll always feel that I'm here for you, like a brother."

Sylvie smiled, not having a reason to distrust Vital. But a *brother?* Possibly not, given the way he had spoken only a short time ago. As she approached sixteen, their relationship could potentially take a new turn. Perspiration tickled her neck, for the room was becoming uncomfortably warm.

When Vital learned she had come into town alone, he offered to ride partway back with her, saying he wanted to look over some wheat fields and talk with a foreman about the coming harvest. As the fur trade shifted farther west, the Jarrots were fortunate they could live from the farmlands and businesses the father had amassed.

"By the way, you need to tell Fernande that the *habitants* have met and decided on the rotation for harvesting the wheat. They want to start with Laurent's fields first, as usual, since they're high up on the bluff. We'll have to wait longer for the fields planted lower, and leave the ones in the floodplain for last."

"I think she's been expecting that, but it's such a huge amount of labor to organize, and Laurent always handled that."

"I will come and help, and I can bring some workers. And other farmers are sure to lend field hands. So don't worry—does that help?"

Sylvie looked down at her hands clasped in her lap. "I will let Fernande know. And thank you so much; all of us will be grateful."

"Let's get a drink of water and head out," Vital said as he began straightening papers and shutting ledger books on the desk.

Soon they clambered down the stairs, almost racing each other. In the back kitchen, which was cooler from facing east and having a flagstone floor, he drew cups of water for them from the stone cistern. He wore simple brown trousers and a blue linen shirt, and he grabbed a dark, wide-brimmed military hat.

Sylvie left by the front to say goodbye, and as she exchanged cheek kisses once again, Madame Julie invited her to stay for a game of cards. "My daughters are leaving soon, and I hear that your skills are becoming interesting; it might make a challenge."

Sylvie said she would be happy to play another day and added jokingly, "But I'm not sure you have enough coin there."

Madame Julie took some silver bits and let them trickle, flashing in the sunlight. "I will make sure I'm well stocked before then, *ma chère.*"

Vital gave Sylvie an amused glance as they continued through the garden. "Just be careful, Sylvie. Maman doesn't lose very often."

Sylvie tilted her face up to meet his gaze. "I think I'm up to it, though I don't have much money for wagering."

On the street, Vital stooped and made a stirrup of his hands to help Sylvie up on her small horse. She stepped lightly on them and drew herself up at the same time that Vital gave a sudden lift. She flew over the saddle, one hand grabbing a handful of the horse's mane, the other grasping the back of the saddle. It was an old game from her childhood, and as her head bobbed down on the other side, she giggled, weak with laughter. Then she felt Vital's hands grasp her waist and lift her a bit so she could steady herself upright. She managed to swing her other leg over and then looked back at him, narrowing her eyes with something more than just laughter.

"You're very badly brought up!" she scolded.

He laughed as he got on his tall horse, which a groom had brought around from the back, and they started down the main street of Cahokia. Both Sylvie and Vital glanced at the cemetery as they passed Holy Family Church. Their fathers had helped to rebuild the church in 1799, from a fire that had destroyed it years earlier. That had been the first project they'd worked on together, and later, both had built businesses and gristmills. Vital's father had become ill and died after working in winter weather on an experimental mill with a horizontal wheel. Sylvie's father had died just two weeks later, on New Year's Eve, 1820. The two men had built big brick houses, platted rival towns, and vied in accumulating lands. Nicolas Jarrot had outdone all of the local French in that regard and left nearly 35,000 acres at his death. The two men's graves lay just yards apart in the cemetery.

The horses stepped neatly to avoid a few wandering pigs and cows, and Vital's mount tried for an apple on a low-hanging branch. Vital checked him, and the horse showed his teeth but kept a smooth gait. Sylvie sat up straight on her pony, picturing how they made a fine sight. Yet their various relatives and acquaintances in the town of twelve hundred souls, glancing from windows or gardens, orchards or outbuildings, saw Sylvie, the little orphan Pensoneau girl, with her dusty shins, hiked-up skirt, and loose black braids, riding next to the twenty-seven-year old colonel and adjutant general, who was also the richest and most eligible bachelor around. Her pony took three quick steps for every two strides by his large black horse.

Chapter 2

**August 1832**
**Cahokia, Illinois**


WHEN SYLVIE HAD RIDDEN UPHILL A WAYS, she paused to turn and look back at the fields of wheat where Vital stood talking with an overseer, his military hat and his black horse forming distinct dark shapes against the shimmering silver-gold wheat. The fields reached to the foot of a tall earthen pyramid called Monks Mound, and as her horse walked uphill, she enjoyed studying its steep, grassy slopes and imagining what must be inside. This mound was the largest of a handful of ancient earthworks in the area. They all lined up, and she liked to picture rooms underneath the grass, possible burial sites holding jewelry, tools, and other precious objects placed nearby the ones who had departed, for their use in the afterlife. While the French had been in the area for a hundred and fifty years, these mounds were created by a civilization much further back in time.

More recently, the main mound had been home to a band of monks from Europe who made a discovery that was changing Cahokia's fortunes. One night during a thunderstorm, a monk spotted a flare of lightning that hit the riverbank to the south and ignited something, which turned out to be a seam of coal. The news produced feverish excitement over the possibility of mining, though Sylvie couldn't imagine why anyone would prefer that to farming the American Bottoms, reputedly the richest farmland in the United States. The monks abandoned the area after perennially falling ill and laying blame on the water from Cahokia Creek, which they said was too polluted to drink.

Sylvie could see no sign of the monks' habitation, and as the horse trod the steeper grade in the afternoon heat, she had trouble coaxing it to more than a slow pace. She was getting hungry from missing the usual midday meal and suspected the family must have noticed her absence by then. She stopped to dismount in a shady spot, shared water from a flask with the horse, and fed it the apple while she chewed the last bit of dry bread.

As they drew near the top of the bluffs, Sylvie could see more of the river channel, as well as grayish-white clouds piling high to the south. A few were forming flat undersides that could signal thunder-storms later. *Please, no heavy rain before the wheat harvest,* Sylvie mentally prayed to the powers in charge of her universe. *Thunder, maybe, and a little lightning, but no rain!*

By the time Sylvie reached Laurent and Fernande's farmhouse on Church Road, both she and the horse were drooping in the heat. She unfastened the gate and led the horse back to the stable. She was tend-ing it when her nephew Etienne arrived and said it would be better for her to get to the house. He was thirteen, the eldest of the children, and was trying hard now to fill his father's role.

Sylvie stopped on the large back porch of the farmhouse and drew a cup of water from the earthenware cistern. Light was turning pale lemon as the sun moved behind looming clouds, and as she drank a second cup, cool drafts from the shadows stirred about her ankles. The smell of rain falling on distant ripe wheat wafted like an aroma of toasting bread.

She felt Amy's presence before she heard footsteps or the rustle of her skirt; the woman's very energy made the air alert. Then Amy was beside her, brusquely snatching the tin cup from Sylvie's hand; the handle scraped her fingers, already chafed by bridle reins. Amy, an African-American about thirty years old, stood a head taller than Sylvie. Under current Illinois law, Amy was an indentured servant, but before that, she had been a slave owned by Sylvie's father.

"You'll not be drinking that water," Amy said, throwing what remained in a sparkling arc toward flowers and vegetables in the kitchen garden.

Sylvie gazed at her, more puzzled by her abrupt action than lack of greeting. Amy had one straight eyebrow and one that quirked high up in the expanse of forehead that Sylvie felt made her look wise.

"This household will be drinking only ginger beer, or tea, coffee—what's been put to boil on the stove. Come in, and I'll get you something."

"*D'accord,*" Sylvie agreed.

"I keep telling you that. And where have you been? We've been wondering about you for hours. You weren't in Belleville, were you? We just heard six more people have died there."

"No, I went into Cahokia to pay a visit. But what do the deaths in Belleville have to do with our well water?"

"I'm just figuring, by way of who lives and who dies around here. Back when my people were on the Islands, cholera came and killed thousands. My family survived because they ate and drank only things that were cooked."

Sylvie didn't want to argue openly with Amy, but those stories about the Islands dated back nearly two hundred years, and who knew if they held any truth? The two moved into the kitchen, and from a large stockpot on the stove, Amy ladled a warm cup of water boiled with ginger root and sugar.

Sylvie thanked her and added, "But everyone knows we get sick from night vapors off water like Cahokia Creek when it gets low in the summer. Then it's pes-til-en-tial." She drew out the word in English.

Amy shook her head emphatically. "You sneaked into town—and rode all that way alone? Everyone was upset, and we didn't need more trouble."

"I am sorry for that. But when did Fernande actually notice I wasn't here?"

"Well, not until we sat down to eat, midday. Etienne said you had mentioned an errand, maybe finding some help with the harvest."

"That's true. I went to see the Jarrots, and Vital said they will help." Sylvie smiled at the idea of Etienne covering for her absence and doing it so well, even when she hadn't shared her plans with him.

Amy's expression softened as she ladled a cup of ginger beer for herself. Amy's ancestors had arrived in the area earlier than Sylvie's own family. A French sea captain coming to mine silver in the early 1700s had brought African slaves, via Santo Domingo and up the Mississippi River, to southern Illinois. But when mines in the area yielded only lead, the captain had left, abandoning the slaves to the care of the small Jesuit mission at Cahokia. Amy's large extended family and network of friends traced their lineage to this one group.

In the spring, Amy's term of indenture would end, and she would become a free, a 30-year old emancipated woman. Recently, she'd been saying she wanted to join relatives and friends in the growing community of free African Americans in New Orleans, *Les Gens de Couleur Libres*. Amy's fate figured into Sylvie's concerns about her own future, for happy as she might be for Amy's coming freedom, it was wrenching to think of losing yet another person in her life. Amy was the one who had held Sylvie's hand during her father's burial a dozen years earlier, and then sheltered her on her lap during the carriage ride to their new home with Laurent and Fernande.

The trip downriver would be dangerous for Amy because outlaw slavers worked the Mississippi, kidnapping free African-Americans and selling them into slavery in the markets of New Orleans. Sylvie knew that Laurent had talked with traders the family worked with, men who transported French wheat flour, wine, fruit, meat, and furs to the city. But now who would make arrangements and find someone trustworthy to guarantee Amy's safe passage? Sylvie sighed, letting her gaze travel out the kitchen windows above the long work table, and toward the grassy area outside shaded by large elms. There were so many things to handle, with Laurent gone.

"We need a bunch of carrots and some onions for the hotpot," Amy was saying neutrally. "Why don't you get them before you clean up for dinner?"

Back outside in the airless heat, Sylvie found shade under an apple tree and looked over the rows of vegetables. Nothing calmed her mind like getting her hands in the dirt. Three onions were just the right size inside their tan, papery skins. She was less selective as she yanked up carrots because any size tasted good, and small ones were often the best. When she returned to the kitchen, she laid the vegetables on the worktable and was able to slip, unseen, upstairs to her bedroom.

Laurent and their father had built the house together, just before Laurent's marriage. It was long and rectangular in the American style, with painted wood siding set horizontally on the outer walls. A pitched roof dropped sharply over an attic, and the bedrooms on the second floor had tall windows and high ceilings. As Sylvie flopped back on her bed, voices drifted in from her young nephews playing outside. She wondered whether she would feel any air currents if only she lay still enough. Soon, her eyelids dropped.

Sylvie awoke to her five-year-old niece, Celeste, tugging her sleeve and trying to drag her to dinner. She quickly rinsed her face, slapped her cheeks lightly to wake up, and went downstairs. The family was at the table with the lamp lit, for the building storm was darkening the evening. Amy served the meal, and after the two youngest boys and Celeste had spooned up a good amount, she took them upstairs to bed. That left Sylvie and Etienne seated with Fernande as they finished a plate of cheese and fruit.

Fernande had soft brown eyes nearly the same color as the curly ringlets edging her forehead. Her hair tended to frizz in the humidity, and the cherry-colored ribbon gathering it back hung limply. She seemed distracted, and once again Sylvie felt Fernande hardly noticed her presence in the continuous stream of urgent situations that she treated like a single consuming calamity. As the family's mourning became tempered by time, Sylvie sensed that Fernande at some point had dropped a tether connecting the two of them; or perhaps all along she had felt less of a family tie to Sylvie. That would only be reasonable, for she and Fernande were not blood relatives.

As Sylvie recounted how Vital Jarrot had promised to help with the wheat harvest, Fernande's eyes filled with tears. Sylvie felt dismay at the pallor of her skin, and the deep rings under her eyes, and wondered how they would manage if Fernande fell ill. This was not the time to mention the other topic, her inquiry about relatives in Missouri.

"I'll take care of things, don't worry," Etienne said. "We're hiring field hands. The overseer brought a list of names today, and we know some of the men. A few are new, though, passing through on their way out West."

*"Ça va, merci, Etienne,"* Fernande said faintly. After a moment, she straightened. "I want the two of you to take the sacks of buckwheat to the Derosches' mill and get it ground so we have more room for the wheat. Can you do that tomorrow? And then someone needs to ride to your Aunt Lizette's and ask all of them to help us, too."

"I'll be happy to do that," Sylvie said and waited as the offer hung in the air. Would Fernande chastise her for riding off alone today, or had Sylvie broken through a boundary, her safe return opening new possibilities for independence?

"That will be good. Yes, Sylvie, plan on doing that one day soon."

Etienne gave Sylvie a brief smile and added, "And you'll tell them that we'll return the favor when it's time to harvest their fields."

Sylvie reassured him, and as they cleared the table and did dishes, they could hear thunder rumbling, coming closer. Later, Sylvie went to check the sheds, stable, and smokehouse, to make sure windows were fastened, doors shut, and tools put away. In the small cottages toward the back of the acreage, where the servants and field workers lived, light from windows cast yellow rectangles onto small, neat gardens.

Raindrops began plopping in the dust, wetting the tops of Sylvie's feet. Her toes were blending drops into the dusty earth, like mixing melted chocolate. This was good rain in small drops, not a punishing thundershower that would pack the wheat against the earth and make it molder. This was nourishing water on her arms, in the cupped palms of her hands.

As she held up the lantern at the smokehouse, the air crashed around her and sent vibrations through the wood. Lightning flared in brilliant planes, and as she headed back, the farmhouse seemed to jump forward as a white, ghostly image of its solid self. Then the sky flapped sheets of incandescence without location, origin, or direction.

Back in the house, Sylvie could hear voices in the parlor. She had dallied on her errands to enjoy the cooler air and now was soaking wet. She stumbled upstairs, suddenly exhausted by the day. After undressing in the dark, she slipped on her muslin nightdress and snuggled in bed next to Celeste, who murmured and turned. A cooler layer of air drifted by as the storm dissipated tension and humidity. Surely she had not breathed enough miasmal night air to fall ill with cholera. Surely this damp air was healthy, a harbinger of the cooler nights coming in September.

Sylvie tucked her hand under her chin. She must have drifted off, for Celeste was prodding her hard, and thunder crashed loudly enough to make Sylvie suddenly alert.

"Sylvie, I'm scared."

"Do you want me to light the candle?"

"No, I want a story," Celeste said. "If it's dark, then we'll go back to sleep."

"What story do you want?" Sylvie propped up on an elbow and could make out Celeste's little face, her huge eyes, the wavy, improbably blonde hair tangled from sleep. No one had found the time to brush and braid her hair that evening.

"About our *grandmère*, the *Fille du Roi*."

Sylvie cuddled an arm around her so they were both comfortable. "Just so you will always know, this is the story of the grandmother of my father—who was your grandfather. His grandfather was the soldier who came to help settlers in Québec, and he married Anne Le Ber, the *Fille du Roi*."

"What was a *Fille du Roi*?" Celeste recited her line on cue.

"Above all, she was a very brave young woman. When she was just a little older than I am now, she left her village in France and began a great adventure. She sailed on a ship to the New World, to *La Nouvelle France*. She and the other young women agreed to leave their homes and families and come to Québec to marry settlers or soldiers. In return, King Louis XIV paid for their travel and education and gave them money."

"How much? Did *Grandmère* Anne get gold coins?"

"Yes, she got fifty golden *livres*. All the women got that much to start their households. So our ancestor Anne sailed away from France in 1672, and after months on the ocean, she landed in Montreal. A woman there named Marguerite de Bourgeoys took the girls in, found places for them to live, and taught them all the skills they needed to make homes in the colonies. They had to learn . . ."

Celeste recited with her, "to spin, to weave and sew clothes, to cook, to grow fruit and vegetables, to make bread, to knit . . ." Sometimes Sylvie varied her lines a bit. "Anne Le Ber made beautiful silk flowers, and all the women wanted them for their dresses and hats."

"Yes, and our cousin Louisa has Anne's tools now, handed down through the family. Louisa makes beautiful flowers, too."

Sylvie continued the story. "All the *Filles du Roi* got dressed up in their gowns for soirées in Montreal. The gentlemen would arrive in their uniforms or dress coats, and they would be introduced to one another. If the girls decided not to marry and stay in Québec, they could go back to France. But the voyage was long, and many people got sick or even died during the trip."

"Anne and François saw each other and fell in love. A *coup de fou-dre*," Celeste murmured sleepily.

"Yes, love struck like a bolt of lightning."

They lay back and listened to the thunder, dimmer now. The air carried an acrid tinge from being burned by lightning.

"Why did she go away?"

"Who?"

"*Grandmère* Anne; everyone says France is beautiful."

"It's beautiful here, too."

"But she was a princess," Celeste murmured, her eyelids sliding closed in spite of her efforts.

"She was not a princess! The king would give the girls chests of dishes and blankets and other things they needed. Some of them were orphans or came from poor families, while others were bourgeois. Grandmère Anne was on the last ship the king sent, with women promised in marriage to the soldiers in the Carignan Salières regiment. But I think, deep in her heart, she wanted more than marriage. She wanted to have some adventure in her life."

Celeste seemed to be asleep, so as Sylvie continued, she was murmuring more to herself. "Perhaps she felt she had little to leave, and more to gain. The women could make better marriages in the New

World, and they could own their own land. Their sons and daughters would have wonderful opportunities."

"Where was her castle in France?" Celeste asked, surprising her.

"She didn't have a castle, *petite chère*. She was from a family of farmers and merchants, like us. You have to be careful to tell your grandmothers' stories just as they are because it's so easy to lose them. Men's stories get written down, but our women's stories are remembered only when we take good care to tell them to each other. Remember this story, and all the names and places, Celeste."

"Did *Grandmère* Anne get married and have a family?"

"Yes, she married François, and he had land claims for his military service. They moved across the river from Montreal, and they always lived near forts because he was a soldier, and Indians or the British might attack them. They had many Pensoneau children, and some of their grandchildren came here to settle."

"We need to have *Filles du Roi* again."

"Why?" Sylvie asked.

"For all the men who are coming here now, from France and Germany and Boston and all those places. There aren't enough women here for them to marry. That's what everyone says."

"Hmm, that could be true. Let's go to sleep, now."

Before dropping off, Sylvie wondered why retelling this story brought so much comfort. How old had Anne been when she made that decision to leave her home for the New World? And was it a difficult choice? Some relatives telling the story would add that she was already betrothed to the soldier and had a good sense of the marriage and land holdings to come. If that were true, she might even have received letters recounting his battles and explorations. In spite of the careful retelling over a handful of generations, some crucial details like that had been lost.

Chapter 3

**August 1832**
**Cahokia, Illinois**

SYLVIE WAS ARRIVING AT AUNT LIZETTE'S HOUSE ahead of the midday meal, and though she hadn't sent word ahead, she counted on being welcome. Her aunt had ten children, and it seemed Sylvie always found room among her cousins at the long oval dining table. Plus, her aunt mothered her a bit, and with her life feeling so unsettled, Sylvie was especially looking forward to the usual warmth and affection.

She had left her horse in the stable at the back of the house, and as she followed flagstone steps through the kitchen garden, she caught aromas of cooking meat and vegetables. The home was in the old French-style, with long, swooping roof lines, deep verandas, and walls of vertical logs. The side door stood open in the heat, and from there she could either go down a half-flight of stairs to the kitchen, or upstairs to the main rooms. The din of voices speaking French—and laughing, protesting, and exclaiming—came from above.

So Sylvie went up and passed through the dining room into the *salon*, where it seemed her cousins were gathered and talking all at once. No one noticed as she slipped in. Aunt Lizette was standing next to a tall man wearing a leather coat, and from the back, Sylvie could see its elaborate beadwork designs.

She spotted Louisa, the cousin closest in age, and edged toward her. The two considered each other best friends, and Louisa grasped Sylvie's arm, almost pinching it. "Sylvie, *tiens!*" She continued in French, "You'll never guess—Paschal is here, and he's getting married to a Kickapoo woman, and they're leaving with her band to live in Missouri!"

"What—that is Paschal?" The man had turned so Sylvie could see his profile, and she felt a sharp pang at how much he resembled his father, Sylvie's uncle, who had died the previous spring. Paschal came home to Cahokia so rarely that he loomed as an exotic figure in Sylvie's life. In recent years he'd been working as a gunsmith, living and trading among Indian tribes allied with the French and Americans.

His father had been a fur trader for most of his life, and after leaving Québec in the late 1700s, had worked as a *facteur* for John Jacob Astor's company. He had traded mainly along the Wabash River, and the family had even lived upriver in Peoria for a time. When Paschal was about twelve, his father had sent him to live with Sac and Fox Indians, and in exchange, a boy from those bands had come to live with a French family.

Sylvie wondered about Paschal's ties to those tribes, and what he had done during the war fought earlier in the summer. And more, how that connected to his coming marriage, and to this rare visit to his childhood home. Two of Sylvie's cousins, Paschal's younger brothers, had volunteered with the Illinois militia and gone to the fighting for several weeks. Surely they would talk all this over at the dining table.

Aunt Lizette was pressing her hands over her ears and announcing, above the other voices, "It's time to eat. The meal must be ready—let's go sit down." She prodded younger children aside to make her way toward the dining room. "Why Sylvie, I didn't realize you were here!" Aunt Lizette bent to bestow cheek kisses. "You'll stay for dinner, won't you? What a day you've picked for a visit—you'll get to hear about Paschal's plans to marry."

Sylvie agreed and thanked her aunt, then held back so she could speak with Paschal when he drew near. After they exchanged kisses and greetings, his demeanor grew serious, and Sylvie realized he was going to express his condolences.

"I was so sorry to hear about Laurent's death," Paschal said. "How very sad for the widow, for their children, and for you. He was like a father to you, I think, the one who was raising you. You may not remember your own father as well, you were so young."

"Yes, he was like a father, the one I've known in my life. And what makes it worse, is that it happened so quickly."

"Yes, cholera strikes like that, a terrible shock."

"He lived barely two days after he became ill in Belleville! And along with missing him, we have to resolve, all of a sudden, how we're going to manage now." Sylvie blinked rapidly and shook her head.

Paschal tilted his head, looking closely at her. "And what happens to you, now? Your older half-sister Jeanne becomes legal guardian; isn't that so?" As Sylvie nodded, he smiled slightly. "I hear she is quite devout and strict with her children. And the American laws we have now give her husband legal authority over you, I think. Are you going to live with them?"

*"Non!"* Sylvie spoke so firmly that Paschal raised an eyebrow. With the hubbub of talk still surrounding them, Sylvie felt she could unburden herself to him. He had been sent off to live with Indian trading partners at such a young age that he might well understand her plight as an orphan. She explained that she would stay with Fernande and the children for now and return to school in the fall. "But I need a plan for my life after that. Come spring, I'll be sixteen, and I want to do something more than stay in Cahokia and get married."

"Life doesn't offer many other choices around here." Paschal sounded so thoughtful that Sylvie wondered if he was imagining broader choices she might have elsewhere.

They began moving toward the dining room, and Sylvie rallied to give him a bright smile. "But I'm so happy to hear that you will be married. *Félicitations!* And I want to hear all about your fiancée."

*"Beh, oui.* After we eat, I'll tell everyone about her and her family."

A servant had set cutlery and plates on the table, and Sylvie slid onto the corner of a bench where Louisa had saved some space. Aunt Lizette was sitting up straight, and she pushed her small eyeglasses up her nose, repeating the gesture several times. Her face was damp, and strands of graying black hair fell loosely from the knot at the top of her head.

Everyone fell quiet as Lizette began to say grace. She thanked the good Lord and Mary Queen of Heaven for this rare visit from her eldest son. "Please bless his union with the bride he has chosen and give all of us the strength to keep this family together as best we can. And please watch over the Kickapoo, and over all the Indians who now must move across the Mississippi River to find new homes, far away in strange lands. Please bless everyone . . . Oh, and thank you for this food we are about to eat." After a pause, she abruptly said "Amen," and the others murmured in response.

Sylvie eyed the china tureens of rabbit stew; several *miches*, round loaves of wheat bread; and creamware bowls holding turnips, carrots, and potatoes sprinkled with chopped *fines herbes*. Though the family typically enjoyed their food for a time without the distraction of talk, Sylvie was so disconcerted by her aunt's blessing that she murmured to Louisa.

"*Alors*, you said Paschal is marrying a Kickapoo woman?"

Louisa nodded vigorously. "A princess—well, actually, the daughter of a chief."

"And why are they going out to Missouri Territory?"

"All the Indians have to leave Illinois now and move west of the Mississippi. The American government passed that law some time ago, and now that the war is over ..." she shrugged.

"But that should just apply to the bands of Sac and Fox that Black Hawk brought back into Illinois when he'd been told not to. The Americans have defeated them, but the Kickapoo were allies for the Americans, weren't they? So why do they have to leave?"

"I don't fully understand it, either." Louisa chewed a piece of torn bread and took a sip of red wine. "*Maman* is very distressed that they're going to live so far away. She's already talking about how she'll miss knowing her first grandchildren."

"But what about a wedding—will they have a big ceremony and a party?"

Louisa looked perplexed and passed the breadbasket. Sylvie tore some from the loaf and was grateful the quiet descending around the table would allow a few moments to absorb the news and try to make sense of it.

Looking around the ring of faces, Sylvie tried to draw comfort from the feeling of family. But so often lately, following Laurent's death, she'd felt distanced from the bonds that made her relatives seem closer to each other than to her. She alone among her cousins was an orphan, and now without Laurent as a kind of stepfather, her future appeared as an uncharted stretch that she would have to shape and manage on her own, a task her cousins didn't have to face, or even imagine.

Except for Paschal. He looked peaceful and at ease, enjoying the meal with his mother and siblings. It made sense that Paschal would marry an Indian woman as so many French had done historically. His own grandmother, Lizette's mother, was part Pottawatomie. The one essential quality was to be Catholic; anyone confirmed in the church became part of the broad community of faith. But Sylvie noticed Aunt Lizette still wiping an eye now and then, and pushing her glasses back up.

Before long, Paschal broke into the scraping of knives, clattering of spoons, and appreciative sighing between bites by asking his brothers about their experience in the war. Two of them had enlisted in June in the Illinois militia after the governor declared that Black Hawk and his band of Sac and Fox had invaded the state and called up volunteers to forcibly expel them. Black Hawk had argued his people were simply returning to harvest corn crops they'd planted earlier on their traditional lands. Other Indians had attacked some settlers out in rural areas, however, and rumors of brutality had stoked public fears.

The brothers had been retelling their war stories over the weeks since they'd come back home, and now they just commented briefly about how the volunteers had been ill-equipped, poorly trained, and barely fed. They still seemed embarrassed their unit had broken ranks and retreated during its first battle against Black Hawk's warriors, an event now derisively called "Stillman's Run."

One of them, Narcisse, then asked Paschal which side he had fought on, and Paschal straightened, looking startled. "The same side as you, of course, with the Americans, and against Black Hawk."

"I thought you were working for the Indian agent who is his main trader."

"I did work with him, and that knowledge proved useful for the US Army," Paschal said. "I did translating and some scouting, and I'll continue doing that in Missouri. William Clark has hired me to work in areas he oversees, out of St. Louis."

Paschal was wearing an old-style muslin shirt with full, gathered sleeves. Over it, he'd tied the *ceinture fléchée*, the red sash of the French-Canadian fur trader, at the waist. His doeskin coat was hanging near the door, where Sylvie could admire its fine fringe and embroidery. The twining vines, flowers, birds, and other motifs looked Algonquian in style. Several women had likely spent years conditioning the leather, making or obtaining the tiny beads and quills, and stitching the elaborate patterns. She especially liked the double white-and-black outlines surrounding main blossoms and leaves, an original and distinctive touch. Was the artist Paschal's fiancée?

As the dishes were cleared, the youngsters tried to keep still so they would get dessert, and Sylvie relaxed with the pleasant heat from the wine she had sipped. Sunlight striped the copper pots and bowls hanging over the deep blue wallpaper, and shadows pooled on the dark green doors, painted with flowers and vines, that enclosed storage shelves. Outside, cicadas whirred in the growing heat. She was certain that this peaceful family life, the love and well-being, and the larger French community, were well worth fighting for. But each person's battle seemed to shape up so differently.

In the quiet, Sylvie suddenly remembered the purpose for her visit. "Oh, I have to tell you about the wheat harvest—the *habitants* decided to begin with Laurent's fields. And we are going to need so much help. They want to start in about ten days, depending on the weather."

As the cousins talked over specific dates and tasks, Edward, Narcisse, and Louisa all assured Sylvie they would come to the farm for several days, and Edward added he could bring temporary workers he had recently hired for his own family's fields. Sylvie had expected they would help again this year, as they had in the past. Typically, workers from all over the area converged on each farm's fields and harvested them in turn.

Lizette was serving tarts made with the summer's first translucent apples, their slices, edged with silvery green, topping apple jelly on a buttery crust. Sylvie held morsels on her tongue to let the juice seep away and the crust melt. Then came coffee, and she was pleased to be given a demi-tasse, like the other grown-ups.

Paschal pulled out a clay pipe with a long stem, and Edward and Narcisse fetched pipes from their father's rack on the wall. Paschal struck a flint to get a spark, and aromatic smoke drifted over the table. The younger children were yawning in the heat, and when Lizette excused them, the boys bounded up to go fishing at the *Grand Marais,* the large marsh; the girls said they would pick currants.

In the lull, Sylvie reminded Paschal, "I want to hear all about the woman you will marry, and your plans. Is she a beautiful princess?"

He laughed. "Well, she is lovely, and her father is a chief. Her name is Shikina, and we can talk more about her family."

But instead, Lizette started bemoaning Paschal's upbringing. "I am sure this is what comes from sending you off when you were so young. Why did I ever allow your father to have his way? You didn't get to know our own customs as you should have, growing up."

"*Maman,* don't trouble yourself like this. I had years of schooling with the village priests, and I learned even more by living with the tribes. I'm lucky to be comfortable among different cultures. And when you meet my fiancée and her family—if you ever do—you will like them all very much."

"I'm sure that's true, and I trust your judgment, Paschal. But the very idea of never knowing my grandchildren!" Lizette's voice choked off, her shoulders sagged, and her hands twisted in her apron like burrowing animals. "What sort of marriage is it, that takes you so far away from us?"

"*Maman,* the Missouri River is not so far away, and the fur trade there is growing fast. I'll be back in St. Louis every spring for the big markets. And it's not the marriage that is taking me away—it's the way the war has ended."

"Last spring, we talked about the war as though it was going to resolve things, somehow," Narcisse said. "We worried the fighting could tear our family apart, with two of us going off. But look at this—it's the peacetime that's pulling us apart, instead."

"With all the Americans coming in, our French way of life is passing, ending before our eyes," Lizette said. "And with the Indians being forced out of Illinois, how will your children, Paschal, get to know our way of life? They won't be able to own land and make their homes here. Thank goodness your father didn't live to see this; it would break his heart."

"At least you are marrying in the Catholic Church—that is true, isn't it?" Louisa asked.

"Oh, yes, don't worry. And if we have to live in a place without a church, we'll build one and get a priest to make regular visits. Remember Cahokia used to be like that—there wasn't always a permanent priest here."

"*Beh, oui*, there always has been. Priests have served Holy Family Church since the 1680s." Lizette spoke sharply, but then she spread her hands and smoothed the air between them. "Paschal, that's a comfort, that you'll attend to your religious lives. But do you not see my viewpoint as a mother and grandmother, God willing? I simply want my family nearby."

She rose, asked them to excuse her, and headed toward her bedroom. Sylvie glanced at Louisa, wondering if one of them should go to her while she had a cry.

Paschal stood as well. "I brought a few gifts . . ." He strode out the door toward the back garden.

Sylvie and Louisa also rose. It was time to head to their favorite place on the north side of the house, where they would spread an old quilt near the flowerbeds. In earlier years, they had played with dolls; later they brought knitting and sewing. Today, conversation would occupy them completely. They had gone down the side steps and were on the flagstone path when Paschal approached, carrying a saddlebag in one hand and a doeskin bundle in the other.

Smiling, he handed the bundle to Louisa, saying, "I saw these and thought of you right away. I hope you'll like them and can use them."

Louisa undid the slender leather thong and found two moccasins of soft doeskin. A decorative cuff covered with intricate embroidery folded down like a collar around each ankle opening. The flowers and vines gleamed in shades of russet, pumpkin, and forest green.

"*Mon dieu*," Sylvie whispered.

"Oh, they're lovely," Louisa said. "Thank you so much. I will wear them with pleasure." She reached up to kiss Paschal on both cheeks.

As he went into the house, the girls continued toward the shade. They lay on their backs after spreading the quilt, and Sylvie kicked off her plain, soft shoes. Louisa preferred the shade because she tended to get freckles; she was fairer, with green eyes and chestnut hair, and Sylvie envied her taller build. Over the years, she and Louisa had shared their innermost thoughts and made a pact to always be sisters for each other.

"I think it's romantic," Sylvie said. "It's a love story. I can understand why Paschal would do that."

"So do I, for love. But there's something . . . not exciting about it, like he's trying to go back in time, to live the *voyageur* past, and that era is gone."

"Not really, not in Missouri. Everyone talks about how wild the plains are, with open land and mountain ranges that have hardly been explored."

"Yes, maybe." Louisa fanned her face with a hand. "But when I marry, I'm going to live in New Orleans, in a city where there's exotic cuisine and books to read and all the latest fashions from France."

Sylvie smiled and propped her hands behind her head. "And who is the handsome, rich, young man who will marry you and whisk you off to live there?"

"I don't know, quite yet. But there are plenty of young men around. More and more arrive every day."

"That's true; they're coming from the East, and from Europe. But you'd want someone who's French and has a profession—a lawyer or an owner of a trading company."

"Someone Catholic and of good family."

"It's so hard to know the truth about their backgrounds. When they get here, they can say anything they want about their families and their past, if they don't have letters of introduction."

"Narcisse says nine out of ten are fleeing drunkenness, debts, or duels."

"Maybe I should take off with one of them and head out west to have an adventure for a while," Sylvie said, and they both started laughing. "Someone from Kentucky who wears bear skins and gets drunk and rolls around on the ground—"

"A 'Kaintuck' who fights other men wearing bear skins, getting drunk, and rolling around on the ground! But seriously, you don't want to leave just when we'll turn sixteen and can finally attend the parties and balls. It's only a month until my birthday, and I can't wait."

"I'm not as excited as you are, Louisa. Think of how much harder it will be for me, with no mother or father. And it's not even clear what my inheritance will be. I'm like an inconvenient scrap of leftover family."

"Oh, Sylvie, what a horrible thing to say! And it's not true—you're like my sister. In fact, maybe you should come live with us now. I can ask *Maman*."

"That's a nice thought. But what if I felt I didn't truly belong here, either?"

"Oh, dear. You're not really going to live with Jeanne, are you, and become all proper and pious and attend mass twice a day? I really cannot picture you doing that, Sylvie."

"No, and I won't have to, right away." They were quiet for a few moments and Sylvie added, "Fernande will probably remarry quickly, though. That's what happens with widows, here. She's not yet thirty, and she's wealthy, with the farmlands and trading business..So, you do see my problem."

"But Sylvie, isn't marriage what you want, too? When you do marry, you'll have your own home, and that's where you'll truly belong. And with children, you'll have very close family ties."

Sylvie gazed up into the branches of the apple tree. "Why does that sound boring at the moment? I want to see a bigger world, just like you saying you want to live in New Orleans. Oh, maybe I should ride off with Paschal. I could imagine doing that, if I didn't have to sleep on the ground. And I'd want good coffee and fresh wheat bread every day."

"No, it would be cornbread. You'd have to learn to eat it, like the Americans."

"*Beh*, corn is food for pigs."

"Sylvie, don't do anything to hurt the family, like Paschal is doing. It's as though we won't know him anymore, once he goes so far away and marries outside the French community."

"You're giving up on him," Sylvie said with wonder.

"No, I'm not. I will always love him and any children he and his wife may have. But they will live mainly in the Kickapoo world, don't you see? The children won't live here, so how will they learn to speak French or attend school with the priests or nuns? They won't even be half French."

Sylvie fell silent on this subject, for her mother had been fluent in English as well as French, and her first marriage had been to an American Protestant. After his death, she had married Sylvie's father, a staunchly Catholic, French Canadian businessman and land agent. First, they'd had a civil ceremony before a justice of the peace. But several months later, they married again in Holy Family Church because otherwise, Jeanne, already grown and quite religious, would not accept the union as legitimate. And her views were hardly unique among the townspeople.

Sylvie could speak English rather well, especially after paying visits to her mother's in-laws in Missouri, the family of her first husband. But Sylvie's extended French Canadian family in Cahokia tended to dismiss that side of her life, as Louisa was doing now. What did "not even half French" mean? She looked narrowly at her cousin, who was shredding a leaf from a hop vine, and changed the subject by asking her to try on the moccasins so she could see them before she left.

Louisa was barefoot, and she slipped her toes into one of the pair. "Way too small, just as I thought. Paschal remembers me as a little girl. I'm not sure I'd wear them anyway. We prefer leather shoes with heels now, in town. Why don't you try them on?"

Sylvie was pleased to slip her foot into one, and then, as it fit so smoothly, into the other. She thought they looked simply beautiful, and she jumped up and pirouetted, to see the beaded blossoms and vines shimmer in the light. The fine thread must be silk to gleam that way, and the sheer glitter of quills was unmistakable. The artistry was unusually fine, making the moccasins a valuable gift.

"They look nice on you. Why don't you keep them? I won't use them."

"Oh, Louisa, I couldn't. What would Paschal think? He meant them for you."

"I'm serious. You seem to genuinely like them."

Sylvie stopped twirling and noted Louisa frowning slightly and gazing away. She waited, and finally Louisa said, "Wearing them would remind people of our ties with the Indians, which is perfectly fine among us French. But I'll be attending my first balls and entering society, and that means dealing with Americans, now. You know they have different views, and they're not as accepting—they lack our history of being *voyageurs* and working the fur trade for so many generations."

"I don't know what to do," Sylvie said after a few moments. "I'll keep them for now, in case you change your mind."

"But they're too small, and they're just not right for me."

"*D'accord.* Thank you, in that case. I will treasure them and wear them, and not worry about what others might think."

"Well, I'm glad. But you're taking a superior tone with me, now. You're acting like you don't see my point, and that's being mean."

"I'm not being mean, and I do see your point, though I think you should be happier for Paschal." Sylvie tried to sound certain, though she was feeling confused herself.

"Well, excuse me for not living up to your expectations." Louisa lay back and pressed her forearm over her eyes. "I'm going to take a little nap, and then I'll feel more like myself. You have a long ride ahead, and maybe you should get started."

Sylvie kissed her fingertips and patted them on Louisa's arm. "Everything will work out well for the family, you'll see."

Leaving the shade, Sylvie made her way back toward the out-buildings and stables. She caught a whiff of tobacco from the garden, where Paschal and Narcisse stood talking. The flowers and vegetables seemed to waver in the heat. Had she and Louisa just had a disagreement, a lasting one? Whenever they had quarreled as little girls, they made up after a few minutes, or hours, at the most. This felt different and more serious.

As she approached, Narcisse was saying, "The Americans seem to view the West as wide-open spaces where they can just relocate tribes, as though other nations don't already own their territories. The Kickapoo will have to head into enemy lands or pass through them, somehow."

"I know it will be dangerous, and we'll face hostilities," Paschal said. "The most traditional of them want to go farther south, into Mexico. But I hope that my standing with Clark, and his military presence, will provide some protection. If I am accepted as a negotiator and translator, I shouldn't have to go that far away, yet."

"You know, our brother Laurent has arranged work with Clark also, doing trading and translating in Missouri Territory," Narcisse said. As he saw Sylvie approaching, he added, "Of course, my own goal is to find land, ideal tracts where new towns can be developed. I want to do what Sylvie's father did when he planned Belleville and Illinoistown."

"Well, that is setting a high standard for yourself to live up to!" Paschal smiled at Sylvie, inviting her into the reminiscence about her father.

She extended the doeskin bundle tentatively toward Paschal, saying that the moccasins were too small for Louisa but fit her well.

"Then I would like you to have them," he said.

"Oh, thank you. They're so beautiful, and I know you didn't intend them for me, but I'll put them away for only the most special occasions."

"Then I'm delighted. And if I'd known you'd be here today, I'd have thought of it from the beginning."

"I'm sorry you have to go so far away." Sylvie's voice quavered and she swallowed, not finding the words for asking him to help her, to envision possibilities for her own future.

"It's not such a bad fate, and we'll make a good life for ourselves." Noting her expression, Paschal added, "We didn't finish talking about what your own fate may be, except that you'll likely avoid living with Jeanne. But I recall you have relatives on your mother's side, in Missouri, including an older half-brother. Have you thought about going to them?"

Sylvie explained how she'd been trying to learn news of David since the war ended and the cholera epidemic broke out. "It's just our Aunt Peggy and her children, and David, at their farm, now," she added. "Her husband is in Mexico; he and his brother have a trading business there, and they go from the American colonies farther west—I've heard as far as Santa Fe. And they're after silver and gold, too, not just furs."

The men nodded as though this was a sensible line of work. "Your aunt's brother is in Mexico, too, isn't he?" Narcisse said. "I've heard he's administrator for the colony Green DeWitt started. That one has drawn a lot of settlers from around here."

Paschal grinned at her. "There you go, Sylvie, if you want a more exciting life. You could join that uncle in Mexico."

"Paschal, do you know that nearly his entire family died of disease when he brought them to Mexico to join him? His wife, his sons— only a baby girl survived."

"Oh, that is tragic. And that is something to consider seriously, that life is difficult and dangerous on the frontier. Plus, they often have to fight the Comanche Indians. At least that's what I've heard."

"So you are just teasing me—that hardly sounds like a reasonable choice for my life."

"Something in between, then; not the safe confines of Cahokia, but also not the rough life of a new colony. Just remember that when you can't find the right place in life, sometimes it's because the choices it offers are too small. They won't fit, like the moccasins when Louisa tried them on."

"You don't really want her to be like you, roaming all over out west," Narcisse said to Paschal. "She should have the chance for prosperity and a settled life, with a husband, and a home, and children. And the pleasures of continuing to live in our French community."

"But that does sound a bit limited to me, right now," Sylvie said. "What about all our family traditions? Think of our legacy, the way our ancestors kept moving, from France to Québec and Montreal, then to Cahokia, doing trade, getting land, and building towns along the way."

"Those family stories can be persuasive," Paschal said. "Sometimes you have to be wary of them, and other times they're a comfort. When I was even younger than you are, Sylvie, and trying to fall asleep at night in an Indian camp, homesick and not even sure sometimes where I was, I'd tell myself a story. My role would be part of a great legend, a tale with me as the hero among *voyageurs*, traveling far away on courageous explorations and accomplishing great things."

"And did it work?" Sylvie asked.

"Usually; but then, the heroes of those stories usually are men."

"But in our family, the women have also made voyages, like the *Fille du Roi* who sailed to Québec to make a new home in the wilderness. But that's so long ago, it would help to know of a real young woman who's done something like that recently."

Lizette appeared in the doorway and was coming outside to join them. Sensing that her aunt should have some time alone with the son she saw so rarely, Sylvie thanked her for the meal. As she said her goodbyes, she told Paschal, "I don't know when I'll see you again—I wish it could be at your wedding. But I will see you and meet Shikina one day. She'll be like my sister, or my cousin."

"If you come out west, Sylvie, or get to the colonies in Mexico, I will make sure to look in on you if I'm anywhere nearby."

Narcisse walked with Sylvie to the stable, where he helped to ready her horse. He gave her a boost into the saddle and gently slapped the pony to start down the allée through the fruit trees and out toward the road.

Chapter 4

**September 1832**
**Cahokia, Illinois**


"Why do we have to bother with this?" Sylvie huffed, edging Louisa away from the little mirror hanging on the wall of her bedroom. It was Sunday afternoon, and the girls were preparing to sit in the parlor for a social call. Sylvie had to stand tiptoe to put in her earrings, while Louisa had to stoop a bit. Louisa drew back and smoothed the wide lace edging the shoulders of her dress. Normally they would change from their church clothes into simpler, looser cotton. They didn't wear jewelry to mass, but they could now, for afternoon tea.

"Fernande means well. She's trying to play the role of your mother and introduce us to eligible young men," Louisa replied.

"But we don't know anything about these two. What if they're not acceptable? What a waste of time."

"Why, what would you rather be doing?" Louisa sounded genuinely curious.

"Cooking. I should be getting food ready with the harvest starting tomorrow."

"But I'm here to help, and we'll have plenty of time to cook later." Louisa laid a hand gently on Sylvie's shoulder. "I like doing this— meeting young men—to a point. It's important to our lives. And these two have letters of introduction from France to some of our acquaintances. So they aren't really unknown; they do come recommended."

"Isn't one of them from Switzerland or somewhere? We don't know any Swiss."

"Hmm, true. But he speaks French."

"Obviously. Fernande may hire these men to help with the harvest, and I don't usually meet the hired laborers. Oh—ouch!" While dragging a comb at her hair, Sylvie had snagged an earring and tugged on her earlobe.

Both girls wore their hair down their backs, the front strands braided or twisted and tied at the back with ribbon. The dresses had puffy, short sleeves, and the necklines, cut low in front, were demure enough for church. The satin—Louisa's sapphire and Sylvie's garnet—glistened, and bars of afternoon sunlight brought lustrous, deep shadows to the folds of the full skirts. They did not wear hoops, a new invention for ball gowns, but rather petticoats starched enough to allow some air underneath and show off their slim black slippers.

Amy knocked briefly before opening the door. "Time to stop primping, *mesdemoiselles*, and descend. You've left Fernande alone with the guests for ten minutes already. Any longer and you will be unforgivably rude, maybe even miss your chance to meet these *messieurs*."

"Are they really worth meeting?" Sylvie murmured.

Amy responded with a small smile and one eyebrow raised as an accent mark. Louisa had already slipped downstairs. So far, to Sylvie's relief, her cousin had acted as friendly as usual, as though she'd forgotten their disagreeable words a week or two earlier. She was shaking hands as Sylvie entered the room. Two young men were standing, and one, who had large, striking eyes and slicked-back hair, was holding Louisa's hand longer than necessary.

Sylvie hesitated, her hand extended, and the other man reached for it. Emile Hubert was florid, perhaps from the sun, and he sparked little interest because he could have been one of the Pensoneau clan with his jutting nose, black hair, and short, trim build. Both men wore stylish jackets with long tails reaching down the back. Their glossy leather boots fit so closely up to the knee that Sylvie thought they must be uncomfortably hot.

Next, Octave Borne politely took her hand and glanced at her before his eyes followed Louisa to where she took a seat, perching lightly on a brocade armchair.

Fernande was wielding the teapot, and Amy passed a plate of pastries. Sylvie helped herself to a tiny lemon tart and then saw that no one else had taken anything. Emile Hubert, noticing this, quickly reached for a sugar cookie. Sylvie appreciated that eating neatly could consume minutes that otherwise would have to be spent conversing.

But the men talked of interesting matters; they had news of the rebellion in France the previous June, and the uprising that brought fighting to the streets of Paris. Sylvie noticed how Octave Borne's large emerald ring glinted in a beam of sunlight and showered hot green dots on the wallpaper and across Louisa's dress.

Fernande sat upright, her corseted torso not touching the back of the chair. The tops of her breasts, plumped up at the low front of the dress, were swathed with layers of chiffon, and she had added fresh rosebuds to the brooch that secured the ensemble. Her hair fell in numerous ringlets on both sides of a wide pink ribbon. Fernande had not borne a child during the past four years, and she was regaining a slim waistline. Sylvie counted the remaining months before she would have to wear a corset for social occasions. It was odd, she considered, how much women thought about these things but rarely spoke of them openly to one another. Her eyes slid to the clock on the mantel and focused again on Emile Hubert, who kept including her, along with Fernande, in his glances.

"I plan to buy farmland here, and I have already purchased oxen, horses, and some machinery and implements," he was saying. "I will make those available to each *habitant* as the harvest goes along. Plus my own labor, of course."

His intentions as a landowner abruptly crystallized, and Sylvie now paid attention, for he would not be deemed unacceptable.

Fernande was saying, "So you'll buy acreage and a home here when an appropriate place becomes available?"

"Yes. This area is so beautiful, and the farmland is the richest I have seen yet in North America. I have been making inquiries." His formal manner of speaking seemed slightly softened and slurred, due to his accent. The French Canadians, especially those from Montreal, bit down harder on the ends of words.

"Have you done farm labor before, monsieur?" Sylvie asked. "The wheat harvest is hard work, with the scything and the bundling."

"A little, though I'm certainly familiar with harvests from my family's estate, and I have supervised dozens of workers at a time. If bad weather threatened, though, my relatives and I were off our horses and down in the fields along with the peasants."

"That is how work gets done efficiently and well," Fernande agreed, cutting off any response from Sylvie, who was mouthing, "Peasants?" In the ensuing pause, the three looked expectantly at Octave Borne and Louisa who, seated across from each other, had not contributed much beyond murmuring back and forth.

"And your plans, Monsieur Borne?" Fernande asked. "Are you also looking to buy farmland here?"

"Possibly, though I am more interested in trade and opportunities in commerce, especially with the markets in New Orleans. My family has run that kind of business in Switzerland. That was such a small country, and at such a high altitude, that they couldn't think of farming thousands of acres at a time as you do here. Fortunately for trading, they don't face the political problems that keep France in turmoil."

"A trading business in New Orleans sounds like a . . . promising future," Louisa said.

By the time Fernande stood to thank the men for their visit, and they leaped up in response, everyone understood she had decided whether they would be allowed to eat meals with the family during the harvest days, and whether they might be trusted to handle themselves well when they encountered the two girls and the younger children about the place. Sylvie suspected the men had gained that approval.

Back upstairs, Louisa undid the tiny jet buttons down the back of Sylvie's dress so she could quickly shed the satin and wriggle out of the petticoats.

"There . . . barely thirty minutes of your time. And now you can leap into peeling potatoes and kneading bread dough," Louisa said.

Sylvie watched her cousin drift toward the window, where she leaned on the sill to gaze out at the young men departing on their horses. Maybe one of them would turn to look or wave. But no, that would have been too familiar.

"Isn't he nice—Monsieur Borne, I mean?" Louisa said when she finally turned toward Sylvie. "He was actually born in New Orleans after his family established their trading company, and he wants to continue living there. And he's good-looking, too."

"Louisa—a tradesman? What good is trade without owning the land that produces the wheat, the wine, or the beef? He'd have to rely on furs, or get into indigo or the slave trade, heaven forbid."

"It sounds like the family deals in European goods. And you can't expect someone from Switzerland to have our kind of farms, just as he said."

"You are already *amoureuse!*" Sylvie started laughing. "But he may be losing his hair, he slicks it down so much!"

"That doesn't really matter. He has such fine eyes; did you notice?"

"Not particularly, since he was staring at you the entire time. What color are they? I didn't have the chance to see."

"Oh, stop it. You're teasing me because you have such huge eyes yourself that you hardly notice them in anyone else—or realize how attractive they can be."

"Do I?" Sylvie stood on tiptoe to check in the mirror and remove her earrings.

"So what do you think of Monsieur Hubert?" Louisa asked.

"That he looks like your brothers or any of our cousins. He'll be exactly like the rest of us, except for his accent, within six months."

"What else would you have?" Louisa asked quietly. Sylvie, in turn, was unfastening the tiny buttons down the back of her bodice. "Sylvie, marrying—or at least becoming engaged—is a way for you to establish firm social standing here in Cahokia. So give it a chance."

"What a strange way to have to think about marriage."

Louisa sighed and stretched up her arms as the last button was undone from the waist of the skirt. "It seems that this is our last chance to take a deep breath before the rush begins—all the cooking, the meals, the endless days—first here, then at other places, and finally at our farm."

It was sobering to think of the unrelenting demand, from dawn until long after dark, during the coming weeks. The hot days rimmed by the lack of sleep, the labor of carrying jugs of beverages and baskets of bread and meat out into the fields under relentless midday sun, the waking up while it was still dark, starry, and hinting of frost, the relighting of fires and lamps to start it all over, yet again. The sheer toil required every able person for miles around to join in one massive effort to get in the wheat, all the wheat on thousands of acres, before the cold rains began.

At a certain point, Sylvie recalled, perhaps after a week, a slight delirium—a sense of everything becoming one long blur—set in, and they would barely discern one day or night from the next. And still they had to milk the cows, gather the eggs, wash giant tubs of clothes, and clean dishes and pans for the next round.

And so the harvest began. Pausing on a fine, warm evening, Sylvie tried to count: was this the fourth day, or fifth, already? Hands on her hips, she stretched her back to ease the pain lodged between her shoulder blades from too much hunching over dishpans or kneading and rolling dough or lugging heavy baskets and jugs. Oh, to rest! Earlier, just after supper, she had actually dozed with her head on her arms atop the kitchen worktable. She couldn't remember that happening before.

She had taken a few moments to consider the news about field workers only a few miles to the south being struck down by cholera. The epidemic was coming closer even as people insisted the cooler weather of September would make it subside very soon. The stories of men dropping as they worked terrified Sylvie. She knew how quickly death could arrive after the first symptoms, a loosening of "rice water" from the bowels. Several victims had been buried at the edges of fields, in graves dug quickly and deep to avoid contamination. Later, their bodies would be retrieved for decent burial. She must have dreamed some such scenes, for their horror jolted her awake, and she returned to her chores.

She and other young people often stayed up later at night, trying to relax so that restful sleep might eventually overtake their nervous exhaustion. They gathered around the fireplace in the kitchen, and one night, she and Louisa cooked crepes as a treat with Octave Borne and Emile Hubert. They were chatting and reviewing the day, sipping cider or wine.

Sylvie was managing the long handles of the crepe press, keeping the carbon-steel plates tightly together and positioned near the coals where the heat was even. She pulled the press back to the hearth and balanced it on the stones, then raised the top handle. Louisa, next to her, carefully peeled off the wafer of golden dough, almost crisp but still soft. She dropped it onto a plate and handed it to one of the men to choose the filling: cinnamon and sugar, stewed apples, or ground chestnuts.

Sylvie, too fatigued to follow the conversation, wondered whether reciting the number of dishes they had prepared that day would help her to sleep later. As she tried to recall this day's menu, she had to mentally correct herself: no, that dish was from the day before or even earlier. She yawned, starting over to get the order right.

Other friends and relatives had slipped off to bed, but Louisa was still laughing and chatting. Sylvie ladled a dollop of batter onto the press, squeezed the plates together, and steered it toward the embers. She glanced again at Louisa and Octave, and at Emile, on the far side.

"Sylvie, aren't getting you tired? Do you need to get to bed?"

Sylvie turned toward the man's voice to her left. She hadn't noticed Vital Jarrot coming in. He eased onto the floor and stretched his feet toward the fire.

"I will soon," she said. "Would you like a crepe?"

"Not at the moment, but I'll take over making them for you."

"You? Making crepes?" Sylvie laughed.

"You forget that I've done a lot of cooking around campfires. Think of all those months on the fur-trade routes. Do you think we men couldn't feed ourselves?"

"I think you didn't cook crepes."

"Etienne says you're to go to bed. I'll stay here and watch over the others."

"Oh, he sent you as the chaperon, did he?"

Vital grinned and nodded. His face was ruddy and tanned, his eyes bright in the firelight. He exuded enjoyment of the fatigue following the long day's work. His brother, François, had not joined the harvesting, however. Vital said he was well enough to resume his rounds as a physician, but not yet to toil under the sun for a dozen hours at a time.

"And you don't mind staying on, after working all day?" Sylvie asked.

"No, I feel fine. I slept a little, earlier."

He did seem content as he leaned back on his elbows to peer around her at Louisa, who was conversing in a low tone with Octave and laughing easily from time to time. Emile, farther away, tried gamely to find moments for joining in. Sylvie pulled the press away from the fire, and this time, as Louisa didn't notice, she peeled off the crepe herself. No one was interested in it, which meant that her work was drawing to a close.

"They could be up all night," Sylvie murmured.

"In that case, I might not stay with them."

"What do you mean? You're supposed to chaperon."

"Yes, Etienne wants me to watch over you, in case the two of them leave."

"Oh, *mon dieu*. Guarding me against . . . him?" She spoke softly and tilted her head.

Vital raised his eyebrows. "No? Not interested? No hint of adventure? Well then, there's no danger."

"Danger? In what way?" Sylvie giggled. "I do need to get some sleep. But you can't leave Louisa and her new *ami* alone together. What kind of chaperon would you be?"

"The kind who lets people's true hearts find each other."

Sylvie watched his expression for a moment. "You like him, then, you and the others? You've had a chance to get to know Monsieur Borne?"

"Yes, there's nothing like scything and bundling side by side for a few days to get to know someone, in the heat and dust. He's all right."

"And what about the other?" Sylvie kept her voice low.

"He's all right, too."

"So do you have a recommendation for me?"

*"Non, pas du tout."* Now Vital watched her expression, his eyes narrowing slightly. "Come, I'll help you up, and you can get to bed." He rose and touched her arm.

Louisa turned as Sylvie stood. "Sylvie, I will be up in a minute. And don't worry about the crepe batter and dishes; I'll clean up."

Sylvie thanked her and said good night to the others. Vital followed her away from the fire, and as she started up the stairs, she stopped and turned.

"Etienne sees you as a chaperon for me," she said. "He doesn't see you in any other possible light?"

"What do you mean?"

"That there's no danger in our being together—the two of us." Sylvie realized, hearing her own words, that fatigue must be allowing her to speak so plainly.

Vital hesitated and glanced away. After a few moments, he said, "It's an informal understanding, Sylvie, but I think a certain young woman accepts, and even returns, my feelings."

"Thank you for telling me. I can keep a secret, if you want to let me know who it is."

"Maybe some other time." He nodded and said good night, then headed toward the porch where the family's friends and relatives bedded down at night.

As she quickly prepared for bed, Sylvie wondered only briefly about Vital's reply. It implied some loss for herself, if only of childish dreams and affections. She resolved to reconsider his words in daylight when she had renewed energy. Despite her resolution to stay awake until Louisa came to bed, she fell into sleep like a stone dropped into a pond.


The next morning, Sylvie was pouring hot water over coffee in the filter of the large metal pot, anticipating the first cup as fragrant steam rose. Amy had brioche ready, and its rich, buttery dough, pulling apart in feathery layers, was a domestic miracle.

Sylvie took her roll and coffee to the edge of the worktable while Fernande began listing the day's tasks. As the end of their part of the harvest cycle approached, she was offering more festive dishes than she had during the earlier days. Roast lamb, to be done on a spit outside; stewed chickens with vegetables on the stove inside; a dozen loaves of bread, to be baked in the brick oven at the end of the vegetable garden; and fruit tartes and walnut cakes, to be baked in the indoor oven.

The men had been gone for some time when Louisa came down to the kitchen. As work progressed and the house grew hot, the girls began packing food to take to the fields for the midday break.

"I will be so glad when you two don't have to go out among those men and boys anymore," Fernande said as she kept up with stirring three pots on the stove, her ringlets frizzing in the steam. "Where is Amy?" she asked irritably.

"Fernande, if you only knew how little you have to worry about," Louisa replied. She was still sipping coffee, so languid that Sylvie had to prompt her to do routine tasks.

"Most of them can't even talk with us," Sylvie said. "They speak German or broken English with such strong accents that I don't understand them. Mainly they just stare at us like we're exotic birds."

"Well, I don't like it. You girls look like day laborers in your work clothes, lugging food and drink out to the fields."

"We are laborers, Fernande; you forget I am an orphan, a poor, landless orphan."

"Sylvie!" Fernande slammed down the wooden spoon and turned, her hands on her hips. "That is no way to talk. Your sister will be fair with your inheritance, but you have to be twenty-one or married, first. So stop making insinuations and get the food packed."

"I am sorry, Fernande. I'm overtired, and I spoke without thinking. Just as you say, everything will work out." As Sylvie apologized, she wondered why people often reacted most strongly to statements that were true. She exchanged a glance with Louisa when Fernande had turned back to the stove; now she would be happy to have them away from the kitchen.

Outside, the sun was so beautiful and the breeze so fresh that Sylvie instantly regretted all the time spent in the house. She might be willing to cut wheat, just to stay out longer. She and Louisa had lugged the baskets of food and jugs of ale and ginger beer into the back of the cart.

"You were late coming to bed last night," Sylvie said as she took the horse's bridle to lead it across the road and into the fields.

"The time with Octave passes so quickly, I lost track."

"Have you had time alone with him?" When Louisa nodded yet kept staring vacantly toward the treetops, Sylvie asked, "Louisa, has he kissed you yet?"

"*Beh, oui.* And I can tell you, that is how you'll know if he is the right one. If fire runs through you when your lips meet, and—"

"Louisa, if Fernande catches you, or your brothers, Narcisse or Edward—"

"I know. They will send him away and tell the other *habitants* that he's not to be trusted. That he's a cad, a handsome, charming, rich . . . cad."

"You are running such a risk."

"All the more delightful!" As Sylvie shook her head, Louisa suggested she should show more interest in Emile. "The way he watches you, I can tell he likes you."

"No, he's so ordinary he's not appealing at all. And it's annoying, the way he says being here in Cahokia is like going back two hundred years in time."

As they reached the workers, they let the conversation die. The swaths of mown field looked oddly dun colored, with the light now reaching to the soil underneath. The remaining stand of golden wheat was narrow, and some men were about to clear it all the way to the field's edge. Their light-blue or white shirts moved with their rhythmical stooping and rising, looking like little boats bobbing on a golden river. Men of the French community, both white European and black African, wore bright red or blue scarves on their heads, while the Germans wore woven straw hats. The air smelled richly of grass, earth, and river.

The harvest of Laurent's fields was nearly over; and then, one day, it was ending. Some workers drove off in carts in the afternoon or just walked down the lane. Everyone was invited to linger in the yard, where long tables were covered with food and drink. At dusk, someone began to play the fiddle, and a harmonica joined in. The mood became festive, even though there would not be dancing that evening. The first ball of the season would be on St. Michael's Day at Aunt Lizette's house, which had been designated the last farm in the harvest cycle.

As night fell, the men concerned themselves with the oxen, horses, and tools. They would take the following day to sharpen blades and make repairs, and to rest before moving on to the next fields. As people went about drinking and talking, laughter rose from pleasure and from relief that the wheat was being safely taken in before the storms of fall, that the weather was holding, that the community would eat well all winter and still have plenty to sell. It was a beautiful crop this year with full, abundant golden kernels, and it would bring a good return in trade.

One final task remained for Sylvie to perform after the last dishes were dried and put away and the leftover food arranged on the table in the kitchen. Celeste had struggled to stay awake until then so the two of them could walk out together in the darkness to the front gate. Sylvie held Celeste's little hand and carried in her other hand a cross fashioned from two handfuls of wheat stalks. Where the small bundles crossed at right angles, she had tied them tightly with other stalks.

Above the girls, the night was clear and starry. Broad wings whooshed overhead, startling them as an owl glided by, intent on finding mice and voles that now had to dart across fields newly shorn of cover. Celeste squealed in delighted fright and grasped harder at Sylvie's hand.

They opened the front gate, closed it behind them, and stood in the road while Sylvie fastened the wheaten cross to the gate. She hung it high, so passersby would see it and know what it signified: The wheat was *en gerbe et en grange*, bundled in sheaves and in the barn, stored for threshing over coming months.

Then the two girls, the younger reaching half the height of the older, their shadows long and wavering faintly in moon and starlight, offered a quiet prayer of heartfelt thanks to the divine forces of sun, earth, water, and the universe's general benevolence. They went back inside the yard and crossed toward the house, where candlelight was shining behind the tall, broad windows downstairs. They could see the moving shadows and faint gleams as family members carried tapers upstairs on their way to bed, and then a candle was placed on the sill of the girls' bedroom window. Etienne had been watching from the porch to witness the girls of the household marking the successful harvest with this ancient rite.

Celeste tightened her grip. "I will remember this night always," she said.

Sylvie squeezed her hand in response. "And I will, too."

As they approached the warm farmhouse, the frosty air dropped like a chilly shawl around their shoulders.

# Chapter 5



**Fall 1832**
**Ste. Geneviève, Missouri**


WITH THE WHEAT HARVEST ACCOMPLISHED, the fall season of balls and parties could begin, and Louisa, who had turned sixteen, was reveling in attending them for the first time. As she recounted all the thrilling details to Sylvie, she focused increasingly on Octave Borne, how they had danced together, and all the things he had said. With time, Sylvie's attention began to wander. Yet as she packed her trunk to return to the school she had attended for several years, she thought of how much she would miss Louisa's company, now that she was not coming back.

Sylvie traveled with her nieces Marguerite and Isabelle, the eldest daughters of her half-sister Jeanne, to the convent school in Ste. Geneviève, nearly sixty miles downriver from St. Louis. Once there, the three shared a large room in the dormitory. That was a second reason Sylvie felt dismayed; this moved her closer to Jeanne's realm, and she worried it would seem natural, when the term recessed for the Christmas holidays, for her to come home to Jeanne's house along with her nieces.

The cholera outbreak had dwindled with cooler weather as predicted, and with mail delivery returning to normal, Sylvie finally heard from her Aunt Peggy. She received a letter at school and took it to the dormitory to read in privacy. The room she shared, up under the eaves, held a deep bay window with diamond-shaped, colored panes across the top. All were slate blue or wine red except for one clear pane near the middle, which Sylvie figured replaced one broken over the years. A long, cushioned seat stretched underneath, where she liked to prop a pillow against the wall, curl up, and read books for hours at a time.

Her reading wasn't always for pleasure; she was taking literature classes in French and English, and she was caught up in a recent book from France about the Cathedral Notre Dame and its hunchback caretaker, who was in love with a young dancer dealing with the woes of being regularly mistreated.

Sylvie sat on the window seat, broke the seal on the letter, and scanned the opening quickly. Her Aunt Peggy wrote that indeed, David had returned from the war sound in body but apparently troubled in mind. Sylvie tried to mentally translate the English phrases. Did "suffering from melancholy" mean the same as *la mélancolie* in French? If so, that indicated a serious loss of enjoyment of life, with possibly long-lasting moods of darkness and inertia.

Sylvie went back to read more slowly, this time also taking in Peggy's condolences for Laurent's death nearly three months earlier, which finished by asking what path Sylvie might choose for her future. That was kind, Sylvie thought; it showed her aunt by marriage considered herself a close relation who might reach out and play a role in her life.

She carefully reread the paragraph about David's condition and paused to wonder what it implied, whether it meant she should not consider a visit or an extended stay. Or perhaps Peggy would like her to offer assistance, to help care for him and possibly raise his spirits.

Sylvie entertained these thoughts only until the next paragraphs, where Aunt Peggy proposed a completely different idea.

> *Now I will share some news regarding plans and opportunities for our family's future, dear Sylvie. You'll remember my brother James, your Uncle Jim, who is living in Texas. He plans to take a wife, a decision that heartens us all. Though both you and David remember your Aunt Angelina fondly, it has been eight years since she died, along with their three poor children, after they joined Jim at Stephen Austin's first colony. It is high time for him to remarry, in my opinion.*
>
> *You undoubtedly will be pleased to learn that Jim's fiancée is Sarah Fulton. She remembers you from your time together at the convent school, and you'll hear from her soon with a proposal that you,*

*with your young, adventurous spirit, will find attractive. But I mustn't divulge details, for she wishes to meet with you in Ste. Geneviève and present the plan herself.*

*We all remain truly saddened by the untimely and lamentable death of your dear half-brother, and I feel it is high time for this side of the family to take a hand in helping you through the difficulties on the path life has presented to you.*

Sylvie leaned back to gaze out at the rain sluicing the yellowing maple leaves beyond the window. Past the garden, brown with leaves and trimmed-back plants, a wall along the riverbank allowed a glimpse of the Mississippi's churning, slate-gray waters. So this was how that family would help, not by inviting her to stay at the farm in Troy, but by proposing something involving Sarah Fulton, Uncle Jim, and the distant colonies in Mexico. Sylvie guessed Sarah wanted her to come along as a travel companion. What else could it be? A woman would need and want female company for such a long and difficult journey.

But what on earth would move Sylvie to agree to such a venture? It would involve hardships and discomforts beyond those she could imagine easily. How ironic that when her cousin Paschal had suggested the colonies in Texas to her in August, she replied that she lacked the example of a modern woman who would take risks as her ancestors had done. Here, apparently, was just such a model in Sarah Fulton.

Sylvie remembered her as an older girl at the school who could run fast, and who often led the girls in games in the courtyard, her curly red hair flying in a wild mass. One time she had even set up hay bales and tried to teach archery. Sylvie smiled at the memory and wondered where Sarah had been for the past few years. And if it wasn't Mexico, how she had managed to form a liaison with Uncle Jim.

Soon Sylvie's nieces came into the room, each with a letter from the day's delivery.

Marguerite, at eighteen, was older than most of the girls, and Sylvie wondered why she had come back to school. Marguerite claimed she wanted to continue her studies in painting and music, but she'd also hinted at the relief of getting away from the strictness and piety at home. As she took a chair by the desk and turned her back while opening her letter, she could have been excited and happy. But Sylvie thought no one would be able to tell, given the demure manner Marguerite always maintained, striving to be gracious under any circumstances.

Isabelle, two years younger, presented a contrast by falling back on the bed and waving her letter in the air before bringing it to her lips for an enthusiastic kiss. She was so close to Sylvie in age that they had been christened together as infants. Sylvie gave her a wide-eyed, curious smile and discreetly pointed toward Marguerite.

"Vital Jarrot," Isabelle mouthed, and sketched a heart in the air with one hand.

Sylvie nodded, having suspected for some time that the two were exchanging letters—without Jeanne's knowledge. At first, she had felt truly irritated that this pretty, mild, ever-unruffled niece who worked dreamily on paintings of birds and blossoms would seem compelling to Vital. But even though Sylvie was younger, she was still Marguerite's aunt, a role demanding fond and generous behavior. Marguerite was closer in age to Vital, their families were closely aligned, and Jeanne would give her approval for the courtship once her mourning period for Laurent drew to a close.

Sylvie mouthed to Isabelle, "And you?" and pointed toward her letter.

"Edward. Our cousin Edward." Isabelle sighed loudly and let her arms drop onto the bedclothes.

"*Tiens!*" Sylvie raised a hand to her mouth. She had suspected a secret suitor, but not Edward, the son of Aunt Lizette. A liaison between such close cousins, even a generation apart, was unthinkable. Though Isabelle was clearly thrilled by the letter, it seemed she was not going to open it in front of the others. Like Sylvie, she was small in stature, with dark hair and eyes. But while Sylvie had inherited her mother's heart-shaped face, large eyes, and petite nose, Isabelle had Jeanne's longer face and smaller eyes, which had to peer past the bony arch of her nose. As Isabelle sat up and turned to gaze out the window,

Sylvie watched her profile—the pale cheek spotted with red—and her heart lurched with sympathy.

"Did you receive a letter also, Sylvie?" Marguerite asked innocently. Though Sylvie insisted she did not have a beau, Emile Hubert had written to her twice since the start of the term. Marguerite patted her refolded letter with both hands on the desktop, smiling in satisfaction, her cheeks creamy pink.

"If you mean from Emile Hubert, no, thank goodness. I have not replied to the second one he sent, so I hope he takes the hint and lets it drop."

In the first note, Emile wrote that Fernande had granted him permission to contact Sylvie so they might begin corresponding. Sylvie had waited as long as decency allowed before writing back a few rote, meaningless niceties. Yet he had written a second time and suggested they might see each other at gatherings during the holidays. She suspected Louisa was egging him on in hopes of making a foursome for the season's parties.

"*Maman* says he calls often at your house, and since you're not there, he stays on to visit with Fernande." Isabelle turned to look fully at Sylvie, her expression thoughtful.

"He does? Why would he do that?"

"Trying to ingratiate himself, I presume," Marguerite said. She had opened a small volume of poetry and was tucking her letter between its pages. "He wants to ensure his social standing among the *habitants,* even though he's not yet a landowner."

Sylvie nodded but gave no further thought to the awkwardness of that situation.

Isabelle enjoyed botany classes and excelled at doing intricate paintings of plants along with concise studies of their culinary and medicinal uses. She and Sylvie also enjoyed the afternoon dance sessions, where young people from town joined the convent students for instruction in etiquette, dance steps, and the manners and morals that would shape them into upstanding members of society. Sylvie liked the history and geography class, and she was still awaiting the promised note from Sarah Fulton when Sister Giroux, the teacher, announced she would begin a unit on colonies being founded in the New World.

When she gathered students soon after around maps from the convent's precious collection, which she had spread out on classroom tables, Sylvie saw the American colonies in Mexico for the first time. Much of Mexico was still labeled Louisiane from when France had claimed it, before Spain took it over. The teacher explained how Mexico had risen up against Spain and won its independence as a country less than ten years earlier. She then pointed toward the northeastern part of the country and asked the girls to look closely at the province Coahuila y Tejas, also called Texas. Someone had drawn circles with a pen around sites along rivers and written in the names of colonies.

"Many of you know families who have gone to settle in these places," Sister Giroux said. "Stephen Austin is licensed as an *empresario*, and he has started two colonies. He grew up here in Ste. Geneviève and even attended this school; I remember him from the afternoon dance lessons and socials."

The girls giggled and nudged one another.

"The first one he founded is San Felipe." She pointed at an inland spot along a river. "He was successful at recruiting the first three hundred settlers needed to establish it. How many of you know people who have left their homes and farms here to become colonists with him, or with other *empresarios*?"

Nearly every student raised a hand. Sylvie thought of Uncle Jim and held hers in the air, though she was picturing Coahuila y Tejas as a place where people disappeared. No one ever seemed to come back, except for occasional traders. She stared at the province's ragged coastline and threadlike rivers and studied the names of Indian nations written across neighboring areas: Karankawa, Waco, Apache.

"Here is where Stephen Austin is building his second colony, a town called Mina." Sister Giroux traced her fingertip in a small circle where a road, El Camino Real, crossed a river, Rio Colorado. The area to the north was labeled Comanche Nation, and so was the vast expanse stretching west to the town of Santa Fe, the northernmost point of Spain's former empire. From there, blank space stretched to the Pacific Ocean, where the mission of San Francisco showed as a dot alongside a huge bay. Not far to the north was the Russian territory called Alaska.

Sister Giroux talked about local French traders who were developing routes from St. Louis to Santa Fe, and Sylvie could make out the dotted lines of two different trails. Both led through Indian lands as well as blank areas. Aunt Peggy's husband must have traveled those routes for his trading, along with his brother, who had been kidnapped and held captive by Waco Indians for several years. Sylvie wondered where the men might be right now.

When her classmates moved to a table holding a different map, Sylvie lingered to look at Green DeWitt's colony, where her Uncle Jim was doing surveying and administrative work. It was marked as a small circle on Rio Guadalupe, to the west of San Felipe and south of Mina. Had Sarah Fulton gazed at such a map and been able to picture a new home for herself? She must have read detailed descriptions in Uncle Jim's correspondence and learned of his views, hopes, and expectations. Sylvie recalled him fondly; both she and David agreed he was the most humorous of the uncles and the most likely to overlook mischief. Surely bright, lively Sarah could find a suitable match closer to home, so she also must be confident of Jim's character and persuaded by his dreams; perhaps they coincided with a yearning for adventure on her own part.

Sylvie went to join the others as Sister Giroux was speaking about the thirteen original American colonies. The map before them had been drawn by the Séminaire de Québec, so it also showed the early French colonies. And there was her hometown, La Cahokie, with its mission founded in 1686. The dotted lines on this map showed the exploratory voyages by Marquette, Joliet, and LaSalle, and once again, most students raised their hands when the teacher asked how many had ancestors who had been on those expeditions as crew, fur traders, or soldiers.

Sylvie peered to see whether the map showed New Design, the Utopian community that her mother's birth family, the Clarks, had trekked west to join. But its location between the towns of Cahokia and Belleville stood blank. She felt uneasy and disappointed, for the colonists' struggles had been severe. Her mother had been orphaned, then widowed, and then had died young; it didn't seem right that the colony her family had striven for should be erased from history, too.

When Sylvie asked about New Design, Sister Giroux agreed that it should appear and added that she might write it in. "Those colonists were quite idealistic. They opposed slavery, and they followed principles that the American president expressed at the time. In fact, one of the leaders was a friend of Thomas Jefferson's, and that's partly how they got the land grant. But half the colonists died from illness in the first year, and it happened so long ago—almost fifty years."

As the class ended, Sister Giroux asked Sylvie to remain for a moment. "The lesson today was not entirely accidental—or coincidental," she said. "I wanted you to have some preparation for this letter that I received, which I am to pass on to you."

Sylvie took the folded paper and glanced at the return address, not greatly surprised to see Sarah Fulton's name. "She was an excellent student here," Sister Giroux continued. "She has a first-rate mind and a keen interest in societal issues. She would make a stimulating travel companion during the voyage she is anticipating. And she speaks of you as a quick child of promising character. I understand the family wishes you to accompany her."

"Do they?" Sylvie's voice was faint, and her teacher looked perplexed.

"You might think of going there as an opportunity. I'd urge you to keep a diary, or a detailed account. Few women get to make such a journey, and when you come back, your observations and reflections will prove valuable. Will you consider doing that?"

"I'll think about it, yes."

"I would look forward to reading such an account; I believe you'd have interesting observations to share."

Sylvie smiled at that idea, but she was startled when Sister Giroux added that Sarah wanted to start downriver in early spring, as soon as the ice cleared and before the typical flooding. The trip—a remote possibility—rushed toward Sylvie with the sudden clarity of a fixed event.

As she walked back to her dormitory room, she recalled encountering Sarah in a dim school corridor years earlier, while a nun was scolding Sylvie and a friend for running and making noise. Sarah had crept up behind the nun and began mimicking her, to the girls' delight. While Sylvie smiled at the memory, when she later sat to read Sarah's letter, she was struck more by the lofty ideals it expressed.

After affectionate and warm salutations, Sarah wrote,

> *I am inspired by the contributions women can make toward building a new society in a entirely new place. Just imagine: what would you choose, if you were creating a new world from its foundations? Women play such a crucial role in starting the more civilizing institutions, such as schools and hospitals. So, Sylvie, you could think of this venture to the young colonies in a similar way.*

Sarah said she wanted to allow more time for correspondence to arrive from Jim and suggested that she and Sylvie meet in Ste. Geneviève after the New Year to discuss the trip.

Sylvie took several days to think over the proposition. One part appealed to her immediately: the voyage to New Orleans. All children growing up along the river dreamed of getting there. And to think she might see the city before Louisa did! The trip could also be a great help to Amy, for the family was still seeking a way for her to get there safely and join her friends and relations. Sylvie decided to ask Sarah if Amy could accompany them that far.

But going on to Texas? She shook her head every time she thought of it. Going so far—to blank areas of the map where tiny colonies existed as mere circles of ink in desolate and raw expanses— loomed as an unattractive prospect. Plus, she had no idea how long a voyage across the Gulf of Mexico would take, or how readily one could return.

Sylvie felt sure that if she stayed on in New Orleans, fate would open up more opportunities for her life. Perhaps she could make use of her language skills to find employment there. Any eventual return to Cahokia would require planning and locating trustworthy travel companions to ensure her own safety, but that could be managed in the future.

When Sylvie replied to Sarah's letter, she wrote the she would be happy to meet in Ste. Geneviève after the holidays and discuss the trip. She said she was looking favorably upon the voyage to New Orleans and explained Amy's plight in some detail. She felt sure that Sarah would agree to her coming along. The rest of the matter, the subsequent voyage to Mexico, she left hanging as an open question.

Chapter 6

**December 1832**
**Cahokia, Illinois**

THE SCHOOL TERM BROKE IN MID-DECEMBER, and Sylvie came home to the farmhouse with Fernande and the family. Frosts were settling overnight on roofs and tree branches, and cold winds smelled of distant snow. The *Grand Marais* was not yet iced over, so she and Etienne slipped off one morning to hunt ducks and geese.

Sylvie was daydreaming of fat roast goose at the *Réveillon* feast, which followed mass on Christmas Eve. Etienne carried a Kentucky rifle, which was newer and more accurate than the old flintlock Sylvie used. Even so, she preferred the older gun's weight and balance and the way its curved wooden parts gleamed with age, compared with the rifle's harder edges and straight angles. They wore moc-boots lined with rabbit fur all the way to the knee.

As they rode downhill, smoke from chimneys rose to bend sideways in the sky, looking like chalk streaks on a slate. Farms they passed smelled wonderfully of bacon and ham curing in the smokehouses. Weeks earlier, the pigs had been driven onto the Commons and fattened on the acorns and mast fallen on the ground. The owners then rounded up the pigs that bore their brands and herded them home for slaughter.

Everyone's spirits rose for the holidays, and the household seemed to be running well, though Fernande looked worn. When she told Sylvie that she didn't know how much longer she could manage on her own, Etienne squared his shoulders and listed the new tasks he was taking on. It made Sylvie's heart ache, and she had wept a bit as she unpacked her things in the bedroom she shared with Celeste.

Sylvie and Etienne dismounted and tied the horses back from the shore in the woods. They separated at the edge of the marsh, and as Sylvie hid behind reeds to watch for waterfowl, she began shivering despite the warm fur and woolens she wore. Clumps of dead grasses bent low, and as she knelt, she hushed her breathing to blend with the quiet setting. She wanted to stay out as long as possible, for Emile Hubert had sent a note saying he might call that day.

Sylvie caught sight of a deer standing motionless across the pond, barely visible at the edge of woods, only the ears rotating slowly. She raised her flintlock smoothly and took aim just as two rifle shots from Etienne punctured the air. The dogs raced to the water and jumped in, splashing loudly, to retrieve any birds plummeting from the sky. Sylvie didn't need to look to know the deer was gone.

More than an hour passed as she and Etienne waited in the cold. Finally, some ducks and geese returned to the quiet pond, and they both got off more shots. When they had a goose and two ducks for their efforts, they agreed to leave. Etienne stepped away to gut the birds, and as she waited, Sylvie could feel her deep chill shifting to overheated discomfort. She had pulled off her hat and mittens when Etienne returned and told her brusquely to put them back on. As he helped her up on the horse, he said her cheeks looked quite flushed and asked if she was feeling well.

The ride back seemed to take longer than usual, and at the house Sylvie went directly to the *salon* to stand by the woodstove, as Etienne took care of the horses, guns, and game birds. She was beginning to feel more normal when Amy came in, carrying a tray stacked with cof-feepot, cups and saucers, and a plate of little cakes.

"So you finally show up! Where have you been such a long time? Fernande has been asking for you half the morning. Get into some clean clothes and watch that you don't track mud. That gentleman is coming to call on you."

Amy set down the tray and gripped Sylvie's shoulder to maneuver her toward the stairs. In her room, Sylvie reached for clean clothes and dressed quietly, for Celeste was sleeping peacefully in the bed, her face rosy and tracked with pink dots.

Was that a sign of measles? If so, that would explain why Celeste had felt so hot and kicked restlessly during the night. As fall progressed, cholera had been replaced by this new scourge. Sylvie had heard that whooping cough, too, was striking children in St. Louis. She sat on the bedside and touched the back of her hand to Celeste's forehead and cheeks. She seemed cooler, and the moments of concern softened Sylvie's mood. But things still weren't quite right: the bedroom walls seemed to swirl quickly when she turned her head, and her stomach lurched in response.

Emile Hubert shouldn't be visiting if the household had measles. Many adults had never contracted the disease because they'd grown up in small, isolated settlements, and it could prove lethal at their age. Now, people living in more populous areas caught it while younger and seemed to survive it better. Maybe he'd had the disease already; one didn't get it twice. Sylvie may have caught a light case the previous spring when Etienne came home after contracting it at the academy he attended in Belleville.

She had barely changed her dress before Amy came to fetch her. Emile was waiting in the salon, and she arrived to see him, dressed in a business suit, chatting with Fernande. He kissed Sylvie's hand, and the three visited for a few moments before Fernande left, saying the children needed her attention.

Emile made comments about the weather, and soon he was launching into expressions of his sentiment. Sylvie gripped the arms of her chair, wondering if he had memorized the formal phrases, given the way he uttered them in fits and starts.

"So happy to find you here alone . . . express my thoughts . . . you must have noticed . . . hold in highest regard . . . evidence of special feelings . . . hope you might reciprocate . . ."

As Sylvie realized that a serious proposal was underway, her tilting stomach sent up waves of anguish and bubbles of giggling, both of which she tried to suppress. The two of them must have looked like stiff marionettes bobbing through a rehearsal.

"I am deeply honored—and much too young to make such a decision," she managed to say when he paused. There was more she was supposed to say, and her mind raced. "With greatest respect for the significance of your regrets . . . I mean respect . . . and your expressions of regard . . ."

"Regrets?" Emile was staring at her.

"Yes, I do regret I am not feeling well. Perhaps another time would be better for this momentous diversion—that is, discussion." She stood up.

"Yes, certainly I am willing to wait. I would not wish to rush anyone into a decision that needs consideration." He stood also, towering above her and tilting along with the stripes in the wallpaper behind him.

"I appreciate your young age, and when you are fully sixteen . . . that is, if my sentiments are reciprocated . . . with reason to remain hopeful . . ."

"That must be Louisa imagining things, in keeping with what she wants." At Emile's expression, Sylvie was suddenly horrified. Hadn't she but thought this? Given his reddening face and firmly set mouth, maybe she had spoken out loud.

"Then we will let time pass before speaking of the matter again." He bowed and lightly touched his heels together.

Sylvie stood in the *salon*, listening as Amy arrived to show Emile to the door. Then Fernande's voice was saying, "I am so sorry, Emile. I do apologize that Sylvie is not herself this morning. We have just come down with measles in the house, and we're at loose ends."

After both had assured each other of their mutual regard, the door shut firmly. Fernande appeared behind Amy, and the two stood, hands on hips, glaring at Sylvie.

"I suppose you believe this is only the beginning, that you'll have many more offers?" Fernande spoke in an unnaturally low voice, allowing space on the vocal register for it to rise with exasperation. Sylvie pictured her pounding lower keys on a piano and charging on to the higher ones. Fernande continued, "He is a fine young man, and you will be lucky to have any better suitor in the future!"

"Do you truly like him that much?"

To Sylvie's wonder, Fernande flushed deeply and lifted her skirt to swish dramatically out of the room. Amy distractedly watched her leave, and when she looked back, she stared Sylvie straight in the eye, her expressive brow arched high.

As though choosing among a range of responses, Amy said mildly, "We need to work on more gracious phrases that you can use. You were abrupt with that young man, even rude, and that causes unnecessary shame. There will be no more responses like that, Sylvie."

"So you think I might get more proposals in times to come?"

"I think you will, and I also think you're wise to wait a few years. But when word gets out about this, your fate is cast into the air." Amy waved an arm, her fingers extended. "You did not actually tell him no; you asked for more time. What if people now think you two have an understanding?"

"Oh, dear. Could I have done any worse? Does he have to ask me again, so I can shout out, 'No and no and no'?" Tears welled up so quickly that they slid down her cheeks before she knew they were coming.

As Amy shook her head and began restacking the coffee tray, Sylvie edged by her to run upstairs. She really was not feeling well, and it went beyond being chilled from hunting and dealing with an unwelcome proposal. She could feel bumps forming under the heated skin of her face, though when she peered in the mirror, she did not yet see the red dots that would soon emerge.

Lamplight during winter storms, staying warm and feeling cozy, more than a week of being entitled to stay in bed and not do chores—having the measles was not all that bad. Though Celeste had recovered quickly and Sylvie also seemed to have a light case, Fernande had sent for a physician, and François Jarrot called several times at the house. Sylvie enjoyed the visits as a relief from social isolation while the family stayed away from the usual holiday visits and parties. He could be quite humorous as he described incidents from gatherings and shared news of friends and relatives.

Sylvie had not seen François for months, given how ill he'd been after the war. As a longtime family friend, he could sit by the bedside and visit at length. Once he even described his own illness, consumption, yet reassured Sylvie it was in remission. At thirty, François was nearly twice her age, but she found him quite comely in spite of being so old. He had regular features, the profile of a Greek statue, and large eyes. He also wore his dark hair long, with its waves reaching the collar of his white shirt.

He would open his medical bag and select small bottles after asking Sylvie to describe her symptoms. One dark afternoon, with wind and sleet beating on the window behind the heavy curtain, he set out two blue glass bottles with stoppers and small labels.

"More laudanum?" he asked.

"No, I don't think so." Sylvie straightened against the pillows and pulled the quilt higher. "The willow bark took care of the fever, and laudanum makes me too sleepy and disoriented to read. And I'm enjoying reading as much as I can right now."

"Did you finish the bottles I left last time?"

"No. I took a bit from one, and Amy took the rest away."

"If Fernande is still taking it regularly, I would advise her to use less, now. She needed its calming effects after Laurent's death in order to keep up her strength. But I've seen how laudanum can weaken people who persist in taking it over time."

Sylvie considered his words as he packed away the two vials.

"You're fortunate to have a light case, and you won't have any scarring." He reached to gently touch her cheek and forehead with the back of his hand. It was an assessment, but Sylvie sensed affection as well.

"I'll be up again soon, to help around the house," she said.

"You need bed rest for two or three more days. It's dangerous to resume daily work too soon, especially in the winter. A relapse would only weaken you for another illness."

"All right; I will obey your orders."

As François got up to leave, he added, "By the way, I was glad to hear that you turned down a certain marriage proposal recently. You deserve a better match, Sylvie. Not only that, you're so young, it's wise to wait a few more years."

He had turned and was getting his things together when he added, "I have tended many new mothers and infants in those precarious weeks after childbirth, when fevers and other dangers set in. I am firmly of the opinion that young women should wait to marry until eighteen, and twenty is even better."

Sylvie was shocked that a man would bring up such a subject, even a physician. When she didn't reply, he glanced at her from where he stood near the door.

"That is how my mother died." Sylvie was speaking almost to herself. "For many years, I did not know that. And later I heard that was how my father's first wife died as well."

"Yes, I remember." François' expression was serious.

"Some people have said that it's due to a curse on the family."

"What? Superstitions and such are idiocy, and I'm surprised to hear you say that. We have scientific understanding now. Whoever would repeat that old story?"

"You have heard it, then—something the servants said, or the slaves, a long time ago?"

"Yes, I admit I have, but it needs to stay in the past. My advice is simple and modern: wait several more years before marrying."

"I will, and for my own reasons." Sylvie smiled and asked, "And do you think I'll grow taller in that time? I'd love to grow two or three more inches."

François laughed and shook his head. "Given your parents—and your father was considered quite short—I'd say that isn't likely. But we can hold out hope."

He nodded goodbye, abandoning during illness the usual cheek kisses.

Sylvie scooted down under the covers. She had several hours before Celeste would appear for bedtime, and she reveled in the solitude and time to think about options for her future. She had been reading newspaper articles about the colonies in Mexico, reports on events in New Orleans, and travelers' accounts of voyages down the

Mississippi River. The news stories about Indian depredations on colonies in Texas, and the mysterious diseases that swept through and killed settlers, discouraged Sylvie in her weakened condition.

But the trip to New Orleans remained attractive. She had mentioned the possibility to Amy, who welcomed the idea enthusiastically. The dangers that Amy would encounter on the river were serious, and both had head heard frightening stories during the previous summer about slavers working the river.

On the day she and Etienne had taken the buckwheat to the local gristmill, he had stopped in line with the cart, its wicker enclosure in back loaded with sacks. Illinois laws reserved certain days for the French to grind wheat, apart from when Americans ground corn. They had pulled up just behind Claude Belanger and his daughter Julia Adeline, in their wagon, and Sylvie noticed Etienne watching them dreamily.

"One day, I'm going to marry Julia Adeline," he said softly.

The girl had long, curling hair and large blue eyes, and she looked demure in a dark, polished cotton skirt and blouse with an embroidered white apron. As she turned to speak with her father, she darted unnecessary little glances back toward their cart. Sylvie could only respect such sincerity, confided by a thirteen-year old. Really, who knew how things might turn out by the time he could marry, five years from now? She envied that Etienne could be sure of inheriting his father's lands and eventually the house where they were all living.

Her own share of her father's property was in a trust whose details remained vague. Jeanne and her husband, Nicolas, now administered it, and they promised they would discuss dividing up the land when Sylvie turned twenty-one, or earlier if she married. As for cash, Jeanne had shrugged each time Sylvie brought up the question.

"Who has money lying about?" she'd asked. "No one, except for the odd coins. Everything is done by barter, by arranging credit in terms of furs to trade, with value defined in bucks' skins. We need someone to start a bank around here. But until then, how could we ever pay you in money itself?"

Sylvie recalled that conversation, from months earlier, as she fingered the lacy edge of her bed sheet. What Jeanne said was true, yet Sylvie would need money for the steamboat fare and for meals and lodging in New Orleans, if she made the trip.

The family also had to give Amy a final payment. Laws prescribed that each woman, at the end of her indenture, was owed a bag of coins, a pair of shoes, and two dresses or fabric for making them. Rightfully, the three siblings—Jeanne, Sylvie, and Laurent, or their estates—should each pay one-third, for their father had incurred the debt when he changed Amy's status from slavery to indentured servitude.

On that day at the mill, Sylvie had gone to the waiting room, planning to visit with friends and neighbors. An animated conversation was taking place about two slavers who had been captured and arrested on the river and their boat impounded. Apparently, they had kidnapped a family recently freed by William Clark, the territorial administrator in St. Louis, and intended to sell them in the slave markets in New Orleans. The men were caught and jailed, while the mother and her children were freed to resume their journey.

Sylvie listened as she watched the operations just beyond the windows, which were large to let in daylight, for any flame from a lantern or candle could ignite the clouds of wheat dust into fiery explosions. Workers carried sacks of grain up a stairway to the top floor, where they poured it into chutes leading down toward the grinding stones. Then the oxen resumed trudging, straining to go round and round to keep the enormous stone burrs turning. The machinery's wooden gears and fittings creaked and squealed as flour dust rose in clouds.

Sylvie wondered if she would see Matthieu, the slave who had worked at her father's mill at Richland Creek near Belleville, a dozen years earlier. After their father's death, Jeanne and Laurent had sold him along with the mill. The other slave had been set free, due to the entangled laws regarding slavery in Illinois at the time.

Sylvie saw Matthieu occasionally at the gristmill, where he often hired out and earned his own wages. He would always inquire after the family and ask especially about Amy.

Sylvie caught sight of Etienne carrying a sack of buckwheat upstairs. He would watch conscientiously over the entire process, for he enjoyed the complexity of the machinery and the workings of the interlocking wooden and metal parts.

Talk in the waiting room turned to the complex laws concerning slavery, which had been outlawed when Illinois became a state in 1818. But an exception had been made for slave owners in the southern counties, many of whom were French. American courts held that laws were not to be applied retroactively, meaning they did not apply to people born into slavery before the area became a US Territory in 1787. Slaves who were currently forty-five or fifty years old could be slaves the rest of their lives, unless their owners freed them, though this predicament and others were routinely debated. Public opinion in Illinois was hotly divided, especially as arguments evolved away from legalistic views toward questions of human decency and dignity, and the religious equality of souls.

No one in Sylvie's family owned slaves, and most of her relatives stood firmly against it. But some longtime family friends, such as Madame Julie Jarrot and even the former governor, John Reynolds, still kept slaves and refused to free even those born after 1787.

Sylvie would flush with shame over an incident that was still retold about her father. During the fierce debate over slavery before Illinois became a state, a minister from the East who was giving an antislavery speech at the courthouse in Belleville referred to a story of Jesus setting free two workers. Her father, who did not have a firm grasp of English, thought the minister was actually heading to his mill on Richland Creek to free the two slaves there. He had taken up a piece of lumber to threaten the minister before the misunderstanding was cleared up. People in Belleville still enjoyed telling the story as a humorous episode involving a fiery Frenchman.

Sylvie decided to slip out of the waiting room, and as she shut the door, the tingle creeping up her neck suggested the group might be gossiping about her family's friends or even retelling that humiliating episode. She stood in the dusty, noisy realm and watched as buckwheat kernels tumbled down the chute and disappeared between the burrs, to be transformed into unappealing gray-brown flour. How amazing that such a drab substance could turn into her appetizing crepes.

Sylvie caught sight of Matthieu with a group of workers nearby and went to greet him. In the shafts of dusty sunlight, his tightly curled hair looked grayer, and the skin at his neck formed folds; his strong build seemed compacted a bit by time. His eyes warmed as he greeted her and expressed condolences over Laurent's death.

"And how is that young Etienne?" he asked. "I saw him carrying up some grain a moment ago."

Sylvie assured him that all in the family were well and mentioned that Amy's indenture would end in the spring. Matthieu already knew that she wanted to join friends and relatives in New Orleans.

"You need to be careful to get Amy's papers from the court when her term is up," he said. "Then she can wear the documents in a locket around her neck, as women do."

Sylvie assured Matthieu that the family would handle the paperwork, and that she personally would make sure that Amy could travel safely downriver. He also had heard the morning's news about the slavers being caught. Sylvie believed she had made him a solemn promise, and as she recalled their conversation while she was tucked in bed on the December evening, she knew she had to keep her word. For what Matthieu had said next still terrified her.

She had told him not to worry, and added, "You know how careful the family is about doing things correctly."

Matthieu had squinted at her and said he didn't want to argue, but that he had been sold as a slave long after slavery was illegal. Laurent had taken the view that Matthieu would stay in slavery because he was born before Illinois became an American Territory.

Sylvie had been too young at the time—only five years old—to understand the circumstances, but Matthieu asked if she grasped the situation now. She said she did, and that it was troubling to think Laurent might do something so questionable, even if it was technically legal. Matthieu had been speaking adamantly that day at the mill, though he had always been a kindly man while she was growing up.

"What about you and your livelihood?" she had asked. "I've heard that you hire out for wages. Will you be able to buy yourself out of slavery?"

"How ignorant you can be when you're a poor orphan child and no one tells you much. I do still hope to earn enough to buy my way free, for as I get older, my value goes down. Already I'm worth less than the *pièce d'Inde* price for a healthy young man. So at some point, I might be able to afford it."

"I don't think of you as so old, but I do hope you succeed."

"You didn't realize I'm actually that old—well over fifty? Born way back then . . ." He chuckled a bit.

"Not many people get to be that age and remain so lively and . . . I am sorry. It's not right—just because you were born at the wrong time," Sylvie said, her words coming quickly. "If it had been . . . what? Just five years later? You would be free already. That's a terrible fate."

"Fate? Fate would be like something God set up in heaven that mere people can do nothing about. If you're truly sorry, just be sure you do right by Amy. There is no fairness in life, Miss Sylvie. Some things are so wrong from the start that they can't be made fair."

She nodded, silent.

"Good, that's settled. No one wants to be like your Papa and bring down more trouble on your family or get another curse put on your womenfolk."

"What are you talking about?"

"Another thing they didn't tell you?"

"I do know about it, if you're talking about that old superstition, about that slave woman who got angry. That was before I was even born."

"Yes, the slave, Frankey, when your Papa sold her and her baby and then bought Amy. He sold that baby as a slave, so he got money for two people, not one."

"That was commonly done; it was legal," Sylvie said faintly. She was beginning to feel nauseated and would not defend her father any longer. "Frankey put a curse on my family because of that? But curses are not real."

Still, Sylvie had grown tenser. The ancestors of many of the area's slaves had lived for a time in Santo Domingo, where she understood some strains of religion practiced a kind of magic. She had heard of slaves years ago in Cahokia who had poisoned their owners, and more recently, of a slave who set fire to the Chouteau mansion in St. Louis.

"But surely they made a legal arrangement for that, and the child became free after a time," she said.

"It doesn't matter, now. That curse, once it's laid, can't be lifted. The mother and child went off with her people a long time ago and aren't around here anymore. They probably have never even thought of lifting it."

"What was the curse?" Sylvie had heard vague references to the incident a few times, but only as whispers among adults that broke off when children were around.

"Well, you know, it has to do with the mothers giving birth to their babies. Think about the way your Papa's wives died, including your own mother."

"Now you are talking about my *Maman*!" Sylvie's voice rose. "How dare you say it was due to some stupid thing someone said years ago. That Frankey, that woman, could not have that kind of power!"

"You can be angry with me." Matthieu shrugged. "It doesn't change a thing."

"What you're saying isn't Christian, and you can't go around frightening people like this!"

Sylvie had fisted her hands, and her arms had trembled. People nearby were glancing at them, looking away, and then turning back to watch when it was clear that she was not paying them any attention. Her voice had risen up and out of control, and when the whining grinding wheels and creaking wooden machinery halted, her words had flown like a bright scarf in the air above their heads.

Now safely alone and at home in bed, Sylvie drew the edge of the sheet above her eyes as she relived her shame. She had not been angry with Matthieu; instead, terror and dread had flowed out with her alarm at finally hearing, in plain words, what had only ever been whispered.

She was thinking through the episode in detail this evening because of François's words earlier. She needed to draw lessons for her own life and take the right actions now, even if she could not rectify the wrongs of the past. She was determined to fulfill the promise she had made that day to ensure Amy's safety.

And to wait several more years before she married, since childbirth arrived so quickly after that event.

Chapter 7

**February 1833**
**Ste. Geneviève, Missouri**

On a Saturday afternoon in early February, Sylvie made her way through raw, cold weather as she left the dormitory for the café where she would meet Sarah Fulton. Wind gliding over blocks of ice on the river drove dampness through woolen clothing, and she clenched her fur-lined cape tightly shut and bent her head into air that felt like a wall she was trying to inhale. It burned her nostrils and made her forehead ache. This amount of ice would surely prevent any travel downriver for several months.

Sarah was already at a small table when Sylvie entered with a gust of wind. She looked much the same, her red hair pulled tightly into a bushy knot at the back of her neck. They exchanged greetings and cheek kisses, and as they settled, Sarah poured tea and offered a plate of *petit gateaux* she'd ordered. Sylvie could see she had gained some weight and thought it becoming.

They settled on speaking English rather than French, and as Sarah chatted enthusiastically about her coming trip and plans to marry, Sylvie caught glimpses of the formerly rambunctious schoolgirl and relaxed into her chair. Sarah spoke as though Sylvie would definitely accompany her for the entire journey, and as she didn't ask this outright, Sylvie had to seek an opening to insert her decision. Sarah described how they would enjoy shopping together in New Orleans for goods needed at the Kerr farmhouse in Texas, which was seven miles from the nearest town, called Edna. And Edna barely qualified as a town, apparently. Jim had sent a list of everyday items that would be helpful.

"Such as a coffee grinder," Sarah said. "Can you imagine—they drink coffee all day in Texas, but hardly anyone owns a grinder. Jim says settlers put coffee beans into a burlap bag and hang it on a tree. Then they smash the beans with a log that's been suspended to swing forward and back so it rams into the bag."

"It's hard to imagine that's effective."

"Coffee and dried turkey meat and cornmeal biscuits—that's the daily fare, especially when Jim goes out surveying." Sarah wrinkled her nose and bit vigorously into a sugar cookie. "I need to enjoy the delicacies in life while I can."

"The affection you two share clearly has grown," Sylvie said, edging into a topic she'd wondered about. "Yet I don't recall that Uncle Jim has visited Missouri in the past few years."

"We've exchanged letters regularly, and you're right—my feelings have developed through that correspondence. You might wonder that I'm marrying a man so much older than myself—fifteen years my senior. But we've been such good friends over time, and his letters describing Texas are so compelling. They pique feelings like curiosity and desire for travel and new experiences. Surely you would agree."

"Maybe I'm not as brave as you are. If I were going there, I might feel frightened at times."

"Ah." Sarah looked serious as she nodded. "I would understand if you're having second thoughts about this trip."

Even as Sylvie heard her doubts acknowledged, she rose to defend her courage. For a moment they were back on the school playfield, and she had to run as fast as Sarah and kick the ball just as hard.

"It's not fear for myself alone, my own safety. I have—we have—another person to consider." As Sylvie explained Amy's situation and asked whether she might accompany them to New Orleans, Sarah agreed to consider the idea.

"Amy says thousands of freed black people are living there, and they have their own world, complete with businesses, shops, schools, and professions," Sylvie added. "Plus her friends and family in that community will help her start a new life."

"So she has family to go to." Sarah spoke wistfully. "You do know that I am an orphan, just like you."

"You would be joining family, though, at least your adoptive brother." Sylvie knew that Sarah had been adopted at a young age by the Linn family after her parents had died. The Linns and the Fultons had sailed together from Ireland to New York, where Sarah's father had a post at a university. Later, the Linns had come to Missouri, and now their son John lived in New Orleans and ran a company that traded regularly with Mexico.

Sylvie asked, "In fact, wouldn't he be taking you on his schooner the rest of the way to Texas?"

"Yes, he will be taking us—you'll be coming too, surely. But I still feel that I'm on my own in the world. Perhaps you, especially, can understand how I want a place, a home, where I truly belong. In Texas, I'll help to create a community that I can be part of from the very beginning."

Though Sylvie recognized the same longing she often felt, she let the possibility hang in the air. She felt submerged in the noise around their table, the voices rising louder. Sarah moved on to talk about school in Ste. Geneviève and memories they shared.

"Sarah, why did you write to Sister Giroux and ask her to talk with me first?" Sylvie broke in after a time. "I also heard about your engagement from my Aunt Peggy, before I got your letter."

"Ah, yes. I should apologize for that." Sarah paused to refill their teacups. "It was presumptuous of me to involve a teacher that way. It's just that . . . she was so important to me. She believes women need to find themselves in life, to exercise the unique, individual abilities each of us has. She'd always say, 'We have to find and develop our characters, and not just by marrying and raising children.' Do you know what I mean?"

"Yes, she does say those things, and I often wish I were a man so I could choose a career and work at something. Is that shocking?"

"Not at all, though it's not the way we've been brought up. Sister Giroux would say we can't shy away from the challenges life offers;

taking them on is how we discover our inner qualities, even if we don't work at jobs."

"*Alors*, she hasn't said quite that much to me."

"Maybe not yet, but I'm sure she's warming up to it. She'll give you the speech as the time for your decision gets closer." Sarah laughed, tipping her head back so her hair bunched in a mass of red curls. "Look at it this way: you'll hear her say it repeatedly if you *don't* come to Texas. In the meantime, it's a compliment that she believes that much in your abilities."

Sylvie took a deep breath and declared, "Going on to Texas is out of the question, unless it's certain that I can make a safe and timely return."

Sarah leaned her chin on her palm and tapped her cheek with her fingertips. "Probably you could get back before long. Remember that my brother runs his schooner both ways across the Gulf of Mexico, and apparently he often stops just a short time in Texas. I hear that only a few months of the year are good for sailing, so it might mean having to return right away. But consider this—wouldn't you like to visit Texas for a while, for the adventure?"

As Sylvie remained quiet, Sarah drew a letter from her reticule. "This is for you, from Jim. He enclosed it in correspondence to me, and he wants to assure you that you are welcome to stay on at the farm in Edna as long as you like. He's looking forward to seeing you and hopes you'll be a companion for his daughter, Minny. She's quite lively, and as you probably know, she turns twelve this spring."

Sylvie took the letter, and Sarah munched another sugar cookie. "It's such a long trip for a quick turnaround, but if that's what you want . . ." She brushed away crumbs and watched Sylvie's expression. "And the way my brother describes the open sea, the way Jim talks about the wildness of the land awaiting the graces of civilization . . ." She straightened and smiled broadly.

"I do like the idea of a sea voyage," Sylvie admitted. "I've always wanted to smell the ocean and see the sunlight on an endless horizon, hear the wind snapping in canvas sails, just like in books I've read."

"And the steamboat ride downriver—is that appealing as well? Or appalling? It will mean nine or ten days in small quarters."

"I am sure I'd like to do that part of the trip." Sylvie realized her responses were edging toward what Sarah desired in spite of her resolutions.

"You'll make an excellent traveling companion; I'm so glad. I'll bring along books and pamphlets that we can read to occupy our minds and aid in shaping our plans."

"No—Sarah, I'll travel as far as New Orleans, but Texas is still a remote possibility. I'm sorry, but I have not decided to go there yet."

As Sarah let the silence grow, Sylvie decided to ask for recent news about her half-brother, David Kerr.

"Ah, David. He's not been entirely well. The malaise he suffers is difficult to describe." Sarah added, after a few moments, "It seems to come and go, marked by periods of deep despair. Going into a bout, he is unable to sleep, and he becomes quite irritable. The family thinks it's related to his experiences in the war last summer. It will get better with time; in fact, it already has."

Sarah clasped her hands before her breast. "And now he has something to look forward to. Did you know he's going to marry his cousin Sally Wells in June?"

"Sally! I've met her, and she's quite nice. But aren't they first cousins?" Sylvie was surprised, and she would have to quickly adjust to this development, for she would not want to go and live with newlyweds.

Sarah shrugged and added that everyone was glad. She returned to her own plans, and as she reviewed details, her delight came like spring sunlight dashing over the dreary winter in the small river town. Sylvie warmed to her enthusiasm and felt Sarah could become a closer friend, even though she was older. The pot of tea was empty, Sarah was assembling her hat, bag, and gloves, and it was time to leave. But they could meet again, and Sarah would seek a booking for three on a riverboat to New Orleans as weather permitted, after Easter.

They parted with fond cheek kisses, and Sylvie walked a longer route to the dormitory to keep the wind at her back and calm her mind. The bustle of the café, Sarah's liveliness, and the prospect of firm plans for a trip to New Orleans all combined to lift her spirits. She was eager to settle the date and buy tickets so she could tell Louisa that she—Sylvie—would be first to get to the city they had dreamed of visiting. And she would get word to Amy right away that they could travel together downriver at the end of her servitude.


The weather warmed and ice broke up on the river before Lent began, allowing boats to resume traveling among the towns. Sylvie and her nieces were delighted they could return to Cahokia in time to celebrate at the Shrove Sunday dance, which would be held at the Jarrot House. Sylvie was eager to attend, for it would be her first ball. She wouldn't turn sixteen for another few weeks, but the women who had a say in her life—Fernande, Jeanne, and Aunt Lizette—had agreed to bend the rules a bit. Sylvie thrilled at imagining an elegant dress and wearing her hair piled up, just as she had pictured that day long ago when she pirouetted alone in the Jarrots' ballroom.

But sadness still intruded: Fernande had not made plans for Sylvie's dress or jewelry. So instead, she would stay with Aunt Lizette, for Louisa had promised that she would like the dress they were preparing for her.

Sylvie and her nieces set off walking from the ferry landing toward the heart of Cahokia. Moments after Marguerite and Isabelle turned off at their house, Louisa came riding up the main street, leading a saddled horse for Sylvie. She dismounted, and the two rushed to embrace.

"Look at you—quite the lady!" Sylvie exclaimed.

Louisa's hair was done up, and she wore a cape, a full-length dress of plaid organdy, and leather button-up shoes with heels. Louisa posed playfully, settling her hat and crossing her hands primly. "Let's get to the house; it's going to rain. But first, I have to stop at the post office—the flag was up."

As Sylvie took the horses' reins, she looked askance at the side-saddles and asked if Louisa was becoming accustomed to riding that way.

"It's all right, and one's skirt does look so nice, spread out. And it's actually easier to sit up straight for that ladylike posture."

"But I'll feel like I'm playing in a costume drama in a St. Louis theater!"

Sylvie waited outside while Louisa went in to get mail. Her gaze traveled toward Holy Family Church and the cemetery in its yard. Enough time had passed since Laurent's burial that Sylvie could attend the ball without appearing unseemly. It would be the last dance until after Easter, for musicians did not play instruments during Lent, and the French fell back on *a capella* singing and more modest entertainment.

"Sylvie! What a pleasure to see you!" Vital Jarrot was coming out of the post office, accompanied by a tall, thin man wearing a black suit. "This is a friend of mine from the war, Abraham Lincoln."

Sylvie shook hands and noticed how distant Vital seemed, speaking English and shaking hands rather than sharing cheek kisses. She knew his English was excellent, for he had studied law in Washington, D.C., among the *Anglais*.

"Tomorrow at the ball, you should feel free to talk with Sylvie as much as you like," Vital told his friend. "She is among the few French ladies who speak English quite fluently."

"I'll be happy to converse with you as long as you can bear it," Lincoln said. "But I'll warn you that I do not dance, so kindly don't entertain expectations of me in that area."

"And why do you not dance, Mr. Lincoln?"

"The main reason is that I am too tall, and as everyone knows, tall people are ungainly. It arises from a deep fear of trampling the shorter people nearby."

"Oh, I see." Sylvie laughed but at the same time noted she barely came up to his shoulder. "And how did you two meet? In the war?"

The men glanced at each other, hesitating over who should speak or which story to begin.

"Abraham was captain of a spy unit, so he reported regularly to John Reynolds while he was commanding the Illinois militia. And as Reynolds' adjutant, I often took reports from him. He also was dispatched to help bury the men from Cahokia who were killed at Kellogg's Grove."

"That was the battle François was in, wasn't it?" Sylvie asked.

"Yes, and I remember him; he was the physician," Lincoln said. "I understand the families took charge of the remains and the reburials have happened, is that right?"

They spent some moments discussing the fate of Black Hawk, the leader of the Sac and Fox who had been captured and sent to the East Coast, where he was being touted as a heroic symbol of courageous loss and treated as the head of a foreign country. His son, often described as quite tall and comely, was causing a flutter in Philadelphia society, where he moved from one soirée to another.

Lincoln sighed. "And here we are, still on the frontier in the woods of Illinois." He quickly added, "I understand, though, that your mother, Vital, entertains with elegance comparable to any hostess back East."

"What brings you to Cahokia, apart from the Shrove Ball?" Sylvie asked.

"I'm trying to convince your friend, here, to consider running for political office, specifically the state Assembly. We share similar views, and in the future, I might need a few allies."

"And I'm trying to convince Abraham to complete his studies of the law before he runs for office," Vital said.

"My more immediate needs, though," Lincoln added, "are supplies and provisioning. I've started running an inn with a business partner in New Salem, and I'm arranging shipments of victuals, brandy, wine, and so forth. It seemed sensible to start here, where friends can advise me and goods don't have to be shipped from across the river."

"After all, you're not quite the one for river travel anymore." Vital laughed and added to Sylvie, "The trip home from Rock River at the end of the war was awful. I don't know if I ever told you about that."

"It definitely went better while I had use of the horse I borrowed," Lincoln said. "My own horse went missing one morning, and I never did find it. I don't know if an Indian is riding him now or another militiaman or even a US Army soldier. It was not a pleasant prospect to travel nearly three hundred miles on foot to get home."

"How did you manage, then?" Sylvie asked.

"After I parted ways with François and Vital and gave back the horse, another fellow and I got hold of a canoe and started downriver. That required several days, and then we had to stop for a day so I could fashion a new paddle. I'd lost mine in some rough water."

"You lost your horse and then your paddle?" Sylvie couldn't help smiling.

"Yes, but for all that, I am a true frontiersman. We put up, and I whittled myself a new one out of a plank of wood."

"Now I don't know whether to believe you," Sylvie said.

Louisa joined them, carrying a bundle of letters and a few newspapers, and she waved a women's fashion magazine toward Sylvie. It was a treasured delivery from Paris, even though months old.

The men took leave, and as Sylvie rode through town with Louisa, she felt nostalgic among the familiar houses and gardens. A beam from the lowering sun broke through clouds and shot golden light across a wiry clematis topping a fence, its green-gray buds held tight as a miser's fists. Primroses—scarlet, periwinkle, and gold—bloomed in the mud at the base of fence posts.

At the house, Sylvie exchanged kisses with Aunt Lizette, who pushed her glasses up to her forehead. "You've grown up more, in just a few months! But every woman is beautiful on the day she enters society. And then just a little more beautiful on the day she marries." She gave a significant glance toward Louisa.

"You two are planning the wedding?" Sylvie asked. Louisa had written weeks earlier that her engagement to Octave Borne would be announced at the ball.

"Octave has to leave soon for New Orleans to handle family business and find a new house—the home he and Louisa will share," Aunt Lizette said. "He'll be back in September, and we'll have the wedding in October."

"You will be here to attend my wedding, won't you?"

"Of course. I could never miss that." Sylvie grasped her carpet-bag and followed Louisa upstairs toward her bedroom. She was telling the truth, for she could easily return from New Orleans by then. Still, her future had an unsettled feeling.

It was time to look at the dresses they would wear the next evening, and Louisa spread out a pink chiffon layered over organdy, cut low in the front. It bore clusters of flowers fashioned of silk and satin, with leaves of velvet. Sylvie knew it had been altered from when Louisa last wore it, but it was so beautiful that she could hardly speak for the ache in her throat.

"Louisa, you made all the flowers, didn't you?"

"Yes. Each one of them, for you. It took hours, and I enjoyed every moment."

"I cannot thank you enough." Sylvie sat on the edge of the bed, fingering the materials. She felt . . . humble—yes, that was the word. This evidence of Louisa's affection sharpened her pain at being an orphan, of not having a mother to prepare her gown, of having to wear an altered secondhand dress and borrowed jewelry for her coming-out ball.

Louisa left briefly and returned with a carafe of wine and a tray of bread and cheese. "Now we have to practice sitting down and rising while wearing these hoops under our petticoats." She poured wine, and she and Sylvie clinked their glasses for *bonne chance*.

Chapter 8

**February 1833**
**Cahokia, Illinois**

THE NEXT EVENING, SYLVIE'S COUSIN NARCISSE ESCORTED HER along the garden path to the front door of the Jarrot House and into the light and the noise of voices and laughter. She had to lift her skirt to mount the stairs toward the ballroom, and with her hair up, the earrings of clustered pearls bobbed against her neck. She was about to enter the dance as an adult emerging into a new world. Men could now consider her marriageable, and she hoped the gradual winnowing of flirtations would last for years.

Narcisse's thick hair grew straight up before falling back, and with his keen eyes and slightly hooked nose, he had the air of a handsome predatory bird. Sylvie knew he was considered quite striking, and when she walked with him in town, girls they passed would turn to glance a second time. Everyone said he was the one in the family who most resembled Sylvie's father, so his role tonight seemed especially fitting, and she suspected Aunt Lizette had instructed him to dance with her if there were any awkward lulls.

They made their formal curtsy and bow before Madame Julie and François, who stood beside her as the eldest son. His dark eyes warmly appraised Sylvie as he kissed her hand. "Save me the first dance," he said, holding her fingertips.

"That is mine, I'm afraid—it's already claimed," Narcisse said.

"Then the second one."

"*Oui, d'accord.*" Sylvie nodded.

Sylvie greeted a few friends and went to say hello to Jeanne and Marguerite. After they exchanged kisses, they fell quiet, and Sylvie sensed coolness, perhaps due to the formality of the occasion.

Marguerite was demurely smiling across the crowded room, and Sylvie said to Jeanne without forethought, "I miss Laurent terribly, at times. And I wish my mother were alive to see this evening."

Jeanne stared at her, tears welling in her eyes. Sylvie regretted making a comment so gauche for the time and place, though Jeanne murmured, *"Moi aussi,"* and briefly clasped Sylvie's hand. Sylvie was struck by how alike she and Jeanne were with their coloring and short stature. Jeanne, at twenty years older, was stouter, having given birth five times. She wore her hair drawn back severely, which Sylvie thought added emphasis to her prominent though well-shaped nose.

The musicians struck up opening bars, and Vital arrived to escort Marguerite in the first dance. Sylvie did not want to watch them, as her childhood fantasy of sharing her first dance with Vital still echoed. When Narcisse arrived, she smiled, took his arm, and stepped as she had dreamed into a clearing on the floor. As they glided in a waltz, Narcisse gave her an amused smile. The dance required changing partners several times, and when they met up again, he asked if she was planning to filch a bottle of brandy and hide under a table downstairs.

Sylvie laughed. "Yes, I just might—and you must join me. You can do your imitations of some of these respectable people." Narcisse was a gifted mimic, and he grinned as he scanned the room.

"I'm trying to hold back. That friend of Vital's already does a good imitation of the governor, don't you think?" He nodded toward a cluster of men, where Sylvie could see Abraham Lincoln's head rising above the others. His black suit resembled the one Reynolds always wore, and he stood leaning forward in the same way.

The dance ended, and soon she was standing breathless on the sidelines, where Narcisse had left her with Louisa and Aunt Lizette. The musicians quickly resumed, this time playing a reel, and François appeared at her side. As he took her hand and she placed hers on his shoulder; they regarded each other, their eyes inches apart. He looked elegant in his dark coat and white, broad collar supported by a knotted cravat.

"You are looking very well," he said. "Life at school must be agreeable, and clearly you've completely recovered from the measles."

"I've been very well, thank you. And you?" A flush was rising on his cheeks as they danced, but he replied that his health was better. They moved side by side for several measures before resuming the closed position. He danced smoothly and led firmly; she could sense each nuance in the hand at the small of her back and in the palm that held hers in the air. As they glided faultlessly, she wondered how she hadn't known that he danced so well. But she had taken her lessons at school and had never danced with either of the Jarrot sons.

The flush on François's cheeks was growing ruddier, and she hoped it wasn't due to illness but to the occasion, even, perhaps, the impression she was making. As the music finished, he walked her to the side of the room and promised to return with a glass of punch. As she surveyed the crowd, she saw almost no one that she hadn't known her entire life. She had really hoped the young men might strike her differently. Would they even see her differently, now that she was a young woman who could be courted?

She caught sight of Emile Hubert threading his way in her direction, and she turned quickly to find someone else she might talk with. François appeared with their drinks, looked at her, and raised an eyebrow.

"I promised Vital I would talk with Mr. Lincoln tonight, as he does not speak French, and Vital was worried he will feel ill at ease," she said.

"Yes, that would be a courtesy." François nodded, and she stepped away. Lincoln noticed her immediately and smiled in greeting; the men near him were speaking French. He was sipping coffee already, before supper. His black suit stood out among the men's knee-length breeches and colorful, long-tailed coats. The room was getting warm, and the doors to the balcony stood open.

"I must confess I'm glad to find someone who speaks English," Lincoln was saying. "Tell me, is 'Mademoiselle Pensoneau' some sort of code name? I must have met half a dozen young women who say they're called that."

Sylvie glanced about to tally her cousins, both close and distant. "Truly, that is the real family name for me and, oh, eight or ten other women here." She had also caught sight of Fernande, who was dancing with Emile Hubert; he must have invited her after Sylvie turned away so quickly.

"Does the name mean anything?"

"I'm told that, long ago, it referred to someone who likes to whistle. But my family's nickname has been 'La Fleur' for a long time, which is more appealing."

"And that means someone who enjoys flowers; I know at least that much French."

Sylvie asked how his visit was progressing, and Lincoln said he'd had interesting talks with Vital about political issues facing the region and the state.

"Ah, politics," Sylvie sighed. "Are you certain you do not want to dance, Mr. Lincoln?"

"No, though I confess I've rarely seen such a collection of lovely young women. I feel my homeliness, decidedly. Why, I could shock someone merely by asking for a dance. And the shock would only increase as they witnessed my poor attempts."

Sylvie laughed. "I am sure you exaggerate."

As the musicians finished a tune, Vital joined them, and the three chatted for a few moments before he invited Sylvie for the next dance.

"We'll have some announcements when it's time for supper tonight," Vital said as they stepped in time to the music, forward and back, then side by side. "You might find them surprising."

"Really?" Sylvie raised her eyebrows, but he just smiled.

After several more dances with various old friends and another with François, Sylvie took a break and went downstairs. As she visited a room set aside for the ladies, she considered she was having a successful evening. Not only that, but the dancing—now that it was real—was also truly enjoyable, much more fun than the years of practice sessions.

She suspected the musicians would break soon, and she went to look over the supper buffet being laid on long tables set against both walls of the main hallway. Each table held several tall Shrove cakes made of crepes stacked into towers. One held a hidden bean, and whichever man found it in his serving would be named the Shrove King. He, in turn, would name his Shrove Queen, and they would wear little gilt crowns and reign over the rest of the party.

Sylvie was tempted to raise an edge of a tablecloth and spy who might be hiding underneath the table. But she decided to ignore the toes of little shoes that peeked out now and then, as well as the smothered giggles. Instead, she admired the stacks of porcelain plates gleaming in the lamplight, and the large silver pitcher filled with red wine. Long ago, it had been a set of silver cups, but after one was lost when the Mississippi flooded the house—and the entire town—one spring, Madame Julie had the odd number of remaining cups melted down and fashioned into the pitcher. She joined Sylvie, and as they moved slowly, she adjusted the position of a platter or a bowl of oranges, making sure all was ready for when the dancers swarmed downstairs.

"I think François will be ill from all the exertion if he keeps dancing," Julie confided. She held Sylvie's eyes for a moment. "No one really sees it, the effects of the illness. One of its cruelties is that it makes a person appear healthy, but the growing redness of the cheek is one sign of an impending attack. And when François has one, he remains at home and out of sight. People simply don't realize how normal activities can tax him."

Sylvie caught the displeasure Julie was expressing. Her usual graciousness had always spread over Sylvie like a warm shawl, infinitely fond and always welcoming. Feeling startled, Sylvie was direct. "Shall I refuse then, if he asks me to dance again?"

"I will remind him," Julie said. "Then he won't ask you again, and you needn't worry about handling the situation."

Her expression was kind, but she stepped away, leaving Sylvie to digest the remark. Several slaves—for they were still slaves, not servants, in the Jarrot House—were bringing in roasted meats from the fire pits in the back, and baskets of hot bread from the ovens. The guests began coming down the stairs, a noisy, ravenous crowd who would eat tonight as they would not eat during the coming weeks of Lent.

The women took chairs as they could, and the men stood, each holding a full plate that included a wedge of Shrove cake. After a few minutes, exclamations rose and ebbed: Vital had found the bean in his slice. Conversations paused as the crowd exclaimed with feigned surprise.

Julie carried the gilt paper crown toward him, and as he placed it on his head, he said, "Really, *Maman*, it is time to get a new one!" Everyone laughed, gave a cheer, and chanted for him to name the Queen.

"*Alors*," he said, crossing his arms and looking about as the young women held their collective breath. Then he extended his hand in invitation to Sylvie. She glanced behind, to see if he were intending someone else, and then laughed with surprise. She came forward, and Julie placed the delicate tiara on her hair.

"The Queen of the Shrove Ball, just for tonight, when you're entering society," Vital said quietly to her. The two of them bowed to the rising cheers, and then, fairly quickly, the others resumed their dining and conversations.

Later, as the empty plates were collected, François stepped to the center of the hall, and others fell back to make a clearing. He asked for their attention, as it was time for announcements. He urged all of them to fill their glasses if they were empty at the moment.

Narcisse stepped forward first. "I am delighted to announce an engagement, which will not be a surprise to many of you. My dear younger sister, Louisa, will marry Octave Borne in the fall, probably October. While they are engaged, he will be returning to New Orleans to see to the family trading business and to establish their home. Then he'll be back for the wedding."

The crowd applauded and shouted congratulations. They raised their glasses for a toast, and as Sylvie glanced around, everyone looked truly happy for the young couple. By fall, Louisa would be seventeen, a good age for marrying, and Octave had become well liked during his time in town. He stepped forward, clasping Louisa's hand and pulling her into the opening. They kissed, and Sylvie felt a thrill of pleasure as she joined in the cheers. When Octave released Louisa, she came to stand near Sylvie in the crowd. As they exchanged a glance, Sylvie thought her cousin looked oddly concerned rather than completely happy.

"I am very pleased, as well, to have the honor of making a significant announcement," Octave said. This time the air of expectation developed into a murmur of puzzlement; the townspeople knew of no other betrothals.

"This good news is that my friend and recent emigré from France, Emile Hubert, will marry Fernande Pensoneau, widowed, as you know, by the death of her husband last summer. Their engagement, happily, will not be as lengthy as my own must be. Fernande and Emile will marry in just a few months, in early May. Please join me in congratulating them!"

After moments of silence, someone began softly clapping. In the  polite applause that rose, Fernande stepped forward, smiling, and clasped Emile Hubert's arm. He then grasped her about the waist and kissed her.

Sylvie felt so jolted that Louisa tugged at her hand, and after a moment Sylvie reached up to pat her tiara firmly into place. So this was what had come of those months of visiting the house and seeing Fernande, while people thought he still was a suitor for her! What about those protestations of affection, and the proposal last fall? However, she truly had been rude when she turned him down.

"Really, what do you expect?" Louisa murmured as though reading her thoughts.

"Decency; a decent time of waiting before she marries again. Maybe that."

"Hush—not here, not now. We'll talk about it later. Endlessly, I am sure."

Sylvie pulled back her shoulders and straightened. "I will not let this affect your wonderful moment, the announcement of your engagement. And I am the Queen tonight; that is what I proclaim. Let no one even remotely suspect that I would feel jilted." She took a breath with her tumult of feelings—relief at not having to deal with

Emile's professions anymore, and disgust at how he had feigned his interests in order to woo Fernande.

She linked her elbow through Louisa's and said, "I will display my complete happiness. Let's go back and dance!"

"You do seem to be taking it well, but I insist that we go over and congratulate the pair. She is your sister-in-law, or was, and if the town turns their back on her now, the marriage will never be accepted."

"Where is Jeanne? She must be . . ." Sylvie stopped, unable to find a word.

"I don't see her anywhere. Come on, we're going to do this."

The girls approached Fernande and her fiancé, and while Louisa hugged her, Emile bent over Sylvie's hand. "I do hope you will forgive me for any possible misunderstanding, and that there will be only amity between us," he murmured.

"I do forgive you—as though there were something to forgive, which there is not." As Sylvie rattled off the conventionally polite phrases, he straightened and smiled. She added, "I trust that you truly love her and that you will make this work."

He nodded. "I do. And I will."

After Sylvie embraced and congratulated Fernande to the best of her ability, the girls moved toward the stairs along with the others returning to the ballroom. Sylvie caught a glimpse of Jeanne nearby, her face white and rigid, her nostrils pinched. Marguerite was clutching her mother's hand. Jeanne would disapprove of the unseemly haste of marrying less than six months after Laurent's death, and for once, Sylvie agreed with her likely views.

Then Madame Julie appeared, trying for a quiet aside. "I am so sorry for you, to see this happening so soon after Laurent's death. *Mon dieu*, everyone believed he was set on you, Sylvie. Now what, now who, dear girl? Oh well, this is just your first dance; you have plenty of time. Years, if you want to take that long.

"But tonight, you are the Queen of the Ball; just live in the joy of the moment. And congratulations to you, Louisa. Your engagement does not come as a surprise, and it's all the more wonderful for that."

Madame Julie swished off, and as Sylvie and Louisa made their way up the stairs, they could hear the musicians retuning their instruments. The men were ready to resume the party and let the women worry about the ramifications of the latest events on the town's society, propriety, and overall well-being. Their wives and sisters would tell them over the next few days how best to interpret everything.

Abraham Lincoln came near as they began climbing the stairs. "Does Vital find the bean and get to be the Shrove King every year?" he asked.

"Not every year, but more often than mere chance might account for," Louisa said.

"Not much of a surprise, then."

"No, not when Madame Julie is managing things," Sylvie said.

Several days later, Sylvie and Jeanne met to walk together between rain showers around the town square. The route took them from Jeanne's house, past Holy Family Church, and near the oldest houses, one of which belonged to their father when he first came to town in the late 1790s. He was married to his first wife then, and Jeanne and Laurent had been young children. The old place was still owned by the family, and Jeanne said that Etienne had recently asked if he could open it up and live there.

"I hadn't heard that, but I'm not surprised," Sylvie said as they paused to look at the house. Standing back behind a fence and untended gardens, it had pleasing lines, with broad porches under a low, swooping roofline. "He won't want to continue living up on the bluff with Emile as his new stepfather. I wouldn't want that, either."

"You're not going up to see Fernande and the children during your time in town?" Jeanne inflected the question as more of a statement.

While Sylvie had planned to visit the farmhouse over the break, she was not yet ready to face the changes in that household, which seemed to close a door on her ever living there again. She and Louisa had sat up late talking after the Shrove Ball, and rather than focusing solely on young men, dresses, or dancing, they had also sorted through options for Sylvie's future. Further talks, over coffee with Aunt Lizette and during long walks to the *Grand Marais,* left Sylvie feeling like one of the oxen trudging at a gristmill, going round and round without discovering a way forward beyond either living with Jeanne or going with Sarah to the colony in Texas.

At the beginning of her walk with Jeanne, Sylvie had broached the idea of bringing Amy along on the voyage to New Orleans, thus ensuring her safety. She was surprised at how readily Jeanne agreed to the proposal, even adding that she and her husband had been worrying for some time about how best to meet Amy's future needs.

Sylvie looked up at the layers of clouds, smelled the damp rising from the wooden walkways, and waited for a break in Jeanne's ongoing talk about finding cash for the riverboat fares to New Orleans—and back, for Sylvie's return trip. Jeanne was also fretting over whom Sylvie might stay with while she was in the city. They knew many merchants, and Jeanne kept sorting among them for families she could trust, discarding this one or that for various reasons.

Finally Sylvie broke in, for the conclusion she had reached would not take on the heft and weight of reality until she pronounced it to her sister.

"Jeanne, please listen for a moment. I must tell you something."

At Sylvie's tone, Jeanne stood still, and the purple umbrella she was holding over her shoulder framed her face like a shadowy flower. Sylvie's umbrella was red, and she kept twirling it behind her, for at the moment there was no rain.

"I am not going to come back here right away. I've told you before how Sarah Fulton wants me to sail with her to Mexico—"

"Which you are not going to do."

"But I am. I will return here; it just will be later than we were initially planning."

"But I have not given my permission, and I am your legal guardian." Jeanne looked her up and down several times, as though assessing whether Sylvie had taken on some unusual physical shape.

"Do I actually need that? Legally, I mean. I would like to have your permission, but I believe I can travel on my own say. I am a free person." Sylvie glanced away, looking about the town square. She and Louisa had settled on this approach; they had chosen the words, and Louisa had coached Sylvie so the sisters wouldn't get into a staring match, or worse, start raising their voices.

"But I don't even know this Sarah Fulton!" Jeanne took her umbrella in both hands and held it before her, vigorously shaking off raindrops.

"Oh, you'll like her when you do meet her. And you certainly know enough to feel certain she is respectable. And so is my uncle, the man she's going to marry. He was in the Missouri legislature, and one of his brothers is a judge. The family owns land . . ."

Jeanne returned her umbrella to her shoulder and began walking firmly, her gaze directed straight ahead. Sylvie stepped quickly to keep up, marveling that an argument just begun may have ended already. Her declaration hung in the air before her wherever she glanced. Like the gold rim of a glass, it shone on the edge of things as though lit by sunlight breaking through clouds.

She was feeling for the first time true excitement for the adventure. Her vision seemed to expand beyond the tidy houses and church steeple of her youth and reach past the recent months of mourning and layers of societal expectation. A larger world lay out there, and its edge was within her grasp.

"That considerably alters the funds you might need," Jeanne said after a minute.

"I don't need to pay a fare from New Orleans to Mexico. We'll have a berth on the trading vessel that Sarah's brother runs between the ports, and he will also guarantee my return passage."

"That is reasonable. You will need money, though, for meals, supplies, and clothing, possibly for several months."

"True. But I would need that even if I lived here."

"That's not the case, Sylvie. When you are here in town, you will live in my house, and we won't need to locate cash. Caring for you is my duty, as set out in our father's will." Jeanne sniffed as she said this, and Sylvie caught the whiff of piety. This was precisely the fate she had foreseen and swore to Louisa she would avoid.

"We have decided, Nicolas and I—as my husband, he naturally has the legal authority, here—on the best source of funding for the entire venture. We'll use proceeds from the sale of our father's mill and the slave some years ago. The total due to you, Sylvie, as one-third of the sale, is an amount we can cover with coin and bank notes.

"It will also be enough to cover the payment due to Amy by law, along with shoes and dresses—plus some extra stipend, purely out of generosity on our part."

"Oh, I am so glad." Sylvie felt genuine relief as she thanked her sister. The talk had gone relatively smoothly, and new buoyancy lifted her steps, as though energy were pouring into her feet from the walkway. She turned to give Jeanne a hug, and they awkwardly bumped umbrellas.

"It is important to make sure Amy gets to New Orleans safely, and with three of you traveling together, it should work out well," Jeanne said as they resumed walking.

As Sylvie talked about arranging travel and packing luggage, Jeanne smiled benignly. "You have been through sad and difficult times, as we all have, and I am glad this trip is working out. Your decision to continue to Mexico does not come as such a large surprise as you seem to think. But you must return quickly, before frontier life has the chance to roughen your character."

After a pause, she added, "Do you know, I have never been to New Orleans? I would love to see the city for myself."

Chapter 9

**Spring 1833**
**On the Mississippi River**

A FRESH MORNING WITH THE SUN BEGINNING TO WARM, iridescent spray
rising above ripples on the river, glimpses of homes, church spires,
and treetops sliding by—all combined to give Sylvie a sense of living
in a long-suspended moment as she stood on the riverboat's deck . She
felt balanced between leaving the past's limitations and moving toward
hopeful opportunities, as though the trip was elongating the delicate
walk up the gangway over water to the solidity of the boat.

Amy stood near her, clasping the handrail, and Sylvie touched her
lightly on the arm. Here was human solidity: the woman who had held
Sylvie's hand at her father's funeral, and who had carried her on her lap
to their next home, was accompanying her now. Amy did not acknowledge the gesture, and Sylvie could only guess at how the enormity of
freedom must be stretching the dimensions of her former servant's
life. Amy did lift a hand to touch the locket hanging from a slender
leather thong around her neck; it carried the court papers that Jeanne's
husband Nicolas had signed attesting to the end of her servitude.

Amy's friends and kinfolk had clustered near the quay to witness
the departure, and she had shared embraces and last words, taking
time with each person. The group seemed more solemn than Sylvie
might have expected, and as the riverboat pulled away, Amy stood
silently weeping as she gazed steadily back toward them.

Sylvie had been learning over the previous weeks how differently friends and family said goodbye. Some were casual and pleased
for her, while others grew worried or even wept. Such a long journey was beyond the life experience of most people she knew, but that
did not keep them from telling fearsome stories of Indian raids and

mysterious epidemics in Texas. Some spoke as though she were dropping off the margins of the known world, while others expected her back impossibly soon. Of all the farewells, the most difficult had been with Celeste and Etienne. They were young enough to feel that such a great distance carried finality with it.

Her last sight of Cahokia was cut off as the boat passed Holy Family Island and its trees and brush blocked her view. Known familiarly as Bloody Island for the duels that had been fought there, its treetops seemed to merge with the rising bluffs behind to form a solid canopy of green. Cahokia might have just been swallowed up whole, and Sylvie smiled at the idea. Sarah had gone to the little cabin she and Sylvie would share, saying she would see to their luggage and do a bit of unpacking. Finally, Amy turned to Sylvie, the ethereal air about her remaining intact as she smiled. Sylvie thought to touch the pouch of coins and bank notes she carried under her cloak, suspended from a belt around her waist.

"It's all there, Sylvie?" Amy asked, her angled eyebrow rising high. "Madame Jeanne was generous?"

"Not particularly, but Nicolas wanted to handle things well for us, and he persuaded her to let go of a larger amount. *Et, voilà!*" Sylvie prodded the bag to make its coins clink. It actually held few coins, the greater part being promissory notes that she could draw on at banks or traders' establishments in New Orleans. She trusted that John Linn would help with the transactions there.

"Did they finally draw on the inheritance that is due to you? I've always believed they should give you some of it before you're twenty-one. And they should show you the ledger books, too."

"I agree." Sylvie sighed as she gazed at the passing landscape, which already was less familiar, only a few miles south of town. Soon she would go to the other side of the boat and watch Ste. Geneviève slide by, with its early flowers blooming above the riverbanks.

"This money is from the sale of my father's gristmill, those years ago," she added.

"The sale of the mill, and of Matthieu, the slave who worked there?"

"Yes, that's right." Sylvie noted Amy's frown and the rare V-shape of her eyebrows pulled down tight. "Why, is that a problem?"

"Humph." Amy crossed her arms and stared ahead. After a moment, she said, "I'm going to look at my quarters on this boat, back there with the other slaves and servants."

"Treating you like a servant is for your own safety until we get to New Orleans," Sylvie said.

"I understand."

As Amy stepped away, Sylvie was thankful they would have more than a week for travel. She and Amy could both use that time to comfortably expand into the newly widened boundaries of their lives. The steamboat *Yellow Stone* held the record for making the trip to New Orleans in only six days, but this voyage would likely last nine or ten, given the current water level and heavy traffic.

Without the daily cycle of household work, the women at first noticed how little there was to occupy them. When Amy found an hour to sit on a bench and watch the river, she lingered in rapturous motionlessness. She commented that if one sat still long enough, the entire world went by. And not just the world above; she spoke of the souls of departed dear ones that flowed deep in the current, just as strains of an older religion flowed beneath teachings of the Catholic faith.

Sarah made sure she and Sylvie had plenty to read and elevated topics to discuss, and at times Sylvie felt she was back at school. But she did get caught up in the questions Sarah posed, such as how women might gain legal and financial equality with men. Surely as slaves were freed, Sarah argued, white men would agree not to continue treating their own wives as chattel. Sylvie heartily agreed with that hope.

One morning over coffee, Sarah shared more of her views on becoming a wife. "Friendship is very important to a marriage, as you know. To successfully create a home on the frontier, the husband and wife each have to offer different skills and strengths. Then they combine those into one forceful unit—a team, if you will—to overcome all the challenges and privations."

Sylvie was thinking how she and Louisa had never viewed marriage in such practical terms during their talks about love and romance. Now she recalled how Sarah enjoyed her past times leading playground games and devising strategies for victory.

As though following Sylvie's thoughts, Sarah laughed. "My views must shock you. Sometimes I forget you're just sixteen. Rest assured, at your age I also dreamed of romance, and my heart fluttered hither and thither among eligible young men."

The boat had stopped at a wharf earlier that morning, and now it navigated through dense traffic of rafts, keel boats, and *pirogues*. Most women coming on board made brief trips between market towns, and today they carried little barrels of butter, live chickens, padded sacks full of eggs, and even loaves of bread tied in dishcloths. Sylvie studied their clothes as she sipped coffee. Their bonnets had brims that reared up like giant scallop shells and were anchored to their heads by wide ribbons tied under their chins in floppy bows. Most wore homespun cotton, and even linsey-woolsey, in the humid heat. Sylvie felt she and Sarah stood out simply because the fabric for their dresses came from France, which had forbidden its colonies to make cloth so it could export it in an effort to balance the imports of food and lumber.

Sarah batted at the cloud of mosquitoes that engulfed the boat when it slowed near shore. She was adding points about men and women respecting one another's opinions and how women might gain ground for decision-making within a marriage, but Sylvie's attention was drifting, and she brought out a small notebook she wanted to show Sarah.

It was a gift from her niece Isabelle, who had labored over it for weeks. The pages listed medications, herbs, and spices that she thought Sylvie would need in Mexico, and Sylvie had marveled at the exquisite little drawings of plants, plus the thorough details for their culinary and medicinal uses.

"I took her advice and packed some things ahead because the same plants might not grow in Mexico," Sylvie said. "And the local residents are sure to have their own remedies. I can get some of those and list them in the notebook, toward the end."

Sarah seemed equally impressed as she leafed through the pages. "This is such beautiful work, she should publish it. It's much better and more complete than what we find at the dry-goods stores or apothecaries."

"I don't have everything she recommended, but I do have quite a few little paper twists of herbs, roots, and teas. If anything helps against fevers, or aches and pains, or even snakebite, it will be worth the effort, won't it?"

"Without doubt. Your Uncle Jim has said that once he's done building settlements, surveying roads, administering colonies, and negotiating treaties, he'd like to study medicine and practice as a physician. You two will have a lot to talk about."

Several days into the trip, Amy presented Sylvie with a dilemma. Late one afternoon, she came to the little stateroom Sarah and Sylvie shared, where they usually rested during the hottest part of the day. She shut the door firmly behind her and announced that she was deeply troubled by the origin of the money Sylvie would give her at the end of the voyage. She called it unacceptably tainted.

"It came from the sale of Matthieu as a slave, and I refuse to take any little bit of it, any single cent."

"Do you mean to wait until New Orleans, then, so I can exchange promissory notes or a bank draft?" Sylvie asked. "I'll try to get Spanish coins, Mexican silver, and some American dollars, if I can. But I don't know what will be available or how long that might take."

"No, I am not waiting. I will take my purse right away when we dock. It is due to me already, and I have made firm arrangements with the people who will meet me."

"Amy, I understand your feelings, but what do you expect me to do? How can I come up with different money on a riverboat in the middle of the Mississippi?"

Amy crossed her arms and said that was not her problem, though she did seem mollified that Sylvie was taking her concerns seriously. The women agreed to think over the problem, and by dinner that evening, Sylvie had come up with one idea, which she confided to Sarah as they ate their meal.

"I can wager for the money. You know that I grew up playing cards, that the French women play all the time, and they play for money. There's a game on the boat every evening, in what they call the 'saloon.'"

Sarah laughed, but when Sylvie continued to look serious, she said, "It's unthinkable. We're among Americans, and with them, only men play cards."

"Think back," Sylvie urged. "Do you remember how well I played at school?"

"I do remember girls complaining that you won too many of their buttons and ribbons. But that was girls, playing children's games. This isn't the same thing."

"But I've kept playing over the years, and even the older women in town say I'm quite good."

By the time they'd finished the entrée and were enjoying rum cake for dessert, the two were chuckling at the idea. Sarah finally said she would front Sylvie a small stake—very small—just to see if she could win a hand or two. And if she did, then she should continue and bet the "tainted money," as they now called it. Even if Sylvie failed to win much, she'd be exchanging coins at the table and could argue with Amy to accept them as proceeds of an entirely different transaction.

"Besides," Sarah added, "No one knows us on this riverboat, and we're hardly likely ever to see any of the men again. If you want to test your playing skills, what better time and place?"

"Sister Giroux would approve, I think," Sylvie said. "I'll mention this when I get around to writing reports for her."

Sarah shook her head, smiling. "I promise never to tell any man in Texas about your playing cards—or gambling. That reputation must not follow us from this boat."


Later that evening, in the tense pause of the card game Sylvie had managed to join, she risked a long glance at the five men clustered tightly with her around the small table. Each studied his cards, held slightly fanned, low and close to the chest. The hanging lamps in the salon emitted smelly kerosene fumes; fortunately, this discouraged mosquitoes. As the boat progressed slowly, Sylvie caught an occasional waft smelling of dark water and damp riverbanks blotted by night. Several men at the table had slicked their hair with Macassar oil, and the flattened locks gleamed brightly.

Amy stood stolidly behind Sylvie's chair, her highly askew eyebrow expressing what a ferocious guard she could be. Sylvie could feel Amy's fingers digging into her shoulder, conveying a hint, or a warning, or, more likely, stern and sustained disapproval.

This group was playing poker, a game recently invented in New Orleans. Sylvie had played it a few times before. She shifted in her chair and pulled her gaze from her opponents long enough to catch Amy with the corner of her eye. "*Arret!*" she mouthed, and Amy's fingers halted their prodding.

Glancing back at the circle of faces, Sylvie caught slight amusement flickering across the face of Mr. Robert Epperson from Virginia, two seats to her left. He must have understood the French, though his expression was now bland. He wore a brocade vest in deep wine colors with a gold watch chain across it, and he had told everyone he was heading to Texas to go into the cattle business.

Sylvie enjoyed deciphering the men's accents. She could now distinguish Kentucky from Virginia or Georgia. But so many Americans kept moving west, who could tell for sure? Recent arrivals from Ireland, Scotland, or Germany had large, raw accents that were easy to identify. But what about this Mr. Epperson, she wondered, as she waited for the first player to make a move; wasn't there a hint of something else, possibly French, in his speech?

Men yielded clues about their cards differently than women typically did, as they tried to mask their dread, confidence, or glee. Sylvie was learning that the frontiersmen, the ones from cabins in the woods of Kentucky, used broad, open gestures. They hadn't learned yet to layer over their frankness with the social conformities of the drawing room, or the protective layers of city life.

The men took sips from small glasses of bourbon, a lovely smelling whiskey from a part of Kentucky named for the French king who had sent troops to help Americans fight their war for independence. It made the men's foreheads trickle drops of sweat and diffused their sharp focus on the cards. Perhaps they also underestimated a mere girl with a French accent—the  mound of cut silver bits on the table in front of Sylvie was growing steadily.

The first player made a modest opening bet.

"What does your slave see in the window's reflection?" Mr. Epperson asked.

Sylvie straightened with a pang of worry. "Nothing more than what any player can see from this side of the table—mainly the backs of your heads."

"That's fine, then," he replied and threw in silver bits to raise the bet.

It took Sylvie a moment to concentrate on her plan for this hand.

"It's unusual for a young woman to be playing cards with a table of men," Mr. Epperson commented as the man next to him tossed in his matching bet.

"Not among the French," Sylvie murmured, then added, "As I think you know."

"Who are you descended from, which group of French?" he asked.

Sylvie mentioned her French Canadian ancestors briefly, including the *Fille du Roi* and regimental soldier, and asked about his.

"I'm descended from a French duke, the Duc d'Epernon, from a son born in England during his exile there. That son came to Virginia instead of returning to France, as that country was extremely hostile to Protestants at the time."

The man on Sylvie's right broke in and asked, his Scottish accent strong, for her to match the bet if she was going to.

"*Excusez-moi,*" Sylvie said primly. She quickly added silver bits to the pile.

Incidental talk ceased during the next round of betting and the one after that. Finally, when the Scotsman called the play and they showed their hands, Sylvie was among the losers. Behind her, Amy gave a small sigh as a cheery Kentuckian scooped the cluster of silver toward his meager stash. Sylvie noted his dusty black suit with distaste. But in Amy's faint sigh Sylvie heard resignation, an acceptance of the inevitability of loss. And it irked her.

Now, her pile of silver dwindling, Sylvie brushed her damp fingertips along the taffeta of her skirt. The cards were growing sticky in her other hand. Against all her protestations, the Kentuckian had poured her a small glass of bourbon, just to celebrate his winning hand. As she sipped, it burned her mouth, and she missed the pleasant fruit flavor of a brandy. She took a second sip, disliking it even more but wanting it to ease her worry. The betting resumed on a new hand, the tenth so far.

"Aha!" The man with the waxed mustache, two chairs to her right, swept up the mound of silver bits. "I am the son of the king of England, don't you know. At least, I feel that way right now!"

"Yea, and I be the son of the prince of Denmark. You ken thon Hamlet, do ye not?" asked the Scotsman, who had lost significantly.

"Didn't Hamlet die before he had children?" Mr. Epperson asked mildly.

They were going to play next without reshuffling the deck, and Sylvie found she could lucidly picture the order in which the cards had been played in the last hand. If she could keep that image clear in her mind, she felt a strong chance of winning. Her confidence rose as she discarded two cards, keeping the core of a straight, nine high. And by a miracle, the replacement cards came through: a ten and a six. Maybe this had something to do with Amy's intense hopefulness at her back.

Each player must have felt more confident about his hand, for the betting rose, round by round. Sylvie could feel her dress dampening with perspiration. Why was the night air not getting any cooler, but feeling warmer now? And then it was over; they slapped their cards on the tabletop. The tension collapsed, and she had won. It was nearly unbelievable.

"*Oh mon dieu, merci, merci, Jésu et Marie—*" Amy's profound prayer came out in a whisper and seemed all the more audible for that reason.

"Oh, that was fortunate!" Sylvie exclaimed loudly in English. "What good luck!"

"*Quelle bonne chance*," Mr. Epperson commented.

As Sylvie scooped the mound of silver bits toward her place, she noted the tone of the men's comments; it seemed fairly good-natured. She wanted to leap up immediately and carry off her winnings, but hard feelings would develop toward a winner who acted that way. It would be even worse if the men felt defeated by a woman who swept off triumphantly. She needed to stay at the table until she lost a few hands and some winnings dribbled away. Then her departure could be seen as staving off the usual losses following a winning streak.

She would have to play carefully and bet conservatively, to lose just the right amount. Amy's hands kept still on the back of the chair, and Sylvie could imagine her holding her breath. She hoped Amy's eyebrow was rocketing up in alarm; that should assuage the men.

And then Sylvie was saved, and her graceful exit assured, by cigar smoke. The Kentuckian, less cheerful now, passed around a box of Cuban cigars. The men took a few moments to light up in a companionable ritual and then puffed heavy blue clouds into the humid air.

"One unfortunate effect of really fine cigars," Mr. Epperson observed, "is that they drive the ladies away. And although we enjoy our smoking, we are then deprived of feminine company."

Sylvie took that as a cue and rose, nudging her chair back gently against Amy's knees. She glanced at Amy, who crossed her arms and glared back.

"Thank you so much, gentlemen, for a fine evening of card playing. You have been very gracious to allow an untalented young woman to take part. And now it is time for me to say good night, *adieu*, and good luck to everyone."

Outside, Sylvie and Amy took the stairs down from the *salon* to the main deck, where the air seemed fresher and less humid, if not cooler. In the night sky, a strip of stars spanned the middle of the river channel. A half-moon was rising, tangled in the treetops of the eastern bank. There was little traffic, and the skipper was trusting to that and to good visibility as he continued running in the darkness. He usually stopped the boat when he couldn't see sandbars or the shoals that rose suddenly like the smooth backs of giant sea monsters lying in wait to snag a vessel's hull, pitch it around at an angle, and keep it stuck for hours until the river rose again.

"Why do you quit just when you are ahead?" Amy spoke in a low voice to Sylvie as they strolled toward the bow. "You were winning, child, and why can't you see that and stay with it?"

"I'd trusted my luck long enough. Aren't you the one who usually tells me to act with more moderation?"

"Not when it comes to silver and to winning streaks. You continue to be a foolish judge of fortune not to recognize the hand of fate, even when it's dealing your cards."

"Maybe you feel that way because your money was at risk, Amy. A gambler always wants more winnings, and I know that feeling. But it can get dangerous. Do you know the term for *la chance* in English? In French it implies good results arriving from a beneficent fate. But the similar word in English is just plain 'luck.' And it can be good or bad."

Two men conversing softly about the price of cotton stopped nearby, their white suits gleaming in the dusk, and the women fell silent. As the riverboat slid past a cluster of rafts and *pirogues* tied up for the night and lit by lanterns, echoes of fiddle music and laughter drifted across the water. Soon, around the next bend, the shorelines fell dark, and the croaking of bullfrogs and whirring of cicadas filled the night. This, too, was musical, and it sounded to Sylvie like hope, or anticipation.


As they neared New Orleans, the women could glimpse large mansions, rows of shacks, and fields of cotton or tobacco past the heavy tree trunks and strands of moss that screened the riverbanks. The smell of the river was sometimes fresh, and other times dank from shadowed, reedy undergrowth in the shallows. Sylvie was eager for the first scent of true salt water.

The riverboat pulled into a wharf at the city's waterfront late in the afternoon, and a stevedore helped the women with their luggage.

Sooner than they expected, they were walking the gangway onto the wharf, then onto land. Sylvie felt the earth rocking slightly under her feet, and her knees wobbled for a few minutes until the sensation passed. They halted amid the laborers, sailors, and townspeople meeting the riverboats and schooners, and Sarah looked around for her adoptive brother, John Linn.

Sylvie turned to Amy, who was scanning the crowd while fingering the leather thong that held her locket. Safely tucked inside Amy's carpetbag was the pouch of coins from the poker earnings. Sylvie felt her heart falling, even as her legs grew steady. Within minutes, Amy's departure would sever completely their daily interactions, conversations, and sharing of events. She wondered whether Amy, as she sorted through the new parameters of her life, would try to establish any connection or pathway back to their relationship.

Sylvie grasped Amy's hand. "Will I see you again—ever?"

"Maybe," Amy replied. "That depends on whether you survive life in the colonies." She smiled to take the edge off the comment. "Just remember that though you might have a hard time finding me in this big city with thousands of us *gens de couleur,* I will always be able to locate John Linn's house or find out when his schooner is due in port."

"Will you do that? I'll be back here in New Orleans within a few months, and you can check when his schooner is arriving."

"What you need is to remember to love the people who come into your life as though they are your real family," Amy said. She pulled her hand free as a black woman, older and just as tall, approached. After exchanging a shy, quizzical greeting, the two embraced. The woman's dress was simply cut and printed with a maze of bright reds and darker tones. A complicated cloth headdress, knotted in front, covered her hair. Something inside Sylvie recognized this woman. She was probably from one of the French community families back home, someone Sylvie had seen in younger years, a relative of Amy's without doubt.

Sylvie could not make out what they were saying. After a few moments, Amy turned and said, "*Adieu,* Sylvie." She was smiling broadly, but a tear seeped down one cheek, and her eyebrows for once held a firm, straight line.

"*Adieu*. Amy, you are so dear to me, I hoped . . . I thought . . . that possibly you loved me."

"I love you, child. I do. And you will continue to grow up straight and fine. Remember that you are smart and brave."

Sylvie began to reply, but Amy turned quickly after briefly touching her shoulder. "My life is waiting for me. It has been waiting many years, and it's time."

As Amy turned away, her companion spoke to Sylvie. "If you ever are hungry or ill and you think your life is over, remember that love abides. That is the force that holds the flesh to the bone. And with any birth, there are the seeds of death. And with death, rebirth. Just look around yourself, and you will see it is so."

Sylvie was startled, faintly alarmed. This was not only an odd thing to say but also echoed her family's old curse. And by speaking that way, the stranger had introduced a dire element into a farewell that was not hers to intrude upon. Sylvie fought back tears; Amy was pulling away into the crowd and not looking back.

But then Amy did turn, and she gave a big smile and a wave before the milling people closed around her. While the gesture looked like a benediction, the finality was unimaginable, so Sylvie did not dwell on it. Instead, she turned to look for Sarah and the brother who would take them on to Texas.

Chapter 10

**Spring 1833**
**Linnville, Gulf of Mexico**

"I AM SIMPLY A VISITOR TO THE COLONY OF AMERICANS," Sylvie said aloud to the walls of her little cabin on John Linn's schooner. She was practicing what to say to the Mexican immigration officials who would meet the crew and its few passengers at the end of their trip across the Gulf of Mexico. She'd been delighted by her week in New Orleans, mainly spent shopping with Sarah for things needed in her new life. Then John had declared the winds, weather, and tides just right for sailing, and they'd made good time on the voyage.

Sylvie would not tell officials that she was a colonist, for she would leave after several months; plus, arriving as a visitor was less complicated. She would explain how she'd stay with her uncle, James Kerr, administrator of the DeWitt Colony. Maybe she should say she came from "near St. Louis, Missouri Territory" because so many Americans came from that area that the Mexican officials would find it quite ordinary. John had warned her that the Mexican government was growing wary of the large waves of American immigrants, suspecting many actually wanted to create an independent state in the Mexican province of Coahuila y Tejas.

Sylvie alternated puckering her lips and grimacing to relax the muscles. She wanted to minimize her French accent, though Mexican officials might not even notice it.

"I am here—heeeerrrre, heeere—to visit my uncle, only." She practiced flattening the *r* on the top of her mouth as she finished repacking the second carpetbag. She folded the final item, a gauzy cotton blouse she had bought for the hotter climate.

A shrill piping sounded, a signal that Sylvie needed to get on deck for the arrival. John owned a home and warehouses in both New Orleans and in Linnville, a settlement on the Mexican coast where the schooner would dock.

She was wearing a silk blouse and a linen skirt, and she pulled on a matching linen jacket and began to button the placket. Immediately she felt too warm and left it open. She stooped to squeeze her feet, enlarged by the humid heat, into heeled leather shoes. She was likely to wear this outfit only for the short trip to John's house, but she was going to enter this new country looking like the lady she was—or hoped to become.

The last items were going into the carpetbag on top of the elaborately beaded doeskin moccasins that her cousin Paschal had given to her. She had never worn them and couldn't easily say why she was bringing them on the trip. Perhaps—beyond being a talisman from a family member who also was venturing in the West—they would prove right for the new climate and culture.

Sylvie shut the final bag and carried both up to the deck. It was the tenth day of sailing, and John said they'd had a remarkably smooth and peaceful crossing for the five-hundred-mile voyage. He spoke Spanish fluently, and he had given Sarah and Sylvie a few lessons during hours when he had set a course and could leave the canvas sails billowing in a steady breeze. Sylvie had memorized Spanish terms to sunlight glinting on ribbons of current.

As she joined the others, the schooner was making its way slowly through an estuary toward a shallow bay. On previous days, the shoreline had looked reedy, low, muddy, and monotonous. Now that they were in shallows, golden bars of light filtered through the top meter of seawater, sparkling on silt and highlighting seaweed furls that shifted from black to greenish brown.

Buildings appeared back among trees, and Sylvie could see a few huge wooden warehouses. Some smaller structures had smooth, white-washed walls, and she wondered if they were made of adobe, which she had never seen. The schooner skirted low-lying banks choked with reeds, and among shadows of trees farther back, Sylvie suddenly discerned shapes of people, a group of men standing motionlessly. Their torsos looked oddly brown above slight clothing, and they were watching the schooner intently. She noticed they carried long bows and spears, and other implements were tucked into belts or straps on their backs.

"Karankawa," John said, noticing Sylvie's look. "They cake on mud as protection against mosquitoes. Very practical and effective."

These Indians looked quite different from the ones Sylvie knew back home, and she wondered how she might meet these people, and whether she might engage in trade for local herbs and medicines. But she drew back instinctively as one man reached an arm and seemed to point at her. Rather than being threatening, though, his comment caused his companions to laugh.

"They are amazed by Sarah's red hair, I think," John said. "They enjoy greeting the boats, and they're not as ferocious as they may look. But when settlers first arrive, they're often fearful of the local Indians, and all kinds of stories fly about."

"How very interesting," Sarah murmured, watching the group intently.

John added, "We have a solid treaty with the Karankawa, which your uncle helped to negotiate, Sylvie. So don't worry. You'll find that bands of them live quite peaceably near our farms and towns."

"I'm sure I'll become accustomed to them," Sarah said quietly. "It's just that the Indians back home wear a lot more clothes and don't carry weapons to greet the boats. Or, at least, not anymore."

Sylvie noticed Sarah's trepidation; after all, she was going to live in Texas permanently. At Jim's farm, a ways inland—apparently four days by ox cart over a primitive "trace"—she would make her home, run a household, and possibly bear children and raise them. Sylvie, though, could enjoy her observations with more detachment.

John was a little older than Sarah and quite a bit taller, and his straight posture exuded command as he began reviewing procedures for docking and passing through Mexican customs and immigration. The officers would examine Sarah's trunk of household items; settlers were allowed to bring in numerous goods that storekeepers would have to pay duty on, so they would likely ask Sarah whether everything was truly for her home, rather than for sale or trade.

Technically, John added, they should be landing at Matagorda and declaring Sarah's immigration status, but they would get around to that later. He was already an established member of the De Leon colony, which was a Tejano settlement, rather than American. Many of the Tejanos, local residents, were descended from Spanish colonists who arrived before Mexico won its independence. All of this would make the process easier.

"Sylvie, your immigration status should be simple as you're just visiting, and they won't be interested in the contents of your bags," John said.

The boat was slowing, edging toward a long wharf, and John began shouting orders for landing and tying up. The crew moved efficiently and quietly; most would escort the cargo as it was unloaded and carted to the warehouses. The ship carried cloth, clothing, finery such as lace and jewelry, household supplies, liquor and brandy, seeds, and farming tools and implements, as well as miscellaneous items like lamps and umbrellas.

Soon Sylvie was stepping from the schooner's gangway onto the wharf, which was shifting side to side on its tether to the land. The plank walkway jolted as she and the others trod upward, and the two bags knocked against her knees. They didn't have to walk far under the hot sun, which was less intense than when reflected off the sea.

A cluster of Mexican guards approached, armed with pistols in their belts. They called out greetings to "Juan Linn" and waved Sarah and the men carrying her trunk toward a small building near the closest warehouse. Sylvie followed, and through the open doorway she watched as two guards opened Sarah's trunk and began exploring the contents. Sarah looked exasperated, her cheeks reddening and damp half-moons forming under the sleeves of her linen blouse, which was ruffled and buttoned high at the throat. John spoke calmly, and the guards began repacking. A different officer arrived and began asking questions and noting responses on a sheaf of papers.

The few words of Spanish that Sylvie recognized stood out like islands in a stream of sounds. The Mexican officers now approaching her out on the walkway had fair skin and dark eyes and hair—coloring much like her own. The younger officer spoke a short phrase in Spanish that included the word *nombre*.

"I don't have a number," she replied in English.

He looked closely at her. "Name," he said.

"My name is Marie Sylvaine Pensoneau."

The other guard, who carried papers and a pen, stepped up. *"Su nombre es Maria Silvia Pensana?"*

*"Non, c'est Sylvaine Pensoneau, un nom français, pas espagnole."* She switched to French without thinking, as it sounded more like their Spanish than her English did.

"Sil-vi-a." He sounded it out while he wrote in the ledger.

"Pensoneau," she repeated.

*"Votre pere soit Pen-son-o; vous êtes la fille; alors, c'est Pen-sen-a. Il faut apprendre à parler Espagnole, mademoiselle."* Sylvie had not expected that Spanish-speaking customs officials would change her last name to their feminine form of Pensoneau. She also was mortified to be instructed—in French—that she needed to learn some Spanish.

*"Oui . . . si . . . bien sur,"* Sylvie replied, wondering how the phrases she had recently learned could simply evaporate from her brain.

*"Votre nationalité?"* The younger one resumed questioning.

Sylvie paused, and the officer looked at her with interest as though he could probe her thoughts. His gaze dropped to briefly scan the shape of her body beneath the linen ensemble. He raised an eyebrow and regarded her not unkindly but as though his compatriots owned this territory, and it was hot here in the full sun. The older guard nudged him slightly and took over.

"Where were you born, and when?" he asked in English.

"In Cahokia, Illinois, in 1817."

"In the United States, so you are American."

"Well . . . It was not a state then, but it was part of Indiana Territory."

"And your father's citizenship?"

"French Canadian, or Québécois; he never became an American."

"Very admirable. And your mother?"

"She was born in England and became an American when she immigrated with her father."

"When, and where?"

"I think they arrived about 1795, and after he died, she went to live with relatives in Missouri Territory."

"So you are French and Spanish."

"*Alors* . . . I believe I am American."

"At that time, Missouri Territory belonged to Spain. We only recently became free of Spain ourselves." He smiled, and she felt the situation shift.

"So you are actually Spanish, Silvia Pensana, through your mother's line. And you have Canadian heritage through your father." He jotted this down in the ledger. "And you are a visitor, not a colonist?"

"That's right. I'm visiting my uncle, James Kerr, for several months. I accompanied his fiancée on the journey. She is the sister of Juan Linn." The guards seemed satisfied that Silvia Pensana now fit into a clear category. But they still needed to give her a warning.

"Many people arrive to settle in Texas, but they claim they are only visiting because Mexico has a strict limit on the number of Europeans and Americans who are allowed to join the colonies. You have to leave at the end of your visit, or you could be subject to arrest and deportation."

"Yes, all right." Sylvie felt her honesty was being questioned.

"Then you are free to go and join your relatives. Welcome to Mexico."

As the officers moved away, Sylvie felt wobbly and vague. How terrifying to have her name changed that way. Did she fully exist here, in a foreign country, without her own true name? And without her actual nationality? She wanted to object, but to whom?

She saw John and Sarah ahead, followed by a porter carting the trunk. The group was moving between the adobe buildings, and as they turned down a lane toward the warehouses, they disappeared around the corner. Sylvie raised her face to the sky and fought back tears. She would follow them, and she could picture her small figure in the cream linen suit, unable to shade herself with her parasol as she hoisted a bag in each hand. She would hurry, stepping quickly until she was almost running, while praying she would not have to call out to prevent being forgotten.

For she was now invisible. If something happened and Uncle Jim tried to find her, would he—or John or Sarah—recognize that she was Silvia Maria Pensana, a woman of Spanish and French-Canadian descent, on the Mexicans' list? Her heart pounding hard, she set off.

# Part 2

Spring 1835 — Spring 1836

~

Coahuila y Tejas, Mexico:
The American colonies
of Gonzales and Mina,
and the Kerr farm near Edna

On the road to the San Jacinto River

Chapter 11

**May 1835 — Two years later
Gonzales, DeWitt colony**

RIDING HORSEBACK THROUGH THE AIRY WOODS, as fast as they could go, Sylvie and Minny, Uncle Jim's daughter, were actually racing. Minny's dark braids flew straight out as her horse galloped on the narrow path through pecan, oak, and scrub pine trees. Sylvie kept sensibly back, though she was urging the horse forward with her knees and leaning over its neck. Dark, light; dark, light: sunlight patched the tangled new green and flashed by. In a clearing, their horses' hooves drummed on grass, nopal cactus, and wildflowers, and Sylvie felt stinging nettles swish against her knees.

Midway across, Minny looked over her shoulder. "Ha! I told you I'd beat you!"

Sylvie pulled forward and her leg jostled Minny's for a moment, but neither was bumped loose. Sylvie was first to reach the faint path that resumed in a dense copse of trees, but she slowed when she didn't hear the other horse close behind her. Minny trailed by a hundred yards and was looking back again. Sylvie slowed till she caught up.

"Wolves! I saw a gray wolf! They're coming after us!" The girl fairly screamed as she rode past Sylvie and took the lead again.

Sylvie watched the path behind, trying to discern any movement of shadow against shadow, and then adrenaline spurred her forward. "*¡Muévete! ¡Darse prisa!*" She was convinced her mount understood Spanish, and it leaped ahead in response to her urgent tone, if not her words. After a minute, Minny, leaning low over her horse's neck, straightened enough to glance back and yell, "Ha, ha! Fooled you!"

"Never cry wolf!" Sylvie scolded, her anger surging on top of adrenaline. And now, her horse turned skittish. It bunched up its haunches, broke its stride, and sidestepped. It turned its head, and after huffing the air, reared its head and neck up and down.

"Easy, easy; it's all right, everything's all right," Sylvie spoke low, in English, and ran her hand soothingly along its neck. The horse lunged forward, and Sylvie barely hung on with her knees. When they settled into a smooth canter, she looked back again.

Something *was* trailing them. Whatever it might be, it was moving quietly, for she could sense only that the patterns of light and dark were shifting differently than they did in a breeze. Feeling uneasy, she let the horse race the last half-mile to the clearing where Uncle Jim was working with the road crew. She had worried before setting out that the five-mile ride north of town might put her and Minny at risk, and now she wondered whether he would be angry with her; she was eighteen and should act like the responsible adult she was becoming. But here they'd be, she and Minny dashing out of the woods like a pair of terrified rabbits.

Sylvie had been in Texas just over two years, and she was increasingly making up her own mind about where to go and when, and whom to see. She hadn't ridden sidesaddle in that time, or obtained many new clothes, though she'd managed to grow an inch taller. And she often didn't bother with bonnets but let her skin be browned by the weaker sunlight of morning and evening. She had lived with Uncle Jim and Sarah for a time after they married, at the farm near Edna. But as she became increasingly restless over the months, he had suggested a move to Gonzales, the main town of the DeWitt colony, where she could work and live with one of his relations.

Uncle Jim and Minny were making an extended visit to the town while he supervised a road-building project, and that morning, Sylvie and Minny thought to pack a lunch as a surprise and bring it to the work site. No Indian attacks had been reported lately, and though everyone feared Comanche raids, those usually came in the late summer and early fall, in time with the hunting season.

Even though Sylvie trusted her intuition and had felt safe when they left town that morning, she now turned uneasily and again tried to spot who—or what—might be following on the trail. It was more a sense of sound than of sight, plus a *frisson* at the back of her neck.

When Sylvie arrived at the work site moments later, Minny had already dismounted, and her father was standing, hands on hips, his expression stolid as they talked. The clearing gave onto a broad meadow, where Sylvie could see a cluster of men working with lumber and small logs, apparently building a bridge across a stream whose banks meandered through tall grass.

Jim waved at Sylvie, and then his glance focused behind her as he smiled and greeted someone else. Sylvie turned to see a rider emerging, and she wondered how long the young man—Texan, not Indian—had trailed them. In another moment, she recognized Armand Fulshear, who was a friend and frequent riding companion. Sylvie hoped that other people, including her Uncle Jim, did not know how often they met, as though by chance, on some evenings at the edge of town.

Armand lifted his gray felt, wide-brimmed hat. "*Bonjour,* Sylvie." He continued in French, keeping his voice low. "I didn't mean to frighten you, and I'm sorry if I did. But I caught your trail a ways back, and I wondered at you and Miss Kerr out riding alone."

"I spotted you, too, though I didn't know who it was. It did give me a bit of a turn."

"If you were able to notice me, then I need to work on my tracking skills."

"Minny thought you were a wolf. She flew right by me, and that's how she took the lead." Sylvie switched to English as Minny approached leading her horse, to include her in the conversation.

"It wasn't a trick, and I was just taking back the lead. But I'm glad it was you, Mr. Fulshear, and not a wolf or an Indian. Papa is annoyed, Sylvie. He says we took too big of a risk riding out here. But I think he'll be happier after he sees the food we brought."

"We need to start setting up." Sylvie caught sight of the men in the distance now leaving their work, some leaning toward the stream to splash their faces and wash their hands and arms. Armand dismounted and helped her down.

"You'll stay and eat with us?" she asked.

"I will, happily, and thank you." He added quietly, as Minny was busy unpacking saddlebags, "At times I think your uncle is right, that you take too much risk."

"You don't seem to mind when it gives us a little time together. If you want me to be completely safe, then I shouldn't ride out in the evening anymore."

Sylvie knew she was taunting him a bit. She wouldn't mind if their relationship were more openly acknowledged, however. With a more formal declaration, they could meet at his home, or the place where she lived. His family was French, and Armand reminded Sylvie of friends back home, with his black hair and deep brown eyes, his skin fair under the weathered tan. As a breeze lifted waves of his hair, worn long to touch the shirt collar, she realized he resembled a younger and more vigorous François Jarrot.

Armand's father, a former sea captain, had amassed considerable land and built up a thriving cattle business. Armand and his brother were considered the best trackers in the area, given the years they'd spent riding open land and minding the herds. Sylvie enjoyed speaking French occasionally, and his family had invited her to join them for several holiday meals during the past year. She thought those occasions had passed quite pleasantly.

The large impediment to their relationship was the threat of war. The American colonies were talking seriously about breaking away from Mexico, and if such a revolt happened, Armand intended to join the fighting. He felt he could not ask her for a commitment at the same time he might be placing his life at risk.

Uncle Jim approached and invited Armand to stay for the meal, then thanked him profusely for keeping his daughter and niece safe on the ride. Minny frowned at that and muttered, as she carried bundles past Sylvie, "We were never in any danger. It's only five miles, and we didn't need him trailing us. *Armando el lobo. El lobo Armando.*"

"His Christian name isn't Spanish, it's French."

"*Beh – oui.*" Minny imitated one of Sylvie's frequent expressions.

Sylvie chose to ignore her and began unloading food and flasks of tea and beer. Men were straggling up from the creek and grouping awkwardly around the fire ring. Minny set a cloth on the ground to the side, as there was not a wide boulder, or even a tree trunk, large enough to serve as a table.

"This actually is thoughtful of you," Jim said to Sylvie. "We're getting low on any interesting provisions, after camping out. Everyone is pretty tired of bacon, cornmeal mush, and coffee. Or dried turkey."

He smiled, his mood softening as Minny had predicted. Jim had a square face with a broad nose so large it was out of proportion, and his small eyes were set close together under a heavy brow topped by thinning hair. He considered himself ugly and often said as much. He would add that he strove to make up for this by offering friendship and trying always to be fair, generous, and slow to take offense.

As administrator for the DeWitt colony, he'd been hired by the town of Gonzales to survey a road that would connect it to Stephen Austin's "little colony" about fifty miles north at Mina. Men joining the colonies were required to give several days of labor each year to road building, though the older men with families often hired younger men to take their places.

In the distant woods past the meadow, Sylvie could see a dark opening like a tunnel, where the crew had hacked away brush and small trees. *Just what I need, a road heading north*, she thought. If a decent road had existed heading east, she could have used it to get to the Gulf, and from there taken passage on a ship to New Orleans. But even then she would have been blocked by foul weather and storms. Hurricanes had struck the coast repeatedly the previous summer and stopped all ship traffic. Inland, deluges of rain had turned primitive tracks into impassable mire—though this happened also in other seasons.

But this summer would be different. Sylvie's plans were taking more definite shape, for Uncle Jim spoke of getting the women of his household—Minny, Sarah, and Sylvie—safely back to the United States in case war against Mexico did break out.

Minny came up and asked about serving the food. "They're hungry. Just look at them holding back, and staring." She bugged out her eyes in imitation.

"I think you should start by cutting the bread, Minny. Then they won't have to tear off hunks," Jim said.

As Minny sliced bread and set it out, the men filed by with tin plates. Sylvie was checking whether she had forgotten anything when one of the group approached her. He was very tall, several inches over six feet, and quite striking. His wide-set eyes under high, sloping brows imparted an open, earnest expression.

"*Mademoiselle* Pensoneau—Sylvie Pensoneau? You're Jim Kerr's niece, I've heard, and I want to say hello because I grew up in Missouri, near your aunt's farm—Jim's sister—in Troy. So I know your brother, David, and others in the family."

"How nice to meet you," Sylvie replied and offered her hand.

He rubbed his hand on his pants before taking hers. "Logan Vandeveer. Please excuse the layer of grime, and these fine clothes." He grimaced humorously at the muddy blue work shirt and misshapen leather pants, both sprinkled with sawdust.

Another man came up to join them. He stood almost as tall and looked leaner, with his large frame. She couldn't help noticing that he was less comely by comparison, but that he had pleasant, regular features. Logan introduced him as his cousin, Andrew Magill, from Kentucky. She shook his hand as well, and as the two were holding back from the meal, Sylvie encouraged conversation by asking how the construction was progressing.

"It's going well," Logan said.

"Fairly well," Andrew said.

"You're building a bridge over the creek, there, I see."

"Yes, we hope to finish that, this afternoon," Logan said. "It's the hardest part, for this stretch. It has to be wide enough for a wagon, plus clearance, and strong enough for heavy loads. We're using the trees we felled while clearing the road grade itself."

"That's the lovely work," Andrew said. "I pulled the best job— hauling logs and digging up the stumps."

He bent back a bit, massaging his lower back with both hands.

"That's because you have such a strong horse," Logan said. "Pity the horses; they do all the heavy work."

"He wants to preserve his own horse for things like pulling carriages and racing on Sunday afternoons," Andrew commented.

"I do have a very fine horse," Logan agreed.

"They both came from Kentucky," Andrew said. "I rode mine, Zeus, all the way here, and he's just as reliable as any human companion. Smarter, too, sometimes. Really, though, we should be using oxen for pulling stumps."

"Zeus?" Sylvie looked at him quizzically, adding, "I have just an Indian pony."

They looked toward the meadow, where a dozen horses were grazing. Logan pointed out his own, a tall black stallion that bobbed its head on an arched neck, as though aware of the attention. As they chatted, the two said they'd been accepted as colonists in Mina, and that they planned to open a mercantile store there. Logan added that his brother had made a start in the cattle business and he also would join that venture.

Andrew added to Sylvie, "Your Uncle Jim was the one who helped me get started here, a year ago. His family knew mine back in Kentucky, before they moved to Missouri and he came out here. And he set me up with a good land claim south of here."

"But you're living in Mina, instead, now?"

"I was impressed by the force of the hurricanes last summer, even as far inland as Victoria. One tore the roof off my new cabin and flooded the bit of field I'd planted. A man can learn from experiences like that, so while I was reevaluating my plans, I decided to visit my cousins up in Mina."

Logan had glanced several times toward the meal set out, and Sylvie said that while was nice to meet them, they should get some food. Thanking her again, they went to join the dwindling line.

After Sylvie served herself, she sat to eat near Minny, apart from the men, several of whom were stretching out in the shade to doze or smoke. She and Minny were packing the empty containers and flasks when Uncle Jim approached.

"I am not sending you back to town alone. My mind won't be at ease unless you have armed men along. Armand will go with you, and I'm adding one more."

"Oh, Papa, we don't need that. At least get someone with a fast horse." Minny crossed her arms and frowned, puffing out her perfectly round cheeks.

Armand approached, leading his horse, as Jim added that Andrew Magill was getting his mount and would join them.

"I don't require any assistance." Armand crossed his arms. "I did ensure that the young women arrived here safely."

"One man in front, and the other at the rear; that's how it's going to be. I'm sending Magill to town also to conduct some business for me. I have surveying to finish this afternoon or I'd come myself."

Andrew came up leading his horse, which really did look quite fine. As Armand watched him talking with Jim, he frowned slightly, and Sylvie turned her attention to her saddlebags, hiding an amused smile. Men acted out their territorial impulses so openly in Texas, and those could be for land, cattle and horses, or even claims to friendship, kinship, and women's affection—or mere attention. She also enjoyed seeing the deference paid to her uncle. He was not only one of Stephen Austin's original colonists, but also had been friends with Austin's father, who had made the initial efforts to start colonies in Mexico. And, as Andrew had said, he was known as the person to see when a young man arrived and wanted to make a start.

"Nobody knows this country better than I do, so I'll take the lead," Armand was saying. His pride, or prickliness, seemed so utterly French to Sylvie, as though he were one of her cousins in a moment of pique. And then, as he caught her eye, the intensity of his look shot a hot streak through her. She sighed lightly and looked away toward the treetops. The undersides of the leaves flickered a pale olive tone that, back home, would signal rain or a thunderstorm. Here, it probably just meant more heat.

"Well then, I will take up the rear," Andrew said, smiling equably. "Let's saddle up!" He held back as Armand rode off first, followed closely by Minny. Sylvie went next, and soon she saw Minny bounding forward, trying to pass Armand. He turned to speak with her a couple of times, and in a wide spot, Minny was able to get ahead. She galloped off and Armand raced after her. Sylvie laughed and shook her head.

"I don't feel like hurrying that much," Andrew said, pulling abreast of Sylvie as their horses walked at a comfortable gait. "Tell me a bit more about how you got to Texas. You didn't come here with your uncle; Jim Kerr has been here ten years or so."

Sylvie explained how she had traveled with Sarah Fulton and stayed on at the farm in Edna for her first year in Texas.

"It's pretty far from Edna to Gonzales. What brought you to this town?"

"I'm helping a relative of Jim's, Nancy Brown. Her husband died, and she's running their place as a boarding house."

"Oh, that's good to know. I may need a room for a night or two. I'm going to check first with my cousin Rachel Berry—Mrs. Flint—when we get to town and see if she has any room to put me up. Do you know her?"

"Yes, in fact, Jim and Minny are staying at her house. And she has five children, in addition to her husband."

"Well, that might make things a bit crowded."

In a clearing ahead, Armand was waiting, looking back at them, as Minny circled her horse around him. She was clearly teasing him, and he looked irritated.

"I think we'd better keep up with them," Sylvie suggested.

"We probably should. I just can't figure out who she is trying to annoy more—him or you."

Sylvie agreed, urged her horse to a faster gait, and they moved quickly on.


Gonzales was a town of barely thirty homes, but as they approached from the north, they passed a wide plaza and several official buildings, for it had been laid out in the Spanish style. The house where Sylvie lived and performed some housekeeping duties was near the center of town, and soon the group stopped before it, a two-story wooden house with comfortable porches. The men dismounted to help Sylvie with the saddlebags and packs. Soon, Nancy Brown's son Duff, about thirteen, appeared to take charge of her horse and lead it back toward the stable.

Armand and Andrew stood talking with Sylvie, neither apparently willing to cede ground first. She thanked them for riding along and said she needed to go in and start preparing dinner, in case Nancy had boarders for the night.

"I was hoping for directions to my cousin Rachel Flint's house, as I mentioned," Andrew said. He held his hat in his hands and glanced toward the side streets.

"But I'm going there myself," Minny reminded him. "I'll ride along with you." Andrew stepped over to give her a boost back into the saddle.

"As you head toward the south side of town," Sylvie said, "watch for a good view across the river, and you'll see some old cabins and buildings. They're what's left of the original settlement, which was burned down about ten years ago."

"I've heard about that," Andrew said. "My cousin was here even then, one of the original settlers along with your uncle."

"Yes, they went through a real ordeal, and they moved away for several years before coming back to rebuild."

Andrew turned to Armand and asked if his family had lived in the area then as well.

"Yes, but not in town. Some miles out on our own spread, which was smaller, then, not the thousands of acres we have now."

"I see." Andrew nodded, said how good it had been to meet both of them, and mounted to ride off with Minny.

Armand, pausing near Sylvie, wished to make plans for when they might meet again, most likely out riding one evening. They set a tentative date, and as he departed, she turned to go in the house.

Inside was dim and cool, and before going up to her room, Sylvie left the last of the containers in the kitchen for the slave, Annette, to take care of. Sylvie felt awkward around her at times, for she'd never lived daily with a young person who was currently owned by someone else. She had known older people still in slavery back in Illinois—several at the Jarrot House, as well as Matthieu, at the mill.

Annette belonged to Uncle Jim, who had loaned her to Nancy Brown to help around the house. Slavery was actually not legal in Mexico, for the new republic had outlawed it when it won independence from Spain. But exceptions were being made for some American colonists who were bringing slaves with them, and Uncle Jim was one of them. He had arrived with seven members of an extended family, and he had explained to Sylvie that he feared they would be separated if he had sold them in Missouri. When Sylvie had asked why he hadn't simply freed them, he said the matter belonged in the past and was closed to discussion.

As Sylvie learned which specific tasks Annette handled around the house, the division of labor lent her some peace of mind. Nancy clearly set out the work she expected of Sylvie and was paying her to perform. These mainly involved cooking and obtaining the necessary supplies and ingredients, often by bartering. She tended a small vegetable garden she had planted in the spring, using seeds she'd brought from Edna. She also dusted the house and helped prepare rooms for let, especially when new boarders arrived and work piled up quickly.

It still struck her as odd to be paid for tasks she had routinely performed while growing up and even while staying at the farm in Edna. Not that she saw much actual cash; the colonies used Spanish money, a trickle of coins from the United States, and their own scrip, which was issued mainly as a way to establish rates for exchange. Sylvie kept a pile of scrip in her bedroom, but the best form of payment she'd received was the Indian pony Nancy had given to her.

Sylvie mounted the stairs, first the broad staircase leading to the second-floor bedrooms, and then the narrow, twisty flight leading up to her own room, the first she'd ever had entirely to herself. It was very small, with a single window, but large enough to hold a bed, desk, chair, and space for hanging clothes. She loved the feeling of privacy that enveloped her each time she closed the door behind her.

Sitting on the little chair, she leaned to undo the buttons of her leather shoes, so faded, rough, and worn. She might be able to stretch out and enjoy some leisure time, for she'd seen no sign of boarders, and Nancy herself seemed to be absent. Sylvie could reread one of the few books in the household, or revisit her small stack of letters from home and from Louisa, who was now married to Octave Borne and living in New Orleans. From her descriptions, the couple's house sounded grand, and Sylvie imagined how pleasant it would be to stay there when she did get to the city.

The walls of her room were covered with sprigged white paper, which Nancy had probably brought along from Missouri. The rolls had run out just short of covering an area below the window, and the gap of bare wall was painted a vivid pink. Sylvie thought that patch perfectly expressed how people made do, here on the frontier.

Other items were of Mexican origin. The little mirror had a frame of tin patterned with intricate cutouts, and the carved wooden crucifix hanging above the bed was painted lavishly to represent blood. Sylvie had protested that it seemed a bit gory, when Duff presented it to her. He was pleased she was Catholic, and she was surprised that he followed that faith as well, for his mother was Protestant, like the rest of the Kerr clan. But Duff had been educated by priests at the mission in San Antonio during the years the family lived there, and he had grown fond of that culture and way of life.

A couple of baskets in the room bore designs that were completely unfamiliar to Sylvie, and she learned they came from Waco Indians. Duff had explained that his Waco Grandmother visited sometimes and exchanged gifts.

This was the woman who had saved the life of his father, John Brown, after he'd been taken captive during a battle fought while he was traveling a trade route. It clearly irritated Nancy that her son referred to her as such close kin, but Duff argued that if the Grandmother hadn't adopted his father to replace the son she had lost, he would surely have been killed. Sylvie respected Duff's views but also understood that Nancy resented the Wacos for kidnapping her husband and keeping him captive in the first place.

John Brown had worked as a trader with his brother, the husband of Aunt Peggy, back in Missouri, the two venturing as far west as Santa Fe. Sylvie liked to think back on the day at her convent school when she'd traced the trading routes on the map of Texas that these men were following. How incredible it was, to be here in the very house of a trader whose work had seemed so remote, nearly mythical then, existing as dotted lines of ink on heavy old paper. She had not imagined surroundings like this: a Midwest wooden-frame house holding Waco wares and Mexican household goods.

The two brothers had died in recent years, both at their homes, following illnesses. Nancy's husband, John, died of smallpox after Annette, whom Jim had just introduced to the household, came down with it first. No one else in the family contracted the disease, as Nancy and Duff had been immunized in Missouri. Aunt Peggy's husband had died of some unknown illness after only a night and day of suffering acute pain in his throat. He was in the process of building a house for his wife and children so they could join him, and Sylvie wondered if Aunt Peggy would still come to Texas and bring the family at some point.

With the deaths of both men, Nancy Brown announced she'd had enough of the struggles on the frontier, for she had also lost two young daughters to illness during winters in Gonzales. She was making plans to leave this summer and go back home to Missouri. She wanted Duff, her remaining child, to meet his familial grandparents, be educated in English, and begin attending a Protestant church. She also wanted to leave before the colonies reached a decision about declaring war against Mexico.

Sylvie planned to travel with Nancy and Duff, at least as far as New Orleans, and with Uncle Jim talking about Sarah and Minny accompanying them, she was feeling more confident that this time her hopes would result in a trip that would actually happen.

She was startled from her reverie by steps pounding up the stairs, and after the briefest knock on the door, Duff rushed into her room.

"Mama sent word—you're supposed to get to Rachel Flint's house right away. The women are gathering there. There's been an attack on some traders west of town. Mama was out visiting and heard the news. I'm supposed to get you there and then come back to guard this house and the horses. The horses, especially."

"They were Comanche, then?" Sylvie sat up quickly.

"Don't know, no word's come back yet. But it sounds like it was."

Sylvie got up and returned to the chair to put on her shoes. She'd been through gatherings like this on two other occasions, and fear clenched at her stomach. If the victims were traders passing through, she wouldn't know them personally. But the search parties that went in pursuit were drawn from men in town and the surrounding areas, and waiting with the womenfolk for word of their safety meant sharing concern for a husband, father, brother, cousin, or even a friend or sweetheart.

Chapter 12

**May 1835**
**Gonzales, DeWitt colony**

As young as he was, Duff carried himself with authority, and Sylvie was glad for his company as they alternately ran and walked toward the south side of town, skirting fenced yards and keeping to the shadows. At Rachel Flint's house, Sylvie went in the side door, and when she turned to wave; Duff had already slipped into the darkness.

Inside, she startled a young woman in the kitchen who was setting dishes onto a tray. It was Susanna Dickinson, a friend whose husband ran the hat factory.

"You scared the living daylights out of me!" Susanna sounded more relieved than angry. "You can go on in." She nodded toward the front room, and through the doorway, Sylvie could see chairs set close together, long skirts mingling at the hem, and women's heads bowed, some leaning together in quiet conversation. The curtains in the room were closed, and the room felt hot with the fire in the grate. As she entered, talk fell quiet.

"Sylvie!" Rachel exclaimed. "I'm so glad you're here. We've been worried sick about you. Minny told us how you both rode out today. And to think that Indians were attacking nearby."

"We rode north of town, fortunately. And the attack was a dozen miles west of town?" Sylvie had already heard this from Duff but posed it as a question.

"That's what we've heard. Come, sit." Rachel indicated a straight-backed wooden chair near the fireplace. "And we heard you had young men accompanying you on the way back. Can you not think about the danger you're putting them in, with an escapade like that?"

Sylvie stayed quiet, surprised at being chided so harshly. She suspected that Rachel was speaking from her own fears and wondered if her husband had gone with the search party. Otherwise, Rachel was hardly one for inflexible propriety, especially regarding customs she often said worked better in more settled places.

With bright, dark eyes and a perfect bow of a mouth, Rachel was pretty whenever she was laughing, and still striking even when stern. Her tight curls bobbed under her white ruffled cap as she gave forth her opinions, which held considerable sway. Not only was she an original settler, but she also was the first woman to own her own land in the colony. She had made the claim on behalf of her late husband, who had died back in Kentucky; she'd been just eighteen and a widow when she arrived at Gonzales with other family members. She soon remarried, only to have that husband die as well, and now she was married a third time, to Dolphin Flint. The couple were raising five young children, and Rachel was not yet thirty.

Most of the women were holding strips of cloth, which they set aside at the sight of Susanna entering with the tea tray. Women were constantly knitting, mending, sewing, spinning, shelling beans, or shucking corn, and it seemed anytime their hands stopped moving, their speech paused as well.

"Please tell me any news you've heard so far." Sylvie wanted to deflect any further questions about her day, especially any mention of Armand. The woman likely wanted to pin down the rumored relationship and discover whether they could call it a courtship, when Sylvie herself wasn't sure. She suspected she was a popular topic of gossip, being of marriageable age, under the protection of an uncle who was usually elsewhere, and of French origin, to boot.

She'd had to adjust to the mores of the colony, over time. This meant she stopped wearing earrings except for a discreet pair once a week, pretended complete disinterest in card games and wagers, and kept to herself how much she'd enjoy a glass of wine with a meal. Those few dinners with the Fulshear family had been a relief, a return to the normality of the way she had been raised.

Rachel repeated what was known, that a hundred Comanche Indians surprised and killed thirteen French and Mexican traders headed to Santa Fe, who had stopped at a cabin farther west. It belonged to a couple, the Castlemans, who had stayed out of the battle by barricading themselves inside. Later, he had sneaked into town to get help, and the search party was mustered. Some of the women named their menfolk who had joined it, mostly from west of the town.

"We won't go into the stockade unless the sentries here decide that's necessary," Rachel said, glancing around at the circle of faces. "Undoubtedly our men are chasing the Comanche yet farther away."

Susanna entered with the tea tray and set it on a table near Rachel so she could begin pouring.

Minny darted in after her and said to Rachel, "I finally got all of your children to sleep. But I had to tell the boys some really scary stories, first. Then they pulled the covers over their heads, and that did the trick."

She looked around for a chair, but all were taken. "Isn't there cake?" she asked. "I thought there was some left in the kitchen."

"Not enough for everyone, dear, but you go ahead."

"My father's not back yet?"

"Not yet, but soon." Minny returned to the kitchen as Rachel explained to the others, "A cousin of mine living in Mina, who is working with the road crew, rode right back out to alert Jim when we heard the news. Jim has a dozen or so men, and they'll be here quickly, I'm sure."

As the women sipped tea, they settled back more in their chairs. Soon they were setting down their cups and taking up the strips of cloth with renewed purpose. Sylvie was wondering about a metal mold with a dozen narrow, deep wells, which stood nearby on the hearth.

"Be careful," said Susanna, who was sitting next to her. "We're making bullets, and the molten lead will take your skin off. You've made bullets before, haven't you?"

"No. Back in Illinois we usually got them from gunsmiths or traded for them."

Susanna, close to Sylvie's age, had been married already for several years. One day, Sylvie had brought some silk flowers, which Louisa had made years earlier, to the hat factory, and she and Susanna had enjoyed using them to decorate hats. Since then, they had visited regularly and become friends.

"Here, Sylvie, make yourself useful," Rachel said, handing fabric to her along with a box of cartridge casings. "You do know how to pack cartridges, am I right?"

"Oh, yes, I've done that many times," Sylvie said. "Are we short on ammunition?"

"Well, not at the moment. But we're sure to need a great deal when we stop putting up with the Mexicans ordering us around, especially when that general who made himself dictator, Santa Anna, brings his army up here."

"*If* that happens," several women chimed in.

"*And*, if the men decide to fight for independence from Mexico," Susanna added.

"Of course they will," Rachel said.

"Rachel, we don't know that for sure," Nancy said.

"You will admit, will you not, that it looks a good deal more likely since the Mexican government saw fit to throw Stephen Austin in prison for months? He was only trying to negotiate. And they've forbidden any more Americans from joining the colonies."

"They had cause," Susanna broke in. "They believed Austin's administrator was giving land to young men in exchange for military service. Maybe he was trying to build an army to fight Mexico."

"It's possible all that is true," Rachel said.

"But it hasn't stopped more settlers from coming in," Sylvie said.

"And that is a huge problem," Nancy said. "Now we have young men from all over the United States and even Europe, thousands of them staking claims wherever they please. They ignore the regulations everyone had to follow when we joined the colonies. And the *empresarios* heading up the colonies have to swear to support the republic of Mexico in order to keep their licenses. What are they supposed to do, now that it's become a dictatorship?

"Just think of all the rules for the colonies that we choose to ignore or even lie about," she continued. "For example, Mexico requires every colonist to be Catholic. Yet, who, here, is actually Catholic?"

A few hands went up, including Sylvie's. She felt compelled to add, "You know my Uncle Jim did convert. He became Catholic just a few days before he married his wife, Sarah Fulton."

Light laughter rippled about the circle, and Rachel said, "Yes, dear, he did finally get around to converting."

"But, seriously, Rachel—war? A real war? And then what?" Susanna protested. "Can the colonists fight off tens of thousands of Mexican Army troops? I don't know if we'll be able to make enough bullets, fast enough. But I'm definitely staying here, no matter what. In my wedding vows, I promised to stay with my husband through sickness, health, poverty, wealth—and I will."

"The wedding vows do not mention war," Rachel said dryly. "I've had occasion to hear them a few times, and nowhere do they say you have to stick it out on a frontier and fight for your lives. We just do it. It's not in a woman's nature to give up."

"Yes, the vows do too cover that. They say, 'Whither ye go, I will go,'" Susanna said.

"Ladies, you know that I am leaving this colony," Nancy broke in. "But the question is easier for me, as I'm not leaving a husband, though I'll be leaving his grave, I admit. My duty is also to my one remaining child and to my parents in Missouri, to tend them in old age. So as I say, my decision is easier. But think of the other women who are taking their children away until the question of war is settled. If fighting comes here, it will be in our cornfields and kitchen gardens. Picture a huge army of Mexican soldiers swarming over our land like hungry locusts."

After several moments of silence, Nancy added briskly, "Well. It's not certain that will happen, though, is it? Staying or leaving—it's a gamble either way."

In the quiet that continued, the women bent their over their hands, which kept moving at their tasks. Sylvie imagined each was holding a lively debate in her mind, and when the conversation resumed, it seemed listless, the pauses growing long. They wanted news of the ranging party that would help them decide how to defend themselves and their homes. Finally, noises came from the kitchen, and they all looked up to see Sylvie's Uncle Jim entering with other men.

"Good evening, good evening." He gave several nods around the room. "We've decided against the stockade—though you can still go there if you feel the need. Since we have the road crew as well as men from town, we'll dispatch them as guards to each home overnight. And tomorrow, probably in the early hours, we'll get word from the ranging party and can make further decisions."

The women rose and began gathering their things, and several expressed their appreciation. Sylvie caught sight of the two young men she'd met that day and nodded toward them. Andrew Magill had been frowning with concentration, but he smiled upon catching sight of her.

Jim began dispatching the work crew to homes where the men were either gone with the search party or standing sentry duty. He assigned Andrew to accompany Nancy and Sylvie back to the house, where Duff was likely still on guard. Soon the three set out walking through the silent streets, past houses where no windows were left uncovered to reveal any occupants huddled inside.

At the house, they found Duff in the kitchen with a rifle, a pistol, and the old blunderbuss lying before him on the table. Their barrels pointed toward different windows as well as the back door. How long he had sat alone; how much planning he had done. Andrew put a hand on Duff's shoulder, a gesture that seemed respectful rather than condescending. "You've done a good job," he said. "I can join you on the watch, now."

As Duff stood up, Sylvie noticed purple half-moons under his eyes from strain and fatigue.

Annette materialized from around the corner to the dining room. "There's no boarders, Miss Nancy. I put by some supper for you."

The girl was about four years younger than Sylvie and often seemed careful with her words, while also appearing observant and thoughtful. A track of small scars made an arc across one cheek, evidence of the smallpox she had suffered several years earlier. With a pang of guilt, Sylvie realized she had not even questioned whether Annette should come along to shelter at Rachel's home, rather than be consigned to guarding Nancy's house along with Duff.

The group was subdued as they ate the cold supper, everyone together around the table in the kitchen. As dusk fell outside, Nancy brewed a third pot of coffee. After a time, Duff seemed to be straining to keep his eyes wide open and said he would go to bed early, if Andrew promised to wake him for guard duty later.

"We'll trade off at what, three in the morning?"

"You're right—six-hour watches." Andrew had added his own rifle and two pistols to the arsenal now stacked on the counter near the stove. "All of you should go to bed and get some rest."

Nancy began bustling with food and drink he might want during the night. "Mr. Magill, it's a true kindness for you to protect this family, whom you hardly know at all," Nancy said.

"Nothing to it, ma'am. This is where I am staying, and I always guard the place where I sleep. And please call me Andrew, or Andy, as my friends call me."

Sylvie felt superfluous as well as tired, and after she also thanked Andrew and said good night to everyone, she wearily climbed the stairs to her little room. The ceiling slanted down so sharply on two sides that she had to stand in the middle to undress and put on her nightgown. She got into bed, and as she leaned against the pillows, she sent a fervent wish, like a prayer, that the men from town would stay safe as they tracked the Comanche. She would not allow herself to picture the battle that could ensue.

Other local Indian nations were mainly peaceable, having signed treaties, and some were traditionally farmers who kept close to their homelands. Comanche, by contrast, were a nomadic, warring nation that was moving in from the Great Plains to expand its territory. Bands attacked other Indians in addition to white settlers, usually to take cattle and horses, which was how they measured their wealth. They were formidable fighters, and the tortures they visited upon captives were gruesome and legendary.

Sylvie chose to think about Armand, as she often did, and her mind drifted to comments Rachel had made that evening. If only the ladies knew how reserved Armand was, how proper, too restrained even to seek a kiss. Yet it was not for lack of feeling. On a recent evening, while tending to a newborn calf and its mother at the edge of a field, he had been so nurturing with the tiny animal, all damp and tottering on its shaky legs, that she found herself holding her breath. He spoke so softly; his hands moved so gently and confidently.

These men could channel their tenderness, their softer feelings, into such treatment of dogs, horses, and even kittens, yet put up their guard and take tough stances with fellow human beings, male or female. They outnumbered young women so greatly that when they did have a chance to chat at a dance or soirée, social convention and formality tied their tongues, forced their hands into their pockets, and brought furious blushes when they did attempt to join a dance or even a conversation. And yet they would quickly volunteer for ranging and search parties and readily engage in battles. What a conundrum was the male nature.

She must have dropped off, for she woke abruptly, her nerves on alert at some sound she couldn't identify. After a time of fruitlessly trying to sleep, she decided to warm a cup of milk. She pulled on a housecoat and buttoned it, picturing the young man in the kitchen, and crept downstairs.

Quiet as she'd been, Andrew's feet hit the floor when he sensed her behind him. One hand was on a pistol so fast that she jumped.

"*Ma foi!*" she exclaimed, and they stared at each other in the dimness.

"Never sneak up on an armed man," he said.

"I thought you were asleep."

He frowned, and she added, "Forgive me. You are clearly awake and on guard."

She explained she wanted to heat some milk and offered him a cup, but Andrew said he'd prefer fresh coffee, if it wouldn't be too much trouble. He wanted to go outside to check the yard and fence line, and after she put pots on the stove, he quizzed her to ensure she knew how to use a rifle. When he returned, he reported that everything seemed quiet, and he carefully replaced the pistol on the table.

Andrew sipped appreciatively at the hot coffee. "Won't you have some, unless you'd rather get back to sleep? A bit of conversation will help me to stay awake." He smiled and held her gaze for a moment.

"Well, maybe half a cup." She added a bit to her hot milk and chose to sit around the corner of the table from him, rather than straight across, where the assembled barrels were pointing. She could feel him watching and looked up to meet his hazel eyes in the closer space.

"What did you say, when I startled you?" he asked. "It sounded like 'fwah.'"

"Oh, it's French for faith—or for one's liver. A *crise de foi* can sound like either kind of crisis." That sounded so inane, Sylvie added, "It's like, in English, 'Oh, my soul.'"

Andrew squinted, as though trying to place the phrase. "It must be a fine thing to be French. My family admires them. My great-grandfather fought with the French against the British in the American Revolution, and my father did also, in the War of 1812. He was even at New Orleans for the big victory."

"That's quite a military tradition."

"Yes, a high standard to live up to."

"Will you join the army here and fight, if there's a war for independence?"

"I don't plan to." Andrew paused and grinned. "I would rather profit from it, unless the fighting comes near Mina. My cousin and I told you earlier that we're starting a mercantile business there, and shopkeepers are needed to supply the army and local militia units—as well as regular townspeople, of course. But I don't mean I wouldn't fight. I will if I need to—but just temporarily, in a volunteer unit. I don't plan to sign up as a regular soldier in an army."

"That sounds like a worthwhile plan." She thought of Armand, by contrast, and how he planned to enlist if there was a war, how military service could take years of his time and send him to distant places. "Tell me about the colony in Mina," she asked. "What is it like?"

Andrew said the town was about the size of Gonzales, but the land was prettier and more varied, with rolling hills to the west and a large lake and pine forest to the east. "The trees grow taller and are less scrubby. You really should see it sometime, and just think, the new road will be done soon."

Sylvie said the area did sound attractive but that she would be leaving with Nancy and Duff later that summer.

"But why leave? Why don't you want to stay?" Andrew seemed genuinely puzzled as he looked steadily at her. She got up to fetch the coffeepot and poured more for both of them. How very odd that she couldn't come up with a simple answer in that moment, with the silence stretching out.

"I've always wanted to spend time in New Orleans," she said, taking her seat again. "My cousin and her husband live there now, and she was my best friend during childhood."

"You're describing something that would just be a visit." Andrew was smiling, which pulled his features into a pleasing alignment. He had fairly large ears that stuck out a bit, or perhaps they just appeared to with his hair so short. He had strong cheekbones, and his eyes looked warmer, crinkled up. He was slouching in the chair, overly at ease for someone on guard duty.

"After that, you'll come back here," he added after a moment.

"I don't imagine I will." She straightened in her chair.

"What about going home to Illinois? Does anything, or anyone, draw you back there?"

The question struck Sylvie as vaguely inappropriate, possibly arising from information she had not shared. Had he talked with Uncle Jim about her or asked questions of Rachel? She hoped he did not yet know that she was an orphan with no true home to claim. It was wonderful, here in Texas, to meet people who did not already bring that dispiriting information to their first impression of her. In this new country, she could leave chosen parts of her past behind, as a great many other settlers were wont to do.

"That strikes me as an impertinent question, Mr. Magill."

"Please call me Andy, or Andrew. And I don't mean to delve into private matters. Would it seem more fair if I told you some of my own background, first?"

Sylvie nodded and sat back, welcoming the idea of a story and curious how well he would tell one. Andrew described setting out in the summer of 1833 and riding horseback with a companion all the way from Kentucky. He delved further back to when he was a boy and first dreamed of Texas when Sterling Robertson, *empresario* of a new colony, had toured farming communities in Kentucky and told tales of the place to recruit settlers.

Inspired by that vision, Andrew and his friend had headed west as soon as their families would allow. However, they arrived to find Robertson's colony failing due to small numbers. Andrew had sought out Jim Kerr, whom his family knew from Kentucky. Andrew said the land claim Jim set up for him had a mix of meadow, woods, arable acreage, and even a stream.

"That sounds like an ideal place," Sylvie said. "It's too bad the hurricanes discouraged your efforts."

"Well, they weren't the only factor …" Andrew looked away for a moment and then grimaced. "It was farming that gave me my real comeuppance. Therein lies a sad story, Sylvie."

She wondered whether his tone of high seriousness was potentially comic, and he continued, "I learned the hard way I'm not cut out to be a farmer. There I was, with one-third of a league, about fifteen hundred acres. The land looked productive at first, but once I got to plowing, the topsoil was only a few inches deep, as well as thin and sandy. It's not much good for crops, other than cotton, possibly."

"And you decided against raising cotton?"

"Yes, I don't want that kind of large, organized system, plus it's built on slave labor, which I also don't want to get into."

"Does your family own slaves, or did they, back in Kentucky?"

"Way back, a few of them did, but they freed the last remaining ones a long time ago. In fact an uncle financed a voyage to return former slaves to Africa, to a place called Liberia."

"I've heard about those efforts," Sylvie said. "I don't want anything to do with slavery, either. And then you decided against farming entirely?"

"I expect to grow my own crops for food, and the claim I'll trade for in Mina includes some farmland on the edge of town. The main parcel, though, will be in grasslands, which I'll put to grazing cattle. That first year, I got to feeling no more noble than the oxen I was driving. In fact they handled the drudgery with more dignity than I did. Fortunately I was in touch with Logan and his brother, and they talked me into going up to Mina."

"So you had only the one season on your claim? My family have been farmers for generations. Also fur traders, and my father liked to design buildings, and plat towns and sell the lots."

"Yes, you see, if you have something else to do, an additional business, that feels like a better balance to me."

"Did your family intend for you to take up an occupation, a certain kind of work?"

"They wanted me to read for the law. But I could not abide sitting still all the time, and I wanted something more active. When I turned twenty, my father honored my decision, and now my younger brother is fulfilling that family expectation."

"You're searching for something that's not as strenuous as plowing land, but not as inactive as being a lawyer." Sylvie laughed as Andrew agreed.

"Now, is that enough of a life story to earn an answer to my earlier question? Is something in particular drawing you back to Illinois?"

"No, nothing in particular, not a liaison or engagement, if that is what you are implying. I do miss my hometown, and my family, and French culture quite a bit."

"You would get back to a kind of French culture in New Orleans. Everybody says that about the city. It's pretty large, though."

"And do you dislike big cities? Maybe you'd like a house set all by itself in the middle of a claim, miles away from any neighbor. That's what Americans seem to prefer, but I could never live like that."

"Well, no. I do like smaller towns; I grew up in one outside of Lexington. And I have to admit my cabin on that first claim was pretty far away from anything else. So was the one we built on my partner's land. He gave up, by the way, and went back to Kentucky. So you see, I do have some perseverance."

Andrew asked her to tell about the trip down the Mississippi River and the voyage across the Gulf of Mexico, and Sylvie enjoyed describing the riverboat journey. She also told about Amy joining kinfolk in New Orleans, but omitted any mention of the poker game and her winnings. Leaping ahead, she shared lasting impressions of the voyage at sea. The memories of huffing sails, warming sun, and the gently rocking boat must have been soothing, for soon Sylvie was stifling yawns and picturing returning to bed.

Andrew suggested that she should try to get more sleep, and she asked if he was going to wake Duff to take guard duty. He said he still felt wakeful but would rouse Duff when it started to get light. Sylvie rose and took her cup to the sink. She did need more rest before the workday began.

They said good night, and as she went upstairs, she reflected how much Andrew had talked about his family background and recent experiences. She had seen that before, with people from Kentucky and other places in the South and East who were proud that their families had lived for generations in a place and that their ancestors had labored and fought to start the United States and preserve it.

Often, questions in Texas began with the humorous, "Who were you, before?" The first steps of friendship involved reciting family lineage and establishing the solidity of the folks back home. Even though she had thought him slightly impertinent, Andrew had taken that approach with her, and actually, she was not displeased at all.

And he had done a fair job of shaping his life into a story for the telling, with humor, irony, and even honesty about failure, along with hope. By contrast, what story had she shaped about her own life, so far? She had told a good tale about the voyages, but those were just pieces cut out from the whole cloth of her life. With so many larger parts omitted that were important to her, she had not actually told Andrew why she had chosen the trip to Texas.

She now realized that decision was largely based on leaving, on getting away from difficult situations back home, rather than on looking forward and reaching for something she desired. Nonetheless, she had found a life of value, here. Back upstairs in the privacy of her room, she could revel in her growing independence, in earning her own money, and in the deliciously secret rides with Armand. Now that she was planning to leave all she'd found in Gonzales, however, she did need something to look forward to. And she was counting on a long visit with Louisa in New Orleans for that.

Chapter 13

**June 1835**
**Gonzales and Mina, Mexico**

Uncle Jim came to call at Nancy's house one morning after mail arrived for him from Edna. He used couriers for colony business, and they also brought along any letters for Sylvie that had arrived at the farm. Jim found Sylvie on the front porch and handed her a letter from her niece Isabelle, who was proving to be her most faithful correspondent from Cahokia. He also asked if she had a moment to stay and discuss something regarding her future plans.

Sylvie held her letter unopened and took a seat in a rocking chair as Jim set out pacing the front porch. She wondered why he seemed so hesitant, and he finally took a letter from his jacket pocked, saying, "Here's the best approach. Sarah describes her situation in a way you'll understand. It is women's business, after all."

As Sylvie began reading, she realized Jim's wife was in what society called a delicate condition. He stood nearby, rocking from heel to toe as she scanned the message, which minded propriety by avoiding any specific reference to bodily matters. Then came the part that directly affected her, where Sarah entreated Jim to ask her to stay at the farm for the anticipated event, due near the middle of July.

Sylvie lowered the letter with mixed feelings. She was flattered that Sarah wanted her company and even wrote that she would be "a companion who brings news and fresh insights to occupy my mind." And what wonderful news this was for the couple, and for Minny, who would now have a brother or sister. However, staying at the farm for a time meant she could not go directly on to New Orleans with Nancy and Duff.

"Of course I'll be happy to stay with Sarah, as she asks," Sylvie said, though her tone sounded hesitant. "This will be a special time for all of you, and you must be very happy. Children are always a blessing, especially when one has suffered losses in the past."

Jim murmured something like "Harumph," as he turned to pace in the other direction, and Sylvie realized she had spoken openly enough to embarrass him. Why couldn't everyone be as practical as the French? Perhaps her reference to the family he had lost, the wife and children who had died years earlier, was upsetting.

Such memories always came with pain, as Sylvie had learned recently. An early letter from Isabelle had told of unbearably sad losses when the cholera epidemic returned to rage in Cahokia during the summer after Sylvie left. It took many lives in town, including young ones. Little Celeste, Sylvie's niece, had died, as had the youngest of Jeanne's children, a little girl close in age. Even now Sylvie grieved at the thought of not holding Celeste's hand again, or telling her their favorite story of the *Fille du Roi*.

But when Jim turned back toward her, he was smiling. "I am so glad that you will join Sarah for this time. She has other women around her, but you play a special role. She misses your conversation, some quality that only you can bring to help pass this time of waiting, which does go slowly. Yes, I suppose I am rather anticipating the event."

"I will need your help to make new travel arrangements, to go later to New Orleans."

"Yes, yes, we'll see to it."

"Do you think a delay will make the voyage more dangerous?"

As Jim hesitated, Sylvie sensed his doubt. In recent weeks, Mexican authorities had boarded American and Texan ships to search for arms and contraband and had even impounded several; reports also told of armed skirmishes breaking out.

"It is possible, and we have to recognize that. But I am holding out hope for peace. If some of the provinces already rebelling against Santa Anna's dictatorship defeat his army, we won't need to fight. Then if Mexico gets back to being a republic, we here in the American colonies can carry on as before."

"Uncle Jim, you are the only person I know who speaks so optimistically."

Jim laughed. "Oh, I know, and I'm often outnumbered. But a slight delay may be beneficial if I can persuade Sarah to travel with you. Then all of you, including Minny, could leave together. I am certain she will consider your feelings, if that's what you want."

Sylvie felt in debt to Jim and Sarah for their hospitality during her first year in Texas, for accepting her warmly and caring for her. Returning to the farm would feel like coming home in a way, and helping Sarah during her lying-in showed she was truly considered a family member. Sylvie realized anew how much she treasured such a bond.

"Yes, I definitely want to get to New Orleans, and having us all travel at once is a good plan. I promised my cousin a long time ago that I would visit, and after tending to Sarah, I do need to fulfill that promise."

"Then let me work on the travel arrangements when the time arrives. And thank you, Sylvie; I am very grateful. Political and military meetings will take me away from home once we get back to Edna. Settlers in the area are planning to gather, and they could take a vote on going to war."

"Do you think peace is possible if it comes to a vote? Do enough others share your views?" Sylvie's question was rhetorical, and Jim seemed to consider a range of responses for a time.

Abruptly, he slapped his leg with enthusiasm at some new idea. "How about a treat in the meantime, a little side trip for you?" he asked. "How would you like to ride the new road to Mina, go along with the new mail service?"

Sylvie was startled. "A long ride like that—is that really a treat?"

"A diversion, certainly. It's a beautiful place to visit, and you should see it if you're leaving Texas for good. You've probably heard that Peter Kerr now has a contract for delivering the mail to Mina. He's a kinsman, and utterly trustworthy. He knows the countryside well, and what better way to demonstrate that people can safely travel with the mail than having my own niece ride along? He's headed out this week. Or you could ride next week, if you want."

Sylvie gazed off, imagining several days of freedom from helping Nancy with housework and packing her trunks. "A trip like that does sound nice."

"You'd stop at Burnam's on the Colorado River for one night, spend two nights in town, and come back."

Sylvie asked where she might stay in Mina, and Jim suggested a couple, Josiah and Margaret Wilbarger, whom she knew from Missouri. Before settling in Texas, they had owned the farm next to her Aunt Peggy's—Jim's sister. Sylvie agreed she would enjoy seeing them again, and Jim announced himself pleased with the plan.

"I'll send Margaret a note in this week's mail, and I'm sure she'll be delighted to welcome you. That also gives you a chance to call on a couple of young men up there, if you'd like."

Sylvie laughed and shook her head. "I don't know which young men you're referring to. You're not matchmaking, are you, Uncle Jim? Men don't know how to do that properly."

"No, of course not. But you can't leave everything to fate, can you?" He reached his arms wide in a questioning gesture.

Sylvie remained on the porch after Jim left, musing over the change to her plans. The ride to Mina was enticing, but it could be dangerous. The town was farther north than any other settlements and lay within lands the Comanche Nation traditionally claimed for hunting in the fall. If one considered only safety, it was surprising that Jim would suggest the trip.

But there had been no further raids after the attack on the French and Mexican traders weeks earlier, in May. The ranging party from town had tracked the Comanche and fought them successfully, with only one man wounded and no loss of life. The group had returned with the traders' goods and horses in tow. As the main administrator for the DeWitt colony, Jim received frequent reports on a range of issues, so Sylvie felt conditions must be safe.

And how interesting that he would suggest calling on Andrew Magill and Logan Vandeveer. She wondered if he had heard that she kept company with Armand Fulshear, and whether Jim preferred one of the others as a suitor. Sylvie enjoyed recalling her nighttime conversation with Andrew. She had felt safe in his presence, and they'd shared an easy manner of speaking reminiscent of being back in Illinois. He wasn't glib, but he also was not reticent to the point of being tongue-tied like so many local young men. She didn't intend to make a comparison, but her talks with Armand did not stretch far, or cover much in the way of politics, history, or ideas. She wondered if it was due to the French they spoke, for otherwise he spoke English. Perhaps his French vocabulary hadn't developed much past everyday terms his family used at home.

Sylvie mused on the coincidence between Andrew's invitation to visit Mina and Uncle Jim's similar proposal. Most likely, there was no coincidence at all. Both had mentioned their families being friends and neighbors back in Kentucky, and they'd had plenty of time to talk while laboring on the new road. She shook her head with a smile.

Finally Sylvie broke the seal on the letter from Isabelle. Her niece often wrote introspectively, as though the accounts stood in for a journal Isabelle might keep if she weren't afraid of her mother finding it and delving into its revelations. Poor Isabelle, still smitten with their cousin, expressed romantic yearnings forbidden and unthinkable in her parents' household. She was careful to make two copies of each letter and send them separately to increase the odds that one would arrive in Texas. And in the small stack of letters that Sylvie treasured, she actually had two copies of a single one from Isabelle.

The others in the stack included several from Louisa--one written in Cahokia after Sylvie failed to return for the wedding, and the others from New Orleans, where the couple had started married life. She had two letters from Jeanne written each year at Christmastime. These were mainly short, dry accounts of births, marriages, and deaths, though one did express great satisfaction that Marguerite and Vital Jarrot planned to marry. When it came to telling about the deaths of the two little girls from cholera, Jeanne's sentences were so brief that Sylvie could sense the pain in each space between words. She had learned the news while still living at the farm in Edna, and Sarah and Uncle Jim had been most understanding and helpful during her bouts of grief.

Sylvie started reading Isabelle's letter, written in March. After relating social news concerning friends and relatives, she moved on to a family business development.

> *Papa and Maman are joining in a venture to build a railroad. It will run only about six miles, but just think, Sylvie—the first railroad in the Mississippi River Valley! It began with John Reynolds promoting a grand idea to lay tracks starting at the coal deposits on his land south of town. The rail cars can bring the coal up to the quays north of town so it can be shipped to St. Louis, or downriver to the iron foundries.*
>
> *Maman says this investment is something your father would have found ideal, and that he would want your inheritances used for such a venture. Papa agrees, and I understand from conversations I've overheard that they will stake part of your share, which Papa manages, to help finance the railroad. They spoke with Etienne about investing your brother Laurent's share—they have to because Etienne got a new legal guardian after Fernande remarried—but Etienne says no. He wants to keep his father's part of the inheritance in the house and farmlands for himself and his younger brothers.*
>
> *It's so strange to watch such a development, to see how John Reynolds calls on the faith and resources of our family and other friends around town. I think he takes advantage of his prestige as a former governor and now a U.S. Congressman. And Vital is very excited about the idea of a railroad, as well. He and Marguerite are making their own stake, drawing on some of the Jarrot family's funds.*
>
> *So Sylvie, imagine this: when you do get back to Cahokia, you might be part owner of a railroad! I don't think they plan on passengers, however—only cars to carry coal.*

Sylvie scanned the rest of the letter, though she barely took in its contents. What did she think, indeed? Isabelle was the first to mention this, and Sylvie resented that her sister had not written to ask her permission or even consult her views. For a moment, she wished she weren't so far away, but then reminded herself she likely wouldn't have much say even if she were in Cahokia. A distant pang of worry began insinuating itself as she wondered about the expense of building the line, and whether it could succeed financially. In Cahokia, she could ask such questions, though undoubtedly she'd hear enthusiasm  from the town's business leaders, as well as anticipation for the profits from shipping coal. She might even be willing to risk part of her inheritance for a handsome return. Though she was given no choice at the moment, she could write to Jeanne and ask to be informed of the amounts of money involved.

Sylvie glanced toward the dusty streets near the house and the hastily built wooden structures along them. How difficult it was, here in Texas, to imagine a railroad, when mere dirt roads were such a rarity that people still traveled mainly by river. And she had never seen a railroad, only drawings of locomotives and cars in illustrated papers. She would enjoy imagining profits, but she also was concerned that such a large financial commitment overlapped so closely with family interests. While Isabelle seemed supportive, Sylvie inferred from the tone that she was maintaining a cautious distance from the project.

Sylvie went inside and climbed the stairs to her room. At the desk, she added the newest letter to the small stack and drew out an older one, the sole letter she had received from her nephew Etienne. *Good for him, to get his own legal guardian and hold on to the farmhouse and land,* she thought. Writing the previous winter, he was still living at home, along with his mother's new husband Emile Hubert, yet had other plans.

*Dear Sylvie,*

*I am fine, how are you? When are you coming home? You're really late from when you said you'd be back. Sometimes I think about going to Texas, and I'd ride horses over the plains and go hunting and chasing Indians. It sounds like fun, but I probably won't do it. I am learning how to run the farmlands, and I handle a lot of important work. Maman says I can live in the old homestead house in Cahokia, so I am fixing it up. The well is still good. When you come back, you can live there too, and you can do the cooking.*

*Aunt Jeanne was here today for dinner. She talks about everyone going to Hell for every little thing. Even me, when she thought I crossed*

*my eyes at her. She is happy, though, that Marguerite will marry Vital
because he's so rich and has lots of business ventures, etc., etc.*

*She doesn't like my stepfather much, but I think he is all right. I
have to go back to the academy in Belleville after Easter. They make us
study Latin and history and home chemistry. You are lucky you aren't
in school and can go riding around the countryside all day. I hope you
are well and happy. You can write back if you want.*

> *Your affectionate nephew,*
> *Etienne*

Sylvie reread his letter several times, feeling that he wrote so genuinely she could almost his voice.

When Uncle Jim decided on travel plans, things moved quickly. The
following week, Sylvie set off on a mild morning to ride the mail route
with Peter Kerr. Settlers along the new road, or trace, had heard about
the service and were eager to pick up their mail at any point along the
way. Sylvie had assumed the mailbag wouldn't be opened before reaching Mina, but Peter seemed happy to stop each time someone rode up
to hand him letters and collect any addressed to them.

Peter Kerr did not look like any postal official Sylvie had ever
seen. Over his white, floppy-sleeved Mexican cotton shirt, two wide
bandoliers holding bullets crisscrossed his barrel chest. With his
sun-darkened complexion and heavy mustache, one might take him
for a Mexican trader or a Tejano cattleman, a descendant of Spanish
colonists.

Peter had removed his large straw hat while they stopped to rest
in the shade of several trees. He was laughing as he talked with a thin
boy who had just ridden up and now stood bent over a pile of letters
Peter had spread out on the ground.

"Do you see your family name on any of these missives, young
man?" Peter asked. "You do cipher letters, do you not, your mother
having taught you a bit, at her knee?"

"I am not certain, sir, but I think to read the name Van den Hoeck on several of these. My mother is longing so for word from her kin back home, that I hope to bring her something from your stack, here."

"Well, son, it won't cheer her if the letter is not actually from her own loved ones. Let me help you—I seem to recall a missive addressed to that name."

Peter got on his hands and knees and shuffled through the pile. Sylvie watched as she sipped water and ate some dried turkey and cornbread.

"There, I knew it!" Peter leaned back on his heels and waved a letter. "This is addressed to any of the family. We can read it right here and now, if you like."

The boy grinned and snatched it. "I will save opening it; my mother will put it on the windowsill and make us all wonder at it. After dinner, we'll read it like it's our dessert, like pie we get at Christmas. Besides, it may be written in the old language, from back in the Alsace, sir, and you might not ken that."

"You are correct, son. Back at home in Pennsylvania, I learned to speak some German, but not to read it. You are quite right about my ignorance in that area."

The boy's pants rose to mid-shin, and his feet were bare. His extra-large plaid shirt was so flimsy that rents had opened around the patches sewn over the elbows. Sylvie guessed he was about twelve; his smile showed perfect white teeth, and his white-blond hair was neatly trimmed. She could offer some cornbread, but he was likely to refuse it—both from pride and a European background. She herself had only recently started eating it, rather than go hungry.

"I must head home directly," the boy said, jiggling from one foot to the other. "Want to see me ride like an Indian? I know how the Comanche ride, and I can almost do it. Here, watch this."

He stuffed the letter into a front pants pocket and approached his horse, a good-size Appaloosa patterned with black on the haunches. The horse had no saddle and only a light bridle. The boy was up on its back so fast Sylvie missed seeing how he did it.

He shrieked, "Yiiieeee!" and tore off, riding zig-zags through the grassy field. On alternate turns, the boy couldn't be seen, having dropped to the horse's far side. Sylvie squinted to spot the one heel, hooked over the animal's spine, that kept him anchored. The pair came closer and turned again, now revealing the boy draped tightly against the horse's side. He raised both hands in the air for an impossible moment and shouted: "See! I can ride like a Comanche!"

Then he hoisted himself upright, somehow, and crouching low just behind the horse's neck, rode away. He turned to wave in farewell.

"That was amazing," Sylvie said after a moment. "I've heard about how the Comanche ride, but I had never seen it done."

"Yes, the warriors can put their horses between our bullets and their own bodies," Peter said. "And they manage to fire a dozen arrows with deadly aim at the same time. You saw how he could keep his hands free and hang on by just one heel. And the Comanche do this while we're kneeling on the ground trying to reload, after we've fired our two precious shots."

He spoke with a discouragement Sylvie had not noticed before. Usually, a glint of humor slightly crinkled his eyes and forehead, as though looking for a way to leak out. Peter swept up the pile of envelopes and began putting handfuls back in the bag.

"Where was that letter from?" Sylvie asked.

"Not the Old Country. The return address was a town in Tennessee."

"Did it have a stamp from Tennessee?"

"No, no stamp at all." Peter glanced at her and grinned. "I know I'm supposed to collect postage if the sender didn't pay, but you won't report me, will you, just because I can't bear to charge an underfed, barefoot lad?"

Sylvie smiled to reassure him. "No, of course not. He might be from one of those European colonies where new arrivals are going hungry. They don't know they can eat squash or potatoes and even think tomatoes are poisonous."

"That's sadly true, and a colony that has endured mass starvation is located just a couple of miles from here. The boy most likely has seen a lot, though his family may be doing all right." He closed the clasp and loaded the bag on his horse.

"That degree of hunger is a danger to the entire area," Peter continued. "With starvation comes pestilence and disease. We need to keep everyone fed in order for all the rest of us to be healthy. And ready to fight, as the need may arise."

Sylvie wrapped her food, regretting she had not simply handed something to the boy. As she repacked her saddlebag, Peter asked if he should ride ahead a bit. She said that would be courteous and watched until he had cleared the trees. As the only female on this stretch of the ride, she missed the way women could cluster during breaks and draw their skirts out wide to shield one another from view as each attended to private needs. But Peter considerately imagined what she might require, and his politely oblique phrases kept them within the bounds of propriety.

After a minute, Sylvie mounted her pony easily, swinging one leg over to ride astride. It was odd to recall her brief period of riding sidesaddle in Illinois, stretching from her first ball to the voyage down the Mississippi River. What was it going to feel like to return soon to French society? Riding sidesaddle might be one of the smaller adjustments. She patted her horse's neck and felt like tearing away at high speed; Peter might not mind a gallop as well.

When she rejoined him along the trail, he wanted to keep a comfortable walk through the trees and said they could run the horses across grasslands farther north. "Let's not tire them until we're close to stopping for the day," he added, "just in case we actually need to dash away from something."

Peter enjoyed conversation, especially if he could spin stories based on his life in Texas, and after a time, Sylvie asked him about a recent visit to New Orleans he'd mentioned.

"That episode was a bitter experience, for it shows how one's fellow man might come to doubt the character of another just because of the fate delivered upon a business venture. That is the sad moral of this chapter of my life," Peter began, his words falling into rhythm with the horses' walking gait.

Sylvie recognized the genre of storytelling that was often used to fill otherwise empty hours. The lofty language shaped life's mishaps into humorous parables whose lessons, properly learned, were sure to lead to success in the teller's latest efforts.

Peter wanted to begin by telling of his business ventures in order, and Sylvie surmised they would be riding a while before the next break.

His first undertaking, ten years earlier, was to bring a cargo of goods down the Mississippi River to the earliest colonies in Texas. After successfully delivering the initial load, he sent the schooner back for a second. He was staying in the town of Victoria, and there he began to court a young woman whose father owned significant land, for their ancestors had settled on a grant from the king of Spain.

"To be brief, I wooed her and was accepted," Peter said. "We planned to marry as soon as my second cargo came to port. Her father insisted that her husband's prosperity be secure beyond any question, and as I was waiting, I decided to take up trade among local Indians, with an eye to establishing a route farther into Mexico.

"Alas, I was, to be brief, robbed of all my goods out on the yellow plains, among the cactus trees and wheeling vultures. This sad outcome showed that the tribe I had imagined warmer to commerce apparently did not share the idea of its benefits. So I returned to Victoria bruised and humbled. But I might have yet retained the hand of my fiancée if my cargo ship had not chosen that particular time to run aground and be lost."

"The ship was lost, and all the cargo? How terrible! But if she loved you, surely …"

"No, everything was lost, my dear, including any hope of marrying. I protested and pleaded with her father, and she did as well; she wept copious tears that would soften most hearts. Ah, she swore she loved me and would always be true. And I love her enduringly; I will never love another."

They rode in silence for several minutes, until Sylvie felt compelled to ask what had happened to her.

"She married another," Peter said. He nudged his horse with his heels, and they picked up their pace.

After a while he slowed, and she pulled close enough to ask,"What did you try next, after the shipping and trading failed?"

"Oh, the shipping turned out *not* to be a failure, my dear, for I had insured the vessel, and I collected ample funds from its loss to start anew. I stayed a spell in Victoria, walked the streets wearing fine clothes, and even bought a span of fine horses to display my prosperity to the hardhearted father. But after some time of fruitless wooing, I headed toward Matamoros to trade the horses. Well, would you guess that in the desert there exists such a thing as a bottomless sandy hole, a great well with unseen water seeping up through it?"

"I've heard of something called quick sand, and how it can swallow up a horse, or even a wagon."

"That is true; I've witnessed it. I watched my fortune sink as those beautiful horses succumbed, one by one, to drowning in what appeared as a flat plain no different from the stretch we had just ridden over. But don't start imagining the tragic scene, my dear, for it is a horror the mind's eye will replay for you more times than you would wish, and always at times when you least wish to see it."

"Oh, Peter, I am so sorry to hear that, and the thought of how the horses suffered—how horrible."

"It was quick, though, and I nearly lost my own life to those watery depths. For some minutes I was willing to let that happen, too. Then a ferocious will took over, and I came to lying on my back, staring at a vast sky where vultures were circling to reckon whether I was ready for sampling. To be brief, I narrowly escaped, and I crawled and walked a long way before ranchers found me and came to my aid."

Peter raised a weather-tanned, wrinkled hand and dragged at the corners of his eyes.

Sylvie wanted to be encouraging. "I can tell you are still keen for more ventures in your lifetime, and I'm sure something will prove successful."

"Yes, I was most fortunate my family back in Pennsylvania would stake me again, and my most recent scheme was to distill alcoholic spirits. In New Orleans I bought all the machinery I would require in Texas to aid in quenching the thirst of the colonists."

"That sounds like it would succeed."

"Indeed. I had engaged the schooner, with a worthy captain and trustworthy mates, and all the equipment was loaded on board. But while I was finishing the requisite paperwork and entertaining associates, the skipper decided to depart. To be brief, I missed the boat."

"They sailed without you?"

"Time and tide wait for no man," Peter said. "You know that a schooner must depart when it can float the tide and find fair weather and steady winds." He described making his way overland with a horse he could barely afford, along with a supply of beans and *tortillas*. Several weeks later, when he arrived near the port in Texas, he found that the distilling equipment had been requisitioned.

"An erstwhile friend, Mr. Sam Houston, had gotten there before me and declared it contraband, arguing that Mexico forbids importation of a distillery. He had the cooperation of Mexican officials, too, for they arrested me and put me in jail. Can you imagine my situation? Houston later said the equipment would go to the Texas army."

"How dreadful! Can an army do that, requisition your goods?"

"They can and they do, my dear. So much is being taken for the Texan army these days, it makes one wonder what they're planning."

"Even so, I cannot believe that an unofficial army of colonists can claim one another's property that way. Or that an army actually needs a distillery."

"Well, I understand that our provisional, somewhat unofficial Texas government will convene for deliberations this fall. Maybe they will take up the issue then, though I suspect they will not." Peter started laughing, and Sylvie joined him halfheartedly, wondering at how he dismissed his misfortunes.

"Texas is the land of starting over," he said. "And these stories are like goods I can trade. They've won me meals and drinks, nights of lodging, and new friendships. The key is to make light of your woes and display unfailing will to succeed."

After a moment, he added, "I am grateful that your uncle has entrusted me with this mail route. Though it is work for wages rather than an entrepreneurial undertaking, it is a godsend, and I'm happy to have the time in Mina. I hope to cultivate contacts among cattlemen there and try that business next. I do not presently have principal for an investment, but I trust the future will show a way to obtain it."

"I understand that Logan Vandeveer and his brother are establishing a cattle business. Uncle Jim says they're making a good start."

"Yes, that's what I've heard, as well. So you and I have a common interest in the destination of our trip. At least I think you want to see a young man or two who are residing in Mina."

"To be brief," Sylvie said, "my uncle would like me to take an interest in either Logan or his cousin. I believe he favors Andrew Magill as a suitor."

"Vandeveer can catch the eye of any young woman near him, his looks are so striking. Magill has more of an air of … readiness and competence, though I cannot say why I think that. If I were riding a dangerous trail, though, I would welcome him along. Perhaps it's *bravado*—do you know that word? It means brashness, just short of bragging, but cheerful in nature."

"One might call it cheekiness."

"Oh, might one?" Peter glanced at her.

"It will be interesting to see the area and gain an idea of what the town is like. One thing I've learned in Texas is that a woman doesn't choose only a husband when she marries. She's also getting his land claims and vision for the place."

"Very well put. You are being sagacious, young lady."

"Sagacious? That must be like *sage* in French—wise, or thinking things through and acting carefully."

"Exactly right. Would you like to practice some Spanish? I'm told my command of the language is excellent."

Sylvie said she would enjoy that, as she wanted to learn more about verb tenses and conjugations. Peter was happy to share what he knew, and the practice helped make the afternoon's ride pass quickly.

Burnam's on the Colorado, their destination for the night, turned out to be a collection of double log cabins plus a trading post. Here, they heard grim news: two shopkeepers from Mina had been killed on the trace coming from San Felipe, Austin's first colony. They'd been driving a wagon loaded with goods. Sylvie felt pangs of dread at the news; Mina probably had few storekeepers, meaning the victims could be Logan and Andrew. As she and Peter separated for the night—the men to one double cabin and the women to another—he tried to calm her mind and asked her to take care with what she said.

"As the women talk tonight, it's likely someone will soon be mourning the loss of a son, a brother, or a husband," he said quietly. "There's only a chance this involves the two young men whom you know slightly, so be courteous."

"I will be *sage*—sagacious, as you say."

"There is little sense in giving in to groundless fear and trembling when we don't know the victims' identities. There's plenty of time for that later, when real sorrows come to test us."

Sylvie agreed, and they bid each other good night.

Chapter 14

**June 1835**
**Mina, Stephen Austin's "Little Colony"**

THE NEXT DAY'S RIDE GREW TEDIOUS. As Sylvie and Peter neared Mina, more settlers met them to claim any mail they might have, rather than make the trip to town. Sylvie paced impatiently during the last couple of halts, wondering at how Peter's joviality and garrulousness did not wane. Back on their horses, they cantered to make up the time, and soon Sylvie felt enlivened by the vista of rolling hills rising above the plains, and taller, more massive trees. As they crested hilltops, she could see blue-black ridges of the Lost Pine Forest to the east.

In the early afternoon, the road began to run straight through homes set closer together, and soon it emerged as a dusty track into a town with regular streets and wooden-frame houses set back in gardens. The homes had picket fences, fruit trees, chicken coops, and curtains on windows that gave onto the street.

"Does this town have a central plaza?" Sylvie asked. "I wonder, because this looks more like a town back in Illinois or Missouri."

"It does, and we'll pass it shortly. That's where they've built the stockade."

Though Mina may have been laid out in the Spanish style, the feel was more American, and as they rode under overarching trees—pecan, elm, maple—Sylvie had a sense of déja-vu, almost like recognition, or homecoming.

"This town has been an important trade site for a long time," Peter added. "A main route, El Camino Real, comes in a few blocks north and crosses the Colorado River off to our left. You'll see it soon, beyond the trees and houses."

Sylvie thought she could smell the river already, a freshness of cool water under heat, of clear water not brackish from the sea. They rode slowly in alternating sun and shade, and soon a few dogs and boys showed up to lope along, practically herding them toward the main street. As they turned by the plaza, Sylvie viewed the stockade's outer wall, which was formed of upright posts set tightly together, their sharpened points raised to the sky. At each corner, a little covered house rose above the perimeter to allow a view for sentries and sharpshooters.

Peter noticed her studied glance. "It is used from time to time, for protection against Comanche raids."

"Has it proven effective?"

Peter looked away, toward the busy street opening before them. "Yes, for the most part."

On Main Street, Sylvie could glimpse the Colorado River between trees and tangled growth of shrubs and vines on its steep banks. They dismounted and tied their horses to a hitching rail in front of a one-story brick building with a wooden false front reaching above it. Sylvie unfastened her saddlebags, which held some coins and items she hoped to barter when she visited the shops.

Townspeople were gathering, mainly young and middle-aged men, and several called greetings to Peter. He said he would start delivering the mail directly and mounted a boardwalk running in front of the building's wide, low windows. A sign declared it an apothecary, and Sylvie imagined a counter inside, shelves with nooks to hold letters, and even a man wearing a white, long-sleeved shirt who would hand out remaining mail when it was claimed later.

For the moment, though, Peter had that job, and he also had to collect postage. He was working open the ties on the postal bag, which had shrunk to half its original volume. Sylvie held back to watch and enjoyed glancing at the women who were starting to arrive. Some were dressed in worn calico blouses and skirts, much like Sylvie's own outfit.

After scanning the crowd for several minutes, she caught sight of an especially tall man who looked familiar. With relief, she recognized Logan Vandeveer, who looked just as eager for mail as anyone else.

Soon he caught sight of her and edged over to greet her and shake hands.

"I confess I'd love to have news from home, and my father does write a letter every so often. How was your ride? Uneventful, I hope. And how do you like the road we built, with our hard labor?"

"It's quite fine, thank you. In the open places we could follow marks blazed on the trees, and it seemed wide enough everywhere for a wagon to pass. There were several good, sturdy bridges over streams—all still standing."

Logan laughed and invited her to stop by the mercantile store, adding that Andrew Magill was there. "I'm getting mail for both of us, since I have to wait till nearly the end of the alphabet for Vandeveer."

"Oh, I don't think Peter alphabetizes anything. And yes, I'd like to come by the store. I'm eager to visit all the shops in town."

"Very good. We brought in a new wagonload of supplies last week, and we're well stocked. But we heard some bad news this morning about another merchant."

"It may be what we heard last night at Burnam's, that two shopkeepers from Mina were killed by Comanches while driving goods up from San Felipe."

"Yes, a father and son. I know them—or knew them; it's a bad loss. Some volunteers are going to retrieve them—the bodies. And the town's Committee of Public Safety plans to call up a bigger group and go after the Comanche raiding party."

The concern that Sylvie had felt earlier for Logan and Andrew's safety was now replaced by imagining new dangers.

"Will you volunteer for something like that?"

"For myself, I'd say probably not. Our *alcalde*, that's like our mayor under the Mexican system, is talking about a long foray, going out for several months over a large territory. I have other plans, between the store and working cattle with my brother. I cannot speak for Andrew though, and what he might do."

"Oh, really?"

"Yes, he enjoys time in the saddle, seeing new vistas and the horizon opening up before him, as he puts it. Plus, hardly anyone has explored much to the north and west of here. But he has other commitments now, too."

Sylvie glanced down at her hands, clasped loosely at the front of her skirt. Peter was dispensing letters to eager claimants, much like a St. Nicholas distributing Christmas gifts from his pouch. When Logan offered to walk Sylvie to their store, he held two letters, one each for himself and Andrew. He tucked them into a pocket so he could carry her saddlebags.

Their store was small, with large, bright windows in the front, and it smelled of freshly sawed pine. A bell tinkled as Logan pushed the door, already ajar, farther open.

"Look at what the mail brought!" Logan waved a letter at Andrew, who stood behind the counter and smiled widely at seeing them.

"My, my. What a welcome delivery." Andrew leaned across to take Sylvie's hand and then grabbed at the envelope Logan held just beyond reach.

As Sylvie glanced about, Logan slung the saddlebags on the counter. "Miss Pensoneau has some trading to do, too."

"Please feel welcome to look around," Andrew said. "But I hope you aren't in need of any food items."

"No, mainly I'd like cloth for a dress or two, and a pair of shoes or boots would be most welcome. I believe none in my size exist anywhere in Texas."

"We don't have any women's footwear, I'm sorry to say," Andrew said.

"Andy, what do you mean about not having food stuff?" Logan asked. "We have ample supplies—or we did when I left for the mail."

"We've had a visitor while you were gone. It seems the Texan army, or the ranging group they're assembling, are requisitioning our flour, coffee, and bacon, and just about everything else. Robert Coleman came in first, and then Matthew Caldwell. They were almost competing with other to lay claim for blankets, rope, pails—and all of our ammunition."

"Can we get one to outbid the other, and gain a decent price for the goods?"

"They didn't talk in terms of money, just their power to make requisitions."

"But, they have to pay us," Logan insisted.

"Maybe in promissory notes."

"Well, that hurts our ability to stay in business." The two shared a grimace. "Promissory notes won't have any value until well after the provisional government meets in the fall—if then."

"I don't know what choice we have at the moment. I gained a little time by telling Coleman and Caldwell that the two of them couldn't argue here, they'd have to decide who gets what, and not come back until then."

"Who are these two men, and why can't they agree?" Sylvie asked.

Andrew explained that Coleman served as the town's *alcalde* and was able to make administrative decisions and order civil actions. But a militia was forming now, as well, through Mina's newly created Committee of Public Safety, and Caldwell said he was representing that group.

Logan stood shaking his head while Andrew leaned, his arms straight and his hands flat on the counter. As Sylvie listened to their discussion, her glance roamed upward to the bolts of cloth stacked high on a shelf behind Andrew. She needed something for everyday dresses, but her eye refused to land on the darker hues. There were only a few plaids, and no calico at all. She did not want to invest in drab colors when she would be in New Orleans so soon. But perhaps she could find something special for a dress nice enough to wear when she arrived in the city, something Louisa would admire. She spied a lovely peach color but couldn't make out what kind of fabric it was.

The two men continued talking about the supplies being requisitioned, but when Sylvie turned her attention to them, they fell quiet. After a moment, Andrew shrugged and smiled, taking on the air of a host.

"You've had such a long ride—I've forgotten myself. Wouldn't you like something to eat and drink? We have pilot bread, a bit of cheese, and a keg of beer that's open. Or we can offer water, of course."

"Good idea," Logan said. "We should enjoy our goods while we still have them."

Sylvie perched on a stool at the counter, and the fatigue of the journey began slipping away as she sipped water and ate some food. The three chatted about news from Gonzales and acquaintances in Mina; Sylvie knew a handful of people in town through their connections to Missouri.

When they finished, Sylvie wiped her hands and asked Andrew if she might look closely at the peach-colored fabric. He stepped on a short ladder to fetch the bolt, which was narrow in width. He spread the loose end on the counter, and Sylvie took it between her fingertips, enjoying the unmistakable sheen of silk.

Andrew smiled and said the length measured the fourteen yards needed for a dress with a full skirt.

"We'll have to talk about the price," she said. "I have only a small amount of coin in silver, plus some colony scrip."

"Hmm. Yes, we can take that."

"I suspect you were hoping for American money. But I do have something almost as good." From the depths of a saddlebag Sylvie drew out three packets of playing cards, adding, "I think these ought to complete what I need for the silk."

"Playing cards!" Andrew exclaimed. "What are you doing with those?"

"I purchased them in New Orleans, when Sarah Fulton and I were shopping for provisions for Texas. Her brother, John Linn, is a trader, and he said playing cards were in such short supply that I'd be able to barter with them to my advantage. And I've been glad to have a pack to use myself, for occasional games."

"He was quite right," Logan broke in. "They'll sell fast, and we'll be happy to take them in exchange. Won't we, Andy?"

But Andrew was staring at Sylvie in such a way that she tilted up her chin. When he did not reply, Logan offered to show her the supply of buttons, saying she might find some suitable for the silk. Touching her elbow, he led her to a set of small drawers, each with a button appended to the front for display. She ran her fingers along their knobby tops as Logan returned to talk with his business partner.

"French women play cards all the time, Andy. It is customary, even in the highest social circles." Logan was keeping his voice low. "If you'd spent any time in their towns when you rode through, you would have learned that. It doesn't indicate anything disreputable, in her case. And for heaven's sake, it was John Linn who advised her to get them."

The two were interrupted by the bell at the door, and a man's voice greeting them and exclaiming what a fine day it was, with mail being delivered. "I'm hoping to get some tobacco," he added. "And Logan, let's set a day for the cattle drive. Oh—you have playing cards!"

Sylvie turned to glance at the man just as he noticed her, and their eyes met and held for a moment; she recognized him but could not place from where. Then she saw the brocade vest, and, when he removed his hat, the oiled, combed-back hair. She remembered it gleaming in the lamplight when they had played poker on the riverboat. She also recalled her winnings, the pile of silver coins.

"Ah!" he said. "Now I know who brought the playing cards!"

Andrew looked hard at her, his eyes enlarged enough almost to balance his ears, which seemed to protrude even more as they flamed red. *How does a man blush with his ears?* Sylvie wondered.

Logan was speaking: "Mr. Robert Epperson, may I introduce Miss Sylvie Pensoneau, though perhaps you two have met." In the silence, he added, "Robert has the ranch north of ours, and he's in the cattle business as well."

"I believe we had passage on the same steamboat coming down the Mississippi River," Sylvie said.

"Indeed," Epperson agreed. "I recall dining at the captain's table with you and your companion, Miss Fulton. It was a pleasure to share the voyage with such cultivated young women." He smiled and bowed his head slightly. "I trust both of you are well? And that you are prospering in this new country?"

"Thank you; we are keeping well, and I will be joining Miss Fulton, who's now Mrs. James Kerr, later this summer. I trust your endeavors are satisfactory, with the cattle business."

"It's off to a promising start, yes, thank you."

Sylvie glanced toward Logan, who looked amused as well as curious, and then at Andrew, whose look sought to delve into her soul and pass judgment. She returned to studying the buttons.

The men went on talking about cattle, the weather, and the ranging party being assembled, and Sylvie had selected buttons, thread, and a few other sundries when another man came into the store. He was as tall as Logan, but leaner. His leather pants bulged at the knee, and in addition to pistols in two holsters, a third was tucked into his wide belt. He quickly took Sylvie in, head to toe, and touched his fingers to his hat brim. His hands, face, and throat were tanned an even red-brown.

"Hello, again," he said, taking a slip of paper from his pocket. He set it on the counter, smoothed it, and pinned it down with two fingers.

"Matthew Caldwell," Andrew acknowledged, with a nod.

"I am authorized to take the goods we discussed before, by order of *General* Edward Burleson, and the black horse out back. That's your horse, I think, Vandeveer."

"No, you cannot take my horse," Logan said quietly.

"Yeah, I am taking the horse. Here's a receipt for him. You'll get him back."

"No, I mean, you cannot do this."

"Military orders. Signed by General Burleson. Look for yourself."

Andrew, who could see the paperwork, looked at Logan and nodded.

"I don't believe you have the right to do this," Logan said, still evenly.

"You don't mean the food—we can take supplies, right? You grant that right to the army of Texas, the troops defending you?"

"Uh, yes. But, aren't you a scout, not a regular officer?"

"You know that Burleson has the authority. And this is for the ranging party he's calling up."

Logan sighed. Hands thrust in his pockets, he shifted from one foot to the other. "That horse is the finest, largest horse in these parts, and you know it. He'd make a valuable prize for the Comanche, and they'll go after him. You're inviting them to seek you out, if you're riding him."

"That's the idea," Caldwell said, and then he smiled. "But that horse will outrun them, won't he?"

Andrew broke in. "Why don't you come back tomorrow, after we've had a chance to talk with Ed Burleson ourselves?"

"Yeah, we'll be back tomorrow for the food, the ammunition, and all the rest of the supplies. We don't have wagons ready at the moment, anyway. Unless you'd like to throw in your wagon as part of the deal. But the horse goes now."

"You are taking my horse while I am here in town?" Logan's voice rose.

"You and your brother have plenty more," Caldwell replied. "I'm not overly worried about how you'll get around." He pushed the paper toward Andrew, touched his hat brim, nodded to the men, and strode out.

"I think he's headed around to the back," Andrew said.

"Well, I'll go make sure he takes the right tack and saddle." Logan went around the counter toward the back door.

"I have an extra pony with me, and I'll make sure you have a ride back out to the spread," Epperson called after Logan.

"Logan is not armed, at least," Andrew said dryly.

"I guess I'll take that tobacco and a pack of playing cards and be on my way." Epperson began counting out some silver coins.

When he also had left, Sylvie and Andrew stood alone, looking at each other across the counter.

"Who is Edward Burleson?" Sylvie asked. "He's the military leader around here?"

"The Burlesons come from Tennessee, and Ed served as an officer under Andrew Jackson. He was head of the commissary for Jackson, and, as you have just seen, it's a good idea to stay friends with the head of the commissary. My father remembers him from the Battle of New Orleans and has great respect for him and his brother, who also served. He strongly advised me to fall in with them, when I got to this colony, that I could trust them as good military leaders."

"You did seem more willing to accept his authority."

"I have to weigh my future, and now I have some hard thinking to do. I've thrown in my lot and plan to stay here. I don't know if you view the situation quite that way, since you're planning to leave, but it does put a different light on things."

They were quiet for a minute, and he fingered the silk fabric. "Let me get this ready for you. I'm now in your debt, since I just sold a pack of your playing cards. I'll give you the length partly in trade, and the rest as a gift."

"Oh, no; I couldn't possibly accept," Sylvie said.

He recognized the ritual rejection for what it was, and she agreed, provided he kept the other two packs of cards. As he measured and cut, Sylvie tried to picture how it might feel to be a man in his early twenties who was trying so many different paths in life, from farming to storekeeping, to now possibly serving in a ranging party. He seemed to still carry the social order from his home and family in Kentucky, though applying it here on the frontier led to some dilemmas.

He had packed Sylvie's goods into her saddlebags when Logan came in, looking grim. "I'll stay here and mind things until Epperson brings that horse," he offered. "I'll also share a piece of my mind with Burleson, if he happens to stop by."

"That will be fine, as long as you're not planning on serving under him later." Andrew gave a wry grin and came out from behind the counter. He took a hat from the rack by the door and offered to walk with Sylvie to the Wilbargers' house, where she would be staying.

They stepped out into a noticeably cooler late afternoon. Shade from trees now extended fully across Main Street, and the air smelled sweet and heavy with summer, redolent of fruits, berries, and vegetables ripening nearby. They headed north toward a part of town she had not yet seen.

"I have arrived at a difficult time for you," Sylvie said. "What an upset, having your store's goods confiscated that way, and now you have all manner of decisions to make."

"Yes, I suppose so." He asked how long she would be in town, and learning she was free the following day, he said, "Tell me, Miss

Pensoneau, would you like to go walking with me in the afternoon? I can show you around, and the pathway along the river can be quite pleasant and shady."

"Yes, thank you, I would enjoy that. And please call me Sylvie, or Marie Sylvaine, if you must."

He tried her longer name, attempting to make the French "r" sound.

Sylvie smiled at his attempts. "It's becoming clear you haven't known very many French people, and you perhaps aren't familiar with the way I was raised. In my hometown, we women enjoy our card games and even wagering. It is a very good practice for mental acuity—and for gaining a little pin money."

"No, I have to admit that all comes as a surprise. Back home, women never think of playing cards. My mother would feel demeaned if she even touched a packet of them."

"What a shame. At first, things that are different can seem wrong. But they are not, really. On later consideration, they're simply different. At least, that is what I have learned." She raised her hand unconsciously to her ear, feeling for an earring that was absent.

"I suppose you're right. Most likely there are customs in Kentucky that would strike you as strange."

"When I was growing up, and we didn't know anyone from there, we said 'Kaintucks' to mean men who were barbarians. We believed they wore animal skins and got drunk and rolled around on the ground." Sylvie felt amused, recalling her talks with Louisa and how they'd teased each other about possible suitors.

Andrew looked at her with such surprise that she laughed. "And here you are, a genuine 'Kaintuck'! Getting to know you, I can see how mistaken we were."

"Well, thank you, I think … I only roll around on the ground when I'm engaged in wrestling—as a sport."

They drew to a stop near a low picket fence that set off a garden in front of a large wooden house. Andrew looked a bit flustered as he hesitated. "This is the Wilbargers' place, and I feel I should warn you, unless you've seen Josiah recently—"

"I have heard about the scalping," Sylvie said. "And I hope he is continuing to heal. My uncle told me about his group of surveyors being attacked last summer. The others were killed, and he is lucky to be alive, with such a serious wound."

"Yes; he often keeps it covered, but it can be shocking if you aren't expecting it. And perhaps even if you are."

"Thank you for thinking ahead to mention it. I am truly looking forward to seeing Margaret—it has been years since I last saw her at my aunt's farm in Missouri."

"Well, then, until tomorrow. And I promise I will call for you wearing clothes like these. I will leave the animal pelts at home."

Sylvie laughed. "I'll wager you will. Until then."

Sylvie enjoyed her evening with the Wilbargers, and the next morning she went shopping with Margaret, for she still hoped to find new shoes. Hers were so cracked and worn that she feared they would fall apart. That would leave her with nothing but the beautiful, beaded moccasins that her cousin Paschal had given her years earlier, and so far they'd stayed tucked at the bottom of a carpetbag. While she bought several small items that weren't available in Gonzales, shoes in her size were not to be found.

When Andrew called in the afternoon, they set out along streets already becoming familiar. Their first stop came several blocks away on Pecan Street, across from the plaza with its stockade. Andrew paused before a one-story house painted white and made distinctive by its large, double front doors. These stood behind columns that supported a graceful roof over the deep porch. Sylvie noticed the front rooms had unusually large windows, which she found appealing.

"What do you think?" he asked. "Is this an attractive house?"

"Yes, I would say so. Why do you ask?"

"I am buying it. I've already done the paperwork, and I could move in shortly."

"You could, but you are not certain you will?"

"Sylvie, I don't know what I'm going to do next. If I sign up for the rangering unit—they say they'll pay the volunteers—it  means six months away from town. I did earn wages hiring out on the road crew, but in addition to buying the house, I also bought the inventory ahead for the store, along with Logan."

Sylvie agreed that was a lot of financing to manage. He said his family in Kentucky was willing to support him with a stake, and added, "In fact, if I make a go of it here, my father might bring out the rest of the family."

"So this could become a place where your family might live." Sylvie nodded, and when Andrew suggested viewing the garden areas and outbuildings in the back, they skirted the south side of the house; sheds and pens for animals were appended to the north side.

Sylvie thought the gardens and the land looked favorable; the previous owner had even started a small orchard. She stood fingering a branch of a young apple tree when she asked, over her shoulder, if Andrew didn't have a fiancée in mind, to be so concerned with establishing a household right away.

"No, no fiancée. What you're seeing is evidence that I want to live here in Mina, as a homeowner and a shopkeeper, and eventually someone in the cattle business. I also recognize that I might serve in a local force, a temporary militia, because we may have to fight to protect our stake; otherwise we'll lose it all. While the military isn't my preference, it seems quite a few are eager to sign up for the new Texan army."

Sylvie agreed, thinking of Armand and his desire to enlist for as long as two years.

"Still," he said, "I would like to find a way to live in this house this summer. I'd offer to show you the inside, but that might not be proper."

"No, it would decidedly not be proper for me to go in, alone with a single young man." Sylvie added, as she joined him, "even in my French society."

They went back toward the street, and Andrew suggested walking by the river.

"You don't mention your family very much," he said. They'd been quiet for a time as they passed the imposing façade of the stockade.

Sylvie took a breath that sounded like a sigh. "You do know that I am an orphan? I expect you've heard that about me." When he nodded, she asked, "Is that the first thing someone says about me, that I'm an 'orphan French girl'?"

Andrew seemed startled, and after a moment he replied, "They usually say 'that pretty young woman whose uncle is Jim Kerr.' That name makes a fellow sit up and take notice, mind his behavior."

Sylvie smiled. "I suppose my larger, extended family back in Illinois is equally influential, but I must say, I do enjoy the sense of respect I get from his name around here."

They followed a footpath downhill from Main Street to the riverbank. There the path grew wide, with dense vines, shrubs, and wildflowers creeping into it, while trees arched overhead. The river flowed green and brown in the shadows extending from the west bank, broken by a few golden beams of light slanting through the trees. To the south was the ferry landing with its poles and ropes to assist carts and wagons. The river was low enough now that some might be driven across at the fording place.

They turned to stroll northward, Sylvie still preoccupied with Andrew's dilemma. She talked of how her own father had served in the militia in Cahokia several times, and that the troops had often been rewarded with tracts of land. He had gained hundreds of acres of farmland that way.

Andrew agreed, saying the same had happened with his ancestors, who had taken large land claims in Kentucky for their service in the American Revolution. And his father had been given grants for serving with volunteer units in the War of 1812. After the battle of New Orleans, he had staked a claim in a parish in Louisiana.

"I think Texas might follow the same practice," he added. "But it's a safer bet to join the local volunteer militia because a colony can award land from what it's been allotted in its contract with Mexico. An army, on the other hand, would be fighting against the Mexican government itself. You'd have to successfully overthrow that government and create a new one in its place. And that's a pretty tall order. First of all, you have to win. Right now, when Santa Anna defeats the forces in a province that's rebelling, he executes the prisoners, kills them as traitors."

"Oh, but that's horrible," Sylvie said.

"Yeah, that doesn't seem like honorable warfare. But is there ever honor in war?"

"I can see what you're saying."

"So how would you place your bets? You're a wagering woman."

"Well, have you been in a battle before?"

"No, not where I had to stand my ground and fire off shots. I've talked my way out of a few scrapes, and once or twice I demonstrated my skills as a marksman, which cooled tempers pretty effectively. And I also trust to having a fast horse."

"Then I would say, hang on to that lovely house you have bought. I would hold onto that home and land with all my might."

Sylvie sounded so serious that Andrew turned to look closely at her. But she didn't meet his eye, for she was looking beyond, at the river, fixing her gaze on something in the distance that perhaps only she could envision.

Soon the two of them were drawn from their talk by other people out strolling who stopped to say hello and be introduced. Sylvie was impressed by the well-dressed women and familiar accents of Missouri. It seemed everyone came from there, or from Kentucky or Tennessee. She could see that they thought well of Andrew, and the women took polite interest in Sylvie without displaying undue curiosity. She could imagine the gossip her presence would engender—only to be cut short by her departure the next day.

The river stretched over shoals of sand eroded from banks it had undercut during high water. Fallen trees were submerged partway, and turtles lined up along the shiny wet trunks just above the water. Dragonflies swooped up and down, hovering in front of the silk flowers on Sylvie's hat and glinting green and blue in rays of light.

"Tell me more about the town," Sylvie said as they began on a path leading uphill toward Main Street. "Do you ever have dances?"

"Yes, and we have several fine fiddle players. With any luck, some-one shows up to play drums, accordion, or banjo, and some young women show up, as well, so the men have a few partners to dance with."

"That's good to hear; I do enjoy dancing."

"I should warn you that, though I can dance a bit, it's not my greatest talent. My parents rather frowned on dancing."

Sylvie planned to ask about his greatest talents, but they had arrived at the Wilbargers' house, and it was time to say goodbye. At the gate, he took off his hat and held it before him with both hands. His ears sticking out looked pale on the top, much like his forehead above the line from his hat.

"So you might be out with a rangering group, or in the militia, this summer," Sylvie said, "while I will be in New Orleans visiting my cousin. It's hard to imagine worlds that are farther apart."

"And after that visit?"

"Hmm. I don't know; I'll have to see what the city offers for my future." She shrugged. "There's always a boat upriver, if I go back home."

"What if you got back to Illinois, and that older world looked small to you? Isn't there something here that you would miss?"

"I don't know what that would be." Her tone sounded as uncer-tain as she felt. Already she was picturing how she would miss riding in open spaces, and simple meals, and very little time spent in drawing rooms or adhering to social conventions simply for their own sake.

"May I write to you? I could send news and try to mention the attractive qualities of life here."

"Yes, I think that would be all right. For now, write care of my uncle at the farm in Edna, as we'll leave Gonzales within the month. Later I can send the address in New Orleans."

As they shook hands, Andrew stooped and gave her a kiss on the cheek accompanied by a searching look. It happened so quickly that anyone watching likely would take it as a mere bow of his head. It was the slightest brush of a touch, and she raised her eyebrows at him and turned to go inside. Within the doorway, she looked back; he still stood with his hat in his hands, where the slanting sun suffused the garden flowers, the fence, and his figure with an edging of light.

Sylvie shut the door behind her, thinking of how Andrew wanted a home and was committed to staying in Mina. She also longed for a home where she truly belonged, and yet to find that, she felt committed to going away.

Chapter 15

**July 1835**
**Edna, Mexico**

RETURNING FROM MINA, SYLVIE FELT STRETCHED between how eager Nancy was to finish packing and begin her journey, and how long it was actually taking to dispose of household goods and say farewell to friends. Uncle Jim, wrapping up administrative tasks for the colony, was also anxious to get to Edna before Sarah delivered their blessed event into the world.

Sylvie reflected that she was not truly sad to leave Gonzales, which now looked rougher and especially flat and brushy after the tall trees and rolling hills farther north. Still, she felt she had gained independence and grown more into adulthood during her year there. She was sad to say goodbye to Rachel Flint, who promised to write letters and then laughed at the idea she would find the time. As Sylvie embraced Susanna Dickinson, there was no such promise, for she had discerned the young woman had not learned to read or write.

Sylvie found no way to say goodbye to Armand Fulshear, which left her feeling unsettled. Though she had ridden out several evenings along her usual routes, he had not appeared. Peter Kerr had let slip that she had "gone walking with a young man" in Mina, and Sylvie suspected Armand had heard the gossip. Finally, she wrote a note to his parents thanking them for the hospitality they had shown her over the year. Armand could make of that what he wished.

The trip to Edna was sixty miles, and the ox cart would force a slow pace. If rains held off and the road dried to hard ruts, the cart might make twelve to fifteen miles a day. Uncle Jim warned that they'd be lucky to go half that far if storms turned the rough trace to mud holes and mire that could suck in wooden wheels and founder the cart.

The group—Jim, Minny, Nancy, Duff, Annette, and Sylvie—planned to ride horseback and take turns driving. They would camp out only a night or two, for enough settlers now lived along the route, and Jim knew so many of them, that they would find shelter in half of a double log cabin or an outbuilding fitted with bunk beds.

Annette seemed buoyant, excited about returning to Edna, and during times Sylvie rode next to her, they chatted about her family. She was looking forward to seeing her Aunt Anise and Uncle Shade, and the couple's four children. The eldest, Jack, was nineteen and did a man's work around the farm. Nelson was next in age, and the youngest two, Caroline and Edwina, had been babies when Annette left for Gonzales five years earlier. Sylvie expected the little girls, whom she had come to know as they played about the farmhouse, had changed a great deal in just the year she'd been gone.

Annette spoke highly of Anise's skill at nursing and assumed Sarah would depend on her as a midwife. Even if their group did not arrive in time for the lying-in, Sarah was in good hands. Sylvie was relieved, for she secretly hoped that when the childbirth arrived, she and Minny might be absent on a long horseback ride.

The weather remained fair as the trek stretched to five days. The group stopped every few miles to rub grease on the wooden axles, which shrieked and smoked against the wheel hubs. Minny liked to ride off ahead, but when Jim became exasperated, she took to looping around the others instead.

Occasionally Sylvie dismounted to walk, and one time when Duff joined her, he confided how unhappy he was to leave his home. Not only did he have friends in Gonzales, but he also had enjoyed going to school and church in San Antonio. "And I am going to miss my Waco Grandmother and her kinfolk," he added.

"I can understand that, especially since I got to meet them," Sylvie replied.

Duff's Waco Grandmother had arrived one afternoon at the house for a farewell visit. She considered herself a relation, since she had adopted Duff's father and thereby saved him. That afternoon, she brought several younger women with her, and they had conversed in

English, Spanish, and Caddo, with Duff doing most of the translating, as they had tea.

The women also brought gifts, and Sylvie was pleased to gain a pouch of dried medicinal herbs in exchange for her last packet of playing cards. She thought it would make a wonderful present for Isabelle sometime in the future.

Then Duff's grandmother had expressed a request, an invitation, actually, for him to come and stay in the Waco Village for some time, possibly a few years. Sylvie had responded with enthusiasm and told how French trading families had followed a similar custom. She added that her own cousin Paschal had lived with Sac and Fox families and benefited from the experience.

Nancy had glared at her as Duff tried to find the words to mollify both his mother and his adoptive grandmother. He finished by saying the invitation was so sudden it didn't allow enough time to make such a significant change in plans. He added that his mother and the girls would need his protection during the coming trip to Edna.

Thinking back on the exchange, Sylvie asked Duff if his mother was still upset with her. Nancy had seemed short recently, and Sylvie wondered if this came from the turmoil of departure, or if Nancy still resented her for supporting the idea of Duff living with the Waco.

Duff said his mother had dismissed that topic. "But Grandmother made another suggestion before she left. We were all outside, saying goodbye, and I think you'd gone inside and didn't hear it."

"You must be right, for I don't recall anything. What did she say?"

"She advised my mother to adopt you because you're an orphan. Grandmother believes that Mama is still grieving for her two daughters who died years ago—my little sisters—and said her heart will heal faster if she adopts a girl child as her own, like a replacement."

Sylvie said simply, "That is remarkable." After a few moments she added, "But Duff, I am eighteen years old, and in many ways I'm already an adult in our society."

"Yes, I know. But I liked the idea."

Sylvie watched him as he stood straighter and directed his gaze toward the track ahead. "You have been like a brother to me," she said, feeling her throat tighten. "I will miss you a great deal." It was true that Duff often reminded her of Etienne, who, though a nephew, was also was like a brother to her.

"Well, good, then." Duff smiled, looking more cheerful. "Maybe you can write me a letter, sometime."

"I will be happy to do that. And which language should I use?"

He laughed and remounted his horse so he could ride on ahead.

It was true that she would miss Duff, but Nancy less so. It seemed they had never gotten beyond a coolness in the relationship between an employer and employee. When they had relaxed at times into amiability, Sylvie would say or do something that threw things off. At first it was wearing earrings on weekdays; then it was preparing French dishes that the boarders found puzzling or worse; finally, it was her tendency to vanish in the evenings for her rides. With their farewell approaching, Sylvie decided to put any regrets about Nancy aside and instead anticipate resuming her easier, warmer, friendship with Sarah.

When the group rode into the drive at Edna and Sarah rushed out to meet them, her red hair flying in a curly mass, it was clear they were arriving ahead of the anticipated event. After a couple of days' rest, Nancy and Duff departed for the coast, and Uncle Jim left for a crucial political meeting. The settlers in the area were gathering at Millican's gin to debate—and possibly to vote on—declaring their independence from Mexico and willingness to wage war.

For Sylvie, Sarah, and Minny, the house suddenly felt emptier. Anise took care of so many household tasks that Sylvie's offers to cook or work with the ripening fruits and vegetables often felt superfluous. Another slave, Rosanah, tended the kitchen garden, orchard, and chickens. So Sylvie concentrated on her main task: conversing with Sarah and keeping her mind occupied as best she could.

The farmhouse was built in the Mexican style, one story high with rooms that rambled from one wing to the next, adjoining each other in straight lines. The thick walls, tile roof, and overhanging trees kept the inside tolerably cool in the summer heat. In the mornings, Sylvie and Sarah could sit in shade on the front porch, and in the evenings, on the back porch.

Sarah worked at copying letters for her brother's Committees of Correspondence. John Linn took a stronger stance than Uncle Jim did that war was inevitable and even necessary. His letters conveyed timely news, including that Stephen Austin, freed from jail in Mexico City, would soon reach San Felipe. Sarah was delighted and said that Austin carried so much influence that the settlers were sure to unify around his leadership in questions of war and peace.

Sylvie listened closely for anything in the letters that might affect their future travel. One day, a private note from John to Sarah related that Nancy and Duff had sailed safely for New Orleans and he'd received word they had taken passage on a riverboat to St. Louis.

When Sarah went to her bedroom each afternoon to rest, Sylvie was glad to get out for a horseback ride with Minny. Wen it was too hot for that, she took up sewing, one of her least favorite occupations. Annette had helped her cut the peach-colored silk from Mina into the myriad pieces required for assembling an elegant dress. So when the hours lagged, Sylvie could stitch numerous yards of narrow strips for ruffles, or blind-stitch insets called facings and gussets. Her neck and shoulders ached, but she still loved the color and feel of the fabric.


With a clatter of hooves out front, Jim arrived home at midday after the meeting of local settlers had disbanded. He clambered inside to greet Sarah, and as he set down his saddlebags and leaned to give her a kiss, they murmured questions and reassurances. Sylvie was setting the table for the meal, and Minny darted in from the yard.

"Tell us the main news, before you even go to wash," Sarah said, not letting loose his hand.

"The vote is for declaring independence from Mexico. And, declaring it *now*—not sometime in the future. I'll tell you more as we eat; please ask Anise and Shade to be here, too."

"That means war," Sarah said softly to Minny and Sylvie as Jim left. "But how does it begin? How do you know it really is war, and not just one more skirmish, after which things quiet down again?"

"Maybe when the fighting is against the Mexican army, and not just some customs officials at the ports," Sylvie suggested.

The four gathered around the dining table and Anise brought in serving dishes. As they began passing food, Jim told them that the first goal would be forming a new government for Texas, the eastern region of the province Coahuila y Tejas.

"We'll start by electing representatives for a Consultation in the fall. Each area that votes in favor of independence is electing men for that, and their task will be to start drafting a form of government."

"Did all the settlers at the meeting favor this?" Sarah asked.

"I could see real differences among the men. The ones who've lived here the longest were mostly reluctant. They tend to speak Spanish and are—or have become—Catholic, and a number are married to women from longtime Tejano families. But the men who've arrived in the last five years or so speak only English, have no interest in Mexican culture, and think of themselves as Americans. They even talked about their rights under the U. S. Constitution—as though those exist here."

"And they favor independence?" Sarah asked.

"Uniformly. They're also young enough to think that war is the best way to get what they want, which is to own their own land. They're too young and feel too invincible to picture that men might actually die."

"What about your own role, Jim? Who did these settlers vote for, at Millican's gin, to represent them?"

"Well, uh … me. I have been elected to the Consultation in early November."

"Why am I not surprised?" Sarah said. "I am proud that the men respect you so much."

"We do need to prepare for war, and it's not clear whether the United States will take a stand, or back us, or become involved at all.

We need to get you, Sarah—when you can travel—and Minny, and Sylvie away from here to a safe place. At least to New Orleans."

"Won't we be safe here?" Sarah protested. "We're so far from the Mexicans' main forts. We're several days' travel east of the *presidios* at San Antonio, and at least a day north of the one at Goliad."

"Maybe the Texan forces could stop one of the smaller armies at either of those places. We can always hope for that," Jim agreed. "But we may look back one day and realize the war has already started. Ships have been firing on each other in the Gulf, and more shots were fired in a tariff dispute at Velasco. If Nancy and Duff made it back to Louisiana safely, they made it just in time."

Sarah's table knife clattered on her plate, and Sylvie glanced at her and then at Minny, who was studying her father. Anise stood listening in the doorway, and Shade and his son Jack, still dusty from the fields, had joined her. A head taller than Anise, Shade draped his arm lightly about her shoulders.

"Very good," Jim said to them. "I'm glad you're here. Let's talk about our situation for a few minutes. Minny, this will become very boring. Why don't you and Sylvie go out for a bit? Maybe pick some fruit for dessert. You'd enjoy that."

"No I would not," Minny said. "It is too hot." She took her linen napkin from her lap and slapped it on the tabletop.

"I would like a walk in the orchard," Sylvie said, rising from her chair. Grumbling, Minny joined her, and they stepped out of the room.

Outside, the hot air was still, and to Sylvie's surprise, Minny walked readily with her under the fruit trees. Heavy scents of ripe peaches and plums, some fallen and split open, filled the air along with the droning buzz of flies and bees feasting on the juices. Sylvie could only imagine what further dire news Jim was sharing and wondered about the odds of getting to New Orleans anytime soon.


Two days later, the twentieth of July, Sarah and Jim's son made his entrance into the world fairly quickly and easily. Anise attended to the birth and Sylvie avoided much of the process without leaving on a ride. After Annette served the midday meal, she and Sylvie took up sewing.

Caroline and Edwina came to play on the porch while their mother tended Sarah, and Minny joined in and guided their games. As afternoon shadows grew longer, the men returned from work in the fields or from hunting, and Annette set out leftovers on a long table under the trees; everyone ate as they pleased. In the slanted, honey light, mosquitoes began to rise, and Jim brought out a few lanterns and candles. Sarah's muffled cries came more frequently, but with dusk falling, members of the household wanted to stay nearby.

And then it fell quiet, a welcome hush. Seven p.m., Uncle Jim noted, drawing out his pocket watch. Anise came to the edge of the porch, drying her hands on a towel and smiling broadly. "A boy!" she proclaimed. "All is well, thank the Good Lord!"

"A son!" Uncle Jim exclaimed quietly. He remained seated in the rocking chair, looking at his clasped hands as though saying a silent prayer. The chair creaked slightly, and everyone watched, forming a circle of light and dark faces, all smiling.

"Once again, after all of these years, I am the father of a son. May he live a good, long life. And may I be a worthy father to him."

Sylvie congratulated him, and Minny stepped forward and laid a hand over his. "A brother!" she said softly, with a wide smile. He raised his arms and embraced her. "I know I did have brothers before," she said, "but I don't remember them because I was just a baby. Now, I'm old enough to play with him and teach him things."

Jim asked when he could go in, and Anise said Sarah needed only a few more minutes. He went to his study to note the birth in the family Bible and soon emerged carrying a bottle of French brandy. Annette followed with a tray of small glasses.

"Let's toast to—it's time to announce his name—Charles!"

The household raised their glasses and cheered. About a dozen people sat on in the lamplight, sipping brandy, talking, laughing, and reminiscing, while Jim and then Minny went inside to Sarah. Sylvie also paid a brief visit and then rejoined the others on the porch to enjoy the evening. A multitude of crickets raised a comforting hum, and soon Rosanah began to sing softly. She had a beautiful alto voice, and she chose the hymns and folk songs they all knew so everyone could join in.

With Jim at home, riders showed up almost daily with saddlebags carrying mail and documents. They rarely arrived alone; young men trailed the mail route in a stream of would-be settlers who wanted land and were eager to fight for it. As a colony administrator, Jim felt obligated to inform them that Mexico had banned any further immigration, retroactive to the previous April. Settlers arriving after that time had to leave Texas or be considered illegal aliens. The young men generally remained respectful toward Jim, but their incredulity was obvious. They were not going to leave, and what was Mexico going to do about it? Jim shook his head in perplexity.

Towns and colonies continued to meet, elect leaders, and enroll volunteers into militia and ranger units overseen by Committees of Public Safety. The provisional government from the previous Consultations continued to organize an official Texas Army. A courier in August brought word that Jim most wanted to hear: Stephen Austin was now back in San Felipe, and a large dinner to welcome him home was planned for early September.

One day in mid-September, the bag contained the text of the speech Stephen Austin had given on that occasion, and Jim read it aloud at the midday meal. Austin had made an open, eloquent call for Texas to become independent, and the family wondered about the ramifications. It stopped short of declaring war, for apparently Austin and others were still wondering about support from the United States.

Sylvie was glad to hear Austin take a stance, if it would help to end her limbo of uncertainty. Surely Jim would now act quickly to get the women and the baby to the coast and on to New Orleans. While Sarah and Charles both seemed healthy, the weeks following childbirth posed dangers from a range of potential fevers and ailments. Sylvie knew it had been prudent to wait—but surely not any longer, now.

The mailbag also brought a letter for Sylvie that bore the return address of Andrew Magill, in Mina. He must have got back from his summer of ranger duties, and she put it in her skirt pocket to read later, when she could be alone in the room she shared with Minny. After the meal and clearing up, she slipped off.

Andrew wrote in a small, tightly packed formal script and began the letter by thanking her for her visit and the later note of appreciation she had sent. She read on quickly:

*… In late June, after I joined the rangers, we caught up with a group of Indians we'd been tracking and found they had some horses that had been stolen. Their leader was a Caddo trader who is well-known around here, and he showed our officers a bill of sale. But one captain, Robert Coleman, didn't believe him and wanted to put them to death on the spot—as horse thieves and likely murderers of the storekeeper and his son from Mina. The captain of my company, Ed Burleson, wanted to bring the Indians back to town for a trial. So their fate was put to a vote by all the rangers, and our side lost. The details of the execution are grim, so I'll move on.*

*I've been in a battle and thank God I am alive to tell about it. We reached Tehuacana Spring and sneaked up on a village there, of Tawakoni Indians. It was night, and we managed to take positions before a barking dog alerted their sentries. But they fought back hard, and our side withdrew after losing a quarter of the 25 men in our company. This was grim, and we went on to the Parker family's fort—a log palisade surrounding their homes—and waited for reinforcements.*

*Once more rangers arrived, we regrouped. My company traveled the rest of the summer, mainly exploring, as far north as the branches of the Trinity River. On our way back to Mina, we encountered a small band of Indians and got into a running fight. This is when I made a fatal mistake that brings me lasting shame and is the reason I am writing to you. You will want to forget me and discard any thoughts of me that may linger* ~~within your breast.~~

*In short, I shot a fellow ranger by mistake, and he died two days later after considerable agony. He was emerging from a copse of trees and I reacted too quickly, to my lasting disgrace. He had already been wounded by an Indian's arrow, but it was my shot that shattered his arm. The surgeon could have saved him by amputating, but the ranger, Smith Hornsby, refused to live like that, without an arm.*

*For this reason I consider my future in this colony is put into question. The other rangers are forbearing, and in their lack of blame I sense both pity and lessened respect, which are anathema to me. I may leave this place, and I will not trouble you by writing again. You should not feel any obligation to reply to this letter, and I also withdraw any expectations that may have been suggested during your visit.*

*I remain your humble servant,*
*Andrew Magill*

Sylvie held the letter long enough that her fingers made damp marks on the thin, pale-blue paper. These were brutal events to absorb—an execution, a deadly attack on a village at night, and then the accidental shooting and agonizing death. Plus, she was stunned by his abruptness in dismissing her and barring any future correspondence.

After several minutes, she began to consider that he was pushing her away out of shame, or hurt pride, or some such combination. And to say he had no future in the colony—how did one relinquish that, and the land claims, and the house he had purchased? Perhaps he had written to Uncle Jim, as well. Anyone would feel horrible, shooting a friend, a fellow ranger. But as she reread the letter, some part of its tone annoyed her. She might call it self-pitying, with further thought. The letter rankled so much that Sylvie decided to talk it over with Uncle Jim that evening; perhaps he could offer insights to ease her mind, and he might even have additional news.

Sylvie found him alone in his study, and he seemed to welcome the interruption. When she described Andrew's letter, Jim nodded and said he'd received reports of those events. He started by saying he had negotiated several treaties with Indian tribes, and that he deplored Robert Coleman's aggressive style of leadership. Coleman should not have attacked a peaceful village at night, without provocation, he added. "And he paid dearly for it, with the loss of so many men's lives."

"Andrew survived the battle, and it seems he kept under different leaders after that," Sylvie said. She told how he had accidentally shot a fellow ranger while fighting a band of Indians, and how the man had died days later. "And now he says his shame is so great he has to leave the colony. Plus, he want to cut off correspondence with me."

To her surprise, Jim laughed. "He can't leave. He signed up for a six-month enlistment. If he left, he'd be a deserter, and that's truly serious business. When he gets over the injury to his pride, he'll think more clearly."

Sylvie unfolded her letter and looked again at Andrew's strongly vertical signature, its letters crammed together. The flourish he had added, lines that normally appeared underneath a name, instead rose jaggedly upward and crossed over his name as though to blot it out. How dark his despair must be, she thought, and how humiliated he must feel.

"What do you think, Uncle Jim? Has he lost your good opinion, and can it ever be gained back?"

"I think he's guilty of being a good marksman who acted too fast. There are worse qualities, and he did survive his first battle. And I take it he was not among the bloodthirsty men who voted in favor of the execution, either. So I would say, with more seasoning and more experience, he might yet made a worthy militiaman. We'll have to wait and see how his peers treat him; that will tell a lot. Men who actually fought alongside him and were present at the scene will have views worth weighing."

"So you expect he will be in more fighting?"

"Oh, yes. I'm going to gather the household tomorrow and let everyone know." Jim motioned toward papers on his desk. "Mina has formed the first company of volunteer militia that will support the Texas Army. I'd say they are ready for war. In the meantime, Andrew will learn how to handle it when life delivers a defeat; he has to." After a moment, Jim asked, "Will you consider writing back to him?"

"No, not at this time. He tells me rather firmly not to write."

"Best give him some time to act like a bear and retreat to his cave. He won't be able to stay there for long."

After a moment, Sylvie took a deep breath and said, "And the rest of us, here in this house—we are not going to New Orleans anytime soon, are we?"

"Not now, and I am sorry, Sylvie. I know this is not what I promised. But the Mexicans are imprisoning even civilians they capture on ships, at this point. It is far too dangerous for you to go on our own, and Sarah isn't ready to travel yet. I am truly sorry."

Sylvie nodded but could feel her anger and disappointment mounting. "You are right, Uncle Jim. This is not what we agreed. I would like you to promise to still try, though. We may not be in an actual war for some time, and the situation can change, depending on the Mexicans' actions. You will continue to try, won't you, to make arrangements? Sarah should be ready to travel quite soon."

"Yes, I will still look for opportunities." Jim kept an even tone, and he and Sylvie looked steadily at each other for a few moments.

Sylvie thanked him for his time and left the room. She crumpled Andrew's letter unconsciously as she made her way to the kitchen and then outside, where she half-ran toward the orchard.

Rain was beginning to fall, and as she circled beneath the trees, it thundered on the tin roofs of the sheds. In her mind, it sounded like bullets. As wetness plastered down her hair, her heart sank with despondency and dread. War was approaching inevitably, and she might have to swallow the bitterness and fear of not getting away in time. And now she had lost even Andrew as a pleasant topic for her musings, from time to time.

She had one last card to play: she could write directly to John Linn to get his help booking a passage for herself, alone. But she'd have a long ride to the coast on a trace she'd traveled only once years earlier, a route now patrolled by Mexican troops. She wondered if such a scheme arose from feelings of panic, rather than reason.

Through the pounding rain, she could hear drumming from the slave quarters, and she paused to listen. She hadn't danced in ages, and soon she tried stepping to the African or Caribbean beat. The tune was not a reel or a jig, and she shortened her steps to keep up with it, speeding up, spreading her arms. Several quick turns, and her toes squished in mud, but she was flinging tension out through her fingertips. She pictured Anise, Annette, and the other black women and girls moving in an arc, their skirts and kerchiefs bright in firelight, the vision merging with memories of Midsummer bonfires back home.

The rhythm was tricky for her, actually several rhythms intersecting and crossing over one another. She tried to count beats, then flung back her head and sang them out loud as rain streaked her cheeks and lips. All the beats, and her steps, came into unity on the sixteenth clear percussive note, and she clapped her hands to mark the moments when the strands of rhythm joined. She stopped thinking and let the music guide her movements, her white forearms glimmering as they swept in wide arcs, while calico hid the rest of her in darkness.

When the music drew to a smooth close, one drum dying out and another following, she dropped her arms and breathed deeply. She felt much better, relieved and energetic, as though she could transform anger and desperation into effective action. Remembering the bonfire dancing in Cahokia reminded her that she had been through war before. The battles against Black Hawk had lasted only a few months and had barely touched the town.

Feeling calmer, she turned to go back to the farmhouse. Even if the fighting stayed far away, though, she still dreaded how it might twist everyone's fate, the way battles had harmed her half-brother David and mangled Andrew's life more recently. Near the back porch, she stood longer in the warm rain, hoping it would wash away streaks of mud.

Chapter 16

**Fall 1835**
**Edna and Goliad, Mexico**

FOR THE KERR HOUSEHOLD, THE WAR WITH MEXICO began one morning in early October. And it was not the pitched battle they'd imagined, but a skirmish over a cannon in the town of Gonzales. A hurried rider brought word that a Mexican army unit from San Antonio wanted to take back a cannon given earlier to the town for self-defense against Indian attacks, but the townspeople had refused to hand it over. In fact, they'd taunted the Mexican soldiers to "Come and get it," and now were anticipating a fight and asking other colonies to send reinforcements.

Jim learned that the Texans planned to attack the Mexican contingent, about one hundred men under a colonel, where they had withdrawn on the west side of the Guadalupe River. He rode off for Gonzales within minutes of hearing the news. The women of the household pulled shawls over their nightdresses and gathered by the kitchen worktable. They brewed coffee, chewed ends of yesterday's bread, and engaged in speculation.

Now that the fighting was on land and within a colony, Sylvie wondered if it could remain just a brief skirmish against local troops. The main Mexican army was still far to the south and would not arrive until after the winter. Part of her thrilled at the idea that the town she knew so well would take such a brave stance against the Mexicans, and she was surprised that her own feelings were so mixed.

"I remember that little cannon," she told the others. "It's quite small, and officials would fire it on the Fourth of July for practice. It would always misfire, and I can't believe the Mexican troops think it's a serious weapon. This must be more about the principle."

"It could be the spark that sets off tinder and feeds the fire," Sarah said. She looked grim and tired.

"Will Papa be in the fighting?" Minny asked. She was standing by the table, cradling a coffee cup with both hands.

"It's possible, dear, though he's more likely to try to negotiate," Sarah said. "But there may not be much fighting, and he probably won't get there in time to be part of it. If the Mexicans fell back right away, they might decide not to fight over such a minor issue. We'll just have to wait and see."

"That's the hard part," Sylvie said. "It feels urgent, as though we need to do something. But what?"

The baby began to cry from his cot in the bedroom, and Sarah left to tend him. It was hours before their usual start of the day, and now time would crawl. Yet they could not expect news to arrive for another day or two, at least. Anise came in to start breakfast, and soon she was joined by Rosanah and Annette.

Jim returned after several days, bringing John Linn with him, both looking weary but also pleased and excited. The battle at Gonzales had remained just a skirmish—half an hour of fighting followed by a parlay and the Mexicans withdrawing to San Antonio. The town could keep the cannon and the right to claim a victory. As Sarah had predicted, this became a spark inflaming the settlers for war.

Jim gathered the household to announce they were officially at war. "Stephen Austin made a declaration to the Committee of Public Safety at San Felipe on October 4. Here, I'll read his exact words to you: 'War is declared—public opinion has proclaimed it against a military despotism. The campaign has commenced!'"

Austin was elected to lead the military forces, which consisted of local men volunteering for militia units plus the regular army authorized by the Texans' provisional government. The next goal, Jim said, was to drive the Mexican military out of the Bexar *presidio* at San Antonio, and hundreds of men remained at Gonzales for that effort.

"What does this mean for you, Jim?" Sarah asked when he paused. "And John—my dear brother, it's lovely to see you—why are you here at Edna?"

"We have some planning to do," Jim replied. "John is now quartermaster for the army, freshly appointed. I was elected major for the militia units in this area, and I'll be attached to Goliad."

"We need to get supplies, wagons, and oxen together by tomorrow and get it all to Goliad," John said. "We may head farther south after that, depending on what happens."

"Why? What will happen in Goliad?" Sarah interjected.

"The *presidio* there, La Bahía, is a key link on the supply line for the Mexicans. They move troops and arms through there from Copano, at the bay, inland to San Antonio. If we can disrupt that flow, we can seriously weaken the Mexican army's ability to fight."

"You're going to do . . . what? Take over the fort at Goliad from the Mexicans?"

Noting the incredulity in Sarah's voice, Jim grinned. "Well, as I say, we have a lot of planning to do."

He and John took seats at the dining table, and Jim began unpacking papers from his satchel. Anise brought them plates of cold meat and cornbread and a bowl of late peaches, then set out several extra candles for the night. The men sat over their papers, keeping their voices low as they drew lists and jotted messages to be delivered around the countryside at first light.

Sylvie found herself drawn to the talk. It was interesting to hear the possibilities discussed, the ideas laid out, and the quantities listed for the food, munitions, wagons, and carts needed to supply a military force that could attack a Mexican fort. John was drawing on his years of leading militia units in New Orleans and running trade schooners, which recently had been ferrying arms and ammunition. He also drew on extensive knowledge of the supplies in warehouses at inlets and bays along the Gulf, and could identify what was ready to move up the rivers leading inland to the colonies.

Sylvie replenished the dishes and brewed fresh coffee; Sarah had gone to nurse the baby hours earlier and probably had fallen asleep.

Minny was in bed, and Anise had left for her family's house out back, beyond the kitchen garden. As the dark hours flowed by, Sylvie saw the plan to attack the *Presidio* La Bahía come into focus. The old Spanish mission, now fortified, was lightly defended, for scouts reported that the Mexican General Martin Perfecto de Cós had moved his troops toward Gonzales and San Antonio. Taking the fort would not require a large force, especially if attack came as a surprise.

John could leave in the morning, and Jim would leave as soon as he could get twenty yokes of oxen ready, along with carts and a few wagons. They wanted to take advantage of a large social gathering in Goliad they'd heard about. A Tejano family, descended from Spanish colonists, was planning an evening dinner and dance and had invited the Mexican officers from the nearby *presidio* to attend.

"Can we trust the hosts with our plan?" Jim asked.

"I know the family well, and I do trust them," John replied. "They often give large parties, and we could use the one on October ninth for cover. It would keep the small number of Mexicans still stationed at the fort occupied and distracted for several hours after dark, when we could move in and secure the fort.

"And if we could get someone inside the party," John added, "we might learn which other Tejano families in the area will stand with us and fight against Mexico."

"You're talking about getting a spy, or a scout, at the party," Jim said. "We can do that, place someone the Mexicans won't recognize as regular army. I've been thinking we can get valuable information from the women, if we could get female eyes and ears there. Women talk over social ties, and they'd know who is friendly with Americans—or with Mexican officers."

Sylvie emerged from the kitchen, and as she poised with the coffee pot, the men looked at her speculatively. "I wish there was something I could do," she said. "I mean, beyond serving food and coffee."

"Are you ready to choose sides and take an active role?" Jim asked. "If you are, we've just been discussing something you might do. It will require dressing for an evening party and dance, plus speaking a little Spanish."

"I do have a silk dress that we've just finished, and I can speak a little Spanish, probably enough for social conversations."

Jim described the party to her and assured her that a Texan scout or two would also be there. "Someone like yourself could mix with the women and pick up information about family allegiances. Maybe she also could keep the officers dancing longer. It's not essential for you to do this, my dear, though it would be helpful. But you should give it careful consideration."

"Your French may also be useful because La Bahía was originally a French colony," John said. "Back when France had the upper hand over Spain in Europe, it tried to rule Mexico as well. Some of the Tejano families in Goliad date back to that period and actually have closer ties to France than to Spain."

"Undoubtedly, some Tejano families will side with an independent Texas, and some will stay loyal to Mexico," Jim said. "They all want a strong local government to protect them against the masses of men rushing in here and trying to get land. Anyway, you would only need to act like your usual charming self—a young woman enjoying a soirée. At first glance, you could easily be Tejana, of either Spanish or French descent."

"Look at it this way," John said. "Wouldn't it be pleasant to attend a party with music and dancing, and excellent food and wine?"

"Well, put that way, yes, indeed." Sylvie smiled at the idea. "It's been a long time since I danced to anything more than a fiddle and a washboard on someone's veranda."

"And remember, we'll place a scout or two inside to keep an eye on things," Jim added. "Can you be ready to leave by tomorrow afternoon?"

Sylvie agreed, and Jim said it was time for all of them to get to bed, though he and John stayed on a while, talking and finishing messages. After she quietly crawled into bed next to Minny, Sylvie had trouble falling asleep. Maybe her nerves were keyed up by coffee, or maybe the prospect of a soirée where she could wear the silk dress and dance with young men was more exciting than she quite let herself imagine.

Sylvie rode out with John Linn and several others the next day, moving at a fast pace. The oxen train with supplies that Jim was assembling would leave later and travel more slowly. It was nearly sixty miles from the farm to Goliad, so they stopped for the night with friends at Victoria. The next day they arrived at the appointed house in time for Sylvie to rest before the party.

John Linn brought her to the door, and the maid who answered their knock escorted them into a large room with a red tile floor and elaborately carved dark wood furniture, all pushed back against the walls in preparation for a crowd. The hostess arrived, a woman in her mid-forties, and she kissed both of them on their cheeks. She also took Sylvie's hand kindly, and as she spoke with John, Sylvie felt challenged to keep up with his fluent Spanish.

Soon, John was translating for her: They would dance in the courtyard that night; would Sylvie find that pleasing? She was assigned her own bedroom; would she like to go there now, to freshen up? A meal would be sent up directly.

John thanked their hostess, and before saying goodbye, he drew Sylvie aside. "Stay here until someone you know comes for you tomorrow morning. Under no condition are you to leave with a Mexican or Tejano."

A maid led Sylvie to her room, and as they went up stairs built into the side of thick, whitewashed adobe walls, she could see the house enclosed a central courtyard. Flowering vines cascaded from ledges, and potted shrubs stood near a softly rushing fountain. On the second floor's walkway, more stairs led up to a flat roof, a patio open to the sky, and they passed several heavy wooden doors. Then the maid paused to unlock one and stood aside for Sylvie to enter.

The bedroom was cool and dim, with light coming through a window on the far wall. It was covered with a jalousie, black, wrought-iron bars set on the outside to deter large creatures—animal or human— from coming in. Sylvie stepped toward it and admired the roses climbing along the bars outside; the breeze carried scents of herbs, flowers, and the river beyond. The maid was unpacking her bag, and as she held up the peach silk dress, they both looked at it critically.

*"Bueno,"* the maid pronounced, adding that she would take it and perform something on it. Watching Sylvie, she made ironing motions with one hand. *"Repasser,"* she finally said. Then she pointed downstairs and said, *"Sala ... siete de la tarde"* and held up seven fingers. Sylvie nodded and the maid left, closing the door behind her. Sylvie was grateful she had several hours to rest, possibly to sleep. She stepped about the room, admiring the intricately worked tin sconces and candle holders and the mirror's elaborate mosaic frame.

After a knock at the door, two boys entered. They set up a small folding table laid down a large tray draped by napkins. With a quick bow, they turned and left. Suddenly hungry and thirsty, Sylvie lifted the cloth corners to find figs and bananas, soft yeast rolls and a sweet pastry, a round of goat cheese, chunks of chocolate and fresh dark cherries in a bowl. *Chèvre et chocolat*—what a miracle!

It was impossible not to relax in such luxury, and after eating, Sylvie ran a hand along the linens of the bed, admiring the handmade lace edging. The sheets were cool and smooth, and she undressed to her shift and turned back the covers. Within moments, it seemed, knocking jolted her awake, and the maid was back. Sylvie saw the light had shifted to dusk as she dragged herself from disorienting sleep. The dress looked fresh and crisp, hanging on the door of the armoire.

The maid bustled about the pitcher and ewer, then the chamber pot, and said something about returning. She soon was back with fresh water, and Sylvie began the process of dressing. On came the corset, laced at the back, then the petticoats. The maid draped a shawl over Sylvie's shoulders in order to dress her hair. She sat before the mirror and watched as her black hair was coiled and pinned, stacked higher and higher, with sprays of little fresh blossoms added fetchingly in several places.

*Do I really look Tejana?* Sylvie wondered. A Mexican officer, meeting her for the first time, would choose which language to speak to her?

Finally, it was time for the dress, and Sylvie stepped into its circular swirl carefully, so the maid could raise the bodice. She helped to slip on its sleeves and adjust the trim on the low-cut neckline to hide any edge of undergarment. Sylvie felt she was as finished as possible, but the maid stood before her, frowning.

She raised a warning finger and left the room abruptly, and Sylvie decided it was best to wait. She had no shoes but her worn black boots, which showed sizable cracks above the toes. They sat by the bed, their button tops hanging limply. The maid returned with purple satin high-heeled shoes in one hand and jewelry in the other. The shoes fit well enough, and Sylvie stooped so the maid could fasten a fine necklace of silver with crystals. Sylvie's silver-filigree earrings suited it, and after a long, critical look, the maid gave a satisfied nod. She held the door open for Sylvie to pass.

In the main room Sylvie had seen earlier, she was introduced to Anita, the elder daughter of the household. The young woman was tall and thin with a long straight nose, and she wore a glittering emerald necklace and a deep-purple satin gown. She took Sylvie's hand and switched eagerly to French, saying that while the family spoke a little French at home, she had learned more at school in New Orleans. She bobbed her head in time with her phrases as she introduced Sylvie to a handful of other young women. These were her sisters and their friends, and Sylvie carefully noted each name, for she would rely on them for conversation and introductions throughout the evening.

"I have to check on the food," Anita told her. "Would you like to come with me and see the dining room and the kitchen?"

The two women passed through rooms that flowed from one to the next in a row. Anita had to duck under doorways framed in wood, though they were high enough for Sylvie. Each room seemed to hold a little recessed fireplace and cupboards with painted doors— much like the French ones in Cahokia. The white walls were decorated with bright, woven blankets, and paintings on wood. Chandeliers of cast iron or pounded tin, whose cutouts and curved edges scattered and reflected candlelight, hung from white ceilings streaked by dark wooden ribs.

Sylvie wondered why American settlers insisted on their log cabins and wood-frame houses, when adobe was so much cooler and prettier and probably stayed warmer in winter. It did make sense for settlers to use logs cleared from the land, and most arrived with little idea of how to make adobe out of mud, clay, and straw.

In the kitchen, cooks and servers worked over copper pots, small braziers, and flat tortilla-cooking stones, conjuring delicious aromas. Sylvie looked about while Anita talked rapidly with an older woman who seemed in charge. A doorway opened onto a patio where the *hornos,* large clay ovens, stood in a row.

When Sylvie and Anita returned to the central patio, Mexican officers had arrived. Wearing bright-red uniforms with decorations, they stood visiting with Tejano men, who wore black suits and elaborately trimmed white shirts. Several musicians wearing bright sashes played guitar melodies that floated as gently as soft conversations.

Using Spanish, Anita introduced Sylvie to several Mexican officers, as well as to Tejano couples and their daughters, nodding vigorously all the while and adding now and then that Sylvie also spoke French. Then at the buffet set with refreshments, they each took a glass of wine.

"This wine is from El Paso and quite nice," Anita said. "Oh, here comes a young man I do not know. He is a Texan, I think."

Sylvie followed Anita's gaze and saw Armand Fulshear step onto the patio and then pause to look around. She was so surprised that she stared, not certain it could be the same person, here, so far away from Gonzales. And he was dressed not in the rough clothes from their rides together, but in a black suit with a high, white shirt collar and a narrow black tie done in a bow. His wavy hair was long enough to brush on the collar and fall a bit in front of his eyes. As he smiled at Sylvie in recognition and approached her, she was frozen into a déjà vu of seeing François Jarrot approach her across the ballroom at the Jarrot house.

Then he stood before her, and with a bow, took Sylvie's hand and looked at her searchingly. They murmured greetings in French, and she hastened to make introductions.

"*Enchantée, monsieur.*" Anita took Armand's hand and curtsied. "But you already know each other!"

"Yes, we met in Gonzales," Armand said.

"And yet we do not know you. So, I surmise, you are here to . . . observe. Please continue to speak French when you wish to remain discreet." Her glance darted toward a cluster of men in uniforms who had just entered. "Oh, here are some Mexican officers I must greet; please excuse me."

"Who are they, do you know?" Sylvie asked Armand. She had the distinct feeling they were at work on the same furtive assignment.

"Captain Manuel Sabriego, on the left, and Lieutenant Jesus de la Garza, commanders at the *presidio*." Armand took a moment to look fully at Sylvie. "You look quite lovely—enchanting. I've never seen you in fancy dress."

"Thank you. And you look so different, I was taken aback."

"I think you didn't recognize me at first."

"Well, we're so far from where we last saw each other . . . What are you doing here, can you say?"

"While no one is nearby, I can mention serving as a scout with the regular army. I'm with two units close to Goliad this evening. So at the moment, I am using my eyes and ears. John Linn said you would be here, on much the same task." He smiled, his dark eyes warm. "Still, even given our assignments, I would like to dance with you once or twice, if I may."

"Yes, I would like that, too."

"Till then." He bowed slightly and moved away to join a cluster of men.

Sylvie wandered toward one of Anita's sisters, who greeted her and included her in conversation among several women. Sylvie could follow most of the Spanish as they discussed parties and social events around town. And here was a rich item: a local girl had just married a Mexican officer stationed at *Presidio* La Bahía. She did not catch the young woman's family name and asked for it as unobtrusively as possible. Anita's sister told her quickly and went on gleefully about who was angry about the marriage, versus who found it acceptable. Sylvie tried to memorize the names of those who kept close ties with the Mexican troops.

When the dancing began, Anita's brother invited her right away, and she was delighted to find herself whirling smoothly about the room. Then a Mexican officer asked her, and though she tried to talk with him, neither could understand the other's Spanish very well. Lieutenant de la Garza himself asked her for the third number, and she found she could chat with him. He danced a bit woodenly, and in her unfamiliar heels, she tripped over the toe of his boot a couple of times. When he escorted her back to a chair, he bowed and said he would fetch something to drink. She wanted badly to rub her sore toes but restrained herself. When the lieutenant returned with fruit punch, he handed a glass to her and stood nearby as though at attention.

"Have you been in town a long time?" Sylvie asked with a bright smile. "And do you plan to stay long?"

"Yes, for a while," he responded. Then he looked away fixedly, and she felt awkward about asking more. He did look quite dashing in the red uniform, and Sylvie sipped at the punch, wondering what a spy's next step might be.

And then Armand appeared to claim the next dance. He danced well, and as he led her firmly, their bodies moved lightly and precisely together.

"You left Gonzales without saying goodbye," he murmured. "I thought I might see you before you departed for your uncle's, following your trip to Mina. How was that? Did you have a nice time?"

His tone struck her as slightly ironic. "I did," she said. "The town is pretty, and it's in a lovely area with a pine forest."

"And what does it offer you, more than you might have in Gonzales?"

"I'm afraid I don't know what you mean."

"I am not afraid to fight for what I want, and I can offer you a great deal in the future. But I thought that by now you would be in New Orleans, waiting out the war. So I did not press my own interests, which surely you must be aware of."

Sylvie grew breathless from dancing while wondering if he was beginning a proposal. She understood there were signs a young woman should give to a man embarking on such a foray, and she had handled this so badly before, with Emile Hubert. Oh, what to say? He was so near, so handsome, and he held her so closely. The wine, the music, and their movements all made the walls, flowers, and colorful lanterns whirl by. Armand's family was wealthy in land and cattle and well respected. The image of Andrew Magill and his pretty house in Mina—followed by his letter full of shame and rejection—flashed through her mind. Everything about Armand was so persuasive, and on occasion over the past several months she had thought longingly about him.

"*Alors,*" Sylvie began. "I now know that with war starting, I could be here a long time, though I dearly hoped to get to New Orleans. I've had to adjust, and it's been a struggle. I still hold faint hope, but I don't know what to say, just now."

He led her through several turns before responding. "War brings uncertainty for all of us and our hopes for the future. But I want to ask about more personal hopes and even affections. Should I continue to have hope in regard to your own feelings?"

"Armand, you are the most charming and promising young man I have had the pleasure of meeting—and riding with, and dancing with—here in the colonies. But please, let's not speak more of a future relationship just now. The thought that harm could come to you is quite painful."

He looked at her closely, his eyes narrowed. In the silence, she thought fleetingly of Andrew Magill and his bravado, his grin and assurance about being lucky. She wondered at Armand's serious look, and at her own fears arising so suddenly.

"All right. This can wait several months while the war plays out. When it's over, I'll come and find you, and we'll go riding again. We'll take up where we left off; consider this a brief interruption. You might come and stay with my family, to have more time with all of us."

"I'd like that."

"As you wish, I'll say nothing and keep my own counsel—and hopes." He smiled at her, looking genuinely happy. As they continued to sway and step quickly to the music, Sylvie noticed people watching them in particular, among the couples circling gracefully over the terra cotta tiles.

The musicians stopped playing while supper was being served, and Sylvie noticed that the Mexican officers began to slip away after quick farewells to the host and hostess. She worried that she had shown obvious interest in Armand and too little toward the Mexican and Tejano men, that she had missed opportunities to make them linger at the party.

Lieutenant Garza was passing by, and she spoke abruptly. "So soon, you're leaving? And I was hoping to enjoy more conversation, perhaps another dance after supper."

"That pleasure will have to wait for another time, *mademoiselle*," he said with a short nod.

Sylvie's cheeks flamed with embarrassment; being so forward was a crude effort, as he had noticed. She hoped no one had overheard, and as she moved with other guests along the buffet table, she became distracted by the food: chicken in *mole* sauce or rolled into thin blue tortillas and covered with green sauce and a sprinkling of cheese, pork simmered with red or green chiles, squashes cooked with herbs or served with sausages. The dessert table held an abundance of local fruits and melons, plus *flan*, pots of hot chocolate, and tarts filled with preserves.

Sylvie found a chair near Anita, who was bobbing along in conversation with some local men and women. As she sat with her loaded plate, they included her in a friendly fashion, and once again she noted their talk about various families, memorizing more names for her lists of potential enemies and allies.

When the music resumed after supper, Sylvie could see no Mexican uniforms among the clusters of men. Armand approached, but instead of asking her to dance, he led her apart from the crowd and up the stairway to the second floor.

"What are you doing?" she whispered urgently. "People are going to notice!"

"You'll be surprised." At the turn for the second-floor walkway, he directed her on up to the rooftop patio. There, in the moonless night, clusters of young people, mainly couples, stood scattered among the potted trees and flowers, enjoying the stars and the views over the town and toward the *presidio* rising on the other side of the river.

"Oh, I see. We're taking the air," Sylvie said.

"Yes, aren't the stars lovely?"

They found a place to stand near a wall where a trellis supported a climbing rose. As Sylvie tipped her head back, Armand leaned and kissed her fully on the mouth; his arm tightened around her and pulled her onto her toes. It was a long, searching kiss, and her blood began to pulse like something melting and running fast and warm. Finally, he let her draw back, and a few thorns on the rose behind her prickled her neck and shoulder.

He had turned to look out over the town, and she took a moment to see if her silk skirt had snagged on any thorns. She delicately unhooked a fold or two, still leaning on his arm.

In a moment, his manner changed; urgently, with barely a glance, he said, "You need to get back inside, right away. I'm leaving immediately. But wait a few minutes, then say good night as you normally would and go directly to your room. Bar the door, if you can." They moved toward the stairs, and he took her hand, preceding her as she gathered up the full silk skirt.

"It has begun," he whispered. "Hell, it might even be over, already."

"You—you were watching for a signal!"

"Shh!"

"Well, and I . . ." They were standing on the second-floor walkway, and she jerked free of his arm and placed hands on her hips.

"Oh, please. You cannot think I was pretending! We did need a good reason for me to come up here. But that doesn't change how I feel about you."

She regarded him, watching his mouth, his eyes.

And he looked long at her. "I can do two things at once, one for my head and the other for my heart." He smiled, and she relented.

"Then take a moment for a proper farewell," she said. She grasped his hand and led him into the shadow of the wall for another kiss, this one with less of an element of surprise.

Back downstairs, he was quickly off, and after a few moments during which no one asked her to dance, Sylvie said good night to Anita and her parents and thanked them for the party and their hospitality. She made her way to her room and found she could slide an iron tongue across the door and snug it into a bracket on the door jamb.

Locked in, she was grateful to be alone with her thoughts. The bedding had been straightened, the pillows fluffed, the sheets turned down, the water jug replenished, and her muslin nightgown laid out. Now, not having summoned a maid, she would have to struggle out of her buttoned bodice and laced corset all on her own. Her fingers seemed clumsier than usual, but soon she draped everything over a chair; it would all be wadded up into her bag in the morning, anyway. She took paper and pen from her bag and jotted down all the names she could recall into two columns, hoping she had gleaned helpful information.

How much wine had she drunk? She could hardly fall asleep, with her head pivoting and the room swaying. And a proposal in the offing! The excitement came in waves, interspersed with worry for Armand, Uncle Jim, John Linn, and the other men. They were fighting; she was sure of it, for why else would she have to hide away with the door locked? She lay in bed, fretting, propped against pillows, until wine and fatigue transported her to a realm of chaotic dreams.

Morning arrived with dim light at the window and a faint, repeated tapping on the door. Sylvie got up and slid the latch, and Anita entered, carrying a tray covered with a cloth. She grinned at Sylvie. "I encountered the maid and took over. Here's breakfast—coffee and rolls."

They sat on the edge of the bed to eat and talk. The space behind Sylvie's eyes seemed packed with cotton wool, but the strong coffee began to cut through it.

Anita kept her voice low. "The household hardly slept, last night. The Texans took the *presidio*—they are in control! They fought for only half an hour. Papa told us; he got the reports. And there were no deaths among the Texans; just one Mexican sentry was killed."

"Truly? That is astonishing. There wasn't much fighting, then?"

"The key, as I understand it, is that our *alcalde*, the mayor, declared that Goliad is neutral. It will not take sides or fight. So no one—no local militia—stood with the Mexicans at the fort, and it had only a few dozen men in it, anyway. Some time ago, General Cós took the rest with him to San Antonio."

"Oh, thank God," Sylvie said. "I am so glad my uncle is all right, and all his friends and your household and everyone."

"If you get to La Bahía—if you go there to meet your uncle—you can say a prayer of thanks in the chapel. It used to be a mission, you know, like the Alamo and other places the Mexicans have converted to military posts. Once you get past the high stone walls and towers, the chapels are often still lovely, though not quite like in the past."

Sylvie said she would try to do that, and when they finished eating, Anita told her to get ready quickly. "This day is off to a fast start, and I may not see you again. So let's say goodbye; I'm happy to have met you."

At the door, they exchanged cheek kisses, and Sylvie thanked her again for her hospitality. When she had dressed and packed, she went downstairs to wait. After a time, Shade, Jim's slave, appeared to fetch her, and he did not say much as he led her to two horses tied in the courtyard. He quietly confirmed the news she had heard and said they would be at the fortress in only a few minutes. They set off at a fast pace along dusty streets leading among tall, white walls of courtyards, some with flowering vines cascading profusions of magenta and purple blossoms.

The walls of the *presidio* were high and imposing. La Bahía was dark, solid and massive, almost foreboding, a place built to survive a siege. Sylvie marveled that the Texan forces had taken it so quickly.

They dismounted in the courtyard, and Shade led her along a hallway to an open area surrounded by grated doors of storerooms. "You'll see for yourself all the spoils of war we've gained," he said. "I have never seen John Linn such a happy man as he is this morning."

Uncle Jim and John Linn were gathered about a table with another man, who was quite tall and had dark eyes and black hair. After a few moments, Jim noticed her.

"Sylvie, we'll leave shortly," he said. "You're going back to Edna with the neighbors who drove the oxen train here. You'll have to explain to Sarah that I'm headed south to Fort Lipantitlan." Jim grinned at her. "I realize she won't be happy with that news, but we think we can take it, too. So be optimistic when you tell her."

Sylvie was picturing Sarah's dismay as Jim went on to introduce her to the third man, Ben Milam. He and others were planning to take the captured supplies to the Texan troops at Gonzales, who were gathering to attack *Presidio* Bexar, at San Antonio.

Sylvie had heard of Ben Milam, for her uncle occasionally handled affairs for a colony Milam had started. Recently, she'd heard he was imprisoned in Mexico because he'd been looking too strenuously into the assassination of an American, General Long, who'd led an exploratory expedition into Mexico. She asked how long he had been back in Texas, and he said he had only recently escaped from prison.

"And in good time, too!" he exclaimed. "I was out on the road last night, coming into Goliad, when I ran into the main contingent of Texan forces headed the wrong way and disentangling themselves from a briar patch. They enlisted me as a private on the spot, and I led them back here to the *presidio*, which I had just passed."

Sylvie looked at Jim, who raised his arms in a shrug. "It's all true. He got Collingsworth's forces back on the right approach. We'd split into four groups for the attack, and the fort had only fifty Mexican soldiers, not enough to hold a perimeter of this size."

"But the walls are so massive," Sylvie said. "How did you get inside?"

"Chopped a hole through the wooden door on the north side," Milam said.

"We borrowed axes from sympathetic townspeople," John added.

"Once inside, though," Jim said, "the fighting was serious. And we sustained one wounded person, a slave belonging to Collingsworth."

"A freed slave," Shade spoke up. "He was free, and he chose to fight for Texas."

"One death," Sylvie said, thinking of the sentry. "While I was at the party, I got some names for you." She drew the paper from her pocket and handed it to Jim. "I learned a bit about local family allegiances, and I hope this is helpful because I didn't succeed at getting the officers to stay longer at the party."

"That's all right," Jim said. "Your information will be useful for the future. Everything turned out well, and we've gained a tremendous amount of ammunition and cartloads of supplies."

John resumed working on a document while Jim looked on. A young man came in and reported that the armorer looking over three hundred captured muskets had found that most were in bad condition. John noted the tally on his list.

Jim's voice rose with the finality of a conversation ending. "So, John, you can provision a force to move south from here, first to Karankawa territory and then to Fort Lipantitlan."

"Yes, no question. Plus we'll send the bulk of the supplies, and the cannons, to the troops gathering outside of San Antonio. And a third portion will be for the forces around here at Goliad."

"We'll meet up, then—you and I—at the fort," Jim said. "Let's try for two weeks from now, about fifteen days, I estimate."

As the men gathered their things, Sylvie caught a glance of the list John had compiled, which noted blankets, clothing, boots, sugar, coffee, whiskey, rum, muskets, cannons, wagons, carts, and cattle.

"I estimate about ten thousand dollars' worth of goods that we sorely need," John said to her. "This was a good night's work."

Sylvie had a little time before departing to search out the chapel in the former mission. The room was small, with a vaulted ceiling and a large cross hanging behind the altar. Painted frescoes to the side showed the Virgin Mary standing on clouds gloriously lit by rays of sunlight. Patches of paint had flaked off, and layers of gilt showed gaps, but still, the chapel felt familiar and reminded her of home. Side areas being used for storage were stacked high with wooden implements and old pieces of furniture.

She dropped to her knees on the floor before the low front railing and searched for words or images that would give form to her uneasiness. She did not have a rosary; she wondered if one was still in the bottom of a carpetbag. She wanted forgiveness for the part she had played, however small, in the betrayal and deception of the night before. She could pray for the soul of the sentry who'd been killed—that kind of prayer was familiar. But she also wanted to ease the guilty feeling that she had taken part in events that led to his death. Could that be handled with prayers for forgiveness for herself, even without a confession? No priest was present to hear one.

Was the battle even morally justifiable? Stephen Austin's declaration of war sufficed as an official decree that connected the attack to a greater, worthy cause. The Texans were refusing to live under a dictatorship—a very cruel one. The fighting had been necessary to gain victory, and no one had acted out of vengeance or for personal gain.

As Sylvie meditated over her questions, she did not see how her presence or absence would have changed the flow of events. The information she had gained might help to save lives in the future. Yet what would happen to that Mexican officer who had married the local Tejana—and what would their life be like as a couple?

Sylvie recalled times in the past when she had been angry with God for allowing little children to die. And yet here she was, among humans dispensing death to one another. At some point, she must have crossed a line separating childhood from this place she now inhabited with adults who issued decrees to align their warring and killing with what they perceived as the will of God. Did people like her uncle really believe that?

Abruptly, she wondered where the sentry's body might be, for it was not lying in a bier here in the chapel. Would it be taken back to his home farther south in Mexico? Her eye was drawn to a wooden statue of St. Francis, standing below the fresco on a side wall. Usually the saint was depicted with birds gathering about him, but this one held little wooden human skulls, with more such skulls stacked about his feet. She still wasn't accustomed to the skeleton costumes and images that integrated death into Mexican holidays and festivals.

In wedding processions, she had even seen the *charrette,* a cart holding model human skeletons dressed as a bride and groom, bringing up the rear. She could make out such a cart in the jumble of the chapel's stored items.

After reciting the Lord's Prayer and several *Ave Marias,* Sylvie stood up to leave, and as she walked a dark stone hallway, she wondered about more earthly matters. What was she up to, passionately kissing Armand after hardly thinking of him for months? And what about her deception with the Mexican officers? Oh, but it had been fun, dancing and drinking wine, hearing music, and enjoying the beauty of the dresses and uniforms, the flowers, and the night itself.

Still, she had become a combatant in her own way. A person with whom she had no quarrel was dead, and others were prisoners. Jim and John Linn had talked of paroling the fifty or so Mexican soldiers captured; this meant making them swear not to pick up arms again against the Texas army or militia and then letting them go away to the south. She wondered how Jim could trust Mexican officers and soldiers that way. Why wouldn't they betray the Texans' cause—our cause, she corrected herself—and return to fight again?

It seemed that battles, and war itself, created confusion and conflict, rather than clearing up much of anything. Someone had said that years earlier, back in Cahokia—it was her cousin Narcisse, she recalled, speaking about the peacetime that followed the Black Hawk war.

Chapter 17

**Fall 1835**
**Edna, Mexico**

During the fall, with the men gone to the war, the women took over work on the farm. Sylvie and Minny picked corn and tended the vegetable garden, fruit trees, and crops such as pumpkins and melons. Rosanah and Annette took on the heavier work of mending fences, chopping wood, and butchering hogs, while Sarah and Anise did household chores and tended to the children. As militia volunteers started returning ahead of the fall Consultation, Sarah was able to hire a few to scythe and bundle the wheat.

The early news arriving cheered the women and gave them hope. In October, a small force of Texans captured a key fort, Mission Concepción, near San Antonio. Militiamen from Mina were involved, and Sylvie wondered if Andrew had taken part in the battle, and if so, how he had fared.

The household learned that after leaving Goliad, Jim commanded forces that captured the fort farther south, at Lipantitlan, and while Mexican troops were killed, the Texans had not lost any men. John Linn had joined Jim there after he delivered the supplies captured at La Bahía to forces gathered near San Antonio.

Making his way back north for the Consultation, John stopped by the farm at Edna and conveyed more news. Sarah wondered why Jim was not with him and also headed to the meeting., and John explained Jim had gone farther south to try to form a treaty with Lipan Apache Indians. He had already negotiated a treaty with Karankawa Indians ensuring that they would not attack Texan forces during the uprising.

Jim finally came home in mid-November, accompanied by Shade and Jack, and the household gradually resumed its familiar routines.

The men's talk was rich with Spanish phrases, the names of forts, towns, and the battles they'd won. More Texan troops were massing near San Antonio, and their leaders were undecided about whether to attack the city. The Consultation did not claim Texas was independent from Mexico, but did declare it was in revolt against General Santa Anna's military dictatorship. If Mexico returned to abiding by its Constitution of 1824, then Texas would remain a republic within the federation. When Jim learned of this outcome, he was pleased.

The Consultation also decided to send Stephen Austin as an emissary to the United States to gain support for Texas. He had been commanding the militia gathered near San Antonio and was replaced by Sam Houston, who also was put in charge of the regular army. Houston combined political experience, as a former governor of Tennessee, and military experience from serving in the US Army under Andrew Jackson.

The question looming by early December was whether the Texans should attack the Mexican forces holding San Antonio before Santa Anna brought his army that far north. With winter coming on, storms and rain would prevent such a large force from moving into the area very quickly.

Austin's officers voted against such an attack. But in early December came electrifying news: some militia units had gone ahead and stormed the city. Following hand-to-hand fighting in the streets, they had won, and they'd also taken both *presidios,* Bexar and the Alamo. The Mexican General Cós had signed a surrender. Now the militia was disbanding, the men heading home, though a small group of volunteers and regular soldiers decided to stay at the Alamo over the winter.

As Uncle Jim assembled the household to convey the latest news, he warned against nurturing a false sense of hope from these early victories. It would be quite a different matter to face General Santa Anna and the main Mexican army, if that happened. So while everyone could not enjoy a full sense of peace, at least the pause in fighting allowed for some peace of mind during the winter months.

*  *  *

Late one afternoon in December, Sylvie was digging potatoes at the far edge of the kitchen garden. She enjoyed working outdoors, and in her hours alone, she inhabited an imaginary life. Sometimes, she pictured Armand appearing for a visit; he was a scout, and didn't that mean he could roam the countryside? In fact, why did he *not* come?

At other times, she moved through fields of nostalgia lit by the heavy gold light that slanted more each day, while breezes wafted ever cooler. Was the harvest bountiful, back in Cahokia? She recalled the frosty, moonlit night when she and Celeste had tied the little cross of stalks onto the front gate. Celeste, dead from cholera. The memory made her chest ache, and at those times it helped to spend time with the baby. Charles was a comfort, a contented soul who especially enjoyed his older sister, Minny.

Sylvie did not hear the riders, but as she straightened in the potato patch, she caught sight of Jack leading two large Kentucky horses to the stable. That meant visitors, and she brushed back her loose hair and shook reddish dust from her skirt. Soon Minny was calling her from the edge of field, and Sylvie carried the basket of potatoes to the root cellar. After washing at the back porch pump, she passed through the dim, quiet house to the front veranda.

She stopped at the doorway and gaped at the guests, Andrew Magill and Logan Vandeveer, who jumped to their feet. She approached to shake hands, noting that Andrew looked deeply tanned and thinner, while Logan seemed unchanged: affable and appealing enough for a second glance. Andrew cocked an eyebrow, taking her in from dusty hemline to dirt-streaked hairline. She did not hold his gaze but turned to Logan, whose calm smile disguised any reaction to her dishevelment.

"I've been digging potatoes," she said. "The other day, Minny and I hunted turkeys and pheasant. I've learned to make my way in Texas."

"What, no dancing for you, lately?" Andrew asked, his smile ambiguous.

"No, not much frivolity around here." Sylvie looked directly at him, then lifted her chin and glanced for an open seat.

"I was telling them about Goliad," Jim said, "and how you helped to distract the Mexican officers at the party while we launched the attack. I believe we're switching now to Mission Concepción for Andrew's story. Maybe we can retell all our battles in order from now until supper time."

"More likely," Sarah said, "that would take till bedtime, the way you men embroider your yarns, revisiting every detail."

Sylvie poured herself a glass of lemonade and sat near Minny, relaxing into the cushions on the settee.

"Andrew was at San Antonio in addition to Mission Concepción, as part of the mounted cavalry," Jim said.

"My goodness!" Sylvie exclaimed, looking at Andrew closely. His own chin rose with a confident air. She turned to Logan and asked, "And you as well?"

"No, I drew the lot of a poor foot soldier since my horse was off serving under an officer somewhere. However, I finally got him back, thanks to the Consultation. And they also voted to repay our mercantile business for the supplies they took last June."

"That's good news. Will you go back to keeping the store?" Sylvie asked, turning to Andrew. She'd felt him gazing at her and noted that his light-colored eyes could seem more probing and less warm or kind than darker ones.

"I doubt it," Andrew said. "The supplies that get through from the coast are mainly for the military. I also need to work on my house and land over the winter. My enlistment is up, but I expect more militia duties are coming soon, too."

"The rangering you did last summer has been officially recognized," Jim said. "Maybe you've heard the Consultation authorized the units you served with as official Rangers for the Republic of Texas, the first ones so designated."

"So I am one of the first official Texas Rangers? Well, that's good, but we're not really our own republic yet. We have a ways to go."

Sylvie felt she had missed a chunk of conversation and wondered what could account for this change in Andrew from the discouraged and shamed man who had written in September, to this seemingly confident one. "And how did these battles go for you?" she asked. "I mean the ones you've recently fought, compared with the earlier ones with the rangers."

"You mean, did I shoot at the right people this time? I did, and I comported myself well enough to gain back some respect after that tragedy of the ranger dying, partly due to my mistake."

"I'm glad for you. Gaining back respect is important."

Jim shifted in his chair. "One's self-respect is surely the most crucial quality. But let's hear about the battles. I want all the details of the action—who led, what strategies you used, how the Mexicans responded—all of it, just as you experienced it."

"Andrew relives his battle scenes with considerable gusto," Logan remarked.

And he did launch quickly into his story, telling how he had ridden day and night to get to Gonzales as soon as news came to Mina about the town's fight over its little cannon. He arrived October eleventh, in time to vote for Stephen Austin as commander in chief but too late for the battle. Sylvie thought he sounded disappointed, but he moved quickly to describe how the volunteers stayed on at Gonzales and elected officers. He was glad he could continue serving under Ed Burleson, who was chosen lieutenant colonel.

"We did a few days of training and then marched west to San Antonio," he continued. "We were about three hundred men, mainly from Austin's and DeWitt's colonies, and with others arriving, we got to about four hundred and fifty. Then Juan Seguin arrived with about forty Tejano fighters. This was good because not only do they speak Spanish and know the countryside well, but also it showed Mexico that some of their people are siding with us. They can't say that this war is just Anglos versus Hispanics. The Tejanos fought well alongside us at Mission Concepción."

Andrew regaled them with a colorful version of how he'd gone with scouts Austin sent to find a good position for the attack on Mission Concepción. The group defied orders to return and instead set up camp at a bend in the river nearby, where they could cross at a shallow ford. Fog rose the next morning, and the men moved under its cover up the high riverbank and into trees. Austin, furious at being disobeyed, had sent army troops to find the scouts. But by then, the Mexicans had spotted the Texans.

"They commenced firing cannons, but the cannonballs went right over our heads through the pecan trees." Andrew jumped up and waggled his fingers over his head to show how pecans had rained down. Logan caught Sylvie's eye and smiled, then leaned back as though waiting through a story he had heard many times.

"The Mexicans couldn't see us from the mission walls and bell tower as we were creeping up the river bank." Andrew squatted down as though he might act out the creeping but stopped and dropped back into his chair. He had got them laughing about the pecans, but his humor flagged as he described the closer fighting.

The first wave of Mexican cavalry couldn't navigate well through the trees, and he and others were able to pick off the riders. He mimicked squinting along a rifle barrel and shooting, his shoulders even rising at the kickback from firing. As Sylvie watched, she wondered if that wasn't the very sequence that had resulted in shooting his fellow ranger. He must have acted more slowly and deliberately this time, though he hadn't mentioned it.

Another militiaman, Jim Bowie, led a company to the mission and soon took the bell tower. The other Texans were still under fire, but Andrew said the Mexican gunpowder was so poor that the musket balls bounced off their buckskin. Their Kentucky rifles had greater range and accuracy, and they'd had time to reload between cavalry charges.

"So we were able to get off half a dozen shots apiece, and once we stormed the walls and got inside, we had some close fighting. I didn't, though—every soldier I came up against was ready to surrender." He clasped his hands, leaned his elbows on his knees, and looked around at his audience.

Everyone already knew the outcome, how the battle had ended after thirty minutes with the Mexicans retreating to *Presidio* Bexar. The Texans lost one man, a volunteer from Mina whom both Andrew and Logan knew. The tally of Mexican deaths varied widely, though, and

Andrew said his unit counted fourteen Mexicans killed and forty-six wounded

"Well done," Jim said. "Both the fighting and the storytelling."

"Yes, thank you for such a vivid recounting," Sarah added.

"You're most welcome," Andrew said. "But I've dominated the conversation long enough, and it would balance things out, Jim, if you'd tell us about Fort Lipantitlan."

Jim begged off, saying that he could tell Andrew and Logan about it at another time, since the rest had already heard the story. For Sylvie, an aspect of that battle remained troubling. Two officers she'd met at the party in Goliad had gone after that defeat to Fort Lipantitlan and fought against Uncle Jim there. Following that second defeat, they'd been paroled again, freed after promising not to fight the Texans. She wondered what would now prevent them from joining Santa Anna's army to the south, but no one spoke of that question.

She was pulled from her thoughts by Uncle Jim asking Andrew to describe the siege of Bexar and how the Texans had fought to take San Antonio. But Andrew had less firsthand experience to relate, as he had served mainly on the supply lines.

"I volunteered to fight, though, when I came back with Ben Milam from doing some scouting. You've probably heard that he was angry with Austin's officers for not attacking, so he stepped forward, roused the spirits of several hundred of us, and led the charge into the city. His death was so strange, though—a single bullet out of nowhere, and at a time apart from the fighting."

"Ben Milam—I met him at La Bahía," Sylvie said. She recalled the tall, dark-haired man who had recently escaped from prison in Mexico. It was a surprise to think of him dying that way; he was the first person she knew personally to be killed in the battles.

"Well, he'd clearly made some enemies in Mexico," Jim said.

Gradually the topic shifted to whether it was wise for troops to stay on at the Alamo mission over the winter.

"That doesn't appeal to me, at all," Andrew said. "The Alamo is so small, dark, and damp, it'd be tough to stay there. I trust Ed

Burleson, and he's resigned his command and advised all of us from Mina to head home."

"I agree with you," Jim said. "I won't go into the Alamo for the winter, either—short of having direct orders, of course."

Sarah and Jim invited the young men to stay the night or longer and made beds available in the bunkhouse. Later in the evening, Logan retired at the same time as most of the family, while Andrew stayed up talking with Jim in his study.

Logan took a moment to tell Sylvie that despite Andrew's bravado at storytelling, he remained troubled. It was nothing more than the usual way men acted, though. "His temper can flare at the smallest things. In that way, he is different from before, since he's always been good-humored and easygoing, like most men in our family."

Logan paused to flash a grin and continued, "Sometimes he swaggers a bit, and sometimes he stares off like he's watching scenes from hell. He swings from one to the other. I try to catch him in between and talk about everyday life, like plans for getting through the winter. It's good he's getting a chance to visit with your uncle."

Sylvie thought over Logan's words while she got ready for the night, and they must have distracted her, for she was in bed before she remembered she needed to put beans on to soak for cooking the next day. She hoped she could slip into the pantry unseen and threw on a shawl over her nightdress. From the kitchen, Sylvie could hear the men's low voices in the study. She moved quietly, and she did not intend to eavesdrop until she heard her name.

"Does Sylvie deserve some explanation or apology, considering the letter you wrote to her last fall?" Jim was asking. "She spoke with me, and she felt you'd barred her from even writing."

"Yes, I owe her that. I figured the only remedy was for me to come in person and make amends. May I ask what you advised her?"

"I did tell her there's a lot of confusion in any battle, and that you might find an opportunity to win back respect. She seemed to listen, and I added some fool words about wounded pride. You seem to have gained back a modicum of self-respect, though it might be a bit wobbly. That forced humor in a man's storytelling …"

Their voices dropped too low for Sylvie to make out words, and she quietly poured water over beans in a large bowl, added salt, and swished it around.

"I will confess I've incurred considerable shame in my lifetime and acted like a damn fool." Jim's voice came clearly. "Did you know I won my seat in the Missouri legislature by running against my own father-in-law? I beat him and took away his seat. That caused my poor wife such consternation that to get away from it all, I brought the family here, to San Felipe. And you will have heard what happened; everyone died of disease but for Minny—my wife, our little boys. I have worked mightily hard since then to perform some good in my life. Maybe someday I'll feel I've crawled out of that deep hole.

"My idea for when the fighting is over and we're back at peace, however that may happen, is to be a physician. I want to do just as much healing as I've done harming."

"I think that sounds quite fine, sir. I'll confess that on certain nights, I hear the dying groans of poor Smith Hornsby, and my conscience smites me. And we've lost men from Mina in battles, several friends among them. So I question whether I should have done something differently. I go over and over the fighting in my head, and even when I did conduct myself well, I still find a reason to be guilty."

"Yes, survivors often do—I've seen that. And you grieve for your friends, but there's little time for mourning in the midst of a campaign. What do you do when it catches up with you?"

"I give up trying to sleep, and when I light a lamp, that puts the world back in order. Or if it's dawn, I go out and start work. I ride hard, work harder. I've been with the rangers or militia from June until last week, so I haven't had much time to brood about things. And it's best not to. My grandpa used to say that scat only stinks more when you stir it with a stick."

"And good Kentucky bourbon can be soothing, at times."

Sylvie heard low chuckles and the sound of clinking glasses.

"I pray most honestly and hopefully that each battle will be the last," Jim said. "I look at all possible alternatives and go forward only if I am convinced it will save lives."

"Oh, the larger picture."

"That, and the moral imperative of war; a just and deliberative body of citizens needs to authorize the action so it rises above personal revenge or aggression."

"And a moral imperative in our case rests with the land itself," Andrew said. "Settlers can put the land to higher use than leaving it open for wandering bands to do some occasional hunting."

"Yes, though the native Indian groups that practice farming have a right to their just portion, too," Jim replied. "That's a principle I have followed as I've negotiated treaties."

Sylvie breathed in sharply as she stood in the kitchen, amazed at the simply expressed right to take other people's land and establish one's own place on it, as though agriculture represented a higher moral order. Probably her own ancestors had felt that way as they took land around Cahokia for farming. But they had left large amounts open for common use and clustered their homes tightly together. *Anglais* settlers usually built a home in the middle of a claim and raised fences around its borders, closing off large amounts of land. The Indians needed a way to make a living, and while Uncle Jim grasped that, Andrew's thinking seemed different. Maybe someday she would have a chance to talk over these views with him.

Sylvie had missed some of the conversation, but the men's voices rose again. "Now that is youthfulness speaking," Jim said. "I forget, sometimes, how fresh life seems to you. My four and a half decades must stretch forever in your eyes."

"I wouldn't say that—maybe a little."

"But you mentioned intentions toward my niece, Sylvie."

"My intentions are most honorable, sir."

"Yes, I've grasped that."

"Well, I believe the next step is to ask her to forgive and forget the letter I wrote and see if she can look past it. If she'll consider me as a suitor, then we can take time to get to know each other better."

"If you're asking for my permission, I gladly give it for spending some time together, properly chaperoned, of course. Sylvie has to agree to your being a suitor, so you'll need to speak with her. And your pride better be way down on the list of things you talk about. I also want you not to ask her for a commitment or even any understanding, just now.

"It's not fair to young women—and I have seen this happen when some mishap befalls the man and he dies—that the community views the young woman as still being tied to him. Then she gets quickly married off, usually as a convenience for some other man. Let's get through the coming war and leave Sylvie without any liaisons, so she can act freely on her own, should any misfortune arise, God forbid."

"I agree, and I'll wait to see if she'd want to marry me, and vice versa. I'm here for the land and for a life. I'd like to settle and marry, head up a prosperous household with lots of children, and run a huge herd of cattle. Not much beyond that."

"Yes, that's not much to hope for, is it?" Jim laughed, and they both chuckled.

"I must set things right with Sylvie. So I have to figure out how to remedy the effects of that letter yet stop short of declaring my intentions."

"You're an intelligent young man, and you'll figure that out if you're worthy. I do think she likes you."

Sylvie's eyebrows shot up, and she realized her feet were growing cold on the terra cotta flooring. "*Comment?*" she murmured. How had Jim arrived at that observation? She tiptoed back to the bedroom and slid under the covers near Minny, who stirred slightly. Sylvie's pulse beat quickly, and she slowed her breathing. How long would Andrew and Logan stay, and could she successfully pretend she hadn't over-heard the conversation?

So here was her next suitor, and he did seem an improvement over the first one, Emile Hubert. Andrew was interesting, and his various approaches to living in Texas kept presenting challenges that were whittling away at his character. It was a shame Logan kept his distance; he was more handsome and affable, though such an even tempera-ment might become tedious with time.

And what about Armand, who had taken his kisses, kept a long silence, and didn't seem to think about permission? This vexed and confused her. At least she would not have to give an answer to Andrew until after the fighting ended, and then only if he survived and was still drawn to her. That combination of circumstances seemed unlikely as she turned restlessly in bed. So many things could happen, and yet she had few options that she could act upon. She needed to create a clear future direction for herself, but how?

The visitors stayed another full day and helped with work around the farm. They would leave early the following morning, and it wasn't until after dinner that Andrew had time to walk with Sylvie in the orchard.

They started chatting about everyday matters, yet the natural pauses grew longer until Andrew finally began his apology for the letter in the fall. Sylvie assured him no apology was needed, but he delved into both his regrets and his wish for a relationship with her.

"Can you ever look past that letter? I'd take it back and eat my words if I could—tear up the paper and swallow every bit."

"Maybe I'll give it back and watch while you do just that!"

"Those feelings came from a deep confusion that followed my first battles and close fighting."

"Seriously, your reasoning makes a great deal of sense. And so much has changed since then." They strolled, enjoying the warm evening, and after a time Sylvie realized that while he spoke about fighting at Concepción and San Antonio, he had not mentioned the attack on the Indian village earlier in the summer. She decided to ask him about it.

"That was your first battle, wasn't it? Yet if you hadn't described it in your letter, I wouldn't know about it."

"That's true. It's not a subject for that kind of retelling, in company. There's no humor in it, no pecans falling or bullets bouncing off. It was desperate and grim, and good men died pointlessly in defeat. Getting back to Mina, being there alone in the house—I found no honor in it, except that my fighting was passable and I survived."

Women were better at understanding emotions, he added; they could even name separate feelings and disentangle them from one another. Sylvie agreed and allowed that it was difficult for her to imagine being in combat and then dealing with the subsequent turmoil.

She wondered if Andrew might continue the discussion of feelings by mentioning what he'd said to her uncle the night before, so she quickly added, "But yes, I can put what you wrote in that letter into the past and move on. Let's see what life brings next."

"Thank you; I am grateful."

"You do owe me a few pleasant conversations and some nicer letters. Then we'll see if the scales can balance, or even start tipping in your favor." Sylvie added a smile to lighten her challenge, and they turned back toward the house.

Chapter 18


**Early Spring 1836**
**Edna and Gonzales, Republic of Texas**


Little mail was getting through, and as Christmas and New Year's passed, Sylvie missed the usual letter from her sister Jeanne; even more, she missed Isabelle's notes conveying personal reflections and news of Cahokia. No letters arrived from Louisa, either, leading Sylvie to picture stalled or embargoed bags of mail. One note came for her from Armand Fulshear, who was able to send it along with military messages arriving for Uncle Jim.

The reports arriving for Jim spurred him to warn the household and their neighbors to prepare for evacuating their homes and farms. The main Mexican army, led by General Santa Anna, was coming north, moving quickly by taking ships to ports on the Gulf rather than struggling along muddy, pot-holed primitive roads. Jim planned to attend the Consultation in March when Texas would declare itself a new country and elect its first president. But when word came that Santa Anna had arrived with troops in San Antonio on February 23, Jim threw himself into planning evacuations. Another delegate would attend the Consultation instead.

Jim argued that settlers needed to leave as soon as ox carts could travel the roads and head east toward Louisiana and safety within the United States. At first, Sylvie found it hard to emerge from winter's listlessness and make effective plans. Evacuation was a vague concept, and the women asked Jim and one another about the kinds of supplies they would need, how long they might be on the road, and whether they could count on getting provisions along the way.

The regular Texas army and volunteer militia units were gathering in Gonzales, ready to fight, and Texans occupying the Alamo stood between them and the Mexican forces in San Antonio. Some well-known frontiersmen had been trickling into the Alamo over the winter, and the volunteers were under the command of Jim Bowie. A young officer, Andrew Travis, was in charge of the regular army soldiers stationed in the old mission.

One day in March, following a delivery of letters and reports, Jim stood in the kitchen doorway, a sheaf of papers in his hand. A rainstorm lashed the trees outside, and budding leaves waved frantically beyond the kitchen window. Sylvie and Minny were at the worktable, wrapping packets of dry bouillon, called pocket soup, in oiled paper, for the household's evacuation. Sarah was spooning cereal for Charles, in his highchair.

"Sylvie, I'm heading to Gonzales as soon as tomorrow, and I'd like you to come with me," Jim announced. "We need to help Rachel Flint pack up her house as quickly as we can and bring her and the children here."

Everyone understood Jim's loyalty to Rachel, one of his first settlers at the DeWitt colony. He added, "Her husband, Dolphin Flint, has gone into the Alamo with the Gonzales Ranging Company, after Travis issued a strong plea for reinforcements. She didn't write about it in detail, in case the note was intercepted. But she has five young children, as you know, and—here's the thing—she is in a delicate condition."

"My word!" Sarah exclaimed. "When is the lying-in, did she say?"

"In a roundabout way, she hints at six weeks, and she hopes to stay at home. She still doubts she needs to leave, and she wrote mainly to tell me about Dolphin. She says the wives of the men who've gone into the Alamo are 'remaining cheerful and hopeful.'"

"Well, of course they have to show faith in their men and hope they will prevail," Sarah said. "Anything else would be disloyal. And on the bright side, look at how the Mexicans haven't put up much resistance in the past."

"But those were small armies, and they weren't led by Santa Anna." Jim held up the papers. "I have other news, and not good, I'm afraid. Our forces lost a battle at San Patricio."

"Isn't that the Irish colony near where you were, Jim, at Lipantitlan? Were the Mexicans able to retake the fort?" Sarah asked.

"Yes, unfortunately. And worse, a company of Texans were taken prisoner."

"They'll release the men soon, surely—just parole them and make them promise not to fight anymore, like you've done with the Mexican prisoners."

Jim began to speak, but stopped as his glance fell on Sylvie, who was watching intently. Armand had written to her that he was serving as a scout for several companies under Colonel James Fannin, based in Goliad. Since the time they'd seen each other at the party, he had gone farther south in Mexico on missions he could not describe, other than to say they had prevented him from writing more often.

Overall, the letter seemed a bit stilted and impersonal, perhaps because it was written in English rather than the French they usually spoke together.

Sarah and Jim had been curious about this letter and gradually realized that a second young man was possibly a suitor for Sylvie. After asking a few questions about Armand, neither mentioned Andrew Magill or the intentions he had confided to Jim. Sylvie wondered whether Armand could be among the troops the Mexicans had recently captured and was roused from her thoughts when she saw everyone looking at her.

"Yes, of course I can help Rachel," she said quickly. "We've done so much packing and planning here that I know what to do. But will she be willing to leave?"

"I'll convince her," Jim said. "The situation is grim. Santa Anna has been shelling the Alamo for a week. Travis's latest plea for reinforcements has an air of desperate nobility. He writes to the people of Texas, and to the entire world, and expresses lofty principles as though history is already preparing a place for him."

As they exchanged apprehensive glances, Minny declared, "I want to go to Gonzales, too! I'm about desperate for something useful to do. And I can drive an ox cart as well as anyone else."

"I cannot spare you," Sarah said. "With Sylvie, Jim, and probably Annette gone, you are needed here. Remember that Rosanah is also in a delicate condition."

"And that's that, young lady," Jim said. "Sylvie, we'll leave at first light and hope the rain lets up. Annette can come along. We'll just take horses since Rachel has her own ox cart."

From a mile or more outside of Gonzales, crowds had swelled fivefold over a typical market day. Wagons and carts moved both toward town and away, and troops were setting up camps, their canvas tents dotting nearby fields.

Jim, Sylvie, and Annette had ridden fast and entered town from the south to avoid heavy traffic on the main road that ran west to San Antonio and east toward Louisiana. Each of them carried a rifle and a pistol. They arrived to find Rachel's house just as full of the children's commotion as ever. She greeted them warmly, and Sylvie had to reach high over Rachel's bulging front to kiss her cheek.

Annette took off her bonnet and eyed the children as they darted about. The eldest, Jane, about ten, seemed able to herd the others, and the youngest, at three, could still be scooped off the floor, which Annette soon did.

"Do you think we'll be ready to go by tomorrow?" Rachel asked playfully. Jim had left right away to check in with militia officers, and Sylvie and Annette had followed her to the kitchen. A meal was on the stove, and lines of washed clothes hung in the back porch. The pantry shelves stood full of sundries.

"You haven't started packing?" Sylvie asked.

"I've been meaning to start, each day of the past week, but then nighttime comes, and well . . . it seems enough that I have simply gotten through the day."

"Ma'am, you have an ox cart, is that right?" Annette asked.

"Yes, and we'll pack that for just a couple of nights, to get us to Edna. That's all we'll need, don't you think?"

Annette raised her eyebrows and looked at Sylvie.

"We'll pack your cart just the same as for everyone else evacuating," Sylvie said. "We have to prepare for leaving Edna and going as far as the Louisiana border."

"You're joking—that's two hundred and fifty miles from here," Rachel said.

Sylvie shrugged. "If we picture that, then we're ready for the shorter trip that is far more likely. Jim says we just need to stay away from towns where the Mexicans might garrison troops."

"I am not running away any farther than Jim's farm in Edna," Rachel said.

"What is the first thing you want me to do, ma'am?" Annette asked.

"Well, pack, I believe. Sylvie can finish cooking the meal, and I'll mind the children, and . . . we will take it from there."

Annette left for the outbuildings. She would locate the cart and start compiling tools and implements, beginning with a shovel, a hatchet, a pail, a lantern, and lengths of rope. Sylvie peeked into the soup pot on the wood stove, surveyed the dishes on the rack, and picked up a long spoon.

The following day passed in a flurry of laundering clothes, cooking food to eat and to pack, and caring for the young children. Sylvie foraged in the kitchen garden, where some radishes, chard, and a few beet leaves showed young and green. She considered clipping the tops of pea plants to eat; most likely no one would be there when the pods filled out.

By evening of the second full day, the women were planning how to pack the ox cart for camping out several nights, starting by placing the least-used items near the bottom. The youngest children were too small to walk far, yet too big to be carried for long, so they needed places to sit among the boxes. Sylvie and Annette worked for a while at attaching storage boxes to the sides of the cart.

Jim reappeared that evening, clearly upset and preoccupied. He had received orders to head toward Edna and then south to Victoria, and he wanted the group of women and children to leave with him by morning.

"But we won't be ready by then unless we work all night," Sylvie said flatly. "And Rachel has gone to a neighbor's house, where the women are talking over the latest news."

"I want to know that you're safely on the road, but I also cannot disobey orders, and we're running out of time. If you do have to leave later, the roads will be filled with settlers, so I know you will be in good company and stay safe. Sylvie, I have faith in you; you have good sense, and you can handle a difficult situation."

"Thank you for saying that. I think we'll be all right."

Jim was already out the front door. "Please say goodbye to every-one and explain as best you can. I feel I'm letting all of you down, and I regret that."

"You don't have a choice, and you'll be helping other people. Goodbye, Uncle Jim, and stay safe."

When Rachel returned from her visit, she took the news of Jim's departure more calmly than Sylvie had expected. "Now we don't have to hurry so much. The other women have decided to stand firm for a while longer, and I will stay here with them. How would it be when our men return, including my husband Dolphin, only to find their wives and children have fled?"

"I can see why you'd believe in the town's men and your own husband, and that they will hold the Alamo. Still," Sylvie urged, "Edna is safer than Gonzales. We are so close to San Antonio here, the Mexicans will fight to control this town."

"Well, I have been a colonist for more than ten years, and I have never run away from anything! Just that one time we had to abandon Gonzales when it was attacked and burned. But that was by Indians, and they'd killed some white settlers. The Mexicans are not going to kill me or my children. Can you even imagine that?"

"Actually, yes, I can, if this town becomes a battlefield. The Mexicans shelled San Antonio; they're shelling the Alamo. What's to keep them from shelling Gonzales? Look at all the Texan troops camped here. And then why would the shells avoid hitting this partic-ular house? Or if there's hand-to-hand fighting in the streets, like in

San Antonio, then what? Will your children be safe? At least think of them."

"I am thinking of them. The other wives and I hardly talked about anything else. Our children, our husbands, and the example we set by showing courage and loyalty. Why, Susanna Dickinson went into the Alamo herself with her child. They have been living there all winter with her husband, Almaron. She sets an inspiring example."

Sylvie tried to control her impatience and speak quietly. "So when will you and the other wives meet again, and will it be soon enough to consider any news that might change your minds?"

"Yes, of course we'll meet again soon. And I do agree with you that it may become necessary at some point to withdraw from town. But we have not reached that point yet."

"So in the meantime, let's make sure we can leave on a moment's notice—since apparently we're going to wait until that very last moment arrives!" Sylvie's voice rose.

Rachel glared at her. "No doubt your plan is correct, and everything you say is God's own truth. Annette should have put the children to bed; I must say good night to them." She turned and left.

Too angry and frustrated to return to any methodical task, Sylvie threw on a shawl and grabbed the coin purse that held household funds. She left the house and walked toward the shops in town. If any place was still open, she could try to buy more coffee, bacon, and possibly a barrel of flour if any was to be had. And salt; they needed to pack lots of salt. The evening still held pearly gray light above orange streaks of cloud. People were milling in the streets and yards, gathering in clusters for animated talk and arguments.

Men by the hundreds filled the militia camps, where campfires and torches burned. Many wore buckskin trousers and coats, while others wore homespun and linsey-woolsey cloth, hand-knit sweaters, and Mexican goat-wool blankets with openings at the neck. Some men had boots, but many wore moccasins or even went barefoot. She tried to keep her eyes cast down and focused shortly in front of her, to avoid drawing attention as a young woman out alone. Still, a few long whistles and "Yooou-hooo's" arose.

Near the stockade, she noticed a flag with words neatly appliquéd reading "First Company, Mina Volunteers." Above the phrase soared the image of a woman, her breasts bared by a loose Roman-style dress; she was flourishing a banner as she floated in clouds. Sylvie couldn't help pausing, and she caught sight of Andrew Magill approaching.

"Sylvie—delighted to see you, delighted!" He grabbed her hand and pumped it, his energy jolting down her arm. "I ran into your uncle a couple of times, and he said you were in town. How are you?"

"Quite well, thanks. And you?"

"Fine and dandy and itching to finally fight. I've been elected second sergeant for the company."

"Well, that's good, I'm sure."

"We elected Jesse Billingsley as our captain. He confers with the first sergeant and me, and then he votes with the higher officers. Logan is here, too, serving as a private."

Logan emerged from a group around the campfire and came to greet Sylvie. He said he had kept his horse was glad he would be part of the mounted militia, as it offered more tactical options.

"And less wear on the boots," Andrew added. "I wonder how many of the men who've arrived barefoot expect to be issued new boots. My father said some Kentucky militiamen did that in the War of 1812, and then they had to march for miles in the dead of winter before the supply barge arrived."

"Oh, how grim." Sylvie looked down at her own dusty, worn boots and noted how the soles were working loose.

Andrew asked why she was still in Gonzales. "Jim said you'd be going back to Edna right away, taking Rachel and her family with you."

"Rachel says she won't leave until all the townswomen agree. And so far, they feel too loyal to 'run away,' as they call it."

"Hmm. I might try to speak with her," Andrew said. "But my experience with Cousin Rachel is that no one can persuade her about anything once her mind is set."

"The situation is serious," Logan said. "We could begin fighting at any time." He glanced around, then leaned toward Sylvie and added in a low voice, "The men at the Alamo cannot hold out much longer.

We think they should fall back, sneak out at night, and join forces with us here."

"Can they do that?"

"No," Andrew said. "First, they'd have to get past the Mexican troops surrounding the place. Also, the army has ordered Travis to stay and fight. He sent envoys pleading for a change in orders, but with no result. The volunteers could leave, but Jim Bowie leads them, and we hear he has fallen ill and taken to his bed."

"That's not encouraging," Sylvie said. "I truly want to get back to Edna right away, and then we'll join the other settlers evacuating to the east."

"Ah, look—there's our general now, Sam Houston. He's been put in charge of the regular army, which is at Goliad, as well as all the volunteer militia units up here."

Logan indicated an ordinary-looking middle-aged man dressed in worn buckskin who was riding a horse so small that his long legs nearly touched the ground.

"He'd look more impressive if he rode a larger horse," Logan said. "There's nothing wrong with buckskin. And he can give a truly inspiring speech." Both he and Andrew wore buckskin coats and dark pants of heavy, store-bought twill.

"I want to shop for a few more supplies and get home before it gets much darker," Sylvie said. "I do sincerely wish both of you good fortune."

"And the same to you," Logan said, with a slight bow.

Andrew grasped her hand. "Get on the road, and get away as fast as you can. Promise me you will do this."

"I will." For one terrifying moment, she knew he was going to kiss her goodbye in front of everyone. Their eyes met, confirming this possibility; then Andrew simply smiled and let go of her hand. Sylvie hurried away, and as she made a few small purchases in the emptying stores, she wondered when she would see the two men again.

* * *

On the evening of March 12, Sylvie's fifth day in Gonzales, dire rumors swept the town. After a siege lasting weeks, the men at the Alamo might have been routed. As soon as Rachel heard this from a neighbor, she joined two dozen other women gathering at Mrs. Charles Braches's house, not far away. Sylvie sent Annette to talk with any servants she knew in other households and return with news as soon as possible.

Word passed quickly through town that scouts on the road to San Antonio had encountered Andrew Travis' slave, Joe, and Susanna Dickinson with her fifteen-month old child, making their way back to Gonzales. The Mexicans had released them so they could report on the defeat and deaths. Annette learned the details in a matter of minutes.

All the Alamo's defenders—about two hundred men—were dead, Susanna Dickinson had told the scouts. Only a few women and children, slaves, and Mexican indentured servants, who had huddled in the chapel, were allowed to live. Susanna's husband, Almaron, Rachel's husband, Dolphin—everyone was dead, either killed in the fighting or as captives. Andrew Travis was dead. The army of men under him had fought bravely, desperately, she reported, as did the volunteer militia. Jim Bowie, who was ill, was killed in his bed. She and Joe and others had taken shelter in the chapel during the furious noise of screaming, firing, and chaos all about them. The only militia survivors included a few Tejano volunteers who convinced the Mexicans they had been taken prisoner by the Texans, and several scouts or couriers who were away from the Alamo at the time.

Annette and Sylvie talked as they stood in Rachel's kitchen. Sylvie had gotten the children to bed, and now the two women simply waited for Rachel to come back. It seemed there was nothing left to do of any importance, especially with the enormity of Rachel's loss.

"Maybe you should go to Mrs. Braches's house so Miss Rachel doesn't have to walk home alone," Annette suggested.

"I don't know. They'll need to talk among themselves and finish in their own time. They'll be in shock and grieving, and they need time with one another."

"That's true. And then they'll need the support of people not so closely connected, who aren't as overwhelmed." Annette glanced at the clock. "Give them one more hour?"

"Yes. I'll wait up. You should get some rest."

"Miss Sylvie, we are leaving here tomorrow. No more delays."

"Yes, I know. Do you realize this is the third time Rachel has been widowed?"

"Are you thinking that will make it any easier?"

"No. But Rachel has learned two times already that life goes on and that she has it in her to survive, especially for her children."

"Wake me up as soon as anything happens, in case I doze off."

Annette left to lie down near the children upstairs, and Sylvie set out the coffee pot and several cups. The kettle was already on the woodstove, which had a small fire going. Then she sat at the kitchen table, her hands idle.

Rachel was not long in arriving. She took off her bonnet but not her shawl, and Sylvie rushed to embrace her. She grasped Rachel's arm to steady her as she moved clumsily toward the kitchen.

"Widowed again. This is the third time. I am not even thirty years old, and the Good Lord sees fit to take yet another husband! And not just mine. The town, the whole town is full of widows." She fell heavily into a chair.

Outside, like a moaning wind came wailing, crying, and children's high screams as the women, in twos and threes, arrived home and confirmed the disastrous news.

"It seems so unreal," Rachel said. "It will take time to fully believe that almost all our men are dead. What a terrible loss; what good men. And oh, their families. All the little fatherless children. And murdering their captives, those Mexican devils; the evil, the pure evil!"

Sylvie watched her, racking her memory for a potion she could brew that would calm Rachel to prevent the baby from coming too early. Once Rachel began to cry, loudly and without reserve, Sylvie worried a bit less. Rachel would exhaust herself, and then Sylvie might get her to rest in bed. She brewed tea with a few herbs, and Rachel sipped at it distractedly. Then Sylvie sat quietly, listening as Rachel repeated her thoughts, her realizations, and even basic facts. She hoped that with each rendition, their plight would become more real to Rachel, and more pressing.

After some time, Rachel numbly agreed that they should get on the road to Edna at first light. "I'd like to be with Jim and Sarah; I want my babies safe, safely away from here." She refused to undress, but she agreed to lie on the bed in the little alcove under the stairs. When she grew quiet and her breaths were shallow and regular, Sylvie tiptoed upstairs for bed.

In the early hours before dawn, Sylvie was awakened from a restless sleep by Annette shaking her by the shoulder. She sat up, wondering at strange sounds of popping and the rumbling of distant explosions. Dread washed over her, and she tried to fend it off as a remnant of troubled dreams.

"Fire, Miss Sylvie. They're blowing up the ammunition depot, I think."

Stabbing darts of orange lit up the curtains, and Sylvie jumped up and thrust them aside. Black treetops stood silhouetted against a wall of flames to the south along the river. A string of explosions ripped through the air, followed by shouts and screams.

"Is it the Mexicans? The Mexicans are here!" Annette, terrified, still kept her voice low.

"I don't know. Maybe they're keeping the Mexicans from getting the gunpowder and arms. I have to find out. Wait . . . button me up; I'd better get dressed."

In the jerking, weird light, Annette fumbled with the row of buttons, but neither felt the need to light a candle.

"Keep Rachel calm if you can," Sylvie said as she dashed down the stairs.

From the front porch, Sylvie saw flames to the north as well, these coming from the main part of town with its stores and houses. The flames rose incredibly high and billowed like waves. Santa Anna's troops must have arrived, for no one else would burn the town and blow up the arsenal. Was it too late for them already? Would they be captured, or would they still be able to leave?

A cluster of men ran into the yard of the house next door. Two were carrying burning torches, and, unbelievably, were shouting in English.

"Is anyone home?" One of them yelled several times and pounded on the door, then on the windows. "Wake up, get the hell out!" He opened the door and stepped inside, while two others methodically touched their flaming torches to edges of wood on the porch, the planks of the house, and, Sylvie could see, curtains and furnishings inside.

She wanted to scream to make them stop, but her voice came out soundless against the roaring wind. One man carrying a burning brand came into Rachel's yard and saw Sylvie on the porch.

"Ma'am, I am from Captain Sharpe's company, and we are ordered to set fire to all the houses. We're coming through, getting everyone wakened up and out. You need to leave—right now."

"We are—we . . ." Sylvie stood gaping.

"How long till then? We can spare your house for a few minutes, but not longer. Get everyone out! We're torching the town from north to south, and the fire is taking over on its own. We're barely ahead of it."

"Why are you—Texans—burning down the town?"

"Sam Houston ordered it. He wants everything destroyed so there's not a single roof where a Mexican can take shelter."

"And the supply depot, too? Is he out of his mind?" Sylvie cried. "We've only just heard the news about the Alamo, and the widow who lives here is mad with grief. Now you're going to burn down her house?"

Annette grabbed Sylvie's arm from behind. "Hush, Sylvie. Try to act like you'll obey. This is a mob, and people get out of control. They can do anything when they're frantic. Please appear reasonable!"

"This is not a mob; it's an army officer."

"I have to go." He automatically lifted a hand to his cap in a salute.

"Sylvie, everyone is awake, and I'm putting the last things in the cart. Rachel is in a hurry, at long last. Let's go. Look at all the neighbors."

In the midst of chaos, people were loading carts, and through the smoke, the women could make out crowds on the street with horses and oxen, the mass moving north to the main road where they could turn east. They were heading toward the flames, now roaring higher into the sky than anything Sylvie had ever seen.

She and Annette went inside, where Rachel was lining up her children and making them hold hands, each older one responsible for a younger one. She explained that their lives depended on all of them keeping one another safe. Then she wrapped shawls around herself, layer upon layer.

"I've fled before," Rachel said. "I know what I'm doing. I hope you girls have packed well and thoughtfully because I don't have time to check your work, and I can hardly think straight anyway. We must go and not stop to look behind. Everything can be rebuilt; we've done that before. But family, loved ones, cannot be replaced. Let's go."

She glanced at the table where they had left the tea. "Sylvie, grab the kettle, the coffee pot, and cups, for heaven's sake. How can you leave those behind?"

Rachel faltered only when it was time to drive away; she shook her head silently and handed the reins of the cart to Sylvie. Annette rode one of the horses from Edna, and Jane, the eldest child, rode the other, holding a youngster in front of her.

Out on the road, they could see most of the houses, outbuildings, and barns burning. Rachel's house, on the south edge of town, was one of the last to be set on fire. A furious, hot wind whipped about them, and the children were coughing. Grayish ash wafted down like blossom petals, and burning embers dropped from the clouded sky to spray them with orange sparks.

Sylvie coaxed the horse to move against the flow of settlers and head south, away from the fire, on the road toward Edna. They had gone a short distance when sentries stopped the cart. One grabbed the bridle to turn Rachel's horse, while another stepped forward to speak to Sylvie.

"You can't go this way, ma'am. You have to turn around. Get on the main road and go east. That's away from the Mexicans and toward the other colonies. Just get across the Colorado River, and you'll be safe."

"The Colorado—that's days away with this cart. Why so far?"

"Sam Houston moved the army out, already."

"What are you talking about? Where are the soldiers? Is no one defending the town?"

"They're on the same road, already going east, away from here." He swung his arm, gesturing.

"They've pulled out ahead of us—leaving the townspeople behind them? We're the ones standing between the Texans and the Mexican army? Is Sam Houston insane?"

"Don't know, ma'am, but he is my commanding officer, and I don't think you will enjoy the Mexican troops when they get here. They'll take all the goods and food and money and everything else, and enjoy the women however they want. Do I need to tell you that?"

At her speechlessness, the sentry's façade of bravery evaporated, and his face transformed to a frightened young man, barely older than herself. "I'd feel awful if it was my own mother and sisters, or my wife. I'd want them to get away, fast. Don't you understand? Please . . . get on the road, out of here."

The other sentry pulled on the bridle to turn the horse, and the cart jolted, its wheels screeching and then locking at the tight turn-around. With difficulty, he backed the horse, and Sylvie did her best to steer north and coax the horse toward the fire. As they passed Rachel's house, now engulfed in flames, Sylvie kept her eyes on the masses of people nearby, concentrating on not running over someone on foot. People of all ages, dozens of them, wandered with dazed, fixed expressions, unaware of others trudging by or trying to pass. Everyone was carrying things, even the children, not only bags and sacks but also family portraits, kittens, and chickens.

Rachel was wailing, her hands clenched onto the rim of the cart. The children sniffled and watched her in terrified silence. Sylvie looked back to see Annette and Jane following closely, and her glance fell on her own carpetbag, which Annette must have thrown in. Near it, the youngest child, John, about three, lay on his back atop a nest of bags, peacefully asleep, his arms spread open toward the smoke-filled sky.

The morning gradually grew gray and took on colors of daylight as they moved slowly toward the east. The cart jolted, and its wheels screeched as the wooden axles and hubs heated up with friction. They would stop to add grease only when the train of refugees ahead of them forced a halt. Sylvie wondered whether the grease would last as far as the Colorado River crossing. Once it ran out, they would have to use soap.

As daylight grew stronger, the older boys asked to walk alongside for a time, and Rachel made them hold hands until they started to tease and shove each other. The younger ones huddled in the cart, dozing when they could lean against their mother. Rachel rarely released her grip on the side of the cart, and she regularly went into sessions of gasping, as though she could not catch her breath. Finally, late in the morning, she fell into a deep sleep.

Their cart had merged into a line with others as the chaos of flight became more orderly. Now, nearly midday, it was clear that neighbors had fled in their nightclothes, and many were barefoot. Entire families owned not a single cart or wagon, as so many settlers had arrived by river and still relied on boats to get around.

When Rachel awoke, she pronounced it time to stop and eat. Sylvie waited until they found a wide spot that offered grass and some trees. With everyone hungry, upset, and already a bit sunburned, it was time to find out how well they had packed and how adept they were going to be at living on the road.

Chapter 19

**Spring 1836**
**On the road, Republic of Texas**


WITH THE SPRING RAINS, EACH STREAM ALONG THE ROUTE swelled to a
river, while the main rivers flowed even higher and became difficult and
dangerous to cross. The rains fell, relentless and cold, chilling people
and turning the muddy road to muck. The refugees' progress slowed
as the wheels of wagons and carts mired in bogs deepened by numerous vehicles grinding their way through. It was difficult to believe the
Mexican army could be moving along the road behind them, and sheer
fright pushed the settlers to keep up their pace.

After several days, Sylvie, Annette, Rachel, and the children
arrived at the Lavaca River, the first main crossing. They would have
to cross one more river before reaching the Colorado. Sylvie remembered riding part of this route with Peter Kerr when they had gone to
Mina the previous June, and how they had cantered through woods
and fields that she and the others now inched through with frustrating
slowness. She had pulled Rachel's cart to a stop in line for crossing
the river and told everyone she would walk ahead to see whether they
could ford the river or would have to float the cart across.

As she walked among the crowds gathered and waiting their turn,
she glanced at campfires where women were cooking meals or washing
laundry. They had strung all manner of tarps and canvases as shelters
from the rain; dogs, chickens, even children huddled on the ground
under wagons, trying to shelter against the damp.

Above, clouds scudded through pearly sky, opening enough here
and there for a bit of blue to show. Sylvie hoped for some sun and
warmth, for a break in the dreariness. One of Rachel's children had
started to cough, always a worrisome sign. It was such a relief to get

away and be alone for a few moments, she almost hoped she would not see anyone she knew and be drawn into conversation. The camps were fairly quiet as the refugees took the opportunity to rest.

She counted twenty-seven carts and wagons that would cross before it was their turn. They might as well plan on spending the night. At the riverbank, she watched one wagon with a team of two horses trying to ford. The driver was skilled, an older man, but the current grabbed the box of the wagon and swung it sharply downriver. The horses were swimming hard, but their strength was not equal to the force. As they moved farther downriver, people shouted conflicting advice, their voices rising higher and higher with the agony of not being able to help. Then the horses regained footing, and they began to pull toward shore. Slowly the wagon came around, its momentum driving it into the backs of their legs. The horses lurched forward, and a wagon wheel caught on the riverbed, tilting the wagon box precariously to its side. Sylvie realized she was holding her breath. Then the wagon swung back down, righting itself and aligning with gravity, and the horses lugged it up the bank on the opposite side.

"Holy Mother of God," Sylvie murmured. How on earth were they going to manage? The people on foot seemed to have better odds, for young boys were rowing boats back and forth, loading up each time with people, crates, and baggage. Well, that was how the children and Rachel were going to get across. Sylvie watched as several men on each bank worked with lines wrapped around tree trunks, stout ropes that could be used to guide and pull on a floating raft or wagon. That was familiar; she had seen it done many times.

Feeling reassured that she understood an approach to take, Sylvie started back. She had spotted a farmhouse some ways off through the trees, and she thought of visiting it to see if she might draw fresh water from a well. She was carrying a pail and some empty flasks; often after setting up camp, someone would go in search of water that hadn't been sullied by horse and oxen hooves, wagon wheels, rinsed-out chamber pots, or soapy laundry.

Along the road, they had passed other abandoned farmhouses. The owners, Sylvie assumed, were well ahead of them on the road.

Stories abounded of unscrupulous men who would ride up to a farmhouse and terrify people by saying the Mexicans were just behind and sure to arrive within minutes. Families fled their breakfast tables, leaving coffee in their cups. They would grab what they could and run, literally, while the thieves remained behind and helped themselves to everything from candlesticks to cows. The threat was believable because no word had yet come back that the Texas army was halting its retreat.

As Sylvie entered the farmyard through a gate, a skinny cat yowled and ran alongside, brushing her ankles. A cow in the front garden looked up at her plaintively, moaning in pain from her swollen udder. Sylvie went to the front door and knocked; she waited and then called out. Everything remained silent.

She went back and talked to the cow, patting its broad, friendly face. Then she carefully squatted down, placing the pail ahead of the cow's back legs.

"Nice girl, good girl," she repeated soothingly. She had to tug a bit, but then the milk released in warm streams. The cat bumped hard against the pail, nearly tipping it over. Sylvie nudged it away with her foot. "Just a moment, and we'll get you a saucer."

She carried the pail of milk to the porch and through the front door into the kitchen. The silence was eerie. Dishes and canisters were scattered about on the table and counters, more likely by vandals than by a sloppy cook. Sylvie peered inside one canister and saw coffee; it smelled so rich and dark that a pain stabbed through her head. She would give almost anything for a few swallows of strong, hot coffee. She had suffered ferocious headaches on the first days after their supply ran out.

From the doorways into the bedrooms she could see clothing strewn, old quilts bunched, and odd shoes scattered. Could she match them up in pairs and take some to Rachel's children? Sylvie considered the urge and wondered if it wouldn't be stealing. On the wall near the kitchen, a calendar hung askew. Days for the first half of March had been crossed off, and Sylvie began counting out her nights on the road, touching a fingertip to each day's square.

Apparently the family had been in this house until four days earlier. And today must be . . . it was her birthday. Sylvie felt uncertain and counted the days again. Yes, today she was turning nineteen years old.

She found a saucer and put out milk for the cat. As she watched it lapping, her hand came to rest on the canister of coffee. When the cat had wandered off to wash, she refilled the saucer. She would not take all the coffee, for that would be too much like stealing. She would borrow some and leave the owners a note with a promise to repay them. Then it would be borrowing from a neighbor, something everyone did routinely.

Paper was strewn about from torn packaging, so she could pour coffee onto a sheet and twist it up. As soon as she pictured this, she found herself following through. Now, she felt in a hurry and failed to look around for a pencil to leave a note. Stuffing the bulging packet into her skirt pocket, she picked up the pail in one hand and the flasks for water in the other.

Back outside, she found the well and its bucket, and she drew up water that looked clear and smelled fresh. She drank some before filling the flasks and waited for any bad aftertaste. She glanced around toward the henhouse but did not see any poultry. Was it worth checking for eggs, and would they still be good? Well, if they smelled bad once they were broken open, they could just be thrown out. Sylvie took a moment to duck inside and feel around a few straw nests but found no eggs.

As she walked away from the farmhouse, she sent silent thanks to the owners. She wished she had written them an IOU, but she was sure they were nice people who would understand. Sylvie would want them to do the same if their situations were reversed. This wasn't theft; it wasn't as though she had taken shoes or blankets or tools. "I am turning nineteen years old," she told herself, "but I'm not becoming a thief."

When Sylvie returned to their camp, Annette was cooking journey cakes, quick-bread dough lumped on wide boards and set near the coals of the fire to cook. Sylvie gave her the pail of milk and suggested heating it for the children.

Rachel was seated nearby, talking with a man who looked familiar. With a shock, Sylvie recognized Byrd Lockhart, one of the early settlers in Gonzales. But he had gone into the Alamo with the other men. How could he be here and alive? Sylvie approached them tentatively, almost fearing he was a spirit incarnated. But he looked up from talking with Rachel and greeted her.

"Yes, I survived," he said, noting her expression.

"Byrd was out getting supplies and recruiting volunteers when the Alamo was overrun," Rachel said.

"I tried to get back in and rejoin my unit. But at every point the Mexican sentries were alerted and kept any of us from returning. Maybe half a dozen of us were gone at the time, and we all tried."

"I am glad to see you," Sylvie said. "It feels like a miracle, somehow. And you're traveling with your family now?"

"Yes; we're a ways ahead of you in line since our farm is outside of town along the route."

"It's a comfort to see you," Rachel said. "Tell your wife and lovely daughters that we must visit sometime soon."

"They'll look forward to that. Remember, Rachel, we have been through this before. Not quite the same thing, but close."

"When we left Gonzales the first time, you stayed back and built the stockade so we could finally return. As I recall, you have not been a refugee before, Byrd."

"But here we are, and we'll make it. I'm joining another militia unit, and we're sure to take a stand and fight before long."

"One can only hope," Rachel said.

Byrd nodded to all of them and said goodbye. The children had been playing quietly and now clustered around Annette, asking when they could eat.

Rachel sat very quietly, fingering a slip of paper. Sylvie saw tears running down her cheeks and waited for her to speak.

"Byrd brought me this voucher. It is for seventy-five dollars, and he thinks the money might be helpful to us, provided we can redeem it from a quartermaster or some such official, for supplies."

"Oh, that's good," Sylvie said. "We can definitely use it for flour, meat, coffee, any number of things."

"The seventy-five dollars is to repay my husband for his horse. When he got to the Alamo, they requisitioned his horse." Rachel beat her hands on her lap and moaned.

"I don't understand," Sylvie said. "Do you want to try to get the horse back instead?"

"No, no, look at the date, March second. He went in on the first of March. They took his horse from him right away. He couldn't have come back home to us even if he had wanted to."

At the end of March, as the refugee train approached the Colorado River, a rumor brought encouraging news: General Houston had halted the army at Burnam's and was letting the civilians pass ahead. And it proved true, for not only did the Texan troops help them cross the river, but they also protected the end of the train. Now the volunteer militia units stood between the settlers and the Mexican army, only a few miles away.

Though Houston had provided a rear guard earlier, led by a Tejano officer who had survived the Alamo, it lifted everyone's spirits enormously to see the full volunteer army, ragtag as it was, massing behind them. When Santa Anna's forces approached as close as three miles to the south, Houston sent out more than a hundred men as a feint; they were to draw fire and distract the Mexicans but were not to engage in battle.

As the refugees passed the army encampment at Burnam's, Sylvie caught sight of Andrew among the groups of soldiers, and he started heading their way. Catching up, he said he had begun watching for her and the others as soon as he returned from scouting and that he would try to stop by their camp that evening. Finding them would be easy, he added, as almost everyone seemed to know of Rachel Berry Flint, widow of Gonzales.

After dinner, Sylvie stayed near the fire while Rachel got the younger children into the tent to sleep, and Annette went with the eldest two to find more firewood. Sylvie was grateful for this time of day when she could sit with a cup of weak tea gradually cooling and watch the first stars appear above the campfire smoke. Each evening stayed light just a little longer. Soon voices would rise in songs drifting from other campfires. Sometimes, when the hymn or folk song was familiar, families would join in all along the line. The unity of their voices singing old phrases of sorrow and hope was deeply comforting.

The toes of the boots she wore, which she'd propped against rocks ringing the fire, were finally dry. But as she pulled back the sole of one to see how loose it was, it broke off in her hand. There was little point in wearing the pair any longer, since they also pulled right off her feet when they got stuck in mud. She unlaced them and checked her stockings, whose holes gaped so large she could fit all her toes through, the fabric too thin to be darned. It was time to let them go and start wearing her moccasins.

The nearly continuous rain meant the cooking fires stayed small, damp, and smoky. Steam rose from anything nearby—clothes, tablecloths, quilts, even the hair on refugees' heads. They tried always to boil water and not drink it until any cloudiness had settled as sediment. Sylvie swirled the dregs in her cup and watched the tea leaves form patterns in the residue at the bottom.

Andrew arrived as it was getting dark and Sylvie had drawn a shawl around her shoulders. He sat on a packing box near her, and when he asked how she was and how they were doing, she gave a listless shrug. He reached to pat her on the shoulder.

"As well as can be expected, I suppose," she said. "At least no one is sick, and I'm thankful for that."

Those with healing skills were busy treating snake bites, diarrhea, fevers, and twisted guts that followed from eating noxious weeds as hunger and fear of scurvy drove some families to forage for anything green.

Water festered in mud puddles, bred mosquitoes, and exhaled fumes at night that caused fevers. Sylvie dipped often into the pouches of medicinal herbs she had from Isabelle and from the Waco women.

"This is a neat camp," Andrew said, glancing around. "You planned ahead and packed well. This looks efficient and as clean as things can be."

"'Clean and efficient.' In other times, I've been called charming. Can you believe that? I don't think you've ever seen me dressed up for a party, or a dance."

"Maybe I will, someday. It's hard to know what to say in these circumstances."

"Did I tell you, Annette helped me sew a beautiful dress with that peach silk that I traded for at your store in Mina?"

"I remember that silk. It was one of the nicest things we had."

"I got to wear it to one party, and it's still at the farm in Edna. When I packed for Gonzales, I thought I would be back within a week."

"I'll wager you looked very pretty in it. Right now, parties seem pretty distant and unreal, like from another time."

"How are you getting along, and how is Logan?"

"We're restless and frustrated. We want to take a stand and fight, get this over with, one way or another."

They grew quiet, and Sylvie commented, "I don't understand how the army could burn down Gonzales and leave people behind like that."

"Yes, it's shameful. Our captain, Jesse Billingsley, and other officers argued bitterly with Houston, and they only agreed to leave town when he said we'd head up the road just a couple of miles. We thought we'd stop and set up a defensive line, but he never ordered a halt. Instead, we marched all night."

"How much farther will we have to travel? Can you make a guess? Do you have any information?"

"We're all pretty weary of this. Houston swears we won't cross the Brazos River without taking a stand and fighting. He expects reinforcements will come from the United States, and some say he has ordered Colonel Fannin to bring the regular army up here from Goliad. We're guessing that he pictures our two armies meeting near San Felipe so we can fight as a major force, maybe west of the town."

"The Brazos and San Felipe . . . at the rate we are moving, that would be . . ."

"We're about halfway there."

"Another two weeks? Of *this*?" Sylvie's outrage vied with despair.

"After the Brazos River, you'll just have one little one to cross, the San Bernard, and then you'll be at San Felipe. I think Rachel still has a place there in Austin's colony from her earlier marriage. You should be able to stay and rest."

"Well, I'm glad Houston has something in mind other than this endless fleeing."

"Sylvie, this is shameful for me and the others. The officers are just short of a revolt, but we also didn't want a battle with you women and children caught in between. We have to fight soon; the militia volunteers keep leaving to help their families. Most come back after a little while. But on any given day, Houston might have as many as twelve hundred men under him, or as few as six hundred. I think as we keep going east, though, we're picking up more and more settlers as volunteers."

"So many men are barefoot, and no one has enough to eat. The longer you march, the worse shape you'll be in when you do fight."

"That's true. Plus the idleness isn't good; what is there to do while we wait around other than drinking, wrestling, and shooting off our weapons? Some of these young men without families get into contests, and that leads to fights. Well, you can imagine."

Sylvie asked if Andrew had heard any news about Jim Kerr and his family, whether they and other settlers had evacuated the towns farther south and managed to stay ahead of the smaller Mexican army in that area. Andrew said he was certain that the Kerrs and their neighbors were traveling, that they had formed another refugee train and were also heading east, hoping to reach the Sabine River and cross into Louisiana.

Andrew needed to get back for guard duty, and as he rose, he left a few small packets of provisions, apologizing that it wasn't much. When he was gone, Sylvie carefully unfolded the corners of wrappings. One held sugar, another rice, and the third, matches. It appeared their ends had been dipped in wax so they might still light after getting damp. How clever, she thought.

When Annette and the children returned and Rachel emerged from the tent, they gathered to hear Sylvie's news. Talking about the second train of refugees turned their thoughts to Jim, Sarah, and the slave families, all of whom must have left the farm.

"I miss Minny," Sylvie said as she poked at embers with a stick. As soon as it stopped hissing steam and dried out, she would add it to the flames. "She has so much energy, and she can seem so certain about what's the right thing to do."

"We're thinking that about you right now, Miss Sylvie," Annette replied.

"Oh! Well, that's nice, but I hardly know what to do other than follow along."

"I miss the farm, my family, everyone. And my man," Annette said, with a sigh.

"You have a suitor?" Sylvie asked.

"Yes, Raymond; you might recall him. He's indentured at the McCarthy's. He'll be free in two years and three months, and then we'll marry. I worry that they don't know where we are, that they've been waiting for us at Edna and we haven't showed up."

"I've thought about that, too," Sylvie said. "But Uncle Jim stays so well informed, I'm certain he knows what happened at Gonzales and assumes we're all together on the road."


One evening, two boys came around, selling cuts of beef to the campers. They told Rachel they lived nearby and had herded their family's cattle ahead of both the refugees and the armies. Their father was now serving in the militia and decided it was time to slaughter a cow and sell the meat as best they could to the army's quartermaster or to refugees. Rachel was dickering, using the $75 chit for her late husband's horse, while Annette examined one opened parcel, smelling the meat and checking for worms.

As Sylvie watched, she noticed armed sentries coming by, escorting a prisoner back to the rear. His hands were bound behind him, but he held his head up and was talking with his captors. Sylvie thought he looked familiar and suddenly recognized the voice: it was unmistakably Peter Kerr's. She had not seen him since they had ridden with the mail from Gonzales to Mina the summer before, and he looked thinner.

She fell into step with them. "Peter? Peter Kerr?"

"Sylvie Pensoneau! By all the heavens, what a pleasure to see you!"

"Can you . . . can you please wait a minute?" she said to the nearest guard. He stopped and frowned at her, still holding Peter's arm.

"And Rachel Berry—Mrs. Flint!" Peter glanced around the camp. "I apologize that this encounter presents me in most unfortunate circumstances."

The other sentry nudged him with his rifle stock, and Peter hunched his shoulders.

"Can you stop here for a moment at least?" Rachel intervened. "We can offer you water, or real coffee."

The sentries stopped abruptly. "Yes, ma'am," one said. "We'd be obliged. Prisoner, be seated." He waved toward a tree stump where the children had been playing, and Peter perched on its edge with a sigh of relief.

As Annette got the coffee, Sylvie went up to Peter and asked what had happened. "Why on earth are you under guard?"

"Oh, my dear, once again my erstwhile friend Sam Houston has seen fit to imprison me for the most wrongful of reasons. This time, he accuses me of being a spy. He's choosing to lash out from disbelief, to protect his mind from absorbing news of the most terrible tragedy."

"Peter, what are you talking about?"

"Prepare yourself for shocking news. I am afraid it will wrench the hearts and drain the courage of everyone, refugee and militiaman and regular soldier alike."

The two sentries were quiet, listening as they sipped from tin cups.

"Start at the beginning, if you can," Rachel said.

"Well, to be brief, I have continued in my occupation of postal delivery and occasional courier for the military. As it happens, I was in the area north of Goliad, heading toward San Felipe, when I was entrusted with news of the defeat of the Texas army serving under Colonel Fannin."

"No—the regular army defeated! How is that possible?" Rachel protested.

"I assure you, it is the sad truth, though Sam Houston himself found it impossible to believe. But brace yourselves for far grimmer events: the Mexicans engaged Fannin's troops out in a poor position, a meadow near Coleto Creek that offered little means for defense. Some men and the commanding officer, Fannin himself, were seriously wounded in the first day's fighting.

"Overnight, they lacked enough water to cool the cannons, and had little food for the men. They barely could treat the wounded. Some men dug revetments during the night, but by daylight, given the size and position of the Mexican forces, it seemed more sensible to call a halt and surrender, and thus live to fight another day.

"The army, about four hundred men, went back to Goliad, this time as prisoners. Fannin was certain they would be paroled and sent back home, and the Mexican general even took him down to the bay to look over a schooner that could transport troops. But it was all a ruse. Or the general had a change of heart, or he received a direct contrary order from General Santa Anna himself."

"Oh, no," Rachel groaned. "It was to give no quarter, again, like at the Alamo. Please tell me that was not the case."

"Oh, madam, as all the saints and angels of heaven bear witness, I would fain tell you otherwise. And the timing for the destruction of these poor souls aligned with one of the holiest days of Christendom, Palm Sunday."

"May Santa Anna's soul burn in hell," Rachel said.

The others—the sentries, Sylvie, Annette, the children—all were staring at Peter.

"This is unimaginable," Sylvie said. "Are you saying the Mexicans killed four hundred men, regular soldiers, who were their prisoners?"

"All but about two dozen who managed to escape. The prisoners had believed they were being released, for they were divided into three groups and marched out along the roads leading away from the fort, *Presidio* La Bahía. Each prisoner had one or two guards on him, and at a prearranged signal, each guard turned and fired at close range, killing his prisoner, pretty much instantly."

The shocked silence continued for long moments.

*"Mon dieu,"* Sylvie breathed and turned to find a place to sit down. She dropped to the ground and leaned on one arm.

"I do not wonder that Sam Houston didn't believe you," Rachel said. "I find it pretty hard to believe myself. Who did you hear this from, anyway? How do you know it's true?"

"Sadly, ma'am, I heard it from two different men who managed to escape. They allowed forty or so men who had skills useful to them—physicians or wheelwrights or blacksmiths—to live so that they might avail themselves of their services. I spoke directly with a physician who is well known to many of us. He told me he was forced to treat the Mexican wounded while leaving the Texans to suffer and die. He and a few others were able to escape while on work details and reached the protection of some sympathetic Tejanos in the area. And a few interceded, such as a Catholic priest who won mercy for some men from around San Patricio, as they were Irish colonists rather than Americans."

"We will wait to hear from Sam Houston or his officers about this before we assign ourselves to despair," Rachel said.

"The official couriers will not be long behind me, I assure you," Peter said. "We will all await their arrival. After that, Houston shouldn't keep me prisoner as a suspected spy any longer."

A sentry set down his empty cup and tugged Peter up by one arm.

"Do not repeat any of this slanderous account," the soldier said to Rachel and included Sylvie in his glance. The women shook their heads mutely. "Thanks for the coffee, ma'am."

The sentries touched fingers to their caps and pulled Peter away and back along the track toward the rear.

Rachel raised her hands in a helpless gesture. "We won't tell a soul," she said. "But everyone will know all about this soon enough."

And that proved true. By morning, rumors sweeping of their own accord were plunging the refugees into despair. The train barely made two miles before stopping at midday when word came back that Houston was officially informed of the surrender of Fannin's army, and of their slaughter at the hands of the Mexicans. Many refugees did not pack up after the meal and move on. Rachel left to confer with others from Gonzales, and she returned saying they would stay put for the rest of the day.

"Some people think we should go north; they think Houston will order his army up that way," she said. "Apparently there's another train of settlers fleeing farther north, and we might join them."

"Let's wait and see which way the army goes," Sylvie urged. "We'd be vulnerable if we headed off north on our own, especially if all the settlements up that way are abandoned."

They spent the afternoon catching up on laundry, mending, and other chores, but the work felt empty and mechanical. With so much death and everyone thinking of someone they knew who was now gone, killed in such a horrible manner, the camps were quiet. Even Rachel's older children withdrew for unaccustomed naps, gaining a few hours away from the harshness of reality.

Sylvie could not sleep; her feelings were in a tumult, with dread keeping her on edge. Finally she decided to head on her own toward the rear to see if she could find Peter Kerr. She did encounter him not far away, for he had since been freed and was visiting with another family. When he saw her, he politely took leave and walked with her back toward their camp.

"I'm glad to see they released you, even if that means the dreadful news is true," she said.

"Thank you, my dear, though my own relief is now mixed with uncertainty. I want to join the militia and serve as I best can. Yet to some I am still branded as a traitor, a Mexican spy. Therefore, I might have to remain a simple civilian for a while."

Sylvie waited until they were seated back at her camp before asking about the information she most feared. He had gladly accepted her offer of journey cake and beans and rice, and he ate as they talked.

"Were men from Gonzales, or Mina, among those captured and executed?" she finally asked.

"Yes, the ones who had joined companies under Fannin after the siege of Bexar. Francis Johnson was popular after he led the charge into San Antonio along with Ben Milam. His men were taken prisoner at the end of February, at San Patricio. Some from the Gonzales area were working as scouts for him at the time. I am sorry."

"I was wondering about Armand Fulshear."

"Yes, I knew him. He was scouting for Fannin's army, and I even met him a few times to exchange courier bags. I have no reason to believe he might be among the few who remain alive. But don't despair; a full list of casualties will arrive, and then we'll have more certain knowledge."

Although Sylvie had suspected this, a desolating shock ran through her. She had pictured Armand as a survivor; he was skilled in tracking, knowing the land, riding fast, and being stealthy. But clearly, Peter believed he had been captured and was now among the dead.

"I will mourn for him, if that was his fate," she said. Peter looked at her quizzically, and then looked down as he set his empty plate on the ground. "I will try to maintain some hope until I see a casualty list," she added. "But my own sense is grim."

"I cannot hold the deaths of four hundred men in my mind," Peter said. "I think of individual men I know and how this puts a finish to the stories of their lives. I'll spend some time recalling their stories; that's one thing I can do. What did their lives mean, with an ending such as this stamped upon the patterns they themselves had created to give meaning to their existence?

"But Sylvie, you're coping with individual sorrow and mourning. Rachel told me—let it slip, and I hope you will forgive my mentioning it—that you may have had a special interest in Armand, and he most assuredly in you."

Sylvie believed that no one really knew of their mutual regard, but of course Rachel knew Armand and his family and would grieve for him. And she'd recall how disapproving she was of the rumors that Sylvie rode out to meet him.

"Yes, he would show up when I went riding some evenings outside of Gonzales, quite often in fact. And we danced together several times at that ball in Goliad when Uncle Jim and the Texans took the *Presidio* La Bahía. And"—she thought of their lingering kisses—"he did press his interest. I think he would have been a suitor. Oh, I feel horrible. It's just terrible."

She began to cry. "Excuse me. I'm so tired and filthy and worn out. When will this accursed fleeing ever end? I would trade away years of my life for a bath and a bed to sleep in. So I'm not at my best, and this is taking a harder toll than it might otherwise."

"Hush," Peter said. "There is no set measure for how hard one's mourning should be, and there's no shame in tears. The women here in Texas must make themselves tough. Yet if you all become as hardened as the men, who will we turn to for those softer feelings? Take some solace in this idea, that you were a comfort to Armand, even up until his last moments. Especially in those moments."

"Oh, I can't bear to think of that. I truly hope he did not realize he was about to die."

Peter let Sylvie sob for several minutes. Then he said softly, "When death first arrives as a certainty before a man, we all cry out for our mothers. And then a moment later, with the next breath we call for our sweetheart or wife. I know this because I myself cried out thusly when being sucked down in that accursed quicksand years ago, and also after other close scrapes. But it is certain that your very dearness gave that young man a transcendence, the spiritual valor of love, that would banish terror and give flight to his soul, upward to heaven."

"Peter, you speak like a religious man, someone with true faith. My own is not as strong. But your sincerity does give me some comfort."

"Think of this: he would have been in the streets of Goliad just before he died, maybe walking past the house where you two danced together. The thoughts of you and your affections might well have been with him, along with thoughts of his family, of course."

"Oh, imagine their grief." She wept bitterly and then couldn't bear to think of his parents any longer. Instead, she pictured the town's streets winding among the whitewashed walls of courtyards, the warm ocher of adobe in the sun, the bright flowers and brilliant blue sky. These were the last things Armand had seen in this world, in his life. He would have thought of her, she was certain. She cried like a child, rubbing grubby fists into wet eyes.

"Do let out the sorrow, my dear. The harder you mourn now, the sooner you might empty yourself of your allotment of grief. That well refills every day, to be sure, but to a lower level each time until it finally becomes bearable. Can you imagine how barren and empty a life would be without love? Even though I lost my own life's beloved, I would far rather have loved her than not had that soul-expanding experience."

"I do not think I loved him back. Not so well, not like that."

"And perhaps that's for the better. That young man always struck me as being in a hurry. He pressed hard with everything; as a courier, he even risked wearing out a good mount. Sometimes I wonder if people who seem in such a hurry have a presentiment they've been allotted a shorter span."

"I agree he had a determined aspect at times, though I liked him very much and he was quite comely. All of that made it pleasant to imagine . . ."

"And a good family, and well off, with property."

"Yes, all those things."

"And yet earlier, I believed your glance had settled a little more northward, toward Mina."

"It must have, for when I returned from our trip there, I didn't manage to say goodbye to Armand before I left for Edna. I simply sent a note to his family. Now that seems so harsh. And I also mourn for the others, such an unimaginable number of men. I am afraid, too, for if we've lost that entire army, what will happen to us now?"

"Why, we persevere. I have lost everything several times. And at the moment, I believe I have nothing. But what is Texas, if not a place where we all start over? Isn't that why everyone came here?" He gestured toward the road and the other camps. "Starting over is one thing we all believe in, and we all know how to do."

"I fear I do not have the strength."

"Hmm. And yet you are so young." After a moment, he asked, "How are Andrew Magill and Logan Vandeveer? Have you seen them?"

"Oh, yes, they're fine. Andrew sees us from time to time, and he has brought a few provisions—that rice, in fact."

She managed a weak smile, and Peter smiled back, though his gaze remained intent and worried.

That night around the campfires, soft wailing and crying intermixed with singing of slow and sad hymns. By their fire, Annette began "A Balm in Gilead," and soon other voices joined in, rising up and down the line, until the phrases echoed one another, a few beats apart. The singing went on and on, the reverberations raising shivers on Sylvie's arms.

Chapter 20

**April 1836**
**Near Harrisburg, Republic of Texas**

RACHEL HELD OUT HOPE THAT HER BABY WOULD WAIT to be born in San Felipe. It was a sizable town, and her second husband had been a colonist there; she still had claim to property and hoped they might be taken in by old friends or neighbors and sheltered during the birth. But the baby had other plans, and the first indications of labor came before the group reached the Brazos River. Rachel alerted her web of acquaintances and asked whether anyone had relatives or friends in the area or knew of an experienced midwife. Talk went forward and back among the wagons and carts and soon produced a piece of valuable advice.

Someone knew of Mrs. Emma Carter, a midwife, who had a farm nearby. She was a widow, and her place was accessible by ox cart a ways up a lane off the main track. The farm was too small and isolated for the Mexicans to bother with, and even if Mrs. Carter had fled, the house would at least offer water, a stove for heating it, and a bed.

With no more assurance than that, Rachel decided to try the place and urged Sylvie to steer the horse up the grassy, winding wagon track. After half a mile, they came upon a clearing with a double log cabin and fenced yard and pasture. At least the horses could graze and rest, for the split-rail fences were still standing. The doors of both cabins, which were connected by a covered breezeway, were closed, and the place showed no signs of being burned or sacked. Sylvie knocked on one door and waited. Two large dogs appeared, wagged their tails, and plopped down without barking.

She turned and knocked on the other door, and after a few moments, it creaked open several inches.

"Good morning, ma'am," she said, to the small, wrinkled face peering at her. "Are you Mrs. Emma Carter by any chance?"

"I am," she replied. "And who might you be?"

As Sylvie introduced herself and described the plight of Rachel and her children, Mrs. Carter listened and nodded, then stepped out to look at the group clustered around the ox cart.

"Then you must come in and make yourselves at home," she said. "I reckon my old hands are still capable of helping at such a time. And that poor woman looks like she sorely needs a bed to lie on. Have you ever seen such famished and exhausted children?"

Sylvie was taken aback as she looked over the group with a fresh perspective. She and Annette had packed so well that they were faring better than most refugees, especially the ones who had run out onto the road weeks earlier with only the clothes on their backs. But she could see that the family did present a sad sight.

She went back and assured Rachel of their welcome, and the children began to troop listlessly up toward the cabins.

"You may take this side," Mrs. Carter told them, as she opened the door of the second one. "There are beds and plenty of room on the floor. We'll cook on the other side, and that's also where I sleep, near the stove."

The children peered into the dimness, and Sylvie glanced about at an orderly interior. Several narrow beds were attached to the walls, and a fireplace stood clean and empty at the far end, flanked by two small windows.

"Go on in," Annette said, gently nudging the eldest two. "I will get us settled while your Mama talks with Mrs. Carter."

In the other cabin, Rachel took a chair by the small table and set about establishing social ties, mentioning the friends who had recommended Mrs. Carter and passing on news of others Mrs. Carter asked about. When they both were satisfied that each came sufficiently well recommended, Rachel asked more about the place.

Mrs. Carter said she had a well with excellent water, and a spring house farther back on the property near a creek. "I'm happy to share all that I have stored, for I have plenty of cheese, eggs, and butter.

Those will be so good for the children. I'd rather you ate my food than the Mexicans. And I'm too old to go fleeing along the road myself."

"Is your husband with the militia, or your son?" Sylvie asked.

"Both my husband and my daughter are dead, some years back. My son-in-law lives here, and he joined the local militia about two weeks ago. They'll be back in another week or two, don't you think?"

"We've been on the road four weeks already," Rachel said. "Whoever could have guessed our ordeal would carry on so long?"

"Where are our soldiers?"

"Our militia troops, under General Sam Houston, are passing along the main road now, so you can feel a bit safer."

Sylvie and Rachel shared a glance, aware that neither wanted to tell Mrs. Carter that the regular Texan army had been destroyed, the men killed after surrendering.

Sylvie asked Mrs. Carter if she might draw some pails of water and replenish the wood for the stove. When those tasks were done and Rachel was resting on the bed, the widow told Sylvie how to find the chicken coop and the spring house. She added that if any Mexicans actually came up the lane, she and the family should go into the woods and hide. Her husband had built a few shelters far back to use while tending cattle or brewing a batch in the still.

As Sylvie explored the outbuildings, she caught one scrawny chicken in the kitchen garden and carried it to the coop, bracing the gate in the fencing behind her. She felt about the piles of straw and located three eggs, one still faintly warm. She set them outside the coop to fetch on her return and went on to the creek. One of the dogs shadowed her, panting slightly and switching its tail.

Sylvie followed a gurgling sound through the trees and soon saw a stream falling clear and bright over a rocky approach to a small pool. She sank down and splashed her face and neck. Then she rose and followed it down to the spring house, a small wooden structure built over a bend and shaded by a dense clump of trees.

Inside, all was damp and clean and smelled faintly of yeast. She found a single wooden cask with a bit of butter, and a triangle of cloth-wrapped cheese that fit in the palm of her hand. She sat on a small bench against the wall and wondered what Mrs. Carter was thinking. She had almost nothing to eat of her own, let alone to share with eight other people. As Sylvie stood up, the bench shifted, and she turned to look more closely. She raised the seat and found a storage area holding half a dozen wrapped parcels, butter to one side and cheese to the other.

Sylvie dropped the lid and plopped back down in relief. She would bring packages back to the house, but right now, nothing could stop her from biting into the morsel of cheese she held. No one would miss it, and she bit hungrily, barely chewing before satisfyingly large globs slid down her throat. It did not just taste good, it *felt* good to eat.

"Where is your cow, fella?" Sylvie asked the dog, which was sitting near the door and cocking its head. She left the spring house to wander in the woods, following narrow, deep paths packed by hooves of cows, or possibly deer. It was so good to be on her own for a little while. The air smelled fresh, with a few trees blooming and others budding vividly green. At last the sun felt warm where it dappled through, and she hoped the seemingly constant rain of the past few weeks might be breaking.

The dog took a jog to the left and looked back. She followed and soon spotted the cow. It was a lovely creature, light brown all over, standing in a meadow and munching grass. After Sylvie spoke to it and petted it, she guided it back toward the cabins.

The travelers shared their cornmeal and flour with Mrs. Carter and put on a pot of beans to soak overnight. They shared three fried eggs, and the older children sucked on their small portions of cheese as though they were candy. The younger ones drank as much milk as they could hold, and then none of them wanted anything but to sleep on a bed, under a roof, surrounded by walls. Annette herded them into the other cabin, and soon all was quiet.

In the dark early morning hours, Rachel woke Sylvie and Mrs. Carter and told them it was time. Having given birth five times, Rachel knew her body's signals. Mrs. Carter awakened quickly and moved about efficiently, giving directions in a low voice. She had stacked clean cloths and bed sheets and kept water heating on the stove. Rachel asked Sylvie to keep an eye on the children, and then she bit down on a knotted rag to keep from making too much noise. Sylvie was relieved she could slip away and watch the children, though she suspected they would sleep through a hurricane at this point.

Annette was awake and said she would go to help Mrs. Carter. "Don't worry," she whispered. "I love helping babies come into this world."

The children barely stirred before noon, and by then, when they went to see their mother, they could also greet their new sister Elizabeth, hale and healthy. Rachel cradled the baby in one arm and reached the other to hug each child while she made introductions. She looked rosy from joy and the effort of a hard but short labor.

That night, at their supper of beans, biscuits, and milk, they all gave thanks by saying a longer grace than usual.

"Can you stay a few more days?" Mrs. Carter asked. "You should rest a spell, Rachel."

Sylvie spoke of the danger of waiting too long and finding themselves once again caught between the armies. Annette argued that the children were getting much-needed rest and that a few more days would return color to their cheeks. Rachel decided it by saying she could use another day or two in bed and that baby Elizabeth needed to start her life by knowing what a house was like.

"If we do stay on, you might go out hunting," Annette suggested to Sylvie. "We certainly could use some meat."


The next day, Sylvie set out hunting and took one of Mrs. Carter's dogs with her. She had roamed a wide area before while foraging for greens and chose a copse of trees to start watching for deer or wild fowl. The dog sat quietly while Sylvie scanned the dim shade, but soon it rose slowly and began a low growl, alerting her that they were not alone. A young man, an Indian, emerged from the trees and stepped toward her, holding his rifle loosely across his chest. She could see, farther back, more men, as well as a pack train of horses and mules. She was being silently surrounded.

Yet as she noted the beaded designs of their clothing, she realized they were not local Indians. Instead, they appeared to be Delaware traders, and as the man began speaking tentatively with Sylvie, she chose French. He spoke that quite well, and she learned the traders were returning to the town of Westport, Missouri, keeping to trails and back roads in Texas to avoid the fighting. Best of all, they knew her cousin Paschal Pensoneau, who worked in Westport as a trader and translator. As Sylvie described the plight of her companions, the men softened and were willing to barter food for her beautiful beaded moccasins. They also anticipated generous treatment from Paschal when he learned how they had helped his cousin in her time of need.

When Sylvie returned to the cabins with freshly killed and gutted turkeys and packets of supplies, the others gaped at her in amazement. After she told the story of meeting the Delawares and bartering in French, they made her tell it again. And as the children asked for the story during quiet times over the next few days, Sylvie began to feel like one of the men retelling his battle stories, or like Peter Kerr spinning his tales of triumphs, failures, and lost love.

The food and rest revived the group, yet even the children were happy to eat lightly and keep some in reserve. Knowing what hunger was like, they wanted to plan against it. When Rachel said she was ready to travel, the children balked. The second eldest asked if they could stay at Mrs. Carter's place and let the adults go on if they felt they had to.

They turned to their mother, to Sylvie, and to Mrs. Carter, their eyes doubting the wisdom of adults. They had trusted without question that their mother would always know what to do and how to keep them safe. Now, grownups had become shadowy figures, with both fathers they had known having died and their mother recently incapacitated by a mystery that produced this tiny, red, wrinkled, crying being that she seemed so thrilled to carry about.

The children lingered; they clung to one another or lay on a bed and fisted up the blankets to resist being lifted. The youngest boy curled up and sobbed, "I cannot, I cannot." Annette and Sylvie coaxed the older boys by promising they could rides in saddles on two horses, like grownups. As she wrenched John's clasp free of Mrs. Carter's skirt, Sylvie silently vowed that her own children, if she ever married and had a family, would never have cause to doubt her this way.

Their goodbyes to Mrs. Carter came with many thanks, and invitations for her to join them, but she wanted to stay in her home. Everyone was wiping away tears, and it really was time to leave. As they walked down the wagon path, Annette shook her head at Rachel's willfulness and marveled at her stamina. She and Sylvie reminisced about how women usually spent ten days in bed and only slowly resumed normal activities, the rest helping to ward off illnesses that could kill new mothers past the dangers of delivery. But the past seemed such a different world now.

Back on the road, they fell in with the last straggling refugees, who reported that the Texas militia units were not far behind. Apparently the Mexican army under General Santa Anna was converging with a second, smaller army approaching from the south. The two sides were likely to meet at San Felipe, so that town would not offer a haven of rest after all. General Houston was keeping his army on the march and might head north to evade the Mexicans yet again. Rumors said many officers wanted to turn south instead, to meet the Mexican forces and fight. But in either case, the refugees needed to hurry.

At the Brazos River, Annette began unpacking the cart so Rachel and the children, and as many stores as possible, could be rowed across in boats. As they had done before, she and Sylvie would drive the horse and the partially emptied cart across the ford.

But Rachel felt rushed and insisted there was not enough time. With the rains letting up, the river had subsided, and she argued they should be able to drive straight across, children and all. Sylvie protested, fearing she could not steer such a load and control the horse if the channel was deep. Rachel snapped at her, and Annette softly urged her to comply. As she reloaded the cart, Sylvie swore strong oaths—in French—and felt better.

They had settled back in the cart, and Sylvie had just taken up the reins, when a sentry slapped the horse hard on the rump; it jumped, jerking the cart forward into the water. Midstream, Sylvie felt the cart begin to float and pull downstream. As long as it floated smoothly, all was fine. But with a tremendous jar, the downstream wheel caught and froze. She felt the current lifting the box on her side and heard the children crying out. She yanked on the reins, but the horse stumbled in confusion with the shifting weight.

Everything whirled then, so fast: the light, trees, land, and water, all in a pinwheel, and she was cold, so cold her breath was gone. The reins were out of her hands as her feet touched shifting pebbles and rocks on the river bottom. She stood up and saw sky, treetops, then burning red streaks across her palms as they broke through the water's surface. Near her, Rachel rose from the water, baby Elizabeth clutched to her chest. Annette was downstream a bit, and she held a bundle of clothes that must be a child. Sylvie looked madly about for bobbing heads. Jane, the eldest, stood holding John, and she was stepping slowly and carefully toward the bank on the opposite side.

One, two, three, four—two more to find—and then Annette plucked a boy by his britches and held him up, as well. She began trudging toward shore.

"I can swim! I can swim!" It was Andy, paddling near Sylvie. She grabbed at him, and he clung to her.

On the riverbank, huddled and shivering, they watched as men waded into the river and tried to calm the horse and right the cart. Sylvie wondered dimly how much of their provisions were lost.

"Sorry, ma'am, sorry," a man said when he led the horse and cart toward Rachel and handed her the lead. She thanked him weakly.

Sylvie and Annette waded back into the shallows to retrieve what they could.

"I'm glad we tied most everything down," Annette said. She had gathered up a packet of dried turkey meat, a tin of flour, and the sewing box. They continued searching until Rachel suggested moving on for a while.

"Let's get going. It will warm us up," she said. And it was true: the sun shone strongly enough to begin drying their clothes as they walked. Resuming their routine almost made the accident seem less of a catastrophe. Everything strapped to the cart remained intact, and

Sylvie found that supplies stored on the side that had floated above the water were passably dry. Annette took a turn driving, to ease the red welts swelling on Sylvie's palms.

When they camped that evening, rather than abandoning the wet flour, they made dough and cooked two dozen journey cakes. Rachel joked that the dousing in the river seemed like a proper baptism for the baby's coming life in Texas.

For the refugees and the militiamen, a fork in the road presented a fateful choice. They could turn north toward Nacogdoches and continue retreating, or south toward Harrisburg and face Santa Anna's army. Andrew had stopped briefly at Rachel's camp and given her and Sylvie a surreptitious message: although General Houston was ordering the army north, nearly all the militia captains had agreed among themselves to turn south and take a stand. Only one company would turn north, and he advised the women to stay with the main group for more protection. And if the refugees moved quickly, he thought they might reach the San Jacinto River and cross it ahead of both armies.

"I've heard," he added, "that the settlers Jim Kerr organized on the southern route have made it to Louisiana. They're safely inside the United States."

"Oh, we could join them at long last," Sylvie said. "How wonderful that they're safe!"

"I would very much like to do that," Annette said.

"Turning south is fine by me," Rachel agreed. "Though I believe we are doing quite well and would manage either way."

When the refugees came upon the fork in the road the next day, most seemed to turn south from what Sylvie could see, and she steered the cart is the same direction. The town of Harrisburg presented a grim site, for it had been burned down. As she drove past fields, Sylvie could see nothing left to forage.

When they did stop, though, they were able to get water from a well. Sentries and militia in the rear guard, whose ranks were thinning as men rode rapidly to and fro, shared brief reports: the Mexicans were moving across open fields toward the San Jacinto River, probably to get to the ferry crossing. The Texan army had kept marching all night, hurrying to catch up with Santa Anna's troops.

The land was becoming low and boggy. When they passed through clearings, Sylvie could see flat marshlands and deltas to the east where the San Jacinto River emptied into Galveston Bay. To the south, farm fields stretched toward a lake that welled up in a low area. Groups of men—possibly a thousand or more from one army or the other—formed dark masses near its shores.

The only place for the refugees to camp lay along the north side of the road on banks rising above a curving bayou. A sentry stopped the cart by grasping the horse's halter and told Sylvie to pull off the road along that side. Though he and the others wore ragtag clothing, she saw that they were heavily armed.

"But why stop here?" she asked. "We want to cross the river."

"See that?" He pointed toward the mass of men, wagons, and horses in the distance, which seemed to be swelling larger. "That is the Mexican army. They're forming up to camp and start crossing the river. It's too late for you to get ahead of them. Our troops are taking positions here, though you can't see the formations through the trees. You'll stay up here near the road because it's behind our forces and it's safer." He grinned suddenly. "Besides, you may not need to go any farther. This is where we'll take a stand and give 'em hell!"

"Is it? In that case, it looks like we'll be close to the action."

"Be prepared, miss," he said less jovially. He tugged the bridle to lead the horse off the road, and soon he let go. Sylvie steered the cart toward trees, and it lurched along until she reached a small clearing that offered some privacy from other camps. Rachel suggested walking ahead to see if there were better sites farther along, so Sylvie and Annette left the others at the clearing.

Many families had already settled in, and the campsites grew denser as the two walked east along the road. They stopped at places where they could peer across the fields, and they spotted the tents Texan troops were setting up not far away. The site teemed with moving horses, men, carts, wagons, and armaments. Across the field at the

Mexican camp, Sylvie could see flags waving in the breeze and sunlight glinting on metal, probably rifle barrels and cavalry swords.

"This is it," Sylvie murmured. "I think we have reached the end of our travel." She and Annette shared a long look.

"They're just setting up, getting into position, and staring at one another?" Annette said.

"This can't last long; somebody's going to start shooting."

"The Mexican camp looks a lot bigger. How many men does Santa Anna have?"

"I don't know, possibly twice as many as our side. Andrew said about fifteen hundred."

Annette concluded they weren't likely to find a better campsite, and as they turned, Sylvie noticed the warmth of the sun and the pleasant breeze. If a battle weren't looming, she would have commented on the beauty of the spring day. Rousing notes from a bugle call drifted toward them, and it took a moment to realize what it could mean. They hurried toward a break in the trees that allowed a view.

Small figures on horseback emerged rapidly in neat rows from the Mexican camp and fanned out as they galloped across the field in the direction of the Texan army and the refugees sheltering in the woods behind its lines. Sylvie could make out the cavalrymen's scarlet trousers and their brilliantly colored, unfamiliar flags.

"My God, they are heading toward us, back where we left the cart!" Annette cried.

"No, wait." Sylvie grabbed her arm. "I think they are charging our cavalry, who are riding out—look over that way."

"Are they fighting, is it actually starting?"

Clusters of men on horseback emerged from the trees and raced toward the Mexicans. Riflemen were giving covering fire, for smoke was puffing above the line of trees. The Texan marksmen would have only a few shots before they might take to horseback as well, or swarm toward the enemy troops for hand-to-hand fighting. As the smoke faded, several dozen more men on horseback galloped toward the fray.

The shouting, cries, clashes of metal, shots firing, and screams of horses floated toward the women. The noise was delayed by distance so what the women heard grew disjointed from what they saw, the gap lending an unreal quality to the fighting. Now they could smell gunpowder. The riders knotted, entangled, and chased one another at the edges of the massed soldiers. Then hundreds more men came running from the Texan camp onto the field. They caught Mexicans who were off their horses and pulled others to the ground among the swirling legs. Swords flashed, rising high and flailing down; rifle barrels gleamed as the butts were used as bludgeons, up and down, then raised high again, until another bugle call sounded.

The Mexicans were turning, retreating toward their camp. A few Texans rode in pursuit, then reined in their horses and began pacing the area as they hesitated and watched. The Texans gathered in clusters, and the clusters formed into a mass. A few riders came from the encampment, and several, probably officers, stayed apart as they engaged in discussion.

"It's over already?" Sylvie asked. "That was quick."

"They're just getting their first taste, I think. Come on, let's get back."

Sylvie and Annette hurried back and found Rachel and the children near the cart, which they had moved deeper among the trees. They had already heard about the battle from militia units moving along the road.

"It was Sherman's Cavalry who led the charge," Rachel told them. "And the First Company, the Mina volunteers, went in, too, to back them up."

"Really!" Sylvie exclaimed. "That was Andrew and Logan out there? Was anybody hurt or killed?"

"I don't think so, just some light wounds as far as we've heard. After they went in, the whole First Regiment got moving."

"What news—good for them!" Sylvie was thrilled. In spite of recognizing the dangers, she felt grim glee at the clashing, the Texans testing themselves against their enemy at long last. Her belly clenched with the rightness of it, as though she herself had been riding along and forcing the Mexicans to retreat.

The women went to work setting up camp. As the evening cook fires began wafting scents of meals, and children darted about playing, women moved along the refugee train to seek out friends and neighbors. Rachel returned from a walk with news about the First Company of Mina Volunteers.

"You'll be interested to know," she said to Sylvie, "that the men from Mina are being positioned at the center of the Texan lines as part of Ed Burleson's regiment. They expect to engage again soon, possibly tomorrow. Apparently a number of the militia captains are ready to order their men into battle, even if General Houston does not."

"And if they win, it will be wonderful. After what we saw today, I am hopeful," Sylvie said. "But should we talk, just among ourselves, about what would happen if, God forbid . . ."

"We must be ready to travel again, and fast," Rachel said. "If the Texans can't stop the Mexicans here, our army will break and retreat and regroup somewhere."

"Where can they go?" Sylvie asked. "That's Galveston Bay just across the fields, the river is on that side, and the bayou is behind us. The idea of surrendering to Santa Anna is impossible. Think what happened to the prisoners at Goliad." She stopped before adding the fate of the men at the Alamo, for which Rachel needed no reminder.

"Well, if our side pulled back toward Harrisburg and the Mexicans went after them, maybe we could wait till it's clear and head across the river toward Louisiana."

Sylvie shook her head at Rachel's idea but did not argue more in front of the children.


As the women went about their chores the next day, they took turns to visit a nearby clearing. As they looked across the fields, they saw soldiers on both sides creating defensive positions, digging breastworks and positioning cannons. In the nearer Texan camp, tents were aligned, campfires burning, wagons of ammunition ready, and men and horses moving in orderly patterns. Now and then, the armies exchanged volleys of fire only to fall quiet again.

The sense of dread, of their lives hanging in a balance, made the morning the slowest and longest Sylvie could recall. The children grew restive, as the adults were too preoccupied to give their usual attention or complete routine tasks. At midday, Annette stoked the fire to rewarm rice and beans.

After the simple meal, Rachel told the children they would gather in the tent for a rest. "If the Mexicans can take their *siesta* every afternoon, we might as well, too," she said.

With the children settled, Rachel lingered to talk with Annette and Sylvie. She had her long-barreled pistol ready; it would give her two shots. Annette showed where she had lined up the kitchen knives and longer hunting knives, and they reviewed their plan for hiding the children in the woods, back from where Sylvie and Rachel imagined they would stand and fight. They recognized their fate as young women could be grim, as even disciplined Mexican soldiers were allowed some time for marauding after a hard-fought victory.

"What do you think about the efficacy of prayer?" Rachel asked.

Annette and Sylvie looked blankly at her. "Couldn't hurt," Annette said finally. "We'll just keep our weapons ready."

"Is it the case that none of us believes our side will win?" Sylvie said.

"Of course they will," both women replied.

Rachel went into the tent to nurse the baby. The children stayed quiet; it seemed they could fall sleep any time they had the chance. The afternoon, hot and sunny, wore on. Sylvie found herself nodding off where she sat before the tent in a bit of shade, her own pistol tucked under her skirt, ready at hand. Annette sat nearby, doing some mending.

Then the air exploded with cannon fire, followed by gunfire. The thunder of artillery shook the ground. Rachel hurried out, and the three women crouched together. Smoke drifted through the trees, and a riderless horse raced by on the road. Their plan to remove the children was not mentioned.

"I am going to look," Sylvie said. She ran toward the clearing and had to nudge through the crowd gathered to watch the commotion of horses, wagons, men, and armaments moving across the fields. After particularly sharp explosions, the crowd drew back collectively. Then rumbling followed, like soft, distant thunder. Sylvie's heart pounded, and her soul rose with tension and hope. Men on horseback slashed with sabers, men on the ground fought in tight clusters, and then a heavy, dark line of men swarmed from the center of the Texan line into the Mexican camp.

The crowd began to roar cries of encouragement, screaming, "Remember the Alamo!" and "Remember Goliad!" A few stretch-er-bearers carrying wounded men approached the near edge of the field, where tents were set up as a field hospital.

"I have to do something," Sylvie said. "I can't just stand here."

"Well, come on, then." A woman nearby tugged at her sleeve. They made their way through the trees and emerged near the hospital tents. Medics were carrying wounded men from the battle and laying them in regular lines on the grass. A man wearing a stethoscope saw the two women approaching and came from a tent. He handed Sylvie a pail of water with a dipper and jammed a roll of bandages ripped from cloth into her other hand.

As Sylvie stepped among the men on the ground, several called to her for water. She went to them one by one, doing her best to ladle water into their mouths as they leaned to the side or stretched upward; a few with leg wounds were able to sit and take the dipper from her. Then someone was asking for her. She heard her name, repeated a few times along a row, a garbled murmur. She looked ahead anxiously, and as she moved, she brushed flies off a few bloodied faces of men who were unconscious or otherwise beyond caring. No one looked familiar, and she realized she was looking for Andrew when she saw, with a start, Logan Vandeveer. He was gazing at her in mute appeal, propped up a bit on one elbow and pressing with the other hand on his lower ribcage. Black blood seeped between his fingers.

Sylvie sank down and offered him the dipper. He raised his head, and the water sloshed a bit around his lips; then as he let his head drop again, it rolled in rivulets back toward his ears. Sylvie could see blood draining in a little stream below his shoulder, puddling up on grassy dirt faster than the earth could absorb.

Sylvie began to say *Ave Marias*, one after the other, as she had following deaths that had visited her life; the urge went far back to her earliest losses, reaching past more recent memories. She pulled at the roll of bandages and ripped more of Logan's shirtsleeve to see the wound near his shoulder. Then she wound cotton flannel strips over and under the upper arm several times as Logan blanched and grit his teeth.

"Just stop!" he finally said.

Sylvie glanced up and saw the physician working his way down the row of prostrate men and boys, coming in their direction.

"*Médecin! Ici, vite!*" she screamed at him. Later, she wondered about reverting to French, but the medic had noted her, apart from all the cries and groans in English and Spanish. He looked sharply at her and Logan and came over, skipping half a dozen men in between. A man next to them was half-sitting up and looked ready to offer help. His foot was bulging in bloody shapes from rents in his leather boot.

The physician leaned over Logan, asking his name, and then began repeating it loudly, slapping gently at his cheeks. As Logan tried to reply, pink foam bubbled out between his lips. The physician checked the bandaging Sylvie had done and let go of Logan's upper arm. He gently pulled Logan's hand away from where it pressed on the larger wound, and Sylvie looked away while the physician reached inside the torn abdomen to feel the organs and locate any bullet. Sylvie, kneeling, lowered her head to fight the blackness tunneling her vision. When she looked up again, Logan's eyes had rolled back, and he fell uncon-scious. The physician looked at Sylvie and shook his head briefly.

"*Non! C'est impossible!*" She was emphatic and frightened that she could not remember any English.

"*Il est votre mari*, your husband?"

"*Non, non; un ami.*" No, a friend.

"*En anglais, mademoiselle*, he has a chance of surviving, as the bullet went through cleanly and has gone out the other side. If sepsis sets in, though, it will be dangerous. His spleen is torn, and I cannot stop all the bleeding. The intestines and one kidney were grazed, but they will heal and will still function. But prepare yourself."

"He is young and strong," she protested, words in English finally arriving.

"We will take him to the tent and get him stitched up immediately. After that, if you can get him someplace where he can be taken care of . . ." The physician glanced about as though something so unlikely might be spotted. He signaled to two stretcher-bearers who were heading back toward the battle. They turned and came over, and the three coordinated moving Logan. The physician's attention quickly shifted to other men in the line. Sylvie walked a ways by the stretcher as the bearers moved toward the surgery area. Logan remained unconscious, but his eyelids fluttered slightly and he took ragged breaths.

Medics shooed her away from the tent, and she returned to offering water to the lines of wounded men. She stopped to bind a couple of shallow wounds until she ran out of strips. Suddenly she realized it had grown quiet; the battle had stopped. Her head still swam with noise, though, and her ears were ringing. The air smelled more of iron than of gunpowder—more of blood and of excrement, foul in the heat. Turkey vultures circled overhead already, rasping their crude excitement.

The stream of wounded slowed, and now men were walking on their own back toward the tents, saying it was over and the Texans had won a resounding victory. They would stop to kneel by their comrades or to help carry others. Sylvie guessed several hours had gone by before she felt she was not needed any longer. As militiamen taking up their duties had nudged her aside, she wandered the trampled grass back toward the surgery tents. She wondered how Logan was doing, but sentries urged her away.

On the road, men caked with blood and grime pushed by in groups, not really seeing her. Many were shouting, proclaiming their victory. Among them, she spotted Andrew walking, stumbling off and on, at the edge of a group. He was streaked with dark dirt, soot, and blood, though his face and hands showed pale moons where he apparently had washed. His hair looked oddly neat, given the overall dishevelment. He carried his rifle in one hand and wore two pistols shoved in his belt. The butt of the rifle looked as though it had grown dark, bloody fur. She realized how thin he was, that he could have shoved yet more pistols in along the belt against his shrunken torso. He carried a pack, and a canteen was slung crosswise across his chest.

Sylvie watched him approach. It was as though he could not see more than five feet ahead and had to look carefully at the road and at each camp he passed. It was so painful to watch that she went to meet him. She took him by the arm and fell into step next to him; he finally looked at her and said, "Sylvie!" in a surprised tone.

"Logan is in surgery, and he is alive," she said. "He's badly wounded, though."

Andrew nodded. "Thank God he's alive. I saw it happen. A Mexican sabered him, after he was shot and went down. We won, did you hear?"

"Yes. So it's over?"

"It's over for now. They have no reinforcements in the area. We've killed hundreds, maybe half the army. Santa Anna has not been found, so his men aren't acting without their commander. Unless it's a trick so they can murder all of us. But we're disarming them to prevent that."

"What about you? How much of this blood is your own?"

"I think I'm all right." He stopped still in the road and looked at her, beseechingly. They moved off to the verge, so others could stream by.

"You might not even realize it if you are wounded," she said. She began to look more closely at his chest. He pulled off the pack and canteen, and she pushed aside torn remnants of his shirt.

"Let's get you to our camp, at least. We can wash the cuts. You were fighting with knives or bayonets, is that right?"

"Yes, toward the end. We were in the middle of the line, so we charged the center breastworks. But we overran them in minutes. After we shot at them all we could, we fought with our rifle stocks. I don't think they'd ever seen starving, enraged Kentuckians screaming and running at them. They were just getting up from *siesta*, and very few of them were ready to fight. Do you realize how stunning this is? We marched for six weeks, avoiding any kind of fight, only to slaughter them in twenty minutes when we finally stood our ground."

"Twenty minutes!" Sylvie was astonished. "It seemed like an hour, two hours."

They proceeded slowly, as Sylvie guided him toward their camp.

"I'll wait here for a minute if you don't mind." Andrew sank to the ground near the tent, sitting cross-legged. "Then I'll report back."

He did not question anything as Rachel and Annette swarmed to check his wounds and pronounced he would live. While they were tending him, the children held back, frightened by his appearance.

"Let me get you something to eat," Rachel murmured.

"Some water, first?"

"Oh, of course. I'm so stupid; forgive me," Sylvie said.

As Andrew sat, bright red bloomed on a pant leg now pressed against his thigh. It became purple, then black, as blood absorbed into the thick, dark cloth. Sylvie watched to see if it gathered more, but the flow subsided.

"Let's get your pants down, and I'll clean the wound," Rachel said. "We'll use black pepper to stop the bleeding. Annette, get the pepper."

"No, ladies; I'll keep my trousers on. It's nothing grave. I would feel it, if it was."

Rachel looked at him doubtfully and handed him a plate with two biscuits. He absently took a bite, but he could not swallow it, no matter how many times he softened it with sips of water. Sylvie tried not to look at the stock of his rifle, it was coated so heavily with blood, hair, and white bits that could be bone or brain. Yet her gaze kept returning to it.

"Annette, take his rifle and clean that off," Sylvie finally said.

Annette had brought the pepper, but as she reached for the rifle, her hand whipped back. "Holy Mother of God."

"Do it, please."

"Coffee," Rachel pronounced.

"Brandy," Andrew said. "Or a couple of shots of bourbon, if you don't mind."

They looked at each other and shrugged, and Rachel got the coffeepot. The coffee did seem to revive him, as if from a dream, pulling his mind into the present from wherever it was roaming.

"How are all of you, Rachel, and the children?" He looked around, as though surprised to find himself among them. "Sylvie, you are looking well, though I see your dress is soiled."

He spoke with such gentility, Southern manners reasserting themselves, that the women burst out laughing. Andrew smiled ruefully. "I hardly know where I am. That was some ferocious fighting."

He placed his hands on his knees, palms up, and stared straight ahead. The women watched and exchanged glances over his gaze, which stared off into the distance again. Gradually, he pulled his attention back.

"What are you planning to do?" he asked. "Now that we've won, you don't have to flee anymore. Everyone can just go home."

After a moment, Rachel said, "We will rest, and then we will go back and see what homes may remain to us. Are you sure it is over? Can we rely on that?"

"Wait a few days to make sure all the Mexicans are captured and securely dealt with. And then, yes, let's go back home. We'll own this land now. I think that's why we just went through this bloody hell. Or we will eventually; sooner, now, rather than later.

He added, "Mexico will attack us again, of course, but not for a while now that their revered Santa Anna is defeated. We just need to capture him; it seems he's disappeared."

Andrew tried to get up, but he moved so stiffly that Sylvie took his arm to help him. He said he needed to report to his unit, and still holding his arm, she began walking with him. At a quiet place, Andrew led them into the trees, away from campsites and people milling about on the road.

They stopped, and he put his arms around her. She leaned against his body; it was so hard now with the bones stretching the skin directly underneath. Her head fit in a hollow under his collarbone. As she relaxed into his clasped arms, she began to weep, the tears flowing on their own. He remained so silent and still, Sylvie wondered if some ranges of feeling had just been burned out of him. She had planned to use a pistol to defend against marauding soldiers, and now that state of fear seemed unreal, so remote it had to be more than only an hour or two in the past.

"Thank you," she said. "*Merci beaucoup.*"

"I love it when you speak French," he said.

"You do?" She looked up at him, releasing an arm to wipe her eyes. They exchanged a smile.

"I need to check on Logan," he said. "As a sergeant, I'm responsible for his welfare. I have to see our captain, Jesse, and get accounted for, and find out our new orders. I'll come back and see you as soon as I can. We have to figure out how to take care of all of you, and where we're going next."

"Let me know where Logan has been taken," Sylvie said. "I can at least make sure that he has water, or food, once he can eat something. We'll rely on seeing you again soon."

Andrew's hand stroked down her shoulder, then her arm, and grasped her hand briefly. He moved off, and she stood still for a few moments, watching him. Then she turned and looked up at the blue sky, savoring the feeling of safety imparted by those brief moments. It was the first time she had felt safe, she realized—for weeks, certainly, but for even longer—perhaps years. How good it was, to lean into his strong frame.

She tried to memorize the sensation so she could call upon it anytime she needed security or peace; would she wear out the memory over the coming days and weeks? For now, the sense of his body was still alive with hers, a comforting energy. She had felt herself come into keen focus within his gaze, when he had hardly been able to take in anything else. As she walked back to camp, she brushed absently at dry blood streaking her blouse and skirt. Some was Andrew's, and some Logan's, and some came from the unnamed others on their side of the battlefield.

Chapter 21

**April 1836**
**Near the San Jacinto River**

Two days later, Rachel and Sylvie were pausing in a clearing to gaze over the site of the battle. It looked like a field again, except where rows of fresh earth rose over the bodies of six hundred Mexican troops quickly buried. The Texans, by contrast, had lost only nine men. Sylvie reflected that Logan was still living, or he would have been the tenth.

This amount of death presaged disease, and the women worried about typhus and malaria, in addition to the dysentery and measles already rampant among the refugees. Nearly two thousand people—the Mexican prisoners, the refugees, and the Texan army—were swarming over this small area, all wanting clean water, food, and firewood. The Mexican army's supply wagons held abundant provisions, and the Texan troops had divided these among themselves, the refugees, and the prisoners. But the supplies would soon be depleted.

"We have to get moving, even though everyone is still worn out," Rachel said. She pressed a handkerchief against her nose as the breeze shifted across the field. "How can the bodies be adequately buried when the land is so boggy and low?"

"I'm worried about measles, that the children could become sick," Sylvie said. "We're all being weakened by dirty water and miasmal vapors off the bayou. Plus they have rashes from mosquito bites."

Several acquaintances from Gonzales had died of measles recently. One small grace arrived, as a woman offered Sylvie a pair of boots, saying her daughter had perished and she hoped someone else could use them. Sylvie accepted the boots gratefully, without fearing contagion since she had already had the measles. After slipping them on and lacing them up, she luxuriated in no longer being barefoot.

"I'm worried about illnesses, too—though my brood are tough little chickadees," Rachel said. "And it's a fine balance between the need for rest and the need to get back on the road."

"Think of the help we'll have for the trip back. The officers are assigning men and sorting out horses and wagons to accompany us. We'll get going soon."

"You'll get no argument from me," Rachel said. "But Sylvie, where will you go, ultimately? Back to Edna, if you can meet up with Jim and Sarah and the others?"

"Yes. If I stay with you in San Felipe, I expect the Kerrs will come by there on their way back. And then I'd continue on with them to the farm."

The two resumed walking, and Rachel glanced several times at Sylvie with a knowing smile. "There's another choice, you know."

"What's that?"

"Mina, my dear girl. But if you can't imagine that as a choice, I'm certainly not going to do it for you."

"That town's been burned, too."

"Not burned down, though—nothing like Gonzales—just a few houses damaged. I do want you to think strongly about your own position after all you have been through. Is Edna really home for you?" Rachel looked at her directly. "It could be Mina if you return feelings for that young man who's been so attentive to us. Seeing as he's a cousin of mine, that's a plus as well.

"Or you may head back home—truly back home—to Illinois. I hear many of the settlers talking about that, getting the women and children back to the States before the Mexicans regroup to attack again."

"Home," Sylvie sighed. "I don't know . . . where is that?"

"Don't just settle for the farm at Edna like a good niece who'll end up a spinster. Home is where a woman makes it. It's where she and her man stake their claim, and where she has a hearth, a stove, and a rocking chair. Where her babies will be born. Why, I've told you about how I ran off with my second husband, Isaac. We were just plumb in love, crazy for each other, and my father was dead set against giving his permission. It's hard to recall why he was, except he thought I should take my widow's claim for my own land. Can you imagine, remaining a widow when I was only eighteen?

"Anyway, there was something bold about the fire in our blood, and it turned everything around. My father finally relented and set us up with the house and land in Gonzales. In the meantime, we had Isaac's place in San Felipe, and that is a home I can return to now, thank the heavens above."

"Rachel, I admire that at this point in your life, you can recall the things you are most grateful for." Sylvie was moved and bent to look at a cluster of wild strawberries, the fruits still tiny and green. She feared her emotion might embarrass Rachel.

"Well, it is as they say: what is the content of your character when you have nothing? And what is it when you have everything? Shouldn't that content be the same?"

"You're right, of course. Yet I think how many times during this trip I've been angry with you. I am sorry for that."

"Yes, it's turned out all right so far." Rachel broke into a laugh. "Imagine anyone being angry with me! But I think of your steadfastness and your help with the children, and I will be forever grateful. I mean this, Sylvie, that you are to think of me as a sister in the future and call on me at any time, whenever you need something and I can be of service."

"Why, thank you, Rachel." They paused briefly to look at each other.

"Don't turn all blubbery on me." Rachel waved her hand as though shooing away a fly. "You'd do the same."

"Yes, I hope so." Sylvie smiled, and they walked on quietly.

At the campsite, Andrew was waiting for them, looking a bit impatient and also a good deal cleaner than the last time they had seen him.

"Sylvie, can we take a walk? I would talk with you for a few minutes."

"Yes, I think so." Sylvie glanced around the campsite, which was orderly and calm in the early evening, and Rachel nodded at her.

"Wherever did you get that lovely shirt?" Sylvie asked, as they set off along the road. It was made of creamy broadcloth with a bit of ruffle and a band at the neck instead of a collar.

"Why? Does it look Mexican to you? And these boots—look at the quality! I wasn't too hopeful that their quartermaster would have a pair big enough for my feet, but what good luck. They're new, and they'll last a few hundred miles, at least." He paused to lift one foot and bobbed it to admire the shine on the black leather that rose nearly to his knee.

"So their supply wagons had not just food but clothing, too."

"Well, uniforms and such—and something even better. Let's get to a quiet place, and I'll show you."

"Andrew Magill, you're in quite a jovial mood. Is Logan doing better?"

"Oh, he is. He's sitting up and able to take a little soup. Not ready for whiskey, yet, but he can croak out a bit of conversation. The sad news is that a man from Mina was killed in the battle. He was a good comrade, and he leaves a wife and children. Jesse, our captain, has a bad wound to his hand, and Sam Houston himself took a shot in the ankle."

As they walked briskly, Andrew said the militia volunteers would soon be free to help the refugees start their return trip. He was scanning the trees farther back toward the bayou, and after a few minutes suggested turning on a side path. They followed a faint trail toward a copse of trees.

"Aren't there snakes back here?" Sylvie's voice rose.

"You'll see; it will be all right."

They stepped over a few logs and around some shrubs and entered a small clearing where sawed sections of log were arranged in a semicircle. Andrew motioned grandly for her to take a seat and sat next to her. They spent a few silent moments looking at the sky and listening to the birds call through the falling dusk.

"Oh . . ." Sylvie sighed. "It's so good to be away from crowds of people. I welcome every moment of quiet, and I hardly know any longer what privacy feels like."

"It is good to be here, especially with you. I can't tell you how different life feels now without the war looming over us. I can go back home, at least for a while. We need to get back, because with so many settlers gone, the Comanche raids probably will be a bigger threat than the Mexicans during the summer and fall."

"How is your house, have you heard? I hope it wasn't burned."

"Apparently it's fine—at least still standing. Boys from town drove off all the cattle before the Mexicans got there and sank all the boats in the river to hide them. The troops passed through pretty quickly; it's so remote, it wasn't worth their trouble. And you? Are you set on returning to Edna?"

"Yes, I think so, for the near future."

She glanced up, and the two looked at each other steadily for several moments.

"Well . . . that gets me to the point of what I want to say. I promised your Uncle Jim that I wouldn't speak to you until I'd survived the coming battles. That was last winter, and here we are, survivors."

"I know. I overheard you two speaking, that night."

"Sylvie—you were eavesdropping?"

"No, not really. I was finishing a chore in the kitchen, and I couldn't help overhearing. You know how it is when you suddenly hear your name."

"And you don't mind?"

"Mind what?" She smiled.

"Well, I wouldn't ask to see you alone if I hadn't received his blessing. I have far too much respect for you to do anything other than that."

"How gallant," she murmured. Tears began to fill her eyes.

"Naturally, what I'm asking is if you'll to agree to . . . uh . . . a courtship. With me."

Sunset was streaking pink and orange through the haze from campfire smoke. Her ears were ringing with the echoing thud coming up from her heart. She suddenly thought of Cahokia, of her dreams from the Jarrot House ballroom, of how her half-brother Laurent would have liked Andrew, and of how Jeanne would disapprove of everything here and now: sitting alone with a young man in the darkening woods, wearing her plain, worn-out dress and secondhand shoes, Andrew in torn, stained pants and pilfered Mexican boots and shirt. Not to mention that he came from Kentucky and was a Protestant.

"Do you?" he asked.

"What?" Sylvie was jarred into the present.

"Like the idea? I mean, of us courting, of having an understanding. I don't know how people do this or what more I'm supposed to say. I'm sorry."

She had to smile, even laugh a little. "I don't know, either, really. I feel like that former world has been ripped away and burned up. Fancy-dress balls, the mothers who arrange everything—it's an artificial place out of some past I can barely recall. How quickly society can collapse." She turned to give him a searching look. "Here what matters is that you are alive; we are alive. And you, Andrew, manage to keep living. That alone does say something."

"May I take it that you are saying yes?"

He moved off the log and dropped to his knees in front of her.

"Yes," she answered hesitantly. Then, "Yes, yes!" A thrill of being alive and a soaring hope started from the same place in her core and ran through her veins in exhilaration; it clenched her hands and firmed her lips in a greediness she had not known before. She breathed deeply, stared at the pink-swirled sky, smelled the woods, the dampness rising from the creek and the dusky ground, the sweat of the human body near hers, the salty, earthy smell of herself.

"I am so glad." Then he was closer, and his arms were so strong, his look vulnerable and sincere. They clung to each other, their bones rubbing through fatless skin and worn fabrics. They kissed, long and exploringly.

She pulled back a bit to see him better, their eyes just inches apart. His were a lovely hazel that shifted color a bit. He loosened her braid, arranging her hair to gaze at her face with the dark tresses tumbling about it. He took a deep breath, and she could feel him tensing. They drew apart, but he sat close and kept his arm behind her, his palm firmly on the log so she could lean comfortably against him if she chose.

She feared she looked dreadfully thin, her big, dark eyes ringed with circles from fatigue, her normally heart-shaped face hollowed at the cheeks. How haggard she felt, yet she tried to maintain a graceful posture, even while her dress bagged at the waist. He looked away, and she tried to remember the thread of their conversation.

"Oh—I almost forgot," he said suddenly. "Now that things are settled between us, I have something for you."

He reached for the jacket and bag he had set aside and withdrew a leather pouch. He tugged the drawstring open and angled it so the contents would pour into her lap. A stream of silver coins ran down, piling up and gleaming on the worn, dark calico. Sylvie was stupefied. It was a lot of money in Mexican silver, but it carried little meaning: they could not eat it, drink it, or take it as medication. There was little they could buy around here, though it held promise of being useful in some future time and place.

"What is all this? Why are you showing it to me?" she asked.

"We divided up the Mexicans' supplies, and that included a chest of silver, probably the payroll. Will you take some for the things you're going to need?"

"Are you certain?"

"Perfectly. Then you can pack a chest full of linens, china, silver, or whatever it is a woman wants to bring to her home, like pillowcases and curtains. I hope there's enough."

"For a courtship? You're running a bit ahead. I'll just want a couple of decent dresses and a pair of shoes, new shoes."

"You don't need those to impress me—unless you want them, of course. I'll need some time, maybe six months, to help defend Mina and make sure the town is a safe place to live."

Sylvie nodded gravely. "By next fall, we should be able to tell whether this courtship is a good idea or not."

"Maybe you can go to New Orleans now, to stay safe and get the goods you want for a household. But the problem would be, I wouldn't get to see you often, which I could do if you're at Edna."

Andrew looked so apprehensive that she laughed and patted his arm. She enjoyed sifting her fingers through the coins, which weighed down her skirt to form a well between her legs. She took his hand, and he grasped hers and leaned against her. "But you earned this, and you will need it, surely," she said.

He looked at her in surprise. "I am keeping some. But I took a hard look all around, and you're the only one who . . . who . . . means something to me, the reason for what I am doing here. There you are, apart. You're just not like anyone else. You are so pretty and smart and steadfast . . ." He lifted his face and shut his eyes. "Oh, I'm no good at saying things like this. You must know what I mean."

"You are becoming so romantic. Would it be easier in French? Try, *je t'adore*."

"I know a little French, and that doesn't mean 'love.'"

"No, not quite. Adoring someone is a good start, though."

They fell quiet as she leaned into his arm and found the place for her head in the hollow of his shoulder. She tried out the idea that he found in her presence the meaning for his striving and suffering. The more she leaned, the more silver slipped out, the coins leaking and falling to the earth, the pile subsiding.

Sylvie began to chuckle. "Look at us, all worn and thin and wrinkled. Is this what we'll be like as old people? Just think, a courtship beginning this way."

He grinned at her. "Don't worry; you clean up pretty good."

At that, she laughed outright, and he joined her. "I haven't laughed like that in ages," he said after a time. "Or felt so happy. Back home in Kentucky, the men in my family have the reputation of being quite good-natured and—take heed—growing to weigh around two hundred pounds."

He waved at his near-skeletal frame and after a moment became more serious.

"I was absolutely ferocious when we finally started fighting, like a madman with all the pent-up fury bursting out. This was different from when I've been on patrol or out rangering. Then I had to think through things and stay alert, scout for signs, follow even the faintest track, watch every bush.

"This was just, 'Get the agony over,' the weeks of marching, wearing out our boots, running short on food, and repeatedly getting sick—plus seeing how pathetic and run-down all the settlers were and not being able to help. It's like I don't know that back-home part of myself anymore, the part that is easygoing, likes a party and fine food, and enjoys races and wrestling. Maybe I felt that way in Mina for a little while."

She was nodding. "We'll do that again, someday."

It was getting dark; time to get back. After embracing for more kisses and carefully retrieving the silver, they started on their way together though the warm and living night.


Two of Rachel's boys became ill during the night and were racked with spasms. Sylvie barely slept, and in the morning she felt drained of energy. Heat rose in flushes up to her forehead, and her stomach wrenched at the first sip of coffee. As she sat near the campfire, she decided she was too weak and shaken to share her news. She would tell Rachel and Annette about the courtship, or informal engagement, as soon as her energy and spirits rose to be worthy of such an announcement. Or, she wondered, should she wait and tell Uncle Jim first? It hardly seemed to matter as she poked a stick at the ashes from the cook fire. She was vaguely concerned by her sweating and listlessness.

"There's a ship! A schooner is coming into the bay!" Annette bolted into the campsite, shouting the news. "Scouts think it's John Linn's ship."

"Our John Linn—Sarah's brother?"

"Yes, and they say he'll bring supplies. He is the army's quarter-master, remember."

"Oh, hallelujah! Can we go and watch? Where is he coming in?" Sylvie jumped up and looked in the tent, where Rachel cuddled a boy under each arm, their faces pale and frowning, their eyes shut tight.

"Dysentery, I think," Rachel murmured.

"Holy Mother of God, protect us. But Rachel, did you hear? I am going to see what's happening and find John, and I'll bring back whatever I can."

Sylvie hurried across the fields toward the shoreline where a crowd of soldiers and settlers was gathering. Everyone was talking freely and sharing yet more news. The Mexican General Santa Anna had been found hiding in a ditch and wearing the clothes of a common soldier. Sam Houston was negotiating a treaty of surrender that the defeated general—and dictator of Mexico—would sign.

Sylvie recognized the schooner anchored in the bay, though three years had passed since her voyage from New Orleans. Crewmen were rowing several long boats toward shore, and as the first arrived, men waded out to pull them up. The crowd gave a rousing cheer but otherwise held back. Soon men were carrying crates and bags toward the army's headquarters, while others launched the boats to shuttle back to the ship. The crowd began to scatter toward different places where they hoped to gain a share of the provisions, and Sylvie wandered among them, hoping to catch sight of John Linn. Finally, she approached one of the crewmen and asked for his whereabouts.

"The captain? He went to the army headquarters early this morning to translate. Sam Houston is negotiating the surrender with Santa Anna. That's what we heard."

Sylvie thanked him and made her way toward the headquarters. Men crowded there more thickly, and she had to nudge her way past groups intent in conversation. When she could see the officers gathered under a canopy, she recognized Sam Houston, who sat on a chair with one leg propped on another, his foot and ankle heavily bandaged. And there was John Linn nearby, looking tall, thin, and serious.

She wondered how she might get a message to him, but she was having trouble thinking. The crowd made her stiflingly hot; why was there no air this morning? She gasped at a sudden clenching through her abdomen, and her knees felt so weak she looked for a place to sit down. There was no such place; she had to return to the camp for rest and some air. Time jagged brokenly as she made her way back; it took mere moments to leave the field as her feet glided lightly. But long, effortful minutes passed on the road as she forced one step after another. More than once, she had to dart into the bushes to empty her bowels, horrified that anyone might catch a glimpse of her.

Annette was serving the midday meal when Sylvie arrived. She declined food and crept into the tent, where she stretched out on her bedroll near the two boys, who were now asleep. Annette brought her tea, which she sipped during moments of wakefulness over the next several hours.

Toward evening, Sylvie awoke and listened for some time to the pleasant rumble of voices outside. Her face was wet and her hair damp, but she felt peaceful and light, at ease and relieved. The man's voice was particularly nice. After a time, she realized it was Andrew's and that she would like to see him. She patted her hair and crawled out, wobbling a bit as she straightened, and stepped toward the group around the fire. Andrew was sitting near a large pile of boxes and packages.

"Food, coffee, and medicine," he said after they greeted each other. "All thanks to John Linn. He would have been here earlier, but his first shipload of supplies ran aground, and he lost the entire cargo. He had to go back and get new supplies, which he did at his own expense."

"We are ever so grateful. We might be using some of the medicine before too long," Sylvie said.

"I already have," Rachel said. "I've dosed the boys, and I think it will be your turn soon, Sylvie."

A circle of concerned faces was watching her: Andrew, Rachel, Annette, and even the children. Sylvie tried to toss her head and say she was fine, but the motion made her dizzy, and no words came out. She sat and listened as the others talked over the day's news. After a time, Andrew stood, saying it was time for him to leave, and looked expectantly at Sylvie.

"I'll walk with you a bit," she said. "Let me get my shawl." As she stepped away from the fire, cold air arrived as a shock on her clammy, damp skin.

"Sylvie, are you very ill? You don't look right," Andrew asked as they set out.

"I don't know. I felt sick earlier, but I'm better now. Still, I'll take some  medication that you brought. Thank you for doing that."

"Good; please do. You can rest tomorrow; Rachel won't leave with the boys so ill." After they walked for a bit, he asked, "You haven't told them about us, have you?"

"No, I'm sorry. I felt so unlike myself all day that I wanted to wait until my head was clear and my spirits were up to . . ." The thought drifted away as she forgot what she had meant to say.

"That's all right; there's plenty of time and better circumstances on the way. But Sylvie, listen to me: John Linn arriving with his ship changes everything. You can leave—he's heading to New Orleans for more supplies, and you should sail with him."

"What? What are you suggesting?" They had moved off the road into a clearing among some the trees.

"I'm afraid for your health, and you have to get away from here. You've told me about your cousin in New Orleans and how much you want to visit her. You could rest and get well there."

"Wait—yesterday told me you love me, I think, and now you want to send me away?"

"Sylvie, you're not listening. That is what most men—husbands and fathers—are trying to do for their families right now. I heard a number of them arranging with John Linn to get the women and children onto his schooner. And it's not just because of the disease here. They'll be safer inside the United States. Now that we're holding Santa Anna, the Mexicans will regroup and attack to try to free him."

"*Alors*, I am not sure what to do. But it doesn't feel right to leave everyone."

"John said he will take you; he's holding a place for you."

"You have already spoken to him!"

"Naturally."

The silence between them stretched out.

"You are telling me what to do." Sylvie stepped away. "You are already acting like—like—"

"Like a husband? Yes, I am. If your Uncle Jim were here, I would defer to him, but he'd tell you exactly the same thing, I'm sure of it."

"Oh, I am not so sure. He has been intent on staying here, being committed to the future of Texas. Do you think Sarah would take the children and leave for New Orleans, or go back to Missouri?"

"I think she might, actually, yes."

Sylvie tugged at the collar of her dress. Her chills had subsided, only to leave her breathlessly hot again.

"You may be right," she agreed. "Sarah likes to think things through, and she can be very logical. Maybe leaving would seem reasonable to her if it's only for a short time."

"John will be here during the day tomorrow, but they'll have to float the ship on the evening tide. You have overnight to decide. And what would keep you here? Rachel will have plenty of help now, including from me."

Sylvie looked at Andrew's lined face, the hardness of his brow and eyes. Where was the warmth, the tenderness she had seen and felt just the evening before? He was not amenable to her wishes now but aloof, even insistent. His large ears sticking out did not look silly, but stiff with determination. Did the prospect of becoming a husband change a man so quickly into being wooden and stern with the new burden of responsibility?

Sylvie did not realize she had spoken out loud, but Andrew was exclaiming, "Wooden? You find me wooden?" and looking exasperated.

"Well, how long do you want me to be gone?" she cried. "To be without you and apart? Do you think nothing of how I feel?"

"Oh, Sylvie." He moved to put his arms around her, but she pushed back. "We have to make sure Mina is a safe place to live, first."

"Answer me: how long? A year, two years? Do you have to defeat all the Comanche, too, before you'll ask me to come back? Not just the Mexicans?"

"No, no—as short a time as possible. But it will be some months, certainly. Here, come here . . ." He caught her arm and pulled her to him. He held her across the shoulders with one arm and stroked her head with his other hand. Then he lowered his arm and grasped her about the waist, reaching easily around her pitiful thinness.

"And am I to trust to your constant feeling—the constancy of your feelings—over that length of time?" Sylvie had her arms up between them, pressing against his chest.

"Yes, Sylvie, you can trust in that. My feelings will not change, and whatever do you mean, anyway?"

"Well, men. You know how men are."

He let go of her and stepped back. "Good Lord. I am not all men. I am me. I just want you well and taken care of, and alive. Is that too much to ask for a relatively short period of time?"

"No, it is not too much to ask. And so I would ask it, too. You will be back on the frontier. You'll be fighting, again, probably a lot. What's to keep you safe for me?"

"Now we are talking about impossibilities. If I am to make a home for us, that is what I have to do."

"Home," Sylvie said bitterly. "You want to send me back home for a while. Don't you see, I don't have a home, not like you have back in Kentucky with your parents and your childhood house—a place you can go back to."

"That's an idea; I could send you to my home. My parents would receive you, certainly, as my intended wife."

"Oh, dear. I don't think I could face that right now."

"Sylvie, you have some tasks to take care of, too. I got the impression from Jim that he is not your legal guardian, that you need to get your sister's permission to marry. Can you take care of that from New Orleans?"

"I don't know, but I can try. At least mail will get to her from there. She also has to settle my inheritance, and her husband will have to sign the legal papers. It's odd, how all along I assumed I would go back to Cahokia, yet now it sounds tiresome, like a difficult chore to be taken care of. Maybe I am not seeing things the right way because I am ill."

"Yes, most likely. Because otherwise an attachment to someone like me wouldn't cause you to feel reluctant."

At his self-mocking scowl, Sylvie had to smile. He did as well, and they stepped nearer each other to embrace.

"Give me a kiss, then, or several, before we part tonight," Andrew said. "And you can make up your mind by morning."

So they clung together for some time in the shadows, until enough people had passed by that Sylvie imagined rumors and gossip fairly flying through the camps. When they parted, she turned after a few steps and watched his figure striding down the road. He had such broad shoulders and moved with so much energy and confidence. Was her own vitality equal to that vigor? He had suffered, yet he was not diminished, as though all of this remained a great adventure.

She knew she would leave on the ship the next day, as John Linn had agreed. Scenes of enjoying Louisa's company—in a home with regular meals, a bathtub, and a bed—floated like a distant mirage. She had no idea until now how much she had been dreading the return trip with Rachel and the ox cart. As her head swam and her guts churned, the idea was loathsome beyond enduring.

Sylvie walked quickly back toward the campsite; at her last glance, Andrew had disappeared. She paused in the dark as a spasm racked her core. And then she began to suspect she was making a mistake, a major mistake. She should go with Andrew, jump on the back of his horse, ride off with him to Mina, and follow this surge of love and courage to make their home together.

That was what Rachel would do. But she would not.

# Part 3

Summer 1836 — Spring 1837

In the French communities of
New Orleans, Louisiana
and Cahokia, Illinois

Chapter 22



**July 1836**
**New Orleans**


SYLVIE RECUPERATED FOR TWO WEEKS at Louisa and Octave's house before she got up to take meals with them, and it was another week before she went outside to walk to the end of the street and back. Louisa had been badly frightened when John Linn appeared on the doorstep supporting a little creature with brown, bony limbs and wearing ragged clothes who turned out to be Sylvie.

The physician who visited periodically said that while she was recovering from dysentery, she might never be free of malaria; it could return anytime she was in a weakened state. He did not cup or bleed her, but instead gave her a powder called quinine, mixed in water. He said doctors in France were finding this new remedy, derived from the bark of a tree, quite effective.

Soon, Sylvie was taking breakfast with the others in the downstairs sitting room. Sunlight streamed in through the garden's trees, vines, and flowers onto a table covered with newspapers and magazines in French and in English, coffee cups, and baskets holding fresh bread, croissants, and beignets. Louisa and Octave enjoyed reading and discussing news each morning until he felt sufficiently informed to don his dark coat and walk to the offices of his family's trading business.

One morning in July, Louisa exclaimed over a page of the *New Orleans Bulletin*. "Here is an advertisement for Narcisse's new townsite! He is selling lots for houses to people from all over the East Coast, and even here, apparently."

"Are you talking about your brother, my cousin?" Sylvie asked. "He has become a land agent?"

"Yes, your favorite cousin, as I recall," Louisa said teasingly. "He's been quite successful with his law practice, and he bought enormous amounts of land for this town on the Okaw River; you can get there by steamboat, up from the Mississippi." Louisa read aloud, "'The location is most salubrious, with the finest soil, and is positioned to become the fastest-growing new town west of the Alleghenies.'"

"I believe all the new towns claim that," Octave said. "The next line will say, 'Lots are selling quickly, attracting the finest citizens,' and so forth. Oh, and, 'The soil is so rich that a family needs only half an acre to grow sufficient food to supply all their needs.'"

Louisa laughed. "Well, you are right, so I'll skip that part. But he has platted streets sixty feet wide, and alleys twenty feet wide. The town is forty-eight blocks, total, with a plaza and a main street that's more than ninety feet wide. How grand."

"It sounds like people would need more than one lot for growing food," Sylvie said.

"But families can't afford much more," Octave said. "Land prices rise higher every day. Many businessmen are getting hold of large parcels near growing cities and dividing them up for lots to cash in on the boom. Narcisse got in at a good time."

Octave wore a white shirt and brocade vest for his coming day of work. As Sylvie glanced at his neatly oiled dark hair and trimmed mustache, she recalled him as the casually dressed young man who had helped with the wheat harvest in Cahokia several years earlier. He'd seemed more attractive back when his work shirt was rolled up at the sleeves and his hair was tousled over a weather-tanned face.

And that brought thoughts of Andrew. She missed him, having grown used to seeing him regularly during their long trek. He should be back in Mina. Had he fallen ill, or worse? She had not heard from him.

"Not all these towns will succeed, mind you," Octave was saying. "Some have proven to be just schemes, even frauds. Settlers arrive to find no water and only hardscrabble, and not even a city hall where they can lodge a complaint."

"When did land become so expensive?" Sylvie asked.

"Everything is becoming dearer and dearer, not just land," Louisa said.

"It's true," Octave agreed. "We see that each week in the business. Cotton is bringing a higher price, and so are wheat flour, corn, whiskey, furs, buffalo hides—practically everything. Silver money is flooding in from Mexico, and it affects the value of money issued here in the United States."

As Sylvie poured more coffee, she noticed Louisa and Octave exchanging a glance as though reaching a silent accord.

"Oh, you must have seen my bag of silver. The fact it was still in my carpetbag shows how honest my fellow travelers were on board the ship. I was so ill, someone could have easily taken it."

Louisa smiled tentatively. "It's just that it is quite a lot of money, Sylvie, and we have wondered—"

"How I came by it?"

"I was going to say, we have wondered about safekeeping for it."

"You know it loses value every day, bit by bit," Octave added. "It takes more money all the time to buy things like bread, clothing, and imports from England and France. So investing your money in durable goods, or in some other manner, would be wise. I'd be happy to advise you."

"Thank you, Octave. I'll give it some thought. I do need to buy clothes, as you know." Sylvie gestured at the frilly housecoat borrowed from Louisa. She was reluctant to bring up buying goods to furnish a household. She wanted to talk with Louisa alone, first, about her possible engagement to Andrew Magill, and the right time had not yet presented itself.

Octave asked, "Where did the silver come from, Sylvie, if you don't mind my asking? News reports say that Texas has been extremely short on coin and long on barter, plus the paper scrip the new republic is issuing."

Sylvie told how the Texas militia had broken into a chest of silver in the Mexican supply wagons after the final battle and shared it out, along with food and clothing. It probably was the payroll for the

Mexican soldiers, she said, but half of them were dead, and the other half prisoners.

Louisa gaped at her. "Do you feel right about keeping it?"

"Yes, I haven't had any second thoughts."

"The spoils of war," Octave pronounced. "I guess that practice holds true even in this day and age."

"You didn't see the burned-out towns and decimated fields, the exhausted old people, and sick children, the refugees dying of illness. We were owed something."

The three sat in silence for a few moments until Octave said it was time for him to leave. Louisa went with him to door and returned to join Sylvie and wait for the morning post to arrive. Sylvie decided to eat another croissant; it was so flaky, buttery, and delicious coated with apricot preserves. Never had she eaten so much, nor so happily, as in the past week. She was beginning to fill out, but she still needed more weight to sustain any energy.

"Sylvie, I haven't really talked to you about our plans for my lying-in." Louisa lightly stroked her belly, slightly rounded under the silk *peignoir,* as she spoke openly for the first time about her pregnancy. "I want to have the baby at home in Cahokia, in *Maman's* house, near my sisters, brothers, cousins, and old friends, so everyone can meet this child. That way it will know that it has a big, welcoming family, even though we live far away from them."

Louisa said it would be ideal for Sylvie to travel upriver with her later that summer. Octave could not leave his work for that long and would join her later. When Sylvie fiddled with the knife on her plate and didn't reply, Louisa looked at her questioningly. A maid entered with the mail, and Louisa flipped through letters rapidly. "Ah, one for you!"

Sylvie reached for the folded paper and was surprised to see the return address was San Felipe, rather than Mina or Edna. She opened the letter, which was from Sarah Kerr.

*June 30, 1836*
*Dearest Sylvie,*

*I am writing from San Felipe, where we—Jim, Minny, I, and the household—have finally ended our trek. It lasted for three months, and you were wise, at the Sabine River, not to join us. I trust you are well and enjoying New Orleans. We spent weeks making our way back toward home, with several lengthy stops due to illnesses and their tragic consequences. When we reached Burnam's on the Colorado, we learned that our home in Edna had been sacked and burned. So we turned around and made our way back to San Felipe, where Jim, as one of the original settlers, still has property and friends.*

*I barely know how to tell you this, other than to write simply. We lost four children on the trip from Louisiana. Our baby Charles died at McKinney's Bluff after we crossed back over the Sabine River into Texas. He was sick twelve days with dysentery and measles. He is buried there, in the holy ground of a cemetery, so I will be able to visit his grave in the future. Anise suffers as well, from the loss of her little girl Edwina. The slave girl who was sick when you visited us during John Linn's stop died soon after, and our fourth loss was a baby just three days old, born to Rosanah. You can imagine how these sorrows compounded the misery of our ordeal.*

*Jim strongly wishes for Minny and me to return to Missouri for some months or longer, depending on how quickly the Mexicans regroup and attack again. So she and I will travel later this month, and she will enroll in the convent school at Ste. Geneviève. We hope to reach New Orleans by early August, and Jim wishes to know if you will travel with us. I assure him that the two of us will be fine, as we will have company among the great numbers of settlers' families traveling back to Missouri.*

*Please do write to let us know your plans, and to assure us of your continued good health. Rachel (the widow Mrs. Flint) gave us this address for your cousin's house and asks me to send her warmest regards. Minny also sends fond greetings.*

*Sincerely yours,*
*Sarah Fulton Kerr*

Sylvie set the page on the table, her hands trembling. She grasped a napkin and held it to her brimming eyes, alarming Louisa, who asked what was distressing her.

"The letter is from Sarah Kerr. Oh *mon dieu*, her baby Charles has died. How horrible for Sarah, and poor Uncle Jim—all the sons he's had have died. And he was so happy with Charles—we all were, and I loved him, too. And now, they cannot even go home because their place in Edna was sacked and burned."

"What a terrible chain of misfortunes! The poor woman, the poor family."

"And they lost three other children to illnesses. Anise and Shade's little Edwina, who was so charming, and her sister must miss her so much. And Rosanah's new baby, and another girl—oh, it's all my fault! I've already had the measles, and I could have stayed with them and helped, and then this wouldn't have happened!"

"Sylvie—Sylvie, get control yourself; please calm down. God dispenses these things, and nothing in this outcome was up to you."

Sylvie took several deep breaths and explained that on the voyage leaving Texas, John Linn had stopped at the Sabine River on the Louisiana border to deliver provisions to the refugees there, who were making their way back home. Sylvie had gone with him and crewmen in long boats out to the delta and asked around until they found the Kerrs' party. The refugees had camped for weeks along the enormous, flooded river area, and illnesses had begun to sweep through, especially malaria, measles, and dysentery.

"It was all so gray and watery, and it smelled so terrible, and I could not stay there."

"Of course you couldn't. You were very ill yourself. There is no question you did the right thing by coming here."

"But Sarah says twice that she hopes I'm in continued good health. She couldn't see how ill I was already? That is so hard to accept; she must think I'm a monster. Charles already had dysentery—everybody did, even me. But when he broke out with the rash, Sarah asked me to stay and help nurse the children. And I didn't. How did I say no? I can't even remember."

Louisa got up and hovered over Sylvie, stroking her shoulder. She murmured reassurances, saying that the situation was so grave nothing Sylvie could have done would have changed it.

"And now she writes so coldly; her tone is like a stranger!" Sylvie exclaimed through tears. "And she says Jim has asked whether I will travel back to Missouri with them. She herself doesn't ask me to, and she adds that Rachel and Minny send warm regards, but she herself does not. She must be terribly angry with me."

"With all the suffering and privations she has been through, the poor woman is likely in a state of shock. It's a wonder she can even write a coherent letter."

"You don't know Sarah. She is reasonable and logical to the core."

"Even someone like that—or especially someone like that— might find it too painful to acknowledge her feelings. I've seen people shut down and deny natural emotions, especially a mother whose baby has died. It can take some time to get beyond it."

Louisa was urging Sylvie up from her chair, saying she should get back in bed for a rest. She offered to read Sarah's letter and provide a separate viewpoint, if that would help. "When someone is tired and worn down, it's natural to take things harder, and messages can seem colder or more critical than they really are."

Back upstairs in bed, Sylvie sat propped against the pillows and resisted falling asleep. She had not told Louisa about her recurring nightmares set in a palette of gray—gray sand and river water, gray skies, gray people wearing colorless rags of clothing. She was at the Sabine River, and as she wandered among the refugees, no one saw her, their eyes fixed wide with horror, their mouths gaping with rotted teeth. And then the figure in the black cloak, who carried a scythe and turned his grinning skeleton face toward her, would make her wake up sweating and moaning.

"Time for more laudanum, I think." Louisa held the blue glass bottle to the light to check its level.

Too disheartened to protest, Sylvie accepted a spoonful. Now that Sarah's letter confirmed Sylvie's fevered dreams, the last thing she wanted was to fall asleep and see the baby, to recognize Charles in all his suffering, and Sarah and Jim's faces, and to see Death hovering gleefully over them all. The laudanum might grant her relief for a time.

Poor Uncle Jim; with all his mistakes and losses and attempts to start a new life, he might be able to forgive her eventually. But how could she make amends with Sarah? She would start by writing condolences, with notes for Anise and Rosanah as well. And those deaths—the children! She would add them to the tally of souls she prayed for whenever she wasn't too angry with God.

People she knew from Gonzales had died, too, with Armand prominently among them. She'd finally accepted the truth of this when she found his name on the official casualty lists published in the New Orleans newspapers. When the laudanum delivered dreams swirling with color and noise, he often appeared, and they went off dancing in a whirl, his eyes always close, regarding her warmly.


Sylvie took longer walks as the weeks went by, and the sunlight seemed to feed her bones. She began awakening with vigor rising in her core and color returning to her cheeks. Now she could often recall events in Texas without the thoughts running wildly and devastating her. Sometimes she was able to put a troubling thought completely out of mind, to be dealt with later.

Sylvie had replied to Sarah's letter, though it took several drafts over several days before her jumbled feelings became clear expressions of sympathy and sorrow, plus a heartfelt plea for forgiveness for deserting the family at the Sabine River. The first few pages soaked up so many tears that she had to keep starting afresh.

Holding a pen felt unfamiliar, and she tried to remember the last time she had written anything. Was it the shopping list she had jotted that final evening in Gonzales? She also answered letters from family in Cahokia, for Louisa had written immediately to let them know Sylvie was safe in New Orleans. Along with notes to Jeanne, Isabelle, and Aunt Lizette, Louisa's mother, Sylvie wrote to her nephew Etienne, saying she would like to stay with him in the old homestead house during her coming visit, if he still liked the idea.

Louisa confided additional news not mentioned in current family letters. Sylvie's older half-sister, Jeanne, and her husband, had suffered the death of an infant just weeks after his birth, in the past year. Louisa's mother had written that Jeanne was becoming yet more devout as a result.

On a brighter note, Vital Jarrot and Marguerite were enjoying married life, and he had served a year in the Illinois state Assembly. The crops were good, and since French wheat, wine, meat, and furs brought premium prices, family members were investing increasing amounts in the new railroad venture. Sylvie tried to imagine the project as Louisa described six miles of wooden tracks running along the eastern riverbank, even through the *Grand Marais*. They expected coal would bring a good price in St. Louis, given the city's rapid growth and the turbulent economic times.

While Louisa seemed to admire the venture, it was from a comfortable distance, as her own family was not involved. Octave called the railroad brilliant and progressive, and he believed the pooled resources of a group of prosperous people should cover the substantial risks involved.

Soon Sylvie and Louisa would see Cahokia and its changes for themselves. They bought tickets on a riverboat for late August.


A letter from Andrew Magill arrived one day while Octave was still at breakfast with Sylvie and Louisa. When Sylvie saw the cramped, vertical handwriting and the return address of Mina, she took a deep breath and opened it quickly.

*June 15, 1836*
*Mina, now Bastrop, Republic of Texas*

*Dearest Sylvie,*
*We arrived back home in Mina and mustered out June 1. The town had been ransacked, and my house was emptied of most of its contents. It is livable, though. We are trying to secure food by rounding*

*up cattle and farm animals, hunting game, and putting in some crops. You were wise not to come back here. The main danger at the moment is Comanche raids. We are so impoverished and distracted, they ride brazenly into town, and people have been killed in their own dooryards. A friend of mine, Conrad Rohrer, was shot by an Indian while he was saddling his horse. I have been appointed executor for his estate. Conrad mustered out with us on June 1, so it is hard to grasp that barely a week later, he died that way after surviving the battles. At times, I fail to understand the ways of Providence.*

*We escorted Cousin Rachel, Annette, and the children safely to San Felipe and left them there with friends. Logan continues to recover, and he receives kind ministrations from the few women in town. (My own rude health merits no similar attentions!)*

*The Texas Army is calling men up again, and I expect to enlist for five or six months. We hear that General Urea has four thousand Mexican troops near La Bahía, and ships are bringing thousands more to Matamoros. Santa Anna is still being held prisoner, and our Texas government is negotiating for complete surrender before letting Mexico have their defeated leader back.*

*This summer, our generals want to establish a perimeter line along the Colorado River and fight there—Mexicans to the south and east, Indians to the north and west. I will continue serving with Jesse Billingsley. I don't know when I will be able to write again if I am posted to some distant area. I obtained this single sheet of letter paper from a neighbor, Mrs. Mays, in exchange for a wild turkey that I shot.*

*My fondest thought is that you are well and safe in New Orleans. Please write and let me know if you go to Cahokia. You should send a copy of any letter to your Uncle Jim, too, as he'll get mail more regularly. Every day I tell myself that the reason for these struggles is so you and the other women can return, and we can have safe and happy homes.*

*With sincere affections, I remain your humble and devoted,*
*Andrew Magill*

*P.S. We've renamed this town so it won't be called by its Mexican name anymore. Now it's Bastrop, for that friend of Stephen Austin's, the Baron of Bastrop. (Though as you know, he's not a real baron of anything.)*

It was fortunate this letter had come through, since Andrew didn't have the paper to make copies and mail them separately, and he wouldn't be able to write again soon. Sylvie was thankful for the good news about Logan and the others but worried about the continued fighting. What a grim summer Andrew was contemplating, besieged on two fronts and scrounging for food. He was right; it was better for her to be in New Orleans. She had already written to both him and Uncle Jim with her travel plans and the address for mail to Cahokia.

The newspapers spread out on the breakfast table carried reports that Andrew had not mentioned. In May, Comanches had raided Parkers Fort, far to the west of Mina. They killed a number of the men and kidnapped two women and three children. The militia men, who were just returning, decided not to pursue the raiders right away because they would already have split up, distributed the captives among small bands, and ridden hundreds of miles to the west. Sylvie tried to integrate the news with what Andrew had written.

"He writes with a very compact hand." Louisa glanced at the letter, now lying on the table.

"Who said this is from a 'he'?" Sylvie asked, and Louisa smiled. With ample time to think while she recuperated, Sylvie had started to question her memory of the conversations with Andrew and their meetings in the copse of trees near the camp. With this letter confirming his regard, she felt more assured that she was not misleading herself with fevered imaginings. She had spoken of the courtship only to Rachel and Annette on her final day with them. Both had heartily approved of her accepting Andrew as a suitor and congratulated her with true happiness.

But here in the parlor in New Orleans, the world looked a great deal different.

"The letter is from a young man you would like," Sylvie said. "Or I should say, you will like him when you eventually meet."

"And how did you two meet?"

"Through Uncle Jim; their families knew one another back in Kentucky."

"*Kentucky!* Sylvie, don't tell me you've taken up with someone from Kentucky." Louisa added humorously, "Remember how we used to joke about 'Kaintucks' and how crude they were? That must mean he is *Anglais*, too, and not French."

"He is *Anglais*, and he is very much a gentleman." Sylvie wished that she had taken the initiative to describe Andrew earlier on her own terms, rather than having to answer defensively now. She told how he had ridden to Texas, gotten a land grant, and then had been accepted as a colonist in Mina. She described how he'd volunteered for the militia and fought in key battles, plus that Uncle Jim had given him permission to court her.

"So he qualifies as a colonist, and that means he can claim a substantial amount of land, now that Texas is a separate country and can distribute it," Octave said. "How old is he, and how much land can he get, do you know?"

"He's twenty-three, about four years older than I am. Under the old system, a man got a headright of one-third league, about fifteen hundred acres, to start. A married man got twice that. Also, Texas might award land grants for serving in the military and the ranger units."

"If they handle that the same way as the US did in the past, a man could get hundreds of acres for each term of military service. So this young man could be looking at thousands of acres. That sounds like a good prospect, Sylvie."

"He has grown fond of you, and do you return his feelings?" Louisa asked.

"I am quite fond of him. He was so helpful to us while we were refugees. He watched out for us and shared his provisions. He has land and a nice house in Mina. I saw the place when I visited in June, a year ago now. He and his cousin were setting up a store in town at the time."

"He is a *storekeeper*?"

Octave glanced at his wife and said, "If it's linked to a trading business, that can be quite profitable. Really, Louisa, men in your family have run mercantile businesses."

"My father had a store at one time—he even owned a tavern, and a hotel," Sylvie said, impatient with Louisa's tendency to cast Andrew in the least favorable light. She told how the military had requisitioned the store's supplies, and how Andrew and Logan were starting in the cattle business.

"There we are," Octave said with an air of satisfaction. "A young man with claims to adequate land, who already owns a house and has the initiative to start businesses. Cattle-raising sounds like a wise investment, given the grasslands in Texas. And Sylvie, you have a couple of years to see how he's doing, once things calm down."

"I need my sister's permission to marry in any case, or turn twenty-one."

"Oh, dear. That's your reason for going to Cahokia, isn't it?" Louisa asked. "You want Jeanne's permission and to get your inheritance settled. But I never imagined that would be so you could marry some *Anglais* from Kentucky and live on a wild frontier."

"Jeanne might see some advantage to your prospects with such a match," Octave said. "What do you think she'll say?"

Sylvie allowed that though Jeanne would favor the land and business prospects, she would object to Andrew not being French or Catholic.

"He is a *Protestant*?" Louisa protested. "Oh, Sylvie, you cannot possibly marry outside of the Church. You have to get him to convert if you are at all serious."

"I have thought about that," Sylvie said. "My Uncle Jim converted to Catholicism just before he married Sarah Fulton, after all. It can be done."

"Well, I must be off," Octave said. Louisa got up to see him off and returned to find Sylvie deeply engrossed in a newspaper.

"I am sure he must be a truly fine young man if you would consider him as a suitor," Louisa said in a conciliatory tone after some silence. She grasped Sylvie's hand. "And I trust you haven't made any promises or commitments, given how ill you were. You can't be held accountable for things you might have said while suffering a raging fever. You haven't been your usual self at all these past weeks."

Sylvie briefly squeezed Louisa's hand. "He was not my only suitor. There was another young man, who was Catholic, French, and from a prominent family. And he was quite comely. Oh, and he could dance so well. We often went riding when I lived at Gonzales."

"Now, he sounds quite nice, very suitable."

"Louisa, he is dead. He was killed at Goliad, along with four hundred other men. All those young men shot dead, murdered by the Mexicans who were holding them prisoner."

"My dear, I am so sorry. It's horrible, and I had no idea."

"He was dear. He was pursuing an interest in me. And now he is dead. While Andrew is alive. Do you see?"

Louisa looked strained. "I wasn't thinking of all you've been through, and I'm truly sorry. We'll talk more about Andrew and about your future when you feel better. The entire subject seems so upsetting it could hamper your recovery."

"It is upsetting to you, isn't it?" Sylvie responded.

As Louisa perused another letter, Sylvie looked about at the shelves displaying china and crystal, the silver tea and coffee services, the dark furniture with plush fabric, the satiny curtains swathed over lace panels at the windows. If any more goods were displayed, a person wouldn't be able to breathe. Yet Sylvie was suspicious of how quickly it all might vanish. Louisa and Octave's ease and security could all be burned at the touch of a torch. She pressed her hand on the table to feel its solidity, but the wood was exactly what made it so vulnerable to fire.

What would Louisa's world be like, if she and Octave lost the house, their possessions, or even the business? Would the content of their characters be the same as it was now? And would they ever be so harshly tested? Sylvie was not able to completely relax in the luxury surrounding her, as she had hoped she might.

Sylvie was copying her reply to Andrew's letter when Mathilde, the maid, announced a visitor. Louisa was out shopping and paying calls, but Mathilde assured Sylvie that this visitor wanted to see her in particular. "She came in the back way and is waiting in the kitchen."

"The kitchen? But why there?"

"You'll want to see her, Miss Sylvie," Mathilde replied, smiling broadly. "You asked for her often enough during your fevers."

Sylvie entered the kitchen to see a tall, well-dressed African-American woman, her hair bound in bright cloth above dangling gold earrings. She turned to greet Sylvie, and the one eyebrow that rose sharply askew could belong to only one person.

"Amy! Oh, is it really you? You look wonderful!" And Sylvie was a little girl again, rushing into Amy's embrace and feeling the motherly arms surround her.

"Sylvie, dear child! And you feel like one, you're so thin. But not as wan and pale as everyone said." Amy pushed her back a bit and looked her over, head to toe. "You're getting well, heavens be praised."

"You look so very well and prosperous. What a beautiful dress—and, oh!" Sylvie, clasping Amy's hand, noted the ring she wore. "You are married?"

"Yes, indeed. Life has been quite fine for me."

"Where are you living, and are you in service?"

"I live across town, in a small house with my husband, where *Les Gens de Couleur Libres* have their homes and businesses." She glanced toward Mathilde, who had turned to tend something on the stove. The maid had come with Louisa from Cahokia, and Sylvie was uncertain whether Louisiana law treated her as a slave or an indentured servant. She would remember to ask and find out.

Amy was adding that she was part owner of a teashop with a bakery, and that she was inviting Sylvie to tea. She had arrived in a carriage, which was waiting for them. Sylvie readily agreed and went to get her things.

She had gone shopping and paid visits with Louisa in areas nearby, and though they rode farther on Sunday drives with Octave, never had they gone to the part of town where Amy lived. The carriage driver, a middle-aged Black man, drove past familiar shops and markets, and then along quieter lanes where the houses were sandwiched in rows and shared adjoining walls. French-style wrought-iron stairways led to upper floors whose balcony rails were elaborately decorative and draped by flowering vines, and Sylvie was charmed by the gracefulness and color.

"Miss Sylvie, you accepted my invitation to tea without a second thought, but do you realize you might be the only white woman in the shop? Will that cause you discomfort?"

"I didn't think about that, but I'm sure it will be fine. I am so happy to see you and I have so much to tell you and I want to hear everything that you have been doing—we could go anywhere. Besides, it's your own place, isn't that right?"

"Well, it's partly my place. I do the morning baking so I can be free from noontime on. I don't have the patience to stay and wait on people all afternoon. I'm old enough to feel pretty tired by the time I get to put up my feet."

"So it's a successful shop with a large clientele?"

"Yes, actually. Free people number in the thousands here. Everyone speaks French, and you'll hear accents from Africa and the Caribbean. We have our own doctors, teachers, and businesses of all kinds. Some people have been to school in France or send their children. There's a fine school in Paris that takes children from the colonies."

"This is all very surprising," Sylvie said. "I haven't heard Octave or Louisa talking about this community. And to think how notorious New Orleans is for its slave markets."

"It is one of the wonders of the world we live in, Sylvie, that such brutality and evil can flourish right next to this new society we are building, full of hope for life after slavery. Of course, some people living here never were slaves to begin with."

The carriage came to a stop in front of a shop facing directly onto a boardwalk. Its door with mullioned glass panes was set between two windows that had flowerboxes below and striped pink awnings above. Amy made arrangements for the return trip and then opened the tea shop's door to usher Sylvie inside. They moved among well-dressed women seated at small, round tables toward an open one near the wall. Sylvie took a chair and glanced about at potted palms on the black-and-white-tiled floor, and sconces and paintings on the walls. The shop was as cozy and pretty as anyplace where she and Louisa had taken afternoon tea, just on a smaller scale.

Sylvie saw women watching her with frank interest; as she smiled, they smiled back and returned to their conversations. Two women behind the counter called out greetings, and Sylvie surmised that Amy had set up their order ahead of time.

"These women are so well dressed and fashionable, I'm lucky that this new dress got done in time; I'd hate to be here wearing my old brown calico."

"Oh, Sylvie—not that old thing from Cahokia? Don't they have any new clothes or dressmakers in Texas?"

"Very few, Amy, and even fewer after the towns were burned down and we had to head out on the road."

"How long were you in those dire conditions?"

"About six weeks."

"Yes, that's what Mathilde told me. And that you were ill, and that you might be engaged to be married. I was quite happy to hear that."

A young woman arrived with a large pottery teapot and a plate of pastries. After she filled their cups, Amy introduced her. The young woman bobbed a curtsy and praised Amy's abilities as a cook and a teacher. Then growing self-conscious, she smiled, bobbed again, and moved to other tables.

"A teacher?" Sylvie asked.

"Yes, I do a bit of instruction several mornings a week here at the shop. The girls need to know how to read and write if they are to succeed in business. Can you imagine being a cook but not being able to read a recipe or write out a menu? Or add up a bill?"

"You read and write," Sylvie said. "I guess I knew that, but it was illegal for indentured servants, or slaves at least, to learn to read, back in Illinois."

"Sylvie, who was it who worked with you, cheek by jowl, when you were little and struggling with your letters and handwriting? In a way, I did some learning right along with you."

"That makes sense, but it's odd we never talked about it."

"That world back in Cahokia is full of contradictions that never get discussed honestly. It's better here, more open and frank, and less bound by tradition."

"That means I can write letters to you, and we don't need to fall out of touch again."

"That's true, we could do that." But Amy said this so wistfully, Sylvie realized she saw the gulf between them enduring over time.

"My life here is fine and good," Amy said, "but doesn't it strike you that I cannot have tea with you in a shop in the part of New Orleans where you are living? You can come here freely, yet I cannot go there. That river flows only one way."

Sylvie thought this over as she ate a *petit four*. Then she asked Amy to tell her about her home life and her husband, who, it turned out, was a dentist as well as a barber. When Amy asked Sylvie about her *beau* in Texas, Sylvie found herself talking about Armand, the deaths of so many young men, and the attractive qualities of Andrew Magill. She was getting better at summarizing her experiences, drawing a few insights from them, and avoiding the events that might cause her to weep at any given moment.

The shop was growing busier, and soon it was time to leave. As they made their way past crowded tables, Sylvie noticed an elegantly dressed, middle-aged woman sitting alone with a small white terrier seated on the chair next to her. She sipped tea in a well of silence, apparently not exchanging greetings with anyone around her.

As they stepped outside, Amy murmured, "That was Mrs. Willetts, the *grande dame* Mrs. Eunice Willetts."

"Why such a *grande dame*, yet no one was speaking to her?"

"Not many are friendly with her in a social way. She comes in for tea and makes her slave wait outside." Amy raised her eyebrow toward a neatly dressed teenage girl standing listlessly to the side of a front window.

"Mrs. Willetts is a Black woman herself, and yet she owns a slave?"

"Yes, she owns several. It's extraordinary to see how people will imitate the customs of society and carry them on, even something as odious as enslaving your fellow man. But Mrs. Willetts was never a slave herself, so she doesn't fully understand. Otherwise she couldn't bear to do it."

"Still, I am astonished."

They rode along, watching the houses and businesses go by, the afternoon sun slanting warm and touching the bougainvillea and geranium blossoms with bright lemon light.

"I'll be going back to Cahokia for a time with Louisa," Sylvie said. "I have to settle my inheritance and get Jeanne's permission to marry so I'll have some say over my life."

"Don't get me started on how those people have treated you, especially your half-sister. I probably shouldn't let on, but your brother Laurent wanted to settle on you when he fell so sick, before he died. Jeanne, though, wouldn't have anything to do with it.

"But you never wanted to marry before twenty-one, anyway. I remember how terrified you were by the curse that slave Frankey supposedly put on your family when your father sold her and her child as slaves."

"Oh . . . I am still terrified by childbirth. That hasn't changed."

"That is just silly, Sylvie. All that hoax and jinx business—you should not pay it any mind. I hear it all the time down here, too. Remember that most of the Black people in Cahokia descended from that shipload of slaves brought around 1700, and we still have our *patois* and stories and dances, and even old bits of religion. It's been very nice to find that familiar world here in New Orleans, but those old customs should not affect you in a place as far away as Texas."

Sylvie smiled at her. "I think you're telling me two different things. One is to pay it no mind, and the other is that a curse cannot travel that far over water."

"You see, my dear, both are true. You are growing up, and a key to adult life, I have found, is being able to hold two contradictory things at the same time in your one mind. Some things are a little more true, others are a little less."

"Excellent advice, I think."

They had arrived at Louisa and Octave's house, and Sylvie gathered her things. She and Amy exchanged cheek kisses, and Amy could not resist one last bit of advice.

"This young man Andrew sounds like a good man, and just the kind of fellow I would want for you, Sylvie. Now go back to Cahokia and wrap things up. But do not stay there too long."

"I'll try not to. Goodbye, Amy, and thank you so much for everything. I've noted the address of your tea shop, by the way, and I will write to you."

"I'll look forward to that."

Chapter 23



**August – September 1836**
**Cahokia, Illinois**

THE TOWN LOOKED SO SMALL, AND THE BLUFFS SO LARGE, as Sylvie stood at the steamboat rail eagerly scanning the landscape of her childhood. Construction work for the new railroad showed as a lengthy scar of cut trees and newly turned earth. From the edge of the *Grand Marais*, a trestle reached on paired legs of pilings, yet stopped partway, an incomplete bridge terminating in air. The formerly wooded shore of the marsh, where she had hunted ducks and geese, was now a broad clearing holding two dozen or more workers' shanties, planted in rows among hundreds of tree stumps.

Louisa, beside her, murmured something that Sylvie could not hear above the thrumming of the boat engine and splashing of the paddlewheel. It was a clear morning of a hot day, and the mist of river-water spray smelled fresh and felt good.

"Cahokia looks so little, so different!" Sylvie exclaimed, as they caught sight of the town's roofs and church steeple through the trees.

"So far, it has looked dreadful!" Louisa shouted back.

Several passengers gathered near them chuckled, and one woman said loudly, in English, "Tut, tut! This is what progress looks like!"

Louisa bit her lip, and she and Sylvie kept silent as they watched the familiar landmarks pass while the boat churned toward the wharf. Most passengers had gathered on the opposite deck to watch St. Louis, ever larger and grander, slip by. The fact they would dock first at Illinoistown spoke to the river's changing channels: It was running deep on the east side, even undercutting the banks, and depositing silt on the west side, where rising shoals were limiting access to the docks at St. Louis.

When the steamboat had maneuvered in, the passengers hurried off. Louisa quickly arranged for a porter to stack their bags in a cart and follow as she and Sylvie walked into Cahokia. They were looking forward to strolling on land after ten days on the boat, and soon they  shared memories triggered by the familiar places and laughed at their recollections. Sylvie was overwhelmed at how beautiful the older houses looked—nestled in their gardens behind fences garlanded with flowering vines—and how closely together they were placed.

Etienne, coming to meet them, looked an inch taller for each year Sylvie had been gone, and she rose tiptoe to exchange cheek kisses. Still a gentle-mannered boy, he wiped at the corners of his dark-blue eyes.

"I'm so glad you're coming to live in the homestead house," he told Sylvie as they resumed walking. "It turned into more work than I expected, but you'll like the changes. I haven't had any luck with the kitchen garden, though, or with cooking."

"Oh, those are my jobs; I see." Sylvie smiled, glancing up at him. "And the laundry?"

"Yes, indeed, that too," he said, fairly seriously. "I am gone much of the time, with all the work running the farm and the woodlands."

Louisa's brother Edward drove up with a wagon to take her home, and after they greeted, kissed cheeks, exchanged news, and loaded luggage, the pair left for Aunt Lizette's house. Etienne picked up Sylvie's carpetbags, and she managed the hatboxes and small carrying case. It was a short walk to the house behind a cedar-stake fence that Sylvie would call home for coming months, or possibly longer.

The homestead house had been built in the French style in the late 1700s, with vertical timbers, a swooping roofline, and deep verandas at the front and back. A single chimney rose from the fireplace, used for both cooking and heating, in the main room. Etienne unfastened the gate, and as they walked through the dooryard, Sylvie mentally listed gardening tasks to do right away.

Inside the house, she quickly noted changes and praised Etienne's improvements. Not only had he cleaned out old furniture and items like the ancient spinning wheel, but he also had added new shelves and repainted the flowering vines on the doors that covered cupboards. A new wood stove for cooking stood near the back kitchen door, with its own little chimney vented out through the wall. Nothing could be done with the windows, though, which remained little apertures in the thick walls supported by cedar posts, filled with stones, and finished with mortar.

"It looks so charming!" Sylvie exclaimed, and Etienne smiled with satisfaction. He was using the bedroom on the main floor and said he had prepared the loft area for her. A narrow stairway against one wall now replaced the century-old ladder, and she went up to view her room, which stretched across half the house. The ceiling slanted cozily on both sides overhead, and light came in two windows set in opposite walls. The chimney from the fireplace below would help to heat the space, and a low wall and railing on the open side would keep things from falling onto the table and chairs on the floor below.

"This is perfect! I love it," Sylvie called out. She set some of her things on the narrow bed and caught herself glancing about for the half-papered wall of her attic bedroom in Gonzales, far away in Texas, in a house that no longer existed. A few of her old things hung behind a narrow curtain: the winter cloak edged with fur and its matching muff and hat, a few everyday dresses, a black lace shawl for church, and a warmer one of finely knitted wool.

She sighed to see the little doll that had belonged to Celeste placed near the pillow on the bed. It had been her favorite, and Sylvie sat down for several moments to stroke the worn fabric cheek and touch the wispy yarn hair as she recalled her niece, Etienne's little sister, gone several years already. Why did so many children die here, Sylvie wondered, when everything was present for a good life? She and Louisa had already been warned that cholera was ravaging the town again that summer.

As Sylvie went about unpacking, Etienne left to see to his cattle grazing on the Commons and talk with the other *habitants* about the crops. Later, they were invited to Jeanne and Nicolas's house for dinner, and Sylvie imagined it would be painful, when she saw the couple, to revisit their sorrow over losing an infant, several months after his birth, during the time Sylvie had been gone. She would put aside all questions of inheritance and the railroad business until later, after she had become more comfortably reacquainted with her half-sister and the family.

The following week, Sylvie was strolling on a warm Sunday afternoon to the home of her niece Marguerite, who had invited her to dinner. Marguerite and Vital Jarrot, married a year earlier, were starting their life together in the large, two-story brick house Sylvie's father had built in Illinoistown around 1810. This had been Sylvie's home for her first four years, when she'd had a family with a mother, father, and older half-brother David. Following her parents' deaths, Jeanne and Laurent had managed the house as a hotel for some years.

The house was to the north of Cahokia, in a townsite that her father had platted and later sold to St. Louis merchants. She spun her parasol on her shoulder, wondering how it would feel to enter her former home, which she had not visited in years. She also wondered that the house had moved so quickly to Jeanne's daughter, a granddaughter, while bypassing the question of whether she herself had any ownership rights. Nonetheless, she would be happy to see Vital again, and curious to see Marguerite as a wife and young mother.

And beneath it all, Sylvie was glad and grateful to have her health back, to feel vigorous enough for the walk of several miles. At times, memories of Texas submerged her, and she would go about distanced and numb to the familiar people and sites of her childhood. At other times, her inner worlds reversed, and Texas seemed remote and dreamlike, with everything around Cahokia so much more compelling. Today she was feeling a restful, pleasant balance.

A maid answered her knock at the door, and as Sylvie stepped inside, she was surprised by nostalgia welling up. She had not expected to recall these specific rooms with their ceilings and cove molding, or the way sunlight fell into the *salon*. And the views out the windows evoked vivid memories; the trees had just grown taller. She was glad to have a few moments to look about, and she caught her reflection in the mirror of the dark wood buffet in the dining room nearby. *I am seeing myself in my home.* The thought felt disorienting in time and space.

Marguerite bounded in on a wave of friendly chatter and cheek kisses. As she invited Sylvie to sit down and asked about the journey, she seemed more vivacious than in the past at school or in her parents' house. And the buoyancy seemed natural to Sylvie, perhaps because she was truly happy. She had grown plumper, her smile even showing a dimple.

Soon Vital came in, grasped Sylvie's hands, and gave her three cheek kisses. Right away he was exclaiming about the adventures she'd had, the new lands she had seen. "And you are thinking you'll go back and start a life there, with marriage in the offing!"

Before Sylvie could say much, Marguerite broke in, looking concerned. "But Sylvie, surely not soon, with the suffering you described in your letters to Isabelle. And the newspapers say Mexico is likely to invade again. You don't have to go back—spend a good amount of time here and become accustomed to our life again."

Sylvie was learning that many of her acquaintances were quick to dispense advice, rather than invest time listening as she tried to answer their questions. True, she still was sorting through a welter of feelings, exploring the contradictions of colonial life, and working out what her experiences of wartime ultimately might mean to her.

Vital maintained an energetic manner, and as they took their places for the meal, he spoke with an air of authority at the head of the dining table. After some discussion of Texas, he switched to telling Sylvie about progress on the new railroad and describing the current challenges. He offered to ride with her to the work site and give a personal tour, if she wished. Marguerite said he often went there twice a day, as crews worked from first light until dark.

"We have to get a lot done during this good weather," Vital said. "Plus prices for materials keep going up so fast that we have to rush to make estimates and place orders."

"I see. So the costs are outrunning the estimated expenses?"

"The situation is quite fluid, subject to rapidly changing market forces," Marguerite said smoothly, and Vital smiled at her fondly.

"Specifically, costs have persuaded us not to use iron or steel," he said. "You'll see that both the rails and coal cars are built of wood. Teams of horses will be able to pull half a dozen cars at a time, as we're keeping to a gentle grade."

"I saw the construction from the riverboat," Sylvie said. "Louisa and I were out watching, and we wondered at the golden color of the track we could see among the trees." She suddenly and vividly recalled the squealing, smoking wheels and axles of the ox carts churning endless miles over rough traces in Texas. The jarring sound and faint smell arrived so palpably that she abruptly set down her wine glass and took up a water goblet for a long drink.

Vital was saying that the wooden parts should function just as well as metal ones, though he paused, noting Sylvie's expression.

"Their ideas are so progressive," Marguerite put in. "So of course not everyone will agree with their methods. The foreman just quit, for example. He came from the East and had worked on railroads before—other kinds of railroads, to be sure."

"It sounds as though he could offer valuable experience," Sylvie said.

"We'll manage," Vital replied.

Marguerite added, "I think it's so wise that my parents as your guardians are investing some of your estate, or your expectations, Sylvie. That way, you'll realize a significant return on your principal." The financial terms flowed in her speech as though she had learned them by rote, reminding Sylvie of their days at school.

"I agree that such a return sounds good," she said neutrally.

Vital took up the theme, telling Sylvie how much he appreciated her investment.

"How much is it, exactly?" she asked.

"A good question," he replied. "Considering the half-dozen main investors, yours is a portion of the amount Jeanne and Nicolas have put in. I'm sure Nicolas will sit down and show you the actual figures."

"I'll make sure to ask him soon," Sylvie said. She took a quick swallow of wine and sought another topic. She dreaded questions about war and her suitor, or fiancé; people here referred to him in various ways. "How is your brother, François, doing?" she asked. "I haven't seen him in town yet, and I've wondered about his health."

Vital shook his head and said François was suffering more frequent bouts of consumption. While he was still managing the estate and the farmlands, the prognosis for his health was not good.

"I'm very sad to hear that." Sylvie was surprised by tears welling up. In spite of herself, she was taken back to Texas, for François resembled Armand Fulshear so much that the memory of Armand's death arrived with its own burden of grief. She had not been able to mourn adequately at the time, and she didn't even know where Armand was buried or whether the family had been able to bring his body home. So much of the truth about her experiences in Texas did not make good conversational gambits over the dinner table.

Marguerite began chatting happily about her baby girl, giving Sylvie time to collect herself. They could go upstairs and look in on her after dessert and coffee. Following that, Vital said, he would walk with Sylvie part-way back to Cahokia, and he suggested a slight detour to view a section of Illinoistown that he was having platted for a new city to be called St. Clair. The surveyor was the same one who had worked with Sylvie's father when he first developed the area.

After Sylvie met the baby, who looked charming while sleeping soundly, Marguerite stayed at the house as she and Vital set out in the warm evening toward the eastern bank of the Mississippi River.

"Have I invested in developing this new town, too?" Sylvie wondered out loud. Vital's dark eyes regarded her seriously, and a flush rose under his deep tan. He lacked the classically handsome looks of his brother, but his manner radiated intensity and nervous energy.

"No. But Sylvie, in our defense, no one heard from you for such a long time. The newspapers were full of the war in Texas, and we read about the dire plight of refugees, the epidemics, the large number of deaths from disease and exposure. Jeanne was very worried about you—we all were. They did ask, most earnestly, 'What would Sylvie want us to do? There is no way to reach her.' I would say a certain hopelessness got mixed in with concern for your best interests, and we needed to move ahead."

"Because the railroad project *had* to move forward?"

"Yes, all the pieces were in place. John Reynolds owns the land where the coal is being mined, my mother owns the largest stretch between the mines and the port, and a cousin of Marguerite's on her father's side threw in his lot, as well. Jeanne and Nicolas invested heavily because they want their daughter's husband—me—to succeed.

He glanced at her and added, "Costs are running high now, but rather than let your potential inheritance just sit there, losing value day by day, it will reap large rewards soon. Trust me."

Sylvie wondered whether Vital made any distinctions between family members and other investors when he promoted his projects. As they walked among surveyors' stakes set on the land cleared for the new town, Sylvie realized that the streets did not align with the grid reaching from Illinoistown, but were set at a sharp angle to them. She tried to imagine houses along these routes and asked about alleys that would run behind them. Vital explained there would be no alleys.

"Then how will people get their carriages and wagons back to the stables?" she asked.

"They won't need those on a daily basis. The men will walk to work."

"Where?" Sylvie glanced about at distant trees and the river beyond.

"At the factories that will come. With all the iron ore in southern Illinois and the coal nearby, we can have a steel-rolling mill. You know about steam power, how that's changing production processes. And we'll be able to ship from here, too. The river is running deeper on our side, which means we'll have a more active port in the future. The western side of the river is silting up, filling with shoals and sandbars, so St. Louis will see its business decline."

As they walked back toward the old town of Cahokia and crossed the nearby creek, Sylvie watched golden light suffuse the treetops and stripe the steeple of Holy Family Church. It seemed she had been gone much longer than three and a half years.

*  *  *

Sylvie was tearing down withered vines and gathering seedpods in the flowerbeds in front of the homestead's cedar fence facing the street. As she fingered some dried cosmos blooms that peeked through a runaway cloud of nasturtium vines, she was startled by a voice coming from somewhere near her elbow and wishing her a good morning.

It was Madame Le Compte, more than one hundred years old, petite, dressed in black, and shrewd as ever. "I just wanted to say, Sylvie, how happy I am to see Pensoneaus back in this house. It does me good to look across the street and see you and Etienne living here."

"It is nice, isn't it, *Grandmère?* We're both enjoying the place." Sylvie addressed her as "Grandmother," even though Madame Le Compte was the mother of Sylvie's Aunt Lizette.

Madame Le Compte congratulated her on her engagement and asked, "Are you keeping it secret? I don't hear people talking much about it."

"No, not really secret. Maybe they stay quiet because my sister insists I can't agree to marry without her permission. So she tells everyone to call it only a courtship. But I suppose I also don't say much because the young man's life is in constant danger. He's serving in the Texas army in case Mexico attacks again, and he goes on ranging missions to fight Comanche Indians. Even when he's at home, the town is attacked. I also don't have recent news from him—only one letter back in June."

"Oh, those are the reasons. I thought it might be because he is a Protestant. That presents a problem for your family."

"Yes, and I've put off arguing more with Jeanne. For her, it's unthinkable for me to marry outside of the Catholic Church. In fact, she forbids it as my legal guardian."

"These people can get so high and mighty." Madame Le Compte shook her head. "Look at some of my grandchildren: They do not accept my grandson Paschal because he married a Kickapoo woman. And here I am, their own grandmother, part Pottawatomie. I love that boy, and he has displayed twice as much character for choosing to live according to his convictions. How people can forget their past—or deny it." She was leaning on a walking stick and now thumped it on the ground for emphasis.

Madame Le Compte, having outlived several husbands, was legendary for saving Cahokia's settlers from attacks in the early days. Her own mother was half Pottawatomie, and her father French, a *voyageur* who had come from Québec with one of Sieur Cavalier de La Salle's expeditions and then stayed on at the stockade they built in the wilderness along the Mississippi River.

When she was grown and married and she heard rumors that Indians were planning raids, Madame Le Compte would head into the woods on her own, carrying a large walking stick. She would parley for a night or two, and back she would come, along with a band of braves and their families who were now feeling peaceful and looking forward to the gifts and feasts the French were only too happy to provide if it meant avoiding a battle. She knew several languages, including the one spoken by the local Tamaroas, and Paschal seemed to have inherited the gift.

"Westport," Sylvie said abruptly. "Paschal is at Westport, on the Missouri River. That's what some Delaware traders told me when I encountered them in Texas. They said he is the main translator there. The *Anglais* call it Westport, but the Indians simply call it Kickapoo Village."

"Yes, I've heard that William Clark calls on Paschal for translating, and I believe he must be doing well. Did you happen to hear about his family or any children?"

"No, and I wish I had asked. I was so happy, at that moment, that they knew him and were willing to trade. They had food, which we desperately needed, and they accepted a pair of moccasins Paschal gave me when he was in Cahokia after the war."

"How fortunate! But as I was saying, this wretched business of turning backs on family members is carrying on with your sister's attitude about marrying a Protestant. She forgets that the Pensoneaus were Huguenots—Protestants—back in France, including the first one who arrived in Québec."

"What? I am sure they were Catholic."

"Your father, yes; he was quite devout. And so were a couple of generations back before him. But remember that my forebears came to New France along with yours, and they always referred to the Pensoneau family as Huguenots from La Rochelle. Why do you think they chose to stay away from France? The country had started persecuting them, even forcing them to leave or be killed."

"I have heard about that. Are you saying our ancestor converted later, in Québec?"

"That's right. New France was being run by the Séminaire de Québec, and the priests made sure everyone who got a land claim was Catholic. Remember, I was born in 1733 or thereabouts, so I was acquainted with the *voyageurs* who came exploring here with La Salle. I even married one. They still knew their family histories from France, and about their grandparents who came to Québec."

Sylvie couldn't help but smile. "That's so much like the colonists in Texas who claimed they were Catholic so Mexico would give them land grants."

"Land and religion. Isn't it interesting how the two are so closely entwined? I wish you good luck in getting Jeanne's permission to marry. I'm sure he is a fine fellow."

Madame Le Compte was turning to leave. "Wait," Sylvie said. "What about my mother? I know that my parents married twice, but I never asked whether she converted in order to marry the second time in Holy Family Church."

"Yes, dear, as I recall. She was Protestant, so they were married first by a justice of the peace. But your father grew uncomfortable, and he was so devout, I think your mother converted in the interests of peace in the family.

"So as far as religion, Sylvie, you can do whatever you need, and as you want. That seems to be your family's actual tradition, if you are looking for one. Does that help, my dear? I hope so, and I'll see you again soon." Madame Le Compte crossed the road to return to her house, and Sylvie watched her pass through the gate in her cedar fence, bordered by a profusion of fall-blooming asters and anemone.

"*Alors*," Sylvie murmured, turning back to the tangle of vines. She could now add family history to her arguments for Jeanne when the time came.


The first ball of the season was scheduled at the home of Sylvie's cousin Narcisse, who had recently married a distant cousin, Félicité—also a Pensoneau. Jeanne had grumbled that a marriage between even distant cousins was unacceptable, causing Isabelle to roll her eyes with exasperation. She had confided to Sylvie that she and Edward were still in love and trying to find a route to a future.

As the ball approached, Sylvie was undecided about attending. She visited Louisa fairly often and was becoming acquainted with her new, healthy baby son. Louisa was delighted with him and with being pampered by her mother and other female relatives. She urged Sylvie to go to the ball and enjoy it for both of them, since she was still taking bed rest.

Sylvie protested that she didn't have a gown to wear, and she and Louisa laughed about the dress Sylvie had borrowed years earlier. "We changed the ruffles and the silk flowers and added different lace, after that night," Louisa said. "You could wear it again, and no one would know."

"Thank you, but I couldn't go unescorted—that's another problem."

"Well, Edward is around, and he'll attend on the chance of getting a few dances with Isabelle. He'll escort you, I'm sure."

As the evening approached, Louisa's plans fell into place, and Sylvie felt buoyant, arriving at the home of Narcisse and Félicité and hearing the familiar exuberant music. Edward walked with her into the room cleared for dancing and left her with Jeanne, who sat surveying the crowd, as he whisked Isabelle away for a dance. Sylvie watched, thinking they made a lovely couple; then she was dismayed to see Fernande and Emile Hubert among the couples moving to the music.

Jeanne gave Sylvie a probing look and said, "Appropriate marriages are the result of careful planning and years of effort. Now that you are back in town, I am reminded to perform the duties your mother would have handled and see to your best interests."

"Jeanne, I have made a commitment elsewhere, as you know."

"But you are not truly engaged. You cannot be, without my permission, at least at the age you are now. And look at the eligible young men right before us tonight."

Sylvie glanced about in hopes of an old friend or distant cousin who might approach and invite her to dance. She did not want an argument, especially since she noticed how Jeanne's hand would settle protectively over the bulge showing among the folds of her black silk dress. Her sister had not mentioned another pregnancy—speaking of it would be improper—but Sylvie was certain Jeanne would be delighted by hopes for another child, even as she entered her forties.

"And also think of young men who are not here this evening," Jeanne continued. "François Jarrot is still available, and he has always been fond of you."

"Jeanne, what are you saying?" Sylvie stared at her sister. "First of all, he is ill. And then you would have me marry him, the elder brother, and cut out Vital, your son-in-law, from the family fortune? I cannot believe you are serious."

"Thank you for clarifying your feelings on the matter, Sylvie. That gives me considerable peace of mind. Let's set a time to discuss several other matches that would be suitable. My dear, we are overdue for a good chat, just the two of us."

Jeanne said this so sincerely that Sylvie's anger withered. Why was it so difficult to talk with her sister? Each time she visited Jeanne's house, they were interrupted by the needs of the young children, questions from the maids, or even calls by other visitors.

François would not be at the ball, given his worsening health, and Sylvie wondered how much Jeanne had heard about Sylvie visiting him. It was no more than friendship, the courtesy of visiting someone ill, but Sylvie knew in her heart that spending time with him was allowing her to grieve Armand Fulshear's death in a more natural and gradual fashion than events in Texas had permitted. It was something she could never explain to her sister.

Sylvie ended up enjoying the evening, dancing several times and filling her supper plate with delicacies she had missed. She wondered, though, how other people could eat such large amounts. But hadn't she herself eaten so much more in the past?

After supper, several Le Compte girls threw on their shawls and said they were going to walk back into town, the night was so beautiful, and Sylvie decided to join them. She trailed a bit behind as they laughed and gossiped, and she admired the arc of moon riding through wisps of clouds that looked like chiffon scarves.

How uninteresting the young men had been at the ball. It wasn't their fault; they were charming—a few good-looking, some others rich. But how did they spend their time? Farming, running the family business, playing cards, racing horses. Few had been as far as New Orleans, and she doubted any had decided to steal coffee or hoard Mexican silver won in battle or even spy on Mexican officers at a party while their fort was being attacked.

Where was Andrew now, and what was he doing? She hoped he was back safely in Mina after his summer of ranger duties. In darker moments, she worried how the news might reach her, if Andrew were killed in a battle or an accident. She did not picture him ever succumbing to illness. Uncle Jim would hear about such an event in an official dispatch of some kind, and he would write to her. While she dreaded receiving any such letter, she also was longing for any word, any message at all.

He was probably at some crude campsite, looking up at the same moon, unless he was snatching a few hours of sleep by a smoldering fire before taking sentry duty. As she approached her street and saw lamplight shining from a window in the old homestead house, she felt a surge of happiness. But why? She looked up at the stars and knew with certainty that Andrew was looking up at them and thinking of her. She missed him, and being alone now let her bring him closer in her thoughts. He might never come to Cahokia and meet all these people. So the part of her attached to him stayed permanently away from here as well.

"I must really love him," she said, breathing it out loud to the night as she unlatched the front gate. "I believe I do."

His absence presented so many difficulties, such as recalling exactly what he looked like and the pitch of his voice. Getting a letter from him would help, but having firm plans for the future would help even more.

At the post office, Sylvie picked up a copy of the *St. Clair Gazette*, a weekly newspaper published in nearby Belleville, along with the mail. Amid business correspondence for Etienne, she found a letter addressed to her from Sarah Kerr. Sylvie was glad but worried, for it was the first she had received. Sarah was staying with family near St. Louis, so Sylvie trusted that both her letters, from New Orleans as well as Cahokia, had been delivered. She still regretted abandoning the family at the Sabine River and grieved the loss of the children. At home, she read Sarah's letter quickly, scanning news as well as an apology, which began partway through.

> *I am sorry, I just could not write before now. I had no idea what*
> *to say. I lost myself for a time, with no sense of who I was anymore or*
> *what purpose my life might still have. Everything I had worked toward,*
> *understood, and built with my marriage and family in Texas was gone.*
> *I felt as though I was struggling underwater in that accursed river, the*
> *endless delta of the Sabine, where you couldn't tell river from lake, or*
> *lake from the Gulf, or marshland from water. A huge tide kept pulling*
> *me this way and that.*
>
> *"Then it was very dislocating to be back here; it was too sudden.*
> *People—even Jim's sister, Peggy—don't understand why I can't just*
> *'forget,' and 'put it all behind me.' But don't they see? I don't want*
> *to forget. If I forgot my little boy, that would be a worse betrayal and*
> *a greater emptiness. I don't want memories that are less real. Once I*
> *began insisting that these people hear my grief and picture for them-*
> *selves the events we survived, I began to recover, or at least to feel a little*
> *better . . ."*

Several times, she assured Sylvie that she did not blame her in any way for the children's fate, and that she now was concerned more about how ill Sylvie herself had been. She asked for news and suggested Sylvie might visit Missouri one day. She added that Minny had come through the ordeal "even stronger and more energetic." She was enjoying school in Ste. Geneviève, though Sarah missed her badly. Sarah also had news from Jim, still in Texas. He said the new republic had pushed hard in negotiations while holding General Santa Anna captive, and he felt Mexico would not invade again soon. But he reported that Comanche attacks were frequent and harsh, especially around Mina, which added to Sylvie's worries.

Putting the letter aside, she took up the weekly newspaper from Belleville. Its bold headlines ran in multiple decks descending in size over the narrow columns of type. Along the East Coast, people were rioting over the price of food. In New York and Boston, huge crowds disrupted traffic and commerce because they could not afford bread, or even wheat flour. Nor could they afford clothing or the wood and coal they needed to heat their houses.

Sylvie tried to imagine a densely populated city, like New Orleans, with unruly crowds venting anger and frustration. Basic items she and Etienne used in daily life were growing more expensive, but so far, the year's crops were fetching high enough prices to compensate.

Etienne had worked hard with the year's wheat harvest, though it required fewer laborers since a couple of *habitants* had invested in threshing machines. Apparently they damaged stalks a bit as they beat on husks to separate the kernels, but the armies of workers that had moved through the harvests in Sylvie's memory had now dwindled to teams of men with horses pulling these machines. She had not been asked to help with the cooking at Fernande's house, but she still had gone to Aunt Lizette's to help for a few days.

Sylvie moved to the newspaper's inside pages and the inevitable reports about Texas. Contrary to what she had just read in Sarah's letter, the articles claimed that Mexico was on the verge of invading the new republic and urged young men to get there and volunteer to defend it.

Over the months, Sylvie had become impatient with the inaccurate impressions of Texas that townspeople gained from local newspapers and relayed when talking with her. How she wished she could give the public different accounts, complete and detailed stories of what women, children, and ordinary settlers of all ages had experienced during the war and as refugees.

With the harvest over and her work in the garden largely done, she had time to muse over memories. But they were growing distant, the details fading. She thought of her geography teacher's challenge from years ago to keep a journal, and she wondered about beginning to write. Beyond buying ink and paper, she would have to think through what she wanted to record for herself and close relations, apart from what she might want townspeople to read.

She began writing in the mornings as she finished her coffee, and soon, spending time each day to record her memories felt like a comfortable routine. She would start with a topic, put down key thoughts, and then reminisce to recall her feelings. She used two different sets of pages, one exploring her heart, with its fears, dreads, hopes, suffering, and joys. These seemed to arrive more keenly, and to gain distinctness and substance, as she wrote. The other set held factual accounts organized by key events, such as the burning of Gonzales and the crucial victory at the San Jacinto River. She toyed with the idea that these could become newspaper articles.

One of the first things Sylvie discovered was that distilling her experiences was hard work. She spent much longer than she expected on a page, and as soon as she reread it, she would cross out parts and rework them. Then came the question of how much personal information to include if her accounts were to appear in the Belleville newspaper. She needed to name the people with whom she had lived, traveled, and suffered, but then she wondered how Rachel, Sarah, or Andrew might feel about that. She was determined to draft at least three articles that drew more on facts than on feelings and opinions before deciding whether to approach the newspaper's editor.

As she began a topic, such as the night Rachel's household learned of the deaths at the Alamo and Gonzales was set afire, she had to guess how much explanation local readers would require. Why had the town's men gone into the Alamo, for example, and what were Sam Houston's reasons for ordering the town to be burned? As she added that kind of information, she encountered gaps in her own understanding. A young woman was not privy to military decisions, after all, and she was relying on what she had heard or learned later.

Sylvie wanted to tell how ordinary people had packed up and fled, and how they suffered for months on the road. As she wrote about the slowly lurching ox carts and how the settlers feared the Mexican army approaching behind them, she would pause and revisit the days and the events. She relived her sorrow over the deaths of the prisoners at Goliad, the illnesses that struck down the children, and the loss of everything they had called home. After reliving the bottomless despair at the Sabine River, she stirred from her reveries to discover an hour had passed and she had written only a paragraph.

The more personal anecdotes she wrote did not arrive in chronological order but sprang from strong feelings in the moment. Rereading these passages after a few days, she began to discern the shape of her insights, findings, and conclusions. Now she was forming stances to answer the questions Sarah liked to ask and finding convictions to share. She wrote about Amy and Annette and concluded that their different fates—one remaining a slave, the other becoming free following servitude—clearly showed how arbitrary and ruthless slavery was, and how it was propped up only by invented laws, which themselves varied greatly from place to place. There was no moral, religious, legal, or even historical justification for the practice.

She thought about the thousands of acres of land claims in Texas being awarded for enlisting and fighting battles, and of the surging value of land in Illinois and other states. Her father had gained hundreds of acres that her family owned around Cahokia by serving in the local militia. Was it entirely right for the generation who arrived first to claim broad swaths of land and compile gains from them, while later generations strove hard just to purchase a toehold? In the 1700s, Cahokia had set up hundreds of acres as Commons that every resident was entitled to use for grazing, hunting, taking firewood, and growing small crops. But in recent years, that land had been sold off in private allotments. What about the Indian nations' original claims to the lands, and the access they lost when the fences went up? At least some men, such as her cousin Paschal and her Uncle Jim, sought to establish legal claims within treaties. But settlers who came later often treated those as meaningless historical artifacts.

Sylvie also mused over how the women had to cope continuously, in uncountable ways, with decisions made by men. Yet they had little say in the Texas Consultations or its new Congress, or even in the Cahokia Assembly, or in a court of law anywhere in either country.

She imagined the newspaper editor quizzing her to see whether her views were consistent with the newspaper's editorials. Should Texas remain an independent republic and stand on its own in the world? Sylvie thought that founding a new country was promising, but that Texas needed a strong alliance with the United States.

After several weeks of regular effort, she had written drafts she felt she could share with readers. But she was not ready to take them to the *St. Clair Gazette*—in fact, she might never be ready for that. She wanted a second opinion, preferably from someone who knew about the publication's politics.

After some consideration, she decided that François Jarrot might advise her well, and she packed her drafts along one day when she went to visit. He was delighted at the idea she would write articles— women did that back East, he said. Given his illness, he spent hours poring over news accounts and following politics. Sylvie intended to leave her drafts with him and come back later, but François asked her to stay while he read them. Her cheeks grew hot with shyness or embarrassment as he went through the articles slowly and made occasional notes. Even so, he read in mere minutes what had taken her weeks to compose.

To her relief, he praised the articles and launched into suggestions. They bent their heads over the work, and when Sylvie returned home several hours later, she felt confident about approaching Robert Fleming, the editor of the *St. Clair Gazette*. Still, it would take time to work up courage for actually visiting the newspaper office.

Chapter 24

**Fall 1836 – Winter 1837**
**Cahokia, Illinois**

FINALLY, IN NOVEMBER, THE POSTMASTER HANDED SYLVIE a letter from Andrew. She slid it in her pocket and clutched it during the walk home, to read it there.

*Aug. 10, 1836*
*Bastrop (Mina), Republic of Texas*

*My dearest Sylvie,*

*We have been allowed a few days leave, so I am back in town and found two letters from you waiting here. They bring me such happiness, especially hearing you are well and back among family in your hometown. We are at our homes so we can vote for the new Congress and President for the Republic of Texas. I was glad to vote for Jesse Billingsley to represent our town. I did not vote for Sam Houston for President (as you might guess), though I hear he is more popular than the other candidates, Sterling Robertson and Stephen Austin. Now we have our own new country, and that feels pretty good. Everyone says Mexico will not fight us again soon because it's chaos there, with continued uprisings.*

*Our company went on a few forays after Indian raiding parties, but we didn't engage any in a decisive way. I am halfway through—my enlistment runs until late November. For serving, we get food rations and goods, like strouding for wool blankets or capes, pantaloons, rope, etc., some pay chits, and a promise of 320 more acres. And lots of time in the saddle for viewing the landscapes north and west of here.*

*This time, Mrs. Mays was willing to trade several sheets of letter paper for half of my military allotment of blue lawn. She wants it to sew clothes. So now I can also write a letter to my parents, which is long overdue. I will tell them about you, and they will be glad.*

*Out of fear of raids, families are living packed together in the houses toward the middle of town. No one visits outlying farms except in large parties in broad daylight. It is good to know that you are safe, even if it means being away from here. With murders and kidnappings, the women pay a terrible price, even if they are rescued later. The army is raising three companies under Robert Coleman to build a large fort about fifteen miles southwest of here. That should help us to defend this area better.*

*Take good care of your health and well-being, and convey my respectful greetings to your kinfolk. My thoughts and hopes for the future reside with you, and I close with continuing sincere affections,*
*Andy Magill*

Oh, what a relief that he was at home in August, even with months left to serve. And the rangers had not engaged Indians in battles, in spite of her vivid, fear-inspired imaginings. How nice that he was going to write to his parents about her. How parsimonious this Mrs. Mays was with her precious paper! Sylvie pressed the letter flat on the kitchen table and reread it several times. The one large omission was any mention of when she might be able to safely return.

On a clear, cold morning, Sylvie decided to go to Belleville. She told Etienne she would shop and do errands, and she rolled three rewritten articles up neatly. She would ride horseback, and she chose a light-colored dress that wouldn't show dust from the limestone road.

After cantering the horse to shorten the riding time, she slowed the pace closer to town. In Belleville, she dismounted and walked the horse to a hitching post near the newspaper office. She swatted dust from her skirt, patted her face with her handkerchief, and rehearsed her presentation. She checked her reflection in several store windows as she passed along the board sidewalk.

The newspaper office had an odd smell, not unpleasant, that must come from ink mingling with paper. The large front room she entered was divided from smaller offices toward the back, and from a large workroom to the right, where reams of paper stood stacked near a letterpress. Light from the front windows shone across wooden chairs and desks toward a table where a man sat facing the door. He wore round spectacles, and his hair stuck up in gray tufts. He greeted Sylvie and asked if she wanted to take out an advertisement, adding, "We still have space in next week's edition."

Sylvie said no, that she would like to speak with the editor, Mr. Robert Fleming, about placing some articles.

"He might be a while," the man said, pointing his thumb toward an office behind him.

Sylvie said she was willing to wait, and he gestured to a row of chairs. She sat down, fearing that if she left she would lack the courage to return. He added that she was welcome to browse newspapers piled on the table nearby, and she glanced at several on the top, which came from cities in the East and South, including Frankfort, Kentucky, and New Orleans. Headlines told of riots over the high price of food and crowds making runs on banks in the East. These stories ran alongside others touting glorious new towns being developed in the West. Sylvie marveled that prices could rise sharply and stay so high when ordinary people couldn't afford to pay them. Surely the cycle would break, and prices would drop as goods and foodstuffs piled up—unless factories and farmers stopped producing them.

Then a man strode out from the editor's office, and Sylvie was ushered in. Fleming was turned away, lighting a pipe, when she stepped inside. The tobacco smelled pleasantly of cherry, and he turned and extended a hand as they introduced themselves.

"I hope you will permit my smoking." He wore a fine white shirt with the cuffs rolled back on muscular forearms. His dark hair was cut short, and his glance assessed her quickly. Sylvie relaxed a bit, feeling this was a person who might listen, if only out of curiosity, rather than simply dismissing her.

"Mr. Fleming," she began, "your newspaper runs numerous articles about Texas, and your editorials discuss what the United States should do if Mexico invades again. I read these with keen interest, as I have recently returned from three years there."

He nodded, and she continued, "I would like to offer you several articles that tell about these events, including the war, from a common person's point of view. I'm concerned at the amount of material from officials and political writers that seems to be . . . not completely accurate or truthful, but often mixed with speculation, rumor, personal interests, and so on."

Fleming shrugged. "It's always that way. What new or special information can you offer?"

"I was present at key events. I was in Gonzales when the town was burned. I was on the road, fleeing as a refugee, for six weeks. I also witnessed the crucial victory—the battle near Harrisburg at the San Jacinto River. And I visited the refugee encampment on the Sabine River."

"Truly? That is of interest. Tell me how you'd like to write about these events. It would be from a woman's perspective?"

"Necessarily, yes, since that's who I am. But people here, in this community, will be interested in detailed and accurate accounts of how ordinary people experienced the events. And that's what I offer, with three articles I've written."

"Well, let me ask you this: do you think the United States should back up Texas and go to war against Mexico if the fighting picks up again?"

"I do, yes."

"And what do you think of the new Republic of Texas being formed, of its government and leaders and so forth?"

"From everything I heard of the plans—especially from my uncle, James Kerr, who is highly involved—the Consultations have modeled the new government to resemble the United States, with a congress, a president, and a judiciary. I saw men being freely elected to the Consultations, and I've heard in letters since that elections are staying open and fair—to men, anyway. So that all seems democratic."

"You are aware, Miss Pensoneau, that this newspaper is Democratic, politically, and favors Jacksonian ideals. We push for western expansion and for bringing Texas into the Union, eventually."

"Yes, and I believe my articles would be consistent with those viewpoints."

"And what about slavery?"

Sylvie took a breath, grateful that François had coached her on what the editor was likely to ask. "I am against slavery in Texas. For one thing, it encourages the plantation system of cotton growing, which will shut out the farming families who want to work the land themselves. It was also illegal during the time Americans were starting their colonies, so it's a debatable point the Texas congress can address—and should, soon."

Fleming raised his eyebrows and smiled. "I was wondering because you come from the old French community, some of whom still hold slaves. You see, I do know of your family."

"That's good because then you'll know that it was my father who bought tracts of land for this town and platted the streets and developed it."

Fleming laughed. "Well spoken, Miss Pensoneau. If you write as directly as you speak, your work will be interesting. But regarding your family ties, we're interested in backing a young lawyer in town, Lyman Trumbull. Cases he is taking could abolish the last remnants of slavery here in southern Illinois. He plans to run for the state assembly. Such legal issues could involve the family of another candidate, Vital Jarrot. His mother, I believe, still keeps slaves who should be free by now."

Fleming watched as Sylvie flushed, thought for a moment, and then shrugged. "Nothing in my articles would take any issue with that stance." As she responded, she stored this new information to think about later.

"I take it you're not advocating abolition, then. What about female emancipation? Do you argue that women should gain more legal rights, perhaps even the right to vote? Some here in our own state assembly believe that as rights are granted to the Negro race, the same should be done for women. I hear that an assemblyman, Abraham Lincoln, is preparing to argue for just that."

"Mr. Lincoln! Why, I've met him, and I would be inclined to agree with him. But Mr. Fleming, I truly am not advancing any political views in these articles."

"All right, Miss Pensoneau, I will cease the cross-examination. It's just that most people who ask me to print their articles are advocating personal and political viewpoints while trying to pass them off as factual accounts and news reports."

"I have been working for several weeks on the articles, and writing and rewriting has developed my thinking; I'm more prepared to take stances because of the work. But I do not do so in the articles."

"Then I'll be happy to look at one or two, if you can leave them with me today. I'll let you know soon whether we'll print any of them."

Sylvie agreed, and thanking him for his time, handed him the scroll of papers. She had got up, yet paused before turning to leave.

"Is there anything else?" he asked.

"Just that . . . I expect to be paid at your usual rate for correspondents."

"Oh—payment! Well, you are taking this seriously." Fleming stood, shoved his hands in his pockets, and came around the desk to stand near her. "We do not usually employ female writers. In fact, I cannot think of a newspaper in this area that does, or that publishes women's writing. I've seen a few back East that do, however.

"And what about the author's name? We'll need a *nom de plume*, if we print any. Everyone will know the writing is from a woman's point of view once they start reading, I'll wager, but we want to get them into the articles, first."

"Could you at least use my initials?"

"I'll consider it. And yes, I will pay you as a correspondent. I'll let you know the rate when I've had a chance to look at these."

They shook hands, and Sylvie passed the next person entering to talk with Fleming. As she went outside, she decided not to stay in town to eat or shop. She had packed some food, and after she had ridden for a time, she stopped at a place that offered a view of the river.

The weather was chilly, and she wrapped her wool shawl tightly as she sat to eat, the horse grazing nearby. She still felt nervous—perhaps more so, having delivered the articles. The spot along the Rock Road was secluded, with wild grape vines hanging among tree branches holding yellow leaves. She watched the river traffic for a while to let her breathing calm before she drew out some bread and cheese, a meat pie, and a flask of water.

As she relaxed, Sylvie began to feel pleased with her venture. But she questioned Fleming's views about publishing women's writing. How would her accounts differ, if written by a man? A man would have been serving with the militia or the army, unless he was too old or infirm. She shook her head at how judgmental it seemed, that her articles would carry a false name or only initials, as though tricking a reader. She wanted to write honestly and in her own voice; otherwise, what was the point? If Fleming didn't like the articles, he didn't have to publish them. She could send them to those more forward-looking newspapers back East.

As Sylvie sat longer, she realized she was enjoying feeling free of fear that enemies—Mexican or Indian—might be lurking nearby. She had the ease to daydream of a possible future as a writer. Soon, though, she was distracted by a deep, repetitive thudding. Pound, pound, pound . . . what was that? It must be more pile-driving in the Grand Marais. The railroad laborers, having finished their midday meal, were resuming the work that shook the air and shivered the ground.

In January, two letters from Andrew arrived in the same post. He had gone to Columbia, the temporary capital for the new republic, to arrange payment and claims for his military service, and apparently mail moved faster there. She was relieved he was well, especially because her worries had been well founded. He wrote that Texans had won a large battle against Indians later in August, with only a few men wounded on their side. In October, Andrew began serving under a new officer after Jesse Billingsley was elected to the Texas congress and left the company. And a month later he had mustered out; he said that he did not foresee another enlistment in the near future.

He wrote that the weather was very cold in Columbia, with "blue northers" blowing, and that Stephen Austin, now the Secretary of State for Texas, had been ill all fall "and looks it." Housing was scarce, and Austin apparently was living in a lean-to attached to a cabin.

Land claims were unsettled, Andrew said, because the new President of Texas, Sam Houston, vetoed the bill Congress had passed to establish a land office. Still, everyone was trying to take the necessary steps to prove their claims, especially because hordes of men were pouring into Texas to get land, now that it was safer and no longer part of Mexico.

He closed by saying he would write again because the town offered abundant supplies of paper. He also was buying legal books, ledgers, and stationery to stock the new courthouse and county government seat planned for Mina—now called Bastrop.

Sylvie had written to Andrew about the Christmas festivities she was enjoying, but he expected bleaker holidays.

> *At times, I fall into nostalgia for the old days in Kentucky.*
> *Christmas will be quite dull, though I may visit Jim Kerr, as he will*
> *gather some people around. I wish I could look forward to seeing you*
> *there. Will you see Sarah and Minny in Missouri? I will find out what*
> *Jim says about bringing the families back here . . .*

The second letter was dated just a few days later and carried the sad news that Stephen Austin had died of illness. Apparently Uncle Jim had made it to Columbia in time to see his old friend at the end. Sylvie wondered what Austin's death might mean for the new republic and for his former colonists, but Andrew's letter sounded hopeful.

> *To prove my original headright land claim, I will have to put*
> *in a crop. I've signed a chit for Jesse Billingsley to handle my military*
> *claims here while I head down to the land. At least the cabin there has*

*a fireplace, so it offers the bare rudiments. Texas is going to honor our claims as original colonists, so I'll get one-third league, about 1,500 acres. A married man gets twice that—something for you to note. They are talking about granting 640 acres for being in the battle at San Jacinto, and 320 acres for each enlistment in the Rangers or military. I will have to pay some fees for these allotments. But first Congress has to pass legislation again to set up a lands office, and everyone hopes that our new president won't veto it. He says he won't.*

*In spite of our battles last summer, Indian depredations on Bastrop (Mina) continue. I have heard of two killings and a kidnapping, just since I have been here. I know the families murdered and the hostages taken, and it distresses me.*

*Nevertheless, I hope to ask you to return sometime in the coming year. I know you are brave and adventurous, and thank heavens for that. I just hope you are not growing so fond of the balls, parties, and French food that you won't want to return to this rough place. Please let me know of your feelings, whether they have changed, whether you have become attached elsewhere, and be assured of my continuing devoted affections,*

> *Sincerely,*
> *Andy Magill*

The last lines started Sylvie worrying. She had tried to write cheerful, hopeful letters and avoid anything that would cause him concern about her fidelity or their faith in each other. On darker days, she wondered if he was hinting of his own doubts. Nothing could be known for sure until she got back to Texas. But when would it be safe enough to return? Not yet, apparently.

Money was getting to be a problem. Sylvie sat at the kitchen table before a pile of coins emptied from her tea tin. She sorted them by metal and origin and tried to guess their current value. She still had the Mexican silver Andrew had given her, though it seemed to be worth less every day, with prices fluctuating. Still, the silver's solid substance made it seem more real than promissory notes or bank drafts, such as the ones that came as payment for her articles in the *St. Clair Gazette*.

In December the editor had accepted all three pieces, and Sylvie got to enjoy a bit of praise and notoriety at holiday parties and balls. Townspeople easily figured out from the initials over the articles that she was the author, and their reactions had been generally positive. Later, a few letters to the editor quibbled about minor points.

Some weeks later, she had gone to Belleville and presented a note at the bank there. But when she asked the teller for hard currency in exchange, he refused.

"But why?" Sylvie had asked. "It says right here on the notes that they can be exchanged at the state bank in Springfield. Surely you do business with that bank."

"We do, but we simply don't have the hard currency, miss. No bank does, right now. If everyone comes in asking to trade notes for silver, we will run far short."

"But what else is a bank for?" Sylvie asked in exasperation.

"Don't you read the news, miss? We are having a Bank Panic, and it's not our fault. It's been happening all over the country since Andrew Jackson closed the national bank while he was president. Regional banks have lost their backing, and in most places, it's worse than here. Come in and try again next week. We might have sufficient silver then, since the amount you want isn't very large."

Feeling personally rejected and confused, Sylvie had walked up and down the board sidewalks of Belleville for some time. Later, she saw that the bank had locked its doors, pulled down shades, and turned the sign to "Closed."

She tried the dry goods store, to see if she could use notes for fabric, gloves, thread, and other items. The merchant said that since she and her family were valued longtime customers, he would do her the favor of accepting her notes at fifty percent of face value. Sylvie had thanked him but demurred and returned home with no purchases and a troubled mind. She talked over the incident with Etienne, who assured her it was typical of what everyone was encountering.

"We are back to a world of barter," he said. "At least the French traders remember how that works, from the old days."

During the winter, Etienne had more time to read newspapers, and that morning he mentioned that the price of cotton was plummeting at American markets. Planters who had taken loans against their future crops were unable to repay them on the pitiful proceeds from sales, and many of them were going bankrupt.

"I think this is going to keep Texas from joining the United States for a while," he added. "The US is talking about going to war with Britain, mainly over setting the boundary with Canada way out west. So Britain is refusing to buy cotton from American growers. However, they're happy to buy from Texas as long as it is an independent country. But the collapse of the cotton market is causing all kinds of havoc with the American banking system."

As long as French wheat still brought high prices, the *habitants* in the area could ride out the worsening conditions. But Sylvie wondered how long that might last. "How will all of this affect us, then?" she asked.

"If banks here begin to fail—with no backing from a federal reserve—they can't extend loans. Then businesses could close, and new ventures won't have the cash or credit they need."

"I wonder what that means for the new railroad that Vital and the others are trying to finish. They were already having problems with loans and cash in the fall, when they switched to using wood."

"I don't know, and I'm glad I don't have anything invested in it." Etienne gave her a long look. "Have you found out yet how much of your inheritance has gone into that line?"

"No, I still have that question, plus others, to settle with Jeanne."

"These are interesting times." Etienne sipped coffee, looking thoughtful. "I'm glad I am staying with humble, reliable farming."

"I've heard that with the value of land dropping, many people around here are giving up and moving away, going back East."

"Plus the huge expansion of new towns is slowing down because people can't get loans for mortgages to buy houses or lots. I'm curious to see how Narcisse's new town will fare, up on the Okaw River."

"Or Vital's new town right near here."

"He's already lost some river frontage. The river's been running so high on the east side that it's cutting away the banks again."

"Oh, the river. Our fortunes rise and fall with it, don't they?"

"That, and other factors, though it does seem the Mississippi is key to anything that succeeds."

As Etienne returned to reading, Sylvie decided to write to Jeanne and insist on setting a time when they could talk as long as needed to clarify points crucial to her future. This could be a fortuitous time, for Jeanne seemed happier, and her outlook brighter, since she had given birth recently to a healthy baby girl who seemed to be thriving.

Sylvie awoke feeling glum and anxious on the morning set for talking with Jeanne. The wind howled outside, and sleet sank wetly into old drifts of snow. So little light came through the clouds that she lit candles in addition to the kitchen lamp, trying to raise her spirits. As she drank her usual coffee, her stomach rumbled.

This should be a favorable time for the talk, but Sylvie even fussed over her clothes, first putting on a dark purple dress that looked right for a funeral. She switched to the plaid taffeta she had worn to parties all fall and winter. It was inappropriate for a morning visit, but worn spots now showing on the black velvet trim gave it an everyday look. She was so pale, though—was she that frightened of her half-sister? She pinched her cheeks and forced a smile in the mirror.

Sylvie pulled on boots and her cloak and made her way through sleet and slush in the front garden. Oh, how much easier this would be if Andrew were here. As she stepped along icy ruts on the main street, she wondered if he could grow to love this town of quaint French homes. She smiled, imagining him in the old homestead, where he'd bump his head on door frames and the kitchen-ceiling timbers. But even if he became a farmer—not likely—he would have to learn French. And the amount of land she might inherit here couldn't equal what he stood to get in Texas. There would be no Comanche attacks, but they'd face Jeanne's continuing disapproval unless Andrew converted to being Catholic. And that he would not do—or at least had not agreed to, so far.

Sylvie tried to retain images of future happiness as the maid took her cloak and showed her to the *salon*, where Jeanne sat behind a small table holding a coffeepot and two cups and saucers. Seeing the set of her sister's jaw and her narrowed eyes, Sylvie suddenly recalled Rachel Flint back in Texas. How would Rachel handle this talk? Sylvie drew strength from the idea as she stooped to exchange cheek kisses.

Their chat began with pleasantries and Jeanne's assurances that the children were doing well. Then she abruptly added that family business ventures, however, now seemed on perilous footing.

"We are extremely grateful that we can continue to rely on your support for the railroad," Jeanne said, calmly pouring coffee for Sylvie. She described difficulties with bank loans and rising costs for equipment and materials. "Of course, the payoff coming will be substantial, and your patience *will* be rewarded."

Sylvie took her cup, barely half filled. "I'd be happy to see documents showing the actual amounts invested, plus any other statements, such as expenses. Then I could more fully appreciate what you're saying. And in addition, I want to see an accounting of my share of our inheritance from our father's estate and my mother's. I am an adult who should be consulted on matters so close to me."

"Oh, you haven't seen a full accounting? I was sure Nicolas went over the records and deeds and so forth with you. Didn't he do that last fall?"

"No, Jeanne, he has never done that, as I'm sure you know." Sylvie kept her voice even and firm to indicate she would not accept the prevarication. Suspecting that Nicolas would be easier to deal with, she added that she would be happy to call on him separately.

Jeanne said she would get that oversight taken care of. Each sister sat grasping her cup and saucer in both hands, and Sylvie noted the resemblance of their posture. Jeanne must be restraining the famous Pensoneau temper inherited from their father—Sylvie had virtually accused her of lying.

"Let's talk more about my land and money. Our father had substantial holdings when he died, and certainly some portion of that can be deeded over to me."

"We cannot cut farmland into pieces and send some with you to Texas," Jeanne said. "But if you marry and stay in the area, title to tracts of land will naturally be transferred to you and you husband."

"You can transfer title to me in any case, and I could sell the land and take the money with me. Cash is portable."

"You cannot make land transactions while you are underage, and these American courts say a woman's land legally passes from her father to her husband. In any case, selling land now would be terrible timing, with values dropping so fast."

After a few moments of silence, Jeanne shifted to another tack, saying the specifics of Sylvie's inheritance would be accounted for at the time she married, since she wouldn't turn twenty-one for more than a year.

"Our father never expected you—or me, for that matter—to deal with complex financial issues while we were young girls, not yet full adults. And I thank heaven every day for my husband's expertise in these areas, I rely so on his decisions. So you see, you are putting the issues in exactly the wrong order. First, we should discuss your marriage prospects."

"As you know, Jeanne, I have made that commitment in Texas."

"No, I do not recognize it as such, for you have not gained my approval as your legal guardian. And your insistence on returning there only continues to harm your reputation with potential suitors among appropriate families in town."

"Harm—in what possible way?"

"The unsavory experiences you have been through change you, roughen you, as a woman. These shadows on your past—that you camped out in close proximity to soldiers, without adequate protection for guarding a woman's purity—these raise justifiable concerns. And you have described these crude circumstances so brazenly—even publishing personal information in the newspaper! A respectable lady simply does not do that."

"Everyone suffers some unfortunate circumstances in life," Sylvie said. She thought of Jeanne's own sorrows over the deaths of a child and an infant but forbade herself from mentioning them. "Saying that suffering brings me, or any woman, into disrepute makes little sense," she continued. "The true question is how we conduct ourselves during misfortunes. I can assure you that my behavior and that of the women I traveled with were above reproach."

"But not above question, don't you see? You were refugees, out on the road, having to steal and beg, for all I know, and traveling in rough company."

"You are saying the fact that I went through an extremely difficult time is itself proof that my character is flawed?" Sylvie was incredulous. "I wish I could persuade you that even in the most raw and uncivilized conditions, one discovers strength of character. And that counts for far more than drawing-room manners and social proprieties." Her voice was rising in spite of her determination, but so was Jeanne's.

"A lady can always find a way to remove herself from dire situations, especially before they develop. You should have come home as you planned, after only a brief visit."

"I sought to do that. And I wanted to. But I did not cause the hurricanes that halted shipping on the Gulf of Mexico. Nor did I bring on the war, or the floods, or Gonzales being burned down, or the Mexican army chasing at our heels."

"That very list displays the crudeness of your recent life. How will you regain the refinement and grace needed for a *salon* of the highest order in our society?"

Jeanne did not flush with indignation; she was a pallid white. Her nostrils pinched so tightly that Sylvie wondered whether she was breathing against her tight stays. She badly wanted to say that she wanted nothing to do with the higher social orders if Jeanne's behavior and values were typical of them.

Sylvie carefully set her cup and saucer on the table and let her gaze drift to a window. She silently flung various responses toward the panes where sleet stuck and melted, then coursed down along wet tracks. After a few moments, she let go of recriminations; they would keep her from her main goal, which was to learn what quality at Jeanne's core was making her so rigid, negative, and insistent.

"What is the real reason that you object to my marrying Andrew Magill?" she asked, almost softly. "Does it have to do with religion, that he is not Catholic?"

"Yes. My deepest concern is for the fate of your soul, Marie Sylvaine. And if you persist on this path of sinfulness, then the souls of your children, my future nieces and nephews, are also in peril."

"It's as simple as that?"

"Yes, it is quite simple, and I am glad you now see that."

Sylvie knew that when it came to religious belief, there was little point in drawing on logic or reason with Jeanne. Her beliefs were passionate and deeply rooted, as Sylvie had seen over her lifetime.

"Jeanne, you do know that our ancestors were Protestant, back when they left France and came to Québec. And that my own mother was Protestant."

"Of course, and that matters little. What does count is that they all found their way to the true Church. Thus, we have been saved. For the sake of our own souls and those of our children, we cannot backslide now."

"It's not backsliding, Jeanne. It is—I don't know how to put this—a vision of a world where such distinctions matter less. We are supposed to be free to practice a range of religions in this country, so why not within a marriage, as well? Andrew loves me and respects me for who I am. He has not asked me to change, and I will not ask that of him."

"Oh, please, do not say such stupid things!" Jeanne's voice rose, and she cleared her throat to continue in a lower tone. "You are describing a world of chaos and loss, where people mistake their baser passions for divine guidance and thereby fall into mortal sin. I will not have such ridiculous premises aired in my house! You have only to look at history to know how absurd your 'vision' truly is." Jeanne worked to take in a deep breath. "If, on the other hand, you take steps to redeem your soul and rejoin your community, the inheritance you deserve will follow as a matter of course."

"Do you mean that would happen if Andrew converted to being Catholic?"

"Not necessarily, for that takes years of study and a serious commitment involving the spirit, the mind, and the heart. Otherwise, it makes a mockery of the church."

"So even if he did that, you still would not approve of the marriage. Do you not see that you offer no way forward for me, with your rules?"

"Of course I provide a way—stay here and make a respectable marriage. Everything falls into place after that."

Sylvie went back to studying the window but could feel Jeanne gazing at her.

"More coffee?"

Sylvie blew out some air.

"Oh, go ahead, scoff at me."

"I am not scoffing. I am frustrated, Jeanne. Your arguments run in a circle. You say both that I should marry here and that no one respectable will consider me, given my current reputation."

"But as you stay here longer, those aspects of your past will fade. However, you will need to keep to the highest society and well within the protection of your family."

"In other words, come and live with you, under your roof and under your complete control."

"Some in town say it is unseemly for you to be living with Etienne in the homestead house. He is, after all, your nephew. If he were your brother, it would be more respectable."

"Etienne is my brother, essentially. We grew up together that way, and he is the closest thing I have to a brother, with Laurent gone."

Sylvie heard the defensiveness of her own tone and realized Jeanne had steered them onto a digression. Surely no one in town cared about this, yet Jeanne went on about the advantages of living with an elder sister, arguing that a young woman should not venture on her own into the world. If she left her family, she lost her social standing, her anchoring in life—even her culture, language, and religion. A woman alone in a strange, new place was an unknown, and open to suspicion and mistrust.

"Our family's standing here is not some trifle to be tossed away. I allowed you to travel to Texas because you needed to become acquainted with your mother's kinfolk, and you were under the protection of a respectable man in James Kerr. But now that you are back, you must resume your rightful life in this community and the Church.

"This world gives your life definition and meaning, plus the background required for an appropriate marriage. You must break off the liaison with that unfortunate man, and do it quickly—it would be easy with a single letter. He is Protestant, an *Anglais*, and from Kentucky—three strikes against him. It has gone on far too long already."

Sylvie looked wonderingly at Jeanne while she delivered the lecture. While she grasped that her sister's religious views were sincere, the rest of it seemed like scaffolding erected for expediency around some fundamental principle that was not yet being spoken out loud. There was money, of course, and land, and Jeanne's clear desire to grasp Sylvie's rightful portion of those as long as she could.

Perhaps that was it, in its entirety. Jeanne's premises were difficult to counter when they were based on such different values and views from the ones Sylvie had learned to trust. And she saw a kernel of truth in what Jeanne was saying, for she actually had little patience these days for the social pretensions that undergirded her sister's life.

With Jeanne not granting legitimacy to a single point she was making, Sylvie was feeling vague, as though she were thinning into an incorporeal being, a mere waif. Her awareness floated toward the ceiling and watched the two women below, one stout and the other thin, hurling words at each other. Her mind even veered toward the window and out through the glass, then watched her figure on the street, already trudging home, in her imagination. Sylvie was anywhere but here, in this room where everything real and true about her reflected no actual existence.

Sylvie murmured as though to herself as she took up her shawl and reached for her bag, signaling her intention to leave.

"What was that you just said?" Jeanne demanded.

"At the basis of all of this, you feel I am rejecting you—you personally—along with the family, and our community. That would be painful." Sylvie found herself standing.

Jeanne stood as well. "Don't be like your unfortunate cousin Paschal, who turned his back on his family. You can see how he has become unknown to his brothers and sisters. When you reject family, Sylvie, your family must cast you out as well, and nothing is graver in this life, except for leaving the holy Church."

"Oh, I know about rejection, how it feels, and not really being part of the family." Sylvie bumped into a chair as she moved toward the door, but it did not budge since she had become so porous.

"What you need is to see a new world, a different place and way of life than here," she said. "We are moving toward a future that you cannot even imagine!" Sylvie had reached the doorstep. "You are so strident, so bound by petty, narrow thinking. As you cast me out, I will be well rid of all of this from my life!"

"Then let it be so, and let it be final," Jeanne replied.

Sylvie had to get out of the house and well down the street before she began not to exist at all.

Chapter 25

**Spring 1837**
**Cahokia, Illinois**

AS SYLVIE THOUGHT OVER THE DIFFICULT LETTER she needed to write to Andrew, she chastised herself for the talk with Jeanne. "Really, could I have done any worse?" she bemoaned when she told Etienne over coffee one morning about the course of the conversation.

Her nephew shook his head in sympathy and said that no one he knew had ever argued successfully with Jeanne in a matter of religion. He had also heard that finances for the railroad were precarious and suspected Jeanne would be defensive about admitting that. Maybe such a talk would go better if Sylvie tried again later, he suggested, after the current bank panic and financial crisis settled down.

"No," Sylvie said. "She is firmly in control of my share of the inheritance, and it's going to take an act of God to make her let go—probably not even court orders could get through to her. I don't think time will soften her views."

"You'll feel better about it once you've finished the letter to Andrew Magill. I trust he'll write that he still loves you and wants you to think instead about all the land you'll get in Texas when you go back there and marry."

"Oh, Etienne, I wish I had your faith in people and such an optimistic outlook!"

"One problem is that you've been through so many troubles and trying times recently, part of you expects more of the same. I've had a luckier life, so it's easier to stay hopeful."

"You are wise beyond your years."

Sylvie concluded what Etienne said was likely true, and after several drafts over the next few days, she finished a letter telling Andrew about her failures. Not only would she not get Jeanne's permission to marry, but she also would not get any inheritance if she married him. She folded and sealed two copies, wondering if the dire nature of the news might encourage him to consider converting—even for a moment. Probably not, she decided. He firmly believed in tolerance for different religious beliefs, and so did she, so why argue against holding fast to such a worthy value?

But given the life-and-death struggles he was facing regularly, her inability to prevail against her half-sister felt particularly humiliating. Would he even still want her as a wife, or consider her a suitable partner for the challenges of the Texas frontier? As weeks went by, Sylvie wondered how soon she might hear back from Andrew, and what the conditions of daily life were like around Mina—now called Bastrop.

Louisa was planning to return with the baby to New Orleans in the spring, along with Octave, who had arrived before Christmas. She urged Sylvie to accompany them, especially after Sylvie told her about the talk with Jeanne. Even if something later prevented Sylvie from going on to Texas, Louisa argued, she could find a new life for herself in the city. Sylvie liked the idea and saw little reason to stay longer in Cahokia.

In late winter, a letter arrived from Sarah, inviting her to come for a visit in Missouri as soon as the weather allowed. And Sarah had more travel in mind. Her husband, Jim, planned to visit Missouri early in the summer and organize a group to return with him to Texas. Sarah wrote that Jim's sister, Sylvie's Aunt Peggy, was ready to move there with her children, and Margaret Wilbarger and her son, who also had fled to Missouri, would come along. Sylvie should think about accompanying them, but they could discuss this more when she came to visit.

Sylvie was amazed at the way fortune, *la chance*, could work. Jeanne had seemingly blocked any route forward to the future, yet here were others offering possibilities. It was cheering and heartening that some friends and relatives—if not her sister—loved her and desired her companionship. She did want to see Sarah and the others quite a bit, and she did not want to land in New Orleans without having heard first from Andrew.

* * *

Card games among the women in town were running regularly at Julie Jarrot's house, and Sylvie had begun to attend more often. Soon her old and trusted method for bringing in cash let her add occasional winnings to the tea tin.

One afternoon, Sylvie was holding a favorable hand of cards and waiting for Madame Julie to meet, fold, or raise her stake. Only the two of them were playing that day, at a small table near the fire in the *salon*.

*Oh, la, la,"* Julie sighed, tossing four silver bits onto the pile.

"And I will raise the wager, just a small amount," Sylvie countered. She let three bits trickle from her fingertips.

*"Alors,"* Julie said with a sigh. "I must ask to see your cards. Mine are not worth throwing away more money."

Sylvie laid down her two pairs of queens and sevens, beating Julie's pairs of tens and fives. Sylvie scooped the coins toward the mound at her elbow as a maid entered to announce a visitor, an unfamiliar man wearing a US Army uniform. Julie said to show him in, that they were done playing, anyway.

"Good day, ladies." The man who greeted them in English stood with military straightness. He had black hair with long sideburns, and Sylvie guessed his age at about thirty. "Please forgive this intrusion into your afternoon." He bowed slightly, and Sylvie placed his accent as possibly from Virginia.

*"Bonjour,"* Julie replied. *"Nous pouvons vous aider comment, monsieur?"*

"Yes, you might be able to help me. My name is Robert Lee, first lieutenant, US Army Corps of Engineers. I am assigned to a project improving the port at St. Louis. As you may know, the Mississippi River has been depositing silt on that side, making the water quite shallow and creating shoals just downriver."

"Perhaps I should translate?" Sylvie asked, looking toward Julie, who nodded. As the women assured him they were aware of the situation, Lee said he was looking into the history of flooding on the Cahokia side. He wanted to know how often, and how deeply, spring floods had inundated the lower levels of the bluffs.

"Part of our project is to control that flooding—in Cahokia, the Common fields, and the lands south." He gestured widely and added, "And this is one of the oldest houses in the area, so I have come to you seeking some history."

Finally divining the purpose of Lee's visit, Julie offered to show him the marks on the kitchen's back stone wall, where the family had recorded the height of floodwaters over the years. Lee said he would be most interested in that, and with a sibilant rush of French, accompanied by nodding and a beaming smile, Julie led the lieutenant toward the kitchen, where he could inspect for himself the tally of the ravaging floods, which had inundated the house not just once but several times.

Soon they were gathered by the wall, where several lines of paint rose at intervals, with the year entered by each one. The maid and the cook looked on curiously.

"Oh, my word!" Lee exclaimed, bending to look at the lowest. He began jotting the year for each mark and its approximate height above the floor.

"And these are typically at what time of year?"

"In the spring, April or May, most often," Sylvie said. "Though there was a terrible flood one summer." She switched to French and discussed with Julie what they could recall.

"Tell him about the time we had a boat tied to the staircase," Julie said. "It floated right here, in the hall! We were packing up my silver cups and the children into the boat."

"The most precious things!" Sylvie had to laugh.

"I remember, too, how one of the children pushed the cook out of the boat—she thought it was funny," Julie said. "The child, I mean," she added with a glance at the cook.

Lee then asked about the large, jagged crack meandering down the wall, and Julie told of the earthquakes that had shaken the region for months at a time, back in the winter of 1811 to 1812. The family had moved to tents in the back garden, even though the walls of the house were quite solid, being two feet thick.

While Lee studied the wall notations, Julie asked for coffee to be served in the *salon*. Lee tried to decline, probably so he could get on with his work, but Julie's hospitality wouldn't allow that.

"You really should talk with Madame Louise Le Compte," Julie said, once they were seated and she was pouring coffee into demitasses. "She remembers everything, and she is more than one hundred years old, now."

Lee was studying the tray of small pastries, and Sylvie was describing the ingredients of several, when François came in to join them. He wore a suit of natural linen and had left his shirt collar open. As Sylvie made the introductions, she noted the hollows visible near his collarbones. She had grown accustomed to his gauntness and fatigue, but today his cheeks showed brilliantly red against the pallor. That could be a sign the final stage of the illness was drawing near.

Once he learned the nature of Lee's visit, François energetically delved into discussing the river channel's flow and silting. As the men spoke in English about possible steps for flood control, Julie sat back, seeming content to have handed the matter over to her son.

Sylvie's attention wandered during detailed talk, but when François concluded that Lee's plans for dikes and levees would shift shipping away from Cahokia's side of the river and favor St. Louis instead, she listened closely and translated for Julie.

François's voice had taken on an edge. "On this side of the river, we are just a final outpost of the East, and an aging remnant of the French empire. To make matters worse, now our port will fill up, and we'll lose shipping from the wharves we've recently built."

Julie asked François to translate and added,. "My younger son, Vital, is building a railroad, the first one in the Mississippi River Valley! And it will transport coal from the bluffs farther south up to Illinoistown for shipping. But if the river is too shallow—then what? Imagine our losses, *mon dieu*."

A silence ensued; the Jarrots had made their point, and Lee did not have a ready response to mollify their concerns. While Sylvie saw the threat to shipping, and to the railroad's future, she wondered if Vital's plan for a new town might be aided by the changes. She described to

Lee how Vital had sold land for a new town to a developer from New York, who platted the new city of St. Clair.

"Investors from the East are lining up to buy housing sites," she said. "Preventing the river from undercutting the banks there could help protect the value of the land."

"It would help the investment if that tract is more stable," Lee agreed.

François gave her a perplexed look as though wondering whose side she was on.

"This is all valuable information that we will take into consideration in our planning." Lee set down his cup, brushed off crumbs, and stood up. "Rest assured that these issues will be studied at length, and the Corps's plans will be announced publicly well ahead of building any levees or starting dredging."

Everyone stood and murmured what a pleasure it had been to meet and talk. Lee thanked Julie for her hospitality by bowing over her hand, rather than shaking it. François accompanied him to the door.

"My dear, that must have exhausted you," Julie said as he returned.

"In a way, *Maman*. But a bit of controversy also gets the blood pumping. I don't think Vital will be happy to hear about this. In fact, I think he will be quite angry and try to fight it."

"It would be good to stop the flooding," Julie said. "But at what cost? I have never seen so clearly how people picture the future as taking place on the other side of the Mississippi."

"*Maman*, business conditions are risky everywhere—in Missouri, too. But remember we have our farmland plus the trading business. We will be all right; don't worry."

"Yes, I know, and you run our affairs so well. What will it be like when Vital has to take over? I wonder about him having a free hand for all his enthusiasms."

Sylvie was surprised to hear Julie acknowledge not just Vital's impulsiveness but also François's coming demise. She looked down in discomfort, and saying it was time to get home, she thanked Julie and kissed her in farewell.

François walked with Sylvie to the door. "Shall I come by tomorrow?" she asked. "I could read to you, if you'd like."

"No, not tomorrow. Maybe wait another day." He leaned back and closed his eyes. She could see it required more effort than usual to take breaths. "I hope, Sylvie, that you are not trusting too fully on this fortune they all expect from the railroad. Even if it proves successful, the gains will come in slowly over time, and not soon, nor all at once, the way the family sometimes talks."

"No, I am not relying on it. It's funny how I don't mind wagering on poker or *vingt-et-un*, but I never, myself, would stake an inheritance on coal mining, or a railroad, or even a new town just up the road. Well, maybe I would wager on a new town because of the land. Look at how your father slowly, steadily accumulated acreage around here, and how that has paid off for your family."

"You're right that land is different and seems to have lasting value, even that is fluctuating just now. You should get your own land, Sylvie, in your own name."

"Yes, I should, and I will, if I ever figure out how to do that."

"Good. Once you accomplish that, I won't need to worry about your future anymore."

"Oh, you worry about me? Please don't." Sylvie had to struggle against a lump in her throat. "I want you to be at peace, and to believe that I will be just fine."

"Perhaps I would have married you, Sylvie, if I hadn't been ill."

"Oh, I wonder. But thank you for your friendship, your affection and esteem." She smiled, and they exchanged cheek kisses. He had made several similar remarks recently, which she believed sprang from a sense of loss as he faced the end of his young life. They were fond of each other, and she would miss François sorely when the sad time arrived. But between them sprang no deeper feelings of the kind she had begun to learn about in life.

Sylvie could not pretend that his death was far off just because it was approaching slowly. She had a role to play in lending comfort to him and the family, if she could. Other deaths—from cholera, measles, and war—had arrived so quickly, this was the first time she could step into the process of mourning in advance. Sometimes it felt as though she still carried grief from earlier times.

Everyone was shocked when news arrived in the spring that the steamboat *Sherrod* had exploded on the Mississippi River. The fire killed nearly two hundred people and burned the cargo, including sacks full of mail. Sylvie was at first horrified by the news and relieved that Louisa and her family were safely in New Orleans. But she was still awaiting word from Andrew, and over time she focused on the mail that had been destroyed. Was it possible that his reply was now fine ash silting the riverbed? How long should she wait before writing and pouring out her heart again?

At last a letter arrived from him, and Sylvie took it to the back garden to sit in the sunshine while she read it. Then she reread it twice. Over the next week, she carried the folded page in her skirt pocket and touched it often during the day, like a talisman. It could not have carried better news. After greetings and good wishes, he wrote:

> *Please come back to me, here. I want us to marry. Please think about this and say you will. Or if not, let me know. I don't care about money or your inheritance. I believe I can provide everything we will need, and you will bring land by being my wife—more than you'd gain in Illinois. You do know that I will not become Catholic, and thank you for not insisting. I hope your sister will come to see the light, so to speak, and soften her rigid attitudes, since she's only making herself unhappy.*
>
> *Finally I can say the town is safe enough for you to return, and it's a more cheerful place now. We've even held a few dances. Noah Smithwick, our blacksmith, plays the fiddle and spins good yarns. A captain of the rangers I've served with plays banjo, sings, and performs skits. We have a couple of physicians and a minister, who can now legally perform Protestant services—no more hiding in the back of the store like we did under the Mexican regime.*

*There aren't many women here, but you can look forward to an amiable group similar to yourself, though not French and not as charming or pretty. At our little dances, they barely get a chance to rest. I can reserve a dance if I ask someone early enough. Logan has more luck with the ladies, especially a certain one he fancies.*

*We are hoping for peace this spring and summer, after pushing the Indians farther west and building that new fort. Your Uncle Jim is heading to Missouri soon and will bring Sarah and others back with him. I trust his good judgment and hope you will travel with them.*

*Ed Burleson says he will call up rangers only for short forays, so I don't expect a longer enlistment anytime soon. Mexico is in too much chaos to invade, and Comanche raids are fewer and smaller, though they still happen in town; I don't want to paint too rosy of a picture.*

*Most importantly, I remain steadfast that everything I am doing, I have done for you, for the land we want, for this house and farmland, and to build my prospects. A man without a wife here is like a cart with a missing wheel. Let me know your decision as soon as possible.*

*I will break off now and make copies to send separately. This is too important to post only one time. I have plenty of paper now, too. May God bless you and keep you safe on your journey—which I hope you will make. With humble affections, I remain your devoted,*

*Andy—(or Andrew, as you seem to prefer)*

As she reread the phrases, Sylvie could nearly hear his voice, so direct and sincere. He possessed so much physical strength and energy, as she'd seen even at the end of their trek and after the battle. The vitality that drove him to fight hard and ride long was very attractive when it was focused on her. She also recalled the intelligent, humorous glint in his eye, which showed awareness and observation, an innate incapacity for boredom. Life would be lively, with him.

Right away, she wrote a note to Sarah, saying she would come to visit and hoped to travel with them. She replied to Andrew with the certainty she was delivering the news he most wanted to hear. After a time, she wondered where the other copies of Andrew's letter might be roaming, for she received only the one.

Sylvie kept in mind one bright point: in March, she turned twenty and had only one year left of Jeanne's guardianship as set in their father's will. She had seen very little of Jeanne over the previous months, though both were polite when they encountered each other on social occasions.


In April, Sylvie traveled to Missouri and enjoyed a visit for several weeks with her Aunt Peggy. The two older sons were leaving soon for Texas to finish the house in Columbia their father had been building when he died so suddenly several years earlier. Peggy had decided to follow later in the summer with the younger children.

Sarah came for lunch or tea most days, and so did Margaret Wilbarger, who reported news about Bastrop that she received occasionally from her husband. Jim would arrive in June, and Sarah expected he would be quite in demand as a speaker, given the acclaim he'd gained from serving as a major in the Texas military, fighting battles, negotiating treaties with Indians, and organizing evacuations during the war. He wanted to get back to Texas in time for elections in August, as he was running for a seat in the congress.

Sylvie agreed to travel with the group that summer and wrote from Missouri to give Andrew the details. While Aunt Peggy was clearly curious about Sylvie's beau, she tried not to pry. Margaret Wilbarger, however, enjoyed telling every story she could recall from Bastrop about Andrew and Logan and their daily life around town.

Sylvie also visited her half-brother David and his wife and was charmed by their two young children. He took her on several longs walks on his farmland, and as they talked, he mentioned his dark moods and bouts of depression, usually attributing them to atrocities he'd witnessed in the Black Hawk War. Time was helping him to heal, but a happy marriage and young children helped even more, especially the youngsters' unclouded affections and pure trust in him. Plus he said their energy was so relentless that he fell into bed too exhausted each night to remember his dreams, troubling or otherwise.

Sylvie hugged him at the encouraging news, and he wished her happiness with the fellow she planned to marry. He expressed no reservations about Andrew's background and even said she was wise to rely on someone so tested by the trials of life.

When Sylvie returned to Cahokia, the time spent with Sarah and Margaret made her years in Texas seem closer and more real. Their optimism about rebuilding their lives in the new country—an independent republic—was contagious. Sylvie felt this hope gave meaning to the suffering they had shared, and she was greatly comforted that she and Sarah were on warm and open terms again.

Daily life became infused with a sense of nostalgia, as though everything Sylvie did now—each place she visited, each person she met—would be for the final time. Often she paused to look hard at something or listen closely to someone, and try to store the occasion as memory. She had not felt this way when she left Cahokia before, for she had expected to return. And while married women did come back from Texas, Sylvie lacked the close ties to parents and siblings that usually prompted those visits.

Cahokia itself was changing, and Sylvie suspected she had a clearer idea of its future than many townspeople did. The traditional French community life was fading: the local courts had shifted from French to English, from the Custom of Paris to American laws, and lawsuits were ending the vestiges of slavery.

And the railroad came to town. The six-mile Illinois and St. Louis Line was completed that summer, and a crowd gathered to celebrate as teams of horses pulled the first cars of coal into town on the wooden railings. Vital Jarrot used the occasion to announce he was running for another term in the state assembly, as Marguerite stood smiling brightly yet demurely at his side.

Vital aligned himself with the Whigs and said he would work with his friend Abraham Lincoln on a range of initiatives, from building roads and bridges to establishing state and regional banks. He also spoke of the lawsuit he'd filed against the Army Corps of Engineers to halt the dredging and dike-building on the Mississippi River. Julie Jarrot was especially proud and happy that day as the crowd cheered her son, and everyone agreed he would win these efforts.

Sylvie was glad the families had something to celebrate and hope for, given recent sad events. Jeanne and Nicolas lost their baby, born the previous winter, when it succumbed to Cahokia's scourge of summertime illnesses at almost six months of age. To make matters worse, Jeanne had to get through the ordeal without a priest, for the one who had recently come from Lyons, France, had fallen ill with cholera and died soon after arriving.

A few weeks after the flurry of the railroad's completion, François Jarrot died quietly at home. He had stayed inside for a week or more, as he typically did during a serious relapse, but this time he did not rally. His death, though expected, still came as a shock.

Sylvie felt his passing as one more change in the landscape of her childhood as she gathered with mourners for a funeral on the morning following his death. Julie stood stoically at the family pew several rows ahead, and Vital, next to her, kept glancing about in a distracted fashion.

Sylvie felt comforted by the way she and François had remained friends. And they had shared quiet times that let her think more easily about Armand's sudden death. At the gravesite, the memory of him slipped further away in time and distance. The losses of the children, including Celeste and now three for Jeanne, remained sharply painful.

As friends departed after the service, Sylvie went to stand over her parents' graves one last time. Silently, she asked their blessing for her journey, and, even more, for her coming marriage. She did not pray, exactly, but she asked her parents' spirits to help her achieve in her life the things they had accomplished in theirs. They would understand and forgive that she would not be returning to this churchyard, to their graves.

Sylvie turned toward the area for Jeanne's family, with its heart-rending small plots, just as Isabelle was approaching with a handful of flowers. She bent to lay down the bouquet, and when she straightened, they exchanged kisses. Sylvie asked if she could do anything to help the family; Jeanne had not attended the service.

"That talk I had with her last spring was dreadful and deeply hurtful," Sylvie confided. "But oddly, I've come to feel freer. How small I would have to make myself, to stay on here and please her."

"Yes, that's exactly how I often feel," Isabelle said. "I would love to come visit you, and see Texas one day."

Sylvie said she would welcome that and asked whether Edward was interested in travel as well. "You could arrive in Texas as a married couple, and no one would ever know that your mother forbade it because you are cousins. Your last names are even different."

"He loves this land and won't leave it, and his family needs him to manage everything. But I will think about it. Even if we never go there, it will cheer me up to imagine it as something possible."

"Do come and visit me, Isabelle. Seriously—it's not so far away, and travel is getting safer and easier. You could become a physician or a midwife with your knowledge of plants and herbal medicines. Why, I ended up using almost everything you packed in the pouch for me, back at school. Your remedies eased many ills during our time as refugees."

"I am so glad." Isabelle smiled but still looked forlorn, and when she said nothing further, Sylvie asked how Jeanne was doing.

"The doctor keeps telling her to get out of the house, to take walks and visit people. But she always says she's too exhausted and needs to rest. I don't know how we will get through the summer months in the future. This is the third death— a tiny brother, two sisters—all in July or August. People say it's because we live near the creek."

"Jeanne has borne so many children, and she's twenty years older than I am," Sylvie said. "One wonders, if there were some way . . ."

"For what, to stop having children? *Maman* would view that as a curse, not a blessing. But these deaths make me not want to marry for some years. A woman should live happily and fully before marriage, since once she enters that stage of life . . ."

"Yes, I agree. But here we are in the churchyard, and are we speaking blasphemy?"

The two young women smiled at each other.

"It would give me a some comfort," Sylvie said, "if I were leaving on better terms with Jeanne. Then the door would be open for her to see what happens with my life in the future and maybe relent a bit or even reconsider."

"I think things are mended between you two as much as they might be. You've met several times since that argument, and you always stay friendly, at least on the surface."

"Yes, I've managed that. But I'm wondering if I should visit her and say goodbye, maybe try once again to gain her approval."

"Quite honestly, Sylvie, I think I can convey your fond farewells, and she will be content. Then she can continue to rest, undisturbed. She views your plans as open defiance, and that does upset her."

"All right. Give her my fond wishes and several kisses."

"That is easily done."

As the two embraced and promised to write often, Sylvie was wiping her eyes, and Isabelle squinted against the sun and her own emotions. As she turned to leave, her head drooped and her shoulders sagged.

Sylvie walked slowly back through town, feeling far away already. The golden light of the summer morning fell on the church and the old houses with their swooping rooflines and deep porches, on the tall, old trees and abundant flowerbeds. What an anomaly, that industry was coming: railroads, houses rising rapidly on grids of streets, maybe even a steel mill. English could be heard as often as French, and Illinoistown was now known by its nickname, East St. Louis.

The most difficult farewell would be with Etienne, even though he was glad for her. A young man still in love with his childhood sweetheart, he believed that Sylvie's happiness was assured by the promise of marriage. But he did look sad as he watched her arrange things in her trunk yet one more time on the evening before her departure. They were visiting quietly when a knock came at the door and Jeanne's husband, Nicolas, entered. He abruptly placed a pouch, which clearly held coins, on the kitchen table.

"Sylvie, this is an advance against your profits, which will be due to you from the railroad earnings. The directors all decided it was appropriate to pay a partial sum to you now, as you are leaving the area. It will be hard to award regular payments once you are away in Texas, which is a foreign country, after all. Vital would have brought this by and said goodbye, but he has gone to Athens to celebrate the new town; he was eager to see the other politicians there."

Sylvie was so surprised that it was hard to find the right words. She did feel grateful, but what did one say about a payment coming in advance of distant profits? She asked Nicolas to thank Vital and the other directors for her.

He shifted uncomfortably, his hands behind his back; he had not taken a seat. "It's not very much, and actually, it was not Vital's idea. His brother, François, insisted upon it, and he argued quite forcefully in your favor just days before he passed away."

"Mon dieu," Sylvie murmured. That made the money more of a bequest, the last wish of a dying man. Tears began to well, for she could just see François bent over the little red chest, as she had seen him as a child when he was fetching coins for the men playing cards. He had wanted to give her something to take into her new life.

Nicolas took his leave, and Etienne watched as Sylvie fingered the leather pouch. It felt almost sacramental, as though it would be disrespectful to count the money right away. "I'll open it once we're underway on the riverboat," she said.

"Maybe it will help you buy the rest of what you need for your household," Etienne said. "You are like the *Fille du Roi*, our ancestor Anne Le Ber, who packed her trunk and left France for the New World."

"Oh, you remember that story?"

"Of course; I heard you tell it so many times to Celeste."

"Me, a *Fille du Roi*," Sylvie laughed. "I do see some similarities, and just now I got my *livres* of gold that the king gave to each of the young women."

"Remember, they could choose to come back if they decided not to marry.. And you can come back here, anytime. When I get married and we have children, you can live with us and help raise them."

"Thank you, Etienne. That sounds lovely." Sylvie did not want to say that life as an aging maiden aunt, a dependent in the household, was not an attractive prospect. She valued his kindness and his caring for her.

She closed the trunk, and they made plans for the morning so he could help her with the luggage and see her off at the quay. She wept as she fell asleep that night, knowing that her final sight of him waving to her as the riverboat pulled away was going to break her heart, that it would be the last time she ever saw him.

# Part 4

Fall 1837 — Summer 1840

≈

In Edna and Bastrop,
Republic of Texas

Chapter 26

**Fall 1837**
**Edna, Republic of Texas**

Sylvie patted her hair one last time and breathed deeply as she stepped out onto the porch, where Andrew rose to approach her. He was so much larger than she remembered. He took her hands, and his probing gaze was exactly the same, strong enough to erase time and distance. He was sunburned red brown, making his eyes more brilliantly blue green. Would he kiss her? Yes, of course, but with the others around, they just touched lips before he veered to plant a kiss on her cheek that minded propriety. And she kissed his cheeks three times—left, right, left—smiling so hard her face ached.

As she turned to find a seat, her side glances perceived a man who was older. It wasn't that Andrew had grown bigger, it was more that he was filling out, with a broader chest and thicker thighs. As he sat down, he tugged self-consciously at a sleeve of his jacket, trying to wriggle the tight cloth across the shoulders. Or maybe he was covering a shirt cuff that needed mending.

She sat near him on the settee, feeling quite small as she perched on the cushion. She wished she could sit across from him instead and keep looking as long as needed to update the images in her mind. He had been so thin when they parted at the San Jacinto River nearly eighteen months earlier. Their clothes in tatters, their limbs so wasted they barely showed any curve of flesh over bone. And now when she did turn toward him, his eyes were only inches away, searching hers.

The October afternoon was pleasantly warm at the farm in Edna. Sylvie had traveled downriver in August with the group including Jim and Sarah, and when the others continued on to Texas, she had stayed with Louisa in New Orleans. There she'd shopped for household goods, a wedding dress, and fabric for several years' worth of clothing. Louisa had given her helpful advice on what to buy to keep a husband respectably outfitted.

Sylvie's voyage across the Gulf of Mexico had passed without incident, and after the schooner docked in Linnville, she'd joined travelers headed toward Edna and nearby towns. How different it was to enter the Republic of Texas as an immigrant who intended to marry and live there, compared with arriving as a visitor to Mexico years earlier. At the farm, Jim and Sarah had welcomed her warmly once again, though the place felt quiet with Minny still away at school in Ste. Geneviève. Jim and Sarah had worked hard to restore the house and replace missing belongings. As Sylvie moved about the rooms, she sorely missed the young ones who had died, especially baby Charles and little Edwina.

As soon as Sylvie had settled in, Jim sent word to Andrew in Bastrop, inviting him to visit. And here he was. Sylvie felt it would be rude to murmur privately with him as the two of them sat with Jim and Sarah on the porch, sipping cider and reminiscing. There seemed to be endless stories to recount since they had all been together, and Sylvie kept noticing little things about Andrew. His hair was trimmed in the current fashion—short on the top with long sideburns—which did nothing to diminish his sizable ears. He was cleanshaven, while she had become used to his beard during their time on the road. As she sipped at her cider, he drank a couple of glasses. She wished the slight amount of alcohol would calm her nerves, but instead it seemed to create a dull space behind her forehead.

Andrew kept glancing at Sylvie, probably also trying to reconcile memories with her current appearance. Her hair was now pinned up in loops and curls, and her dangling earrings glinted, casting light. He couldn't see even her lower legs, with her skirt sweeping the floor. Maybe he recalled her hitching up her shorter, old skirt as she crossed a stream or straddled a horse. As though reading his mind, she flushed.

"Sylvie—Sylvie, I was saying maybe you two can gather some pecans." Sarah was speaking to her. "Then we can make the cakes we talked about. Take Andrew with you—he's tall enough to knock down some nuts off higher branches."

"All right." Sylvie and Andrew got up and left the porch. He followed her silently around the house toward the orchard, and from the back door, Sarah called after them to wait a moment; she came out with large baskets.

"Don't feel you need to come back until these are full," she said, smiling. "Dinner won't be ready for an hour or more, so you have plenty of time."

Sylvie and Andrew walked toward the end of the orchard where it met fields and skirted some woods. They still glanced diffidently at each other.

"Are you happy to see me?" he asked.

"Oh, yes! What makes you ask?"

"It's just that you seem so formal, and everything is so different from what I recall."

"I probably do look a lot different. When I think of how sick I was, and how thin and hungry, and my clothes in rags . . . I don't want us to forget those times, but I do want to start again with newer impressions."

"I'll agree to that. Look at you, with your finery and your hair." He gestured in vague swirls around his head. "You look very . . . French. Attractive, I might add. Your eyes are still so big, and . . . shiny."

"You look different, too, you know."

"Yes, no more beard. And I guess my clothes are better. But I am afraid I've actually grown rougher over time. Summer, a year ago, I was out riding and sleeping on the ground, eating army rations off a tin plate around a campfire. This past year, I've mainly lived in my house. And while that's better, I've pretty much forgotten what it's like to have a woman around, like a sister or a mother. I'm bad at cooking, mending my own clothes, even growing a kitchen garden."

"You look like you're in good health, though. I feel smaller next to you—have you grown taller?" She asked in a humorous way, but they glanced at each other, noting the different levels of their eyes.

"Yes, maybe I have since life has gotten easier and we can eat regular meals again. That first summer after the war was very lean till we got livestock rounded up again and got a few meager crops planted. Even with army rations I felt hungry all the time until last spring. Since then, I've been eating to my heart's content, making up for it."

"It took me a long time in New Orleans to get any appetite back. I didn't know then how ill I really was. But back in Cahokia, when the balls and parties started, I truly enjoyed the suppers. I still couldn't eat as much as before, but I spent more time tasting things than dancing."

"And were you still the belle of the ball with all the young men asking you to dance?" He stopped walking, and after a step or two, she did as well. He was watching her closely again.

"No, I just danced a bit, mainly with cousins. Other girls were younger and prettier, and so excited about coming out in society. I held back, and truthfully, I wasn't interested in being courted by those young men."

"Is that truly the case?"

"Yes; you were often in my mind, and so was Texas. I always felt that my future lay here and I'd find it only by coming back. Sometimes I felt split between two worlds, but most often, the one back there seemed dull and narrow. That must sound strange to you—you have more of a home back in Kentucky, with parents and siblings."

"Hmm. I think I can imagine it." He started to walk again at a meandering pace. As though remembering their errand, they continued toward the edge of the orchard where the native trees encroached.

"And you?" she finally asked, her heart thudding. "You mentioned dances and young women in your letters."

"I haven't been courting at all." He laughed, adding, "Sylvie, you have so little to be concerned about, it's humorous. You'd have to spot me in the lines of men leaning against the walls, our hands in our pockets. And no, there is no one who strikes my fancy. My heart belongs elsewhere, as I learned very well, over the past year and more."

"Ahhh. That is nice to hear."

"Come here," he said. "I see pecan trees just beyond these oaks." They stepped into the grove of trees, out of direct sight of the house.

He took her hand, and they stopped and put down their baskets. They held hands and looked at each other. She felt extremely, painfully, shy, and she hoped he had the courage to act.

He gently pulled her to him and gathered her in his arms, and they held each other for a time. Then she pushed back and looked up so they could have a soft kiss, and then another. Then they separated, still casting glances.

"Things are different after all this time," Sylvie said. "And some things feel the same."

"Thank goodness for that." He grinned at her. "But maybe things seem less different for me because I've stayed here—though we rode all over the north and west of Texas. And last summer, the work on the house and land felt like getting things ready for you. It'll be your job to revive the garden, though. I planted several times, and then I'd go off with Logan and work cattle for a while. What did come up just withered and died."

She smiled at his kindness, the vulnerability he showed by directing humor at his efforts. "You're speaking of us being at home together, but what exactly is your plan?"

"How soon can we marry? I can try to find an official tomorrow, a minister or a justice of the peace."

"No, I won't be ready! Two trunks of household goods are still at Linnville, and I have to finish the wedding dress. I also need Annette's help making garments for you that will be part of my trousseau. We should start out with clothes for several years. And then I need to know which household implements you have already, and which we need to order while I'm here, and . . ."

"Good Lord. You aren't throwing up roadblocks, are you?"

"*Mais non!* No, all of this is genuinely necessary." He looked so perplexed she said, "Can you take off your jacket?"

"Certainly." He let it drop on the ground, and she reached up to feel along his shoulders and arms. He let her hands explore for a few moments, then bent to kiss her more firmly, his own hands sliding down her back to her hips.

When they broke off, she said, "I'm searching for the man I remember, and you feel more familiar than you look."

"I'd say the same about you. What happened to your braids, your old calico dress? You used to have a sun-browned face and a sassy way of delivering repartée."

"I never want to be barefoot and ragged again. Or hungry, at least not like that."

"You never will be, I promise, as long as you're with me. But can you wear your hair in braids once in a while?"

She smiled, and looking down at their feet, noticed they were trampling pecans. "Maybe we should pick up some of these."

"Oh, let me knock down some fresh ones." He found a long stick and began thwacking at branches in the canopy overhead.

"I am so sorry that I failed with my important tasks. I never got Jeanne's permission to marry, and in fact we ended on worse terms than ever. I don't know what to say about my inheritance. I honestly think Jeanne will disown me if I marry outside the Church, but does she have the power to do that? I don't know if that's legal. Her husband did arrive on my last night in Cahokia and gave me an advance against my earnings from the railroad. It wasn't much, and I spent most of it in New Orleans buying household goods."

They stooped, moving about and picking up pecans. After a few minutes he said, "I wrote to your sister and formally asked for your hand in marriage. I haven't heard back from her."

"You did?" Sylvie straightened and looked at him. "I am amazed. She never said a word about it. Well, thank you, though, for trying."

"I wonder if my letter got through. There's always the chance it wasn't delivered."

"It wouldn't make a difference—nothing will except converting to Catholicism."

"Which I will not do. We created this country—I mean, the United States—in order to have religious freedom, and I believe in it. My family immigrated because of persecution. If I converted or gave in to religious intolerance now, it would be a huge step backward. But

I meant it when I said that when we're married, you can practice any religion you want."

"Yes, you've been very good about that. But do people have to convert to become Protestant? Or does that happen just by lapsing from being Catholic?"

"Oh—just by backsliding; yes, that probably works."

Andrew looked so puzzled that Sylvie had to laugh. "I'm sorry. I just realized that sounds a bit . . . arrogant."

"There you are. We'll be married by a minister, or if you object, by a justice of the peace. And just think of the land: a wife brings fifteen hundred more acres. We can call it your land, if you'd like."

"Wonderful! I do like the sound of that. And maybe that's where I can lay the section of railroad track that's my rightful inheritance. I've been worried about where to put it."

"Then it's settled." They both started laughing, and when Sylvie kept giggling, Andrew brushed leaves off a fallen trunk so they could sit. They leaned against each other, still chuckling. And then she was back in that moment when they had been hungry, dirty, and victorious, and he had poured Mexican silver coins into her lap. At last, at last, his arms were strong around her again.

After a time, he straightened and said, "Eighteen minutes."

"For what?"

"That's how long the battle took at San Jacinto. We were that close to dying and losing everything—all the colonies, the land claims, our lives. We had nothing, you and I, except our lives when we declared our . . . mutual affection."

"Love," she said, looking down at her open, empty hands. "It felt so real, the most real thing during all that unreal time. The fighting and the fleeing don't seem as real, thinking back. But was our connection only for that moment, for that time and place, or does it endure and transcend?"

"You sound like one of those romantic poets."

"No . . . no, that's not what I mean. Are you angry with me? Sometimes you seem so stern."

"Oh, not at all. I'm sorry, and I don't mean to sound that way. Sylvie, I've had a lot of time out chasing Indians—riding, fighting, and shooting, and all of it spent only with other men. I think that makes a fellow grow hard, or rough. It has to show up in some way."

"Then I'm glad I'm here to bring out the gentler sides of you." She smiled and raised her eyebrows.

"Yes, thank you; I'll enjoy that. But seriously, living in Bastrop will require courage from you, beyond attachment to me. The Comanche attack pretty often, and constant danger affects women's lives in ways you need to consider. Here in Edna, a hundred miles south, there's more peace and a sense of security."

"As I recall, your house in Bastrop is very close to the stockade."

"That's true, and it must seem like a haven to you, a place of protection. I wouldn't be spending much time there, though, since I get called up to give chase."

He said this ruefully, his good humor returning, perhaps even bravado. It might sound naive if she admitted that her own courage depended on his standing between her and danger.

"I'll have time to think more about that," she said. "Since we're waiting until spring to marry, when I turn twenty-one, we have a long engagement coming, and a nice courtship."

"Oh, that long. What will I have to do?"

He looked at such a loss that she had to laugh. "Nothing different, really. Keep getting the house ready, maybe try again to start a kitchen garden. In the meantime, I'll finish my trousseau. There's a great deal of sewing, and I'll warn you I don't enjoy that much."

"Are you likely to become bad-tempered?"

"Yes, exceedingly."

"Then I'll have to go on a few rangering missions, just to cope."

"Oh, don't even joke about that. Don't you have work to do with Logan and the cattle?"

"Yes, actually; we'll be very busy with the herds come spring."

"Isn't this wonderful? We're talking about ordinary life, everyday things, not matters of life or death—more the pleasures of life."

"With what we've been through, Sylvie, the ordinary things are the real pleasures. But how did you put together such a large trousseau—did you use the Mexican silver I gave you?"

"Yes, plus that advance on the railroad and some money for writing the newspaper articles, and a bit I came by here and there. And it's only three trunks."

"What could possibly fill three trunks?"

He looked so puzzled that Sylvie had to smile and give a reassuring kiss. And that led to several more.


Running stitch, slip stitch, hem stitch, whip stitch for buttonholes—Sylvie sewed on and on, fashioning sheets, towels, aprons, pillowcases, shirts, skirts, blouses, dresses, and even men's undergarments—a new effort for her. While she did not enjoy the work, it was satisfying each time she folded a finished item and placed it in a trunk. Annette helped, and they enjoyed sitting in a sunny spot to stitch and reminisce. Sylvie wondered about her peach silk dress, which had disappeared when the farmhouse was ransacked. Annette said she had been watching for it, in case a local woman showed up wearing it. She also told about accompanying Rachel and the children on their return trip to San Felipe from the camp near the San Jacinto River. She said Andrew had helped them a great deal along the way.

Rachel corresponded with Sarah and Jim, and apparently she and her children, including baby Elizabeth, were staying well. She had returned to Gonzales and was helping to build the town for the third time. Jim had shaken his head, saying he wasn't going to try once again. He learned about the town being burned while their household was on the road, fleeing, and he had written a document renouncing his claims there.

Sylvie had also talked with Anise and Shade and expressed her condolences for their loss of Edwina, one of the four children who had died on the trek. She enjoyed seeing Caroline, now eight, and Nelson, two years older, as they played or did chores. Rosanah was living away with her husband but came back during the day to work.

She seemed to be recovering from losing her infant and was expecting another child soon.

In the evenings during Andrew's visits, conversation ran late under the lamplight. Jim had been elected to the Texas Congress, and he shared news about legislation and political efforts. Sylvie and Sarah did sewing while Jim and Andrew enjoyed a glass of brandy. The life that Andrew described in Bastrop contrasted with the peacefulness at Edna, especially when Jim asked about the Comanche, who still considered the town an illegitimate outpost in the midst of their fall hunting grounds.

"What they're mainly after isn't game but our horses," Andrew said. "That's how they figure their wealth." He told of a raid in daylight the previous summer when Comanche had driven off fifteen horses. Men gathered quickly and caught up with them about eight miles out of town.

"We got into a running fight, since we were in trees and had dismounted to shoot. We chased them off, and we came back with our own horses plus theirs as well. Not every skirmish ends that successfully, though."

Jim asked about another raid, in which several settlers had been killed and others kidnapped. As Andrew recounted the events, Sylvie's expression grew solemn.

"Not long after that raid, Indians robbed a house below Bastrop." He said that Ed Burleson and some others had driven the Comanche into a cedar brake on a creek near town and sent back for more men. Andrew arrived with the reinforcements, and they tracked the group. They caught up with them in the afternoon and chased them into a ravine, but the Indians escaped and made it back to their camp.

"But here's the strange part: most of them died there. We arrived later, expecting to fight, but instead we found dead bodies and the remains of a huge feast. It looked like they'd gorged on pigs they'd killed in the woods, and something about the meat—or the fat, which they're not accustomed to—killed them."

"How very strange," Sarah said. "I haven't heard of that happening before."

"Andrew, just how many ranger missions have you been on?" Sylvie asked. "It sounds as though the fighting is nearly continuous, and I don't think you've told me about all of them."

"Half a dozen, I'd say, since last November. But on a couple of those, I never fired at anyone. We just went out in pursuit, or were tracking and were too far behind."

"I find this a little troubling," Sylvie said. She had put down her sewing and was pressing the fabric flat with her hands. "Are you always someone who goes out when men are called up? And do you always have to be?"

"I'm hardly the only one who responds. I have a fast horse, and I'm considered a good shot. And I'm not married; other men would have to leave wives and children at home, where they too need to be defended."

"So when you are a married man, will you go out less often? Or when you have children, would you be more likely to stay back?"

"That's not a fair question, Sylvie," Jim interjected.

"Why not?" Sarah asked. "It's important; let him answer."

"Let me put it this way," Andrew said. "Protecting women and children makes the ranger duties even more important. What if my home were attacked and my wife and children were taken? I would want—I would expect—other men to ride out and help me. Therefore, I have to be someone those men can count on, too."

"I guess I can see that," Sylvie said.

"What the women suffer when they are kidnapped is terrible," Sarah said. "Since Rachel Plummer was ransomed from the Comanche and has come back to live among us, everyone talks about the abuse and the beatings she endured. You may not know, Sylvie—she was kidnapped at Parkers Fort shortly after the war."

"Yes, I saw stories about her in the New Orleans papers," Sylvie said. "She was forced to walk barefoot in snow, in very high mountains out west. Other torments were hinted at."

They glanced among one another, not comfortable discussing openly the veiled references to rape and tortures.

"What amazes me," Jim said, "is how far the Comanche can get with their prisoners in just a few days. As Mrs. Plummer describes it, they made a hundred miles a day or more."

"They probably are that fast," Andrew said. "I met her and the others on my first foray with the rangers in July 1835. We were in pretty bad shape after attacking the Towakani village, and we went to the Parkers' compound to regroup. Everyone treated us kindly. When we all came back after the war, a ranger unit did try to find the Comanche band that is still holding Cynthia Parker and the children. No luck, though."

They sat in silence for a minute, and then Jim spoke of an effort in Congress to establish the new Texas capital near Bastrop. "That would bring more settlers up there and make it clear to the Comanche that our presence is permanent. Plus we'd name the new capital for Stephen Austin."

"I like that plan," Andrew said. "I've heard some people in the San Jacinto area donated land for a capital on Buffalo Bayou and are calling it Houston."

"Austin reserved good tracts of land for himself on some hills along the Colorado River," Jim said. "It seems a fitting tribute to his memory to use some of it for a significant site, like a capital. He would have liked that."

As the men talked more about land claims and military allotments, Sylvie pondered the recent raids on Bastrop and the amount of fighting Andrew was doing. What did that portend for her married life? He seemed distant at times, often withdrawing from conversation only to look sternly at her and others before emerging from his thoughts. She wondered if she could persuade him to stay in town more often and defend it, rather than always answering a summons. Clearly, Andrew needed her presence to bring some balance into his life.


Christmas was going to be festive at the Kerr farm. After the years of war and separation, the household was eager to celebrate being together and enjoying renewed prosperity. They had plenty to eat and drink, friends and family to share with, and a new country pulling itself together, even though actual money was scarce and government-issued scrip nearly worthless.

Sylvie gladly switched from sewing household items to knitting scarves, hats, and socks intended as gifts. She also helped with cooking. The brief visits with Andrew were becoming more relaxed and natural, as he stopped by occasionally between his other obligations. He was tending to the house in Bastrop, herding cattle on land west of there, and minding his original land claim, located south of the Kerr farm near Victoria. Sylvie could see how much Andrew enjoyed riding hither and yon, how happy he was in the saddle, going places. After a few days at the farm, he became restless and needed to be off on the next task.

Sarah announced that Christmas dinner would be ham, served late in the afternoon. Dessert came afterward, and everyone was expected to contribute to the evening's entertainment, including friends and neighbors who planned to stop by.

"But I don't have any talents," Sylvie protested, when she caught Sarah alone. "I don't sing well, and I can't play the piano at all."

"That doesn't matter." Sarah spoke firmly. "Surely there is something you can do."

"I like to dance," Sylvie said doubtfully. "*Alors*, I'll think of something."

Annette took Sylvie aside and suggested talking with some of the slaves. "We have good musicians, and we all know the old French songs and dances from back home. There's a banjo, flute, drums, fiddle—and Anise and I love to dance. Rosanah might like to, also, and it would remind us of good times in the past."

"I like that idea," Sylvie said. "People here don't know much about French customs. We'd need to practice ahead. Let's keep it as a surprise, though, in case it doesn't work out."

Annette arranged times for Sylvie to visit the slave quarters when they were practicing Christmas songs and dance music for reels, jigs and waltzes. As the rhythms of the djumba drums moved from one tune to the next, Sylvie shed her self-consciousness and danced along with Annette and Anise. The music lifted her spirits like nothing else, and she worked to keep up as the others stepped to African or Caribbean beats.

Andrew arrived on Christmas Eve day, amid the flurry of preparation. When Sylvie warned him that he also would be expected to contribute a performance the next day, he looked startled and then grew thoughtful. He agreed but said he'd need to rehearse, and Sylvie wondered what talent he was planning to display.

Sarah wanted a religious service on Christmas Eve; even without any clergy, she said they could say prayers, read scripture, and sing hymns. As family gathered in the parlor, Sylvie had trouble concentrating on the familiar words and songs. Her mind kept reviewing details of preparing meals and gifts, and her glance kept traveling toward Andrew's boots. She had knitted a pair of wool socks for him and was worrying they might be too small. Several times she had started to form the heel, only to rip out the stitches and start again with a larger size. Had she overdone it, or failed to make them wide enough? Oh well, there was nothing she could do now.

On Christmas morning, in the warm kitchen smelling of cinnamon rolls, coffee, and bacon, Andrew and Sylvie caught a moment to exchange gifts. Others in the family were surprising one another with small packages as they came and went. Andrew pronounced himself delighted with the burgundy-red socks and admired the fine, tiny stitches. And Sylvie gratefully accepted the two reels of trim he presented, one a narrow black ribbon, and the other ivory lace. She smiled to think how that one would look on a nightgown she was sewing. And at a moment when no one else was around, Andrew handed her a small leather pouch.

"Open that later, when you are alone," he said, kissing her quickly on the cheek.

The farm chores and cooking proceeded, and late in the afternoon, everyone gathered for dinner. Neighbors arrived in the evening, bringing cakes and pies, and the entertainment began. One woman played the piano rather well, and Sarah sang several songs to much applause. After that, Jim recounted some humorous stories. Another neighbor sang country tunes while accompanying himself on the banjo, followed by a violinist who played old Irish airs.

"Now, Andrew, what will you perform for us?" Sarah asked. Everyone looked expectantly at him as he stood up, tugging at the sleeves of his jacket.

"Back home at holiday time, we children were often asked to recite," Andrew replied.

"Ah, poetry? We haven't had literary contributions yet, tonight," Sarah said.

"I think these count as poetry, though I'm not sure about literary quality. My uncle, John Magill, wrote verse. He published a book on the history of Kentucky, and he added some of his poems at the end of it."

"I knew your uncle, and I've heard about the history work," Jim said. "But not about any poetry. Well, well!"

"These don't have much to do with Kentucky; mostly they mention Athens, or Rome, or Greece. When I was young and we had to memorize them, I thought those were places just down the road." Andrew smiled sheepishly as several people chuckled.

"I'll give you a choice. Do you want to hear 'The American Revolution,' or 'Brittania'? How about, 'Man's Fall and Punishment'? No, too grim. We could try, 'Praise Ye the Lord,' or 'Progress of Religion'?"

"Which is the least dour, or solemn?" Sarah asked.

"They all strive earnestly toward high ideals. But I'll recite one suitable for Christmas, 'Come, For Ye are Called.'" Andrew grasped his lapels and bounced slightly on his toes, and Sylvie could picture him as a young a boy trying to please his family.

"After each stanza, you can join in saying the refrain, if you'd like. You might have guessed, it's 'Come, for ye are called.' All right, here we go."

And he began declaiming the poem in a slow cadence, emphasizing the words that rhymed.

*But mouths of babes and suckling*
*Are fit to render praise*
*We'll follow their example*
*And shout in loudest strains—*
*Come, for ye are called!*

The group obligingly shouted the refrain on cue, and as Andrew finished, Sarah stood and thanked him. "What a wonderful recitation. It was so marvelous that I believe just one selection will do. We would not want to dilute its effect, after all."

Hearing the round of applause, Andrew sat down with clear relief.

Sarah then called on Sylvie, who stood and said, "I am going to beg. That's what we do at home, in the winter holidays. Back in Cahokia, we dress in costumes and ride in a sleigh from house to house. Homes that have soup ready, *bouillon,* leave their shutters open, and we go in, warm up, and eat and drink. Then we beg an item to take to the next house, for the soup pot at that party. It really is a lot of fun." All along, we sing a begging song, *'La Guiannie.'"*

She paused while the musicians finished assembling their instruments near the piano. "You might want to stand up so you can join in," she told the audience. "Those of you who don't know the French lyrics might just want to tap your toes."

As the musicians struck up the tune, those originally from the St. Louis area began clapping and even singing some of the lyrics. Sylvie began dancing lightly, holding up the edge of her skirt. Her shoes from New Orleans had fairly high heels, and she liked the clicking noise they made in time with the music.

Everyone was laughing and clapping at the end of the song, so Sylvie decided to proceed with the encore. She asked Annette and Anise to join her and announced that the next dance came from the Caribbean, its origins possibly dating back to Africa. The beat began fairly slowly, and the three women slid their hips side to side and gracefully raised an arm high overhead. Their dresses looked festive, with Annette in green, Anise in red, and Sylvie in deep blue. As the tempo picked up, so did their steps, and they moved faster and faster.

Sylvie lost herself in the thrill of music and movement synchronized with the others. They whooped a few times as the complex, shifting rhythms reached crescendos, and Sylvie was perspiring, holding her skirts high, whirling now so the room was a blur.

When they finished, out of breath and laughing, they gave one another hugs. Everyone was still on their feet and clapping, but the applause died out fairly quickly. Jim and Sarah looked pleased but surprised, and some of the neighbors murmured comments to one another. Sylvie glanced at Andrew, whose eyebrows arched high in his pale face.

She tossed him a wide smile, but his expression remained fixed. Was he so struck by her talent, she wondered, that he was simply amazed? She glanced down to see one hand still holding up her skirt, with plenty of petticoat showing. She let it drop.

The guests moved on to singing Christmas carols, and Sylvie returned to her seat near Andrew. When he nodded at her but did not speak, she said, "That was a nice poem you recited."

"Thank you. And that was some fine dancing."

"That's one thing I do well. I love to dance."

His eyebrows, no longer raised high, had dropped low. "So I see."

She gave him a *moue*, a humorous frown, and turned her attention to the woman playing a hymn on the piano.

Alone in her bedroom later that night, Sylvie reached for the soft leather pouch Andrew had given her in the morning. She worked apart its knotted cord and slid out a golden chain with a locket. Both were simply but beautifully fashioned, and they gleamed in the candlelight. The only design was an embossed *fleur de lis* on the front of the locket.

"Oh," she breathed, stroking it with her fingertip and feeling the weight of the chain. She wondered where Andrew ever could have found such beautiful jewelry, out here. Maybe he had made arrangements with John Linn, who was bringing more fine things all the time to his warehouses. She clicked open the locket and saw the inside was bare of any likeness or lock of hair. A bit of paper bore small handwriting that said, "To be filled."

She sat back, smiling dreamily. What a lovely, valuable, romantic gift! And then she was embarrassed that she had given him only the knitted socks. She had bought many goods in New Orleans that they would need, such as plates, lamps, and cutlery, and she had worked hard all fall sewing household linens and clothing, including garments for him. But she could not make gifts of those things while they were not yet married.

Oh, well. He would have to be patient and trust to the future, enjoying her charm and spirited dancing in the meantime. She suspected he had been slightly shocked by her performance and hoped he would view it more favorably as he thought over the evening, out in the bunkhouse. She also hoped she was not the topic of too much comment by the other men staying there.

Chapter 27

**January – March 1838**
**Edna and Bastrop, Republic of Texas**


ONE MORNING IN LATE JANUARY, SYLVIE AND ANNETTE looked over the
assembled household goods that had to be transported to Bastrop.
Three trunks were crammed full, wooden crates carried kitchen gear
and utensils, and several boxes held supplies of seeds, candles, salt,
spices, medicines, kerosene, and more. Sylvie felt this mass of goods
could propel her life forward on its own momentum.

"I suppose we can ask Sarah to store some things here, if we can't
bring it all," she said.

"True. But you and I really know how to pack an ox cart, don't
we? And this time we have two, plus pack horses."

Sylvie had to chuckle. "How many times did we unpack, and
repack, Rachel's ox cart, do you think?"

"A hundred times, I suppose, though I was going to say thousands. We owe each other a happy trip now, to make up for that awful
trek, don't you think?"

"To balance things out? I agree, and I am so grateful that you're
happy for me, and my coming marriage. I'm also extremely grateful
for the work you've done to sew things, get everything ready, and now
bundle it all up."

"You're welcome," Annette said quietly. "My life here will go on
much the same, but it will be a bit duller, with you gone."

"I wish you could come with me, or that more in life was changing for you, especially after our struggles as refugees. Your hard work
is always done to benefit others." Sylvie broke off, feeling sad and at
a loss for words. More than once she had wished she'd taken Annette
with her on John Linn's schooner when she fled Texas, and had found

some way to get her to Illinois, or any possible path toward freedom. But when she had hinted at such thoughts, Amy closed off the topic as pointless, with Sylvie back in Texas. Plus she shuddered at the idea of being a runaway, a fugitives from the law, and insisted she would not have left Anise, Shade and the rest of her family behind.

Now Annette said, "Your efforts, and Miss Sarah's, aren't working out quite the way you both imagined, either, I think. I remember in Gonzales sometimes you'd say that women might get more rights once slavery was completely abolished in Texas. And we all held out hope."

"Yes, and slavery was abolished officially—by Mexico. But that was overwhelmed by the sheer numbers of Americans coming in, and their will to keep slavery going here. And now Texas is copying all the same structures and practices that hold inside the United States. Or nearly all—though not quite. My life will be better here, but it took that long trip back home to fully realize that."

"I'm glad for you, and for your hopefulness. And here I am with family I love, my aunt, uncle, cousins. I do value that a lot."

Though Amy did not make a comparison explicit, Sylvie still felt the absence of family in her own life as a void that stuck to her like a shadow. Even Uncle Jim was fairly distant, as an in-law. But by marrying, living in a new town where she would make friends, and starting a family of her own, she hoped to redress that constant sense of loss.

As she finished dividing the loads, Sylvie was determined not to leave behind her small stack of novels from New Orleans, including *The Last of the Mohicans*, by James Fennimore Cooper, and *Edgar Huntly*, by Charles Brockden Brown. She imagined Andrew would be interested in how these authors described life in western wilderness, if he had any time to read.

Andrew had visited the farm several times since Christmas, and as Sarah and Jim relaxed their vigilance as chaperons, he and Sylvie found more private times together. He showed affection in a natural way, as though it flowed from a fundamental part of his personality, and that put her mind at ease. She watched for any dark periods of anger or despair, and saw that he became stern and withdrawn on only a few occasions. She figured this was how he found the resilience to counter the effects of the fighting he'd done.

During a stop on his way south to his original land claim, Andrew asked Sylvie if she wanted to ride there with him. Though he planned to swap that land for a claim closer to Bastrop, in the meantime he needed to tend to the cabin and put in a crop—literally "a few hills of beans." The weather was fair, the roads hardened by frost, and the idea of a day away from sewing was appealing. Sylvie packed food, and they set out early one morning. They returned quite late and in good spirits, and Sylvie hoped any rosy coloring or disheveled hair would appear normal for the end of such a long ride. Sarah smiled at them as she went about turning down lamps and lighting candles for use at night.

Several days later, she approached Sylvie and asked for a few minutes to talk quietly. When they were alone, Sarah suggested it might be wise to move the date for the wedding forward by a month or more. Sylvie blushed furiously and disagreed. She was determined to wait until she was twenty-one and could marry in her own legal right. If she adhered exactly to the terms of her father's will, she hoped that one day in the future, either she—or her husband or a son—could go back to Illinois and establish a valid claim to her inheritance. Jeanne's power as legal guardian would terminate soon, and her influence over the prevailing opinion in town would diminish with time.

Sarah nodded and agreed with Sylvie's thinking. She added that she probably would not travel to Bastrop, however, for the wedding. Already they were having to work around Jim's busy schedule to make sure he could get there to give her away. But Sylvie understood that Sarah's reasons were entirely different and more personal. She threw her arms around Sarah wished her continued good health as she mentally counted the months before the blessed event would arrive.

In February, all the colonists of Bastrop had to appear in town to make their land claims official under the new government. Andrew planned to be present, and other colonists would serve as witnesses for him, as he would in turn for them. After that, he had to visit his original claim and have an official survey made and recorded. He and Sylvie planned that on his return to Bastrop, he would stop at Edna.

Then he and Sylvie and her pack train could travel north together. Once in town, Sylvie would stay with Margaret Wilbarger again, and that would lead smoothly toward her birthday on March seventeenth, with the wedding taking place shortly after.

When Andrew arrived at Edna and Sylvie proudly showed him the household goods bundled and ready to load, she was disappointed by his reaction, after all her work.

"I go rangering for months at a time with just two saddlebags." He stood, scratching his head. "With all this, you're going to make quite an entrance in town."

"I think that's all right. People already know that I'm an orphan, and a few could have heard I'm disinherited as well." She lowered her head and looked up from under her brow. "I couldn't bear it, if our marriage appeared quick, or offhand. I want to look like a woman from a respectable family, with property, so that I can form friend-ships and enjoy a certain social standing."

Sylvie looked back down, amazed that she sounded so much like her sister Jeanne. Yet she persisted, "Does that make sense? Think of how men respect you if you fight and shoot well. It's the same thing with women, only they put stock in different things."

"All right. I'll leave female friendships and questions of social standing up to you."

"Besides, you're going to like our new things, like nightshirts and linen sheets with lace trim. And I even have fabric for curtains."

"I'm just not sure how we'll fit all this into my house—our house."

"We'll make it work, though you might have to build shelves and cupboards."

Andrew had left his boots near the outer door, and Sylvie noticed he was wearing the socks she had knit for him, the wool bunched around his toes. "Oh, I made them too big, didn't I?"

"No, they're great. The extra room in the toes lets them stretch wide enough. Thank you again." He kissed her on the cheek, then he added a longer kiss on the lips.

"You do love me," she marveled.

"Do you have any doubt? Is a firm date set for the wedding?"

"Yes, March 29. Uncle Jim committed to it before he left for San Felipe."

Jim had to be present there to establish his own land claims as a colonist, and later he planned to go to Gonzales and serve as a witness for the numerous surveys he had done for DeWitt's colony. After that, he would head north to Bastrop.

With everything ready for departure, the group set out on a sunny, dry day in early March. Shade and his son Jack planned to drive the carts with their high, teetering, strapped-down loads. Andrew, Sylvie, and Annette would ride horseback and lead two horses packed with bags and parcels. Andrew had arranged for friends to meet them at Burnam's on the Colorado River and help them get to Bastrop, so the others could return to Edna.

Sylvie rode her own horse, Sheba, a little pinto with an unusually long blond mane and tail that Uncle Jim had given her as an early wedding present. Whenever she was in the lead, she felt like a princess of old leading her wedding procession through the Texas countryside.

After the night at Burnam's, Sylvie rode close to Andrew so she could ask about the farmhouses and cabins they passed as they neared Bastrop. Those families would be neighbors in her new life. As he spoke of where they had come from and how they were faring, he often mentioned ensuing deaths, some from accidents or disease—even a couple of duels—but a number following Indian raids.

"I need to tell you about the warning system we have in Bastrop," he said. "When someone spots a raiding party or other danger, he fires off two quick rifle shots. A man in the next field over—we always stay within hearing distance—fires another two. And then the next man, and so on. In town, it makes a distinctive kind of volley, and the women know to gather the children and head for the stockade."

"And then what happens?"

"A rider brings a report to the courthouse at the north end of town as soon as possible, and we form a posse to ride out. Others stay back and defend the town."

"That sounds like a good system." Sylvie nodded. "So let me ask you, after we are married, will you try to be one of the men who stays back and guards the town?"

"Hmm." Andrew's mouth set firmly and his eyes kept straight ahead. "Let me figure out how to present your wishes to the other men," he said finally.

"Maybe like this: 'I've done my turn, and now I have a wife . . .'?"

"That won't work. Lots of men could say that."

"How about, 'My wife insists, and I had to promise to get her to marry me'?"

"Worse!"

Sylvie smiled. "I'll find a way to persuade you, Mr. Magill."

Andrew laughed. "I have no doubt that I will strongly prefer staying nearby."

"I know you'll be there to protect me. But at what cost to you?" Sylvie smiled sadly at Andrew and wished she could reach across the space between their horses and touch his arm or leg.

Noting her expression, he said, "I will always come back. If I can't outshoot them, I can outrun them."

After a moment, Sylvie said, "I just wish that the one party that really needs to honor the land claims had been at the courthouse as part of your formalities."

"You mean the Comanche, and I agree. We have good treaties with most tribes, but assuredly not with them. If it's any comfort, they attack other Indian nations as often as they attack us. They want to expand their empire at any cost."

"That's not actually a comfort, no."

"Well, let me tell you more about the land claims. You'll enjoy how the day went. We were all gathering at the courthouse on February first, dozens of us in our Sunday best. We were so anxious we were hovering over the three land commissioners, who were seated at a table. But then, no one wanted to be the first to step forward—we waited and deferred to the very first settlers, and to our military leaders.

"But once the signing and the witnessing and the swearing to this and that got started, we all rushed in. Everyone had to have two witnesses, so we were all offering, 'Here, let me bear witness for you,' and, 'Why yes, I'll serve as witness for you, too. And here is your claim, and now let's get this man his claim.'"

Andrew laughed as Sylvie smiled, picturing the scene. "And where did you end up, in the order of registering claims?"

"I was number thirty-three. And my claim to one-third league is duly registered. Josiah Wilbarger served as a witness for me, and afterward, I served as witness for several others."

"And you'll register your land survey from farther south, so you can make the swap later?"

"Yes, right away. The surveyor found the right witness trees—a blackjack and a live oak—and the same corner posts. Even the pile of rocks marking the southeast corner, which fortunately hadn't migrated somewhere else."

"I'm surprised you didn't move your pile of boundary rocks to a safer place, maybe inside the cabin." Sylvie grinned, teasing him.

"Better than that—you'll see them at home in Bastrop, stacked under the bed." They chuckled, and Andrew added, "Let me tell you about another land claim. I'm administrator for the estate of Conrad Rohrer, a settler who was killed in town about two years ago. I registered his along with my own, that day. He was a single man, so I'll manage his one-third of a league of land and make sure it's next to our two-thirds league. I'll have to arrange that survey soon, as well."

"Did you just say '*our* two-thirds league'?" As he nodded, she added, "I will want to see those acres of grassland we'll have. Maybe we can make a trip out there before long."

"We could if we got together a party of half a dozen or so, to be safe. Logan's land is near mine—ours—and so is Peter Kerr's, and Noah Smithwick's. You haven't met Noah yet, but you'll like him. Both he and Logan plan to marry soon."

"I remember Noah Smithwick, unless there are two men with that unusual name. He was the blacksmith at Gonzales, and just before the war, he was pounding every broken tool or odd bit of metal into some form of weapon."

"I'm sure it's the same man, and last year he spent several months living with the Comanche. He was trying to learn the language, and he hoped to set up a trading post."

"That's hard to imagine, though I admire the approach."

"It didn't last long. It was difficult for him to see the stolen horses and cattle, and the white captives taken. Plus he was suspected of spying whenever they discussed upcoming raids."

Andrew added that each colonist also claimed a *labor* of land, one hundred and seventy-seven acres, near town. His allotment was long and narrow, with frontage on the western bank of the Colorado River. It was intended for farming, but he wanted to use it mainly for grazing.

Right away, he could see Sylvie had other ideas. She was planning a good-size kitchen garden at the house and suggested raising larger crops on the other land—maybe wheat, corn, pumpkins, and even grapes. They could hire help, she argued.

Andrew said that when his land grants came through for military service, he hoped to group those with their three thousand acres of grassland. He had heard lately that his two longer enlistments, plus fighting the battle at the San Jacinto River, would bring another twelve hundred and eighty acres.

Sylvie took a minute to add up Andrew's allotments. If she included the acreage that would come with marriage, plus Rohrer's estate, her husband would be managing nearly six thousand acres and owning most of it. She enjoyed a moment of glee as she compared that with what she might have inherited in Illinois. How satisfying it would be if she could throw those numbers back at Jeanne.

On the second morning of her stay with the Wilbargers, Sylvie dressed and fixed her hair carefully, for Margaret planned to introduce her to women in Bastrop who Sylvie hoped would become her own friends over time. She picked up a silver earring, but her hand stopped in midair. Most American women here did not wear earrings, and she wondered what they might imply—that she was still quite French, or, worse, a loose woman? First impressions were so important.

A sharp knock came on the bedroom door, and Margaret stepped in, looking worried.

"Quick, grab a shawl and hat. Did you hear the volley of shots just now? We may be heading to the stockade. Come and get some food in case we have to run there."

Sylvie got her things, and moments later she was standing in the kitchen with Margaret and Seth, who was around eight. Margaret handed her a cup of coffee and pointed toward a pan of cornbread on the table. "Help yourself, and you can bring some along."

She returned to the window, standing back and peering outside, scanning to the left, then the right. One arm corralled Seth behind her. "Two men were killed in town last night," Margaret said. "They just found the bodies and think it was an Indian attack. Josiah went out at the first warning shots and came back to let me know. He's off again, helping to search the town. They'll also decide who will head out after the Indians—if anyone saw the direction they took."

Sylvie sat at the table to sip coffee, holding the cup with both hands. How strange it was, the way danger and fear slowed the passage of time, especially for women who had to wait. She saw a rifle leaning against a wall, a powder horn near the cornbread, and Seth's little fist reaching toward the box of shells on the table. Sylvie slid the box away, and as Margaret sensed his squirming, she straightened her arm to anchor him more firmly.

"When do you think we'll know what to do?" Sylvie asked.

Margaret laughed dryly. "How quickly I was able to forget how this goes, while I was away. But if it's a serious attack, we'll hear more shots."

Soon, two shots rang out in quick succession nearby, then two farther away, and then another two, from a greater distance. Echoes of the final two came faintly. Sylvie imagined the warning fanning out from the center of town.

"We'd best go to the stockade," Margaret said. "The signal means the men are still here—but not fighting here in town—so we'll make it just fine."

Outside, a few other women were scurrying, pulling children by the hand and heading in the same direction. Margaret, Seth, and Sylvie had to run about six blocks, and they arrived nearly breathless at the outer wall of tall, vertical posts. The single narrow door, guarded by sentries, was propped open just enough to let them through.

Sylvie glanced toward the closest blockhouse, one of four that rose high above the corners of the perimeter wall. She could discern dark figures moving inside, visible through narrow openings that gave sharpshooters a view. Sun glinted on a protruding rifle barrel, and an arm waved briefly at her. Or did she imagine it? Maybe Andrew was up there, rather than riding off after the raiding party. She hoped so.

Inside the fence, they crossed a field of trampled grass and approached a single rough building made of logs. Other women clustered near the front, as though seeking shade under its overhanging roof. Seth wrung free from Margaret's hand and went to lope about with other children.

"What a way for you to meet the women in town," Margaret murmured. She and Sylvie stopped to straighten their dresses and smooth their hair. They had put on hats, though Sylvie's had blown back and hung by ribbons tied at her throat.

"Give me a moment." She freed the knot so she could shove her hair back and resettle the hat.

"You look lovely," Margaret said. "Or lovely enough. The women are going to be just as interested in your state of mind right now as they will be in your dresses and teacups later on. At the moment, they'll want to see what mettle you're made of."

"The metal?" Sylvie asked, puzzled.

"You know, courage. Will you shrink back all aflutter and grow fainthearted, or will you pick up a rifle and give the bastards a taste of their own hell?" Margaret grinned. "Put on your brave demeanor, my dear, and let's go say hello."

Introductions ran quickly as they joined the other women, who eagerly shook Sylvie's hand. They seemed to know about her already, for no one asked what had brought her to town. She met Abigail Mays and recalled how Andrew had bartered with her for letter paper. Then she met her daughter, Lucinda, who was engaged to marry Logan Vandeveer.

Sylvie and Lucinda smiled at each other as they clasped hands and paused for a moment. "Our future husbands are such close friends, I hope that we will be, too," Sylvie said. The line sounded rehearsed, which it was.

"I am sure that we will be," Lucinda replied with such genuine good will that Sylvie warmed to her right away. Her handshake was soft, and her face still round, her large blue eyes framed by soft brown curls. Sylvie was taken aback by how young Lucinda seemed at fifteen years old, and how much older she felt.

Margaret was talking with others about the two men killed during the night. The attack came on the east side of town, where a Mr. Weaver and a Mr. Hart apparently had been guarding a pen of horses. As each woman shook her head slightly to signify that she did not know them, they speculated that the victims were either hired hands or recent arrivals. Town was so full of newcomers just now, it was hard to know everyone's background.

As time dragged by, more families arrived from farther away and were admitted to the stockade. The women were frank, open, and friendly. All had rushed from household chores and were wearing everyday dress when they abandoned churning butter, gathering eggs, or hanging laundry to dry.

The most recent arrivals also brought news of a second attack, this one on two men working at the sawmill east of town. One was killed while mounting his horse to escape, but the other, a Mr. Dollar, leaped off his horse at the river, swam across, and ran the rest of the way into town. He reported the Indians numbered about fifteen and were driving a dozen stolen horses. A group of settlers had organized to go after them.

"We might be able to leave here pretty soon, then," Abigail Mays said.

Several women agreed, and they turned to watch the children, who were kicking a ball and running around the dusty yard.

Lucinda was standing nearby, and Sylvie asked her quietly, "How often do you have to come in here?"

"Just about once a month, I'd say, over the past year or so."

"Do you ever get used to it?"

"It's not something you want to get used to, is it?" Lucinda smiled wryly. "But it does start to feel routine after a while. And since no one has been killed inside the stockade—even the time the Comanche attacked it—I usually feel safe here."

"I wonder if I'll ever feel that way."

"The worst part is wondering who has been killed or kidnapped. When it's women and children, we almost always know them."

"That will be a new experience for me," Sylvie said. "I knew men who were killed in the war, but the Mexicans didn't kill or kidnap women and children."

Lucinda nodded. "We stayed here during the war; we didn't evacuate. My mother says the risks we take are worth it, to settle the land and keep it. But I think each woman has to make that decision for herself." Lucinda's eyes were solemn, and Sylvie wondered whether she was reflecting her own doubts or urging Sylvie to be cautious.

"The men never seem to want to give up," Sylvie said.

"That's true. As soon as they've fought and killed to stay here, they feel they cannot back down, ever. My father argues that if he did give up and go back to Alabama, it would make all the sacrifices meaningless; they'd have been done for nothing."

"Yes, I think that's the case for Andrew," Sylvie said.

"And the same for Logan. When you marry, you're saying 'yes' to the man, the land, and this life, all three together. There's no separating them out. But it's easier for me. I mainly grew up here, so I don't have another place called home in the back of my mind."

As she said this, Lucinda smiled, and they fell quiet. Sylvie stepped toward the wall to peer through a gap between the pine logs toward the house across Pecan Street that would be her future home. *Do I have the courage to do this?* she asked herself. She estimated the number of strides needed to run from the porch of the house to the doorway of the stockade. It would require mere seconds, but what about children?

If she were carrying a young one and leading another by the hand, the trip would take longer, and each moment was precious. Maybe by the time she had children, a treaty with the Comanche would be in place and bring some peace.

The pine trunks were rough-hewn, and sockets where branches had been torn off oozed sap that had dried in white streaks like tracks of tears. Sylvie pressed a fresh blob, and it came off onto her fingers, sticking them together as she tried to rub it off on rough bark.

The women nearby were sharing stories about their hometowns and how recently they had returned to Bastrop, as only a few had stayed during the war. They seemed well spoken, many referring to farms and prosperous family backgrounds. Sylvie wondered if the other women's knees felt as spongy as her own, their intestines just as unsettled.

Soon, sentries in the blockhouses reached out and waved a signal. The stockade's gate opened to admit a messenger who announced it was safe for the women to return to their homes. The town was clear of Indians, and no more victims had been found. A party of rangers had left to in pursuit, off to the east.

Margaret looked closely at Sylvie as the two emerged with Seth onto the street. "This is the way your life will be for a time, though please note that I am alive and well after nearly ten years here. Just remember that we're doing this for the chance to build a better world, the one that we want."

"I think I can bear that in mind," Sylvie murmured.

"Oh, look, here's your young fellow. He must have been up in a blockhouse. That's good; he's a good shot. I'll leave you two to talk. I want to find Josiah, and we'll see you back at the house, later today."

As Andrew joined them, he still held his rifle ready, across his chest. They assured each other they were all right, and he said that among the victims, he knew only the man who had made it back to town. He and Sylvie started toward his house, and she suggested making coffee and taking a few minutes to calm her nerves.

When they went inside, she continued out through the back door to the garden and the privy beyond it, among the outbuildings. Her insides felt queasy as jelly. Why was she so afraid? She could not remember fear taking over like this before. Maybe it was not just for herself, she reasoned, but for children she might bring into this world. Would she be able to protect them and provide a good life?

She thought of Margaret, and of Abigail and Lucinda Mays, and the equanimity they showed. "Mary, holy mother of God, please give me strength," she murmured, a bit shocked that she was ready to pray again. But she did feel better after sending a plea heavenward, and soon she was ready to return to the house. If she could keep from telling her future husband that she wanted to leave, this time, then she could do it again in the future. Her staying on in Bastrop could gain the momentum of a habit, of a risky decision renewed daily in many small ways, which would continue to prove right.

As she stepped back in the house, bars of sunlight glowed on the smooth pine-board kitchen floor, and a breeze freshened the air. She traced a shoe along a strip of light and instinctively took a few dance steps. They evoked nostalgia for the Jarrot House ballroom, and she was delivered to the morning years ago when she had danced there all alone and conjured a vision of her future. The years in between fell away, and she let the sadness, trust, and childhood joy of those moments flow into her and this new home so far away. She took a few more steps across the alternating stripes of honey light and shadow, sensing that peace and security welled inside these walls; she was certain she and Andrew would be happy here.

Andrew came in from the front room, and after watching her sway, stepped closer and reached his arms around her. He tried to move his long legs and feet along in time. How surprising that they had never danced together, yet would soon be married. He was right when he had told her he wasn't good at dancing, but his strong arms were comforting, and soon they were simply standing together.

When he released her and went to put a kettle on the cook stove, Sylvie sat at the table. She watched how he moved about the space and studied how it was organized. "I'm very glad that you didn't go out after the raiding party," she said.

"Enough men had already banded together, east of town. And to tell the truth, I wanted to make sure you were all right. All at once, it seemed important to stay nearby and protect someone. That did feel different. It's not bad—it feels good." Andrew scooped coffee into a tin coffeepot and poured boiling water on top of it.

"What are you doing?" she asked skeptically.

"Making camp coffee—that's how we do it. I can add an egg, if you'd like."

"An egg?"

"Yes, it settles the grounds nicely. Except I don't have any eggs." He set the pot on the table and produced two brightly glazed Mexican mugs. "We'll let it steep a minute, and I'll pour yours off first. I like to spoon mine up, nice and gritty." At her horrified look, he laughed. "I was joking."

Still, she watched closely as he poured a stream into her cup. "This is not how we're going to make coffee in *my* kitchen."

"I suppose you have a French-style coffee pot in one of those trunks?"

"As a matter of fact, I do."

"Are you going to stay awhile today and do some unpacking? Maybe locate it in time to brew a second pot?"

"First, I need to measure windows. I left some curtains without hems, though I trusted the widths from the dimensions you gave me."

"I'm still amazed that you put together so much finery—china, crystal, and even some real silver pieces—with those few sums of money."

"I also bought a lot secondhand from people who were moving away from Cahokia during the financial crises. And Andrew, there is something you need to know about me."

"Something I don't already know; what might that be?"

"I grew up playing cards; all the French women do, back home. And I'm good at it. We play for money, I often win, and that's how I bought some of these things."

After a moment, Andrew said, "I knew about the card playing, but gambling? That skill should prove useful here in town. But can you stay out of the taverns?"

Sylvie had to laugh. "I got most of my winnings at Julie Jarrot's house in Cahokia—the most respectable place in town. But one time—on my first trip to New Orleans, years ago—I played poker with men on the riverboat."

Andrew's eyebrows rose, and he cleared his throat. "And you won?"

"Mainly. I had to lose a bit, now and then, to stay in the game long enough. One of the men who played that night lives near here, and I saw him that day at your store. His name is Epperson, and clearly he recognized me. But he's never mentioned the wagering?"

"Not that I know of. I remember he commented about your playing cards that day, but I didn't catch any other reference. I'd advise you not to mention this to ladies in town, or invite them to play. I don't think they'll take it the right way."

"Oh, I won't, believe me."

"Do you think we could play a bit of poker, though, sometime? Think you'd beat me?"

"Oh, Andrew, I don't want to play against you; I can think of better things to do."

He shook his head. "I love the way you hint, future Mrs. Magill. Why don't we get married today? We have a justice of the peace just up the street, unless he went out after the Comanche. We could be back here in half an hour. I can pick you a bouquet from people's door yards, as we walk to the courthouse."

"No. We'll wait until I'm twenty-one and no one can ever question the marriage because I lacked a guardian's permission. One day, I'm going to claim that inheritance."

"You do play for high stakes." He paused, then added, "While I've invested too much here to let it go, you could still back out. And after today, you must be thinking of it."

"Oh, that's why you want to marry at this moment—you're afraid I'll back out! No, I'm not going to do that." Her voice stayed firm, and she crossed her arms. "Besides, you've arranged for a Protestant minister to marry us, and that seems important to you. We don't have to settle for a justice of the peace on short notice."

"I do prefer the minister. But that rather closes the door for you with your family. And if you want to avoid that, a civil marriage will be fine with me."

"My fate is already set, either way. Let's stick with the minister. You are a good man, and I want you to have what you need and want."

He leaned over, and they shared a long kiss. After a few moments she broke away to add a final thought. "You should be grateful for my card-playing skills, and even my dancing. If I didn't know how to take risks, or put on a show of—what do you call it—bravado, I just might not be the kind of woman who is willing to stick it out here with you."

"Heard and understood, Mrs. Magill." Though his tone sounded lighthearted, the look they shared was serious.


Sylvie turned twenty-one on a Saturday, and Uncle Jim arrived in town the following Monday. Late the next afternoon, Sylvie held his arm as they walked from the Wilbargers' house to the courthouse on Spring Street. She wore a dress of creamy lawn sprigged with tiny embroidered violets and tied with a lavender sash, white gloves, and a lace mantilla as a veil. She held a bouquet of fresh-cut lilacs and raised it several times so she and Jim could enjoy the scent. With her other hand, she touched the golden locket, Andrew's gift at Christmas. The blue sky was streaky with high white clouds from a morning shower that had freshened the air, and the sun was feeling warm but not hot.

Margaret and Josiah Wilbarger trailed behind, talking and laughing; the wedding party was invited to their house for dinner afterward. Sylvie wished that everyone she loved could be present: Etienne and David, Louisa and Isabelle, Sarah and Minny, Amy and Annette. Uncle Jim's presence was a comfort, and he had brought a gift from Sarah and several notes from members of the household. He also conveyed good wishes from friends in Gonzales, including Rachel Flint, who had recently remarried.

Andrew had arranged for Noah Smithwick to play the fiddle during the ceremony, and he stood with Andrew on the porch of the courthouse, watching for Sylvie and Jim to round the corner. When they came into view, Noah raised the violin, clamped it under his chin, gave a broad smile and a wink at Sylvie, and began playing an old French tune.

The minister, Hugh Childress, was waiting inside, and Sylvie heard him clearing his throat repeatedly as they entered. Andrew led the way, and they gathered near an alcove set off by a carved wooden railing. The space it enclosed had served judges, juries, and land commissioners. No Protestant church had been built yet in town.

Logan and Lucinda arrived a few minutes later, and Logan took his place beside Andrew. All the men wore dark suits and were looking more at ease than the groom. Lucinda, dressed in muslin with lace trim, stood farther back, her gloved hands clasped, her expression wistful and dreamy.

"This is only my third wedding," the minister said, clasping his hands around a Bible and smiling tensely.

"That's all right; this is my first," Andrew said.

For Sylvie, time slowed nearly to a halt. Her gambles and risks, her past and her hopes, her romantic yearnings, her pragmatic fortunes— how amazing that they could crystallize so clearly into one moment in time and combine into such a propelling force. The currents flowing in her life had delivered her to this little town in Texas, where she was now joining her life with this man. And as she looked up at Andrew, his regular features were so lit by pride and hope that they shone more attractively than even Logan's striking looks.

Sylvie glanced at Uncle Jim and was startled to see tears in his eyes. She wished only that her wedding service could have lasted longer than ten minutes—and that included two Irish ballads that Noah Smithwick coaxed from his fiddle. She and Andrew exchanged plain wedding bands that had been passed down through his family, said their vows, and then Andrew bent to share their kiss. Afterward, she handed her bouquet to Lucinda, who whispered, "We're next, and soon!"

Sylvie could not have been happier if she'd been in a cathedral with a thousand people gathered, instead of a frontier courtroom with half a dozen good friends. Dinner at the Wilbargers' house passed enjoyably, and they all drank a bit too much wine. The men followed it with brandy and soon began joking about the *charivari*, a Texas wedding custom.

"Usually the parties include a barbecue," Josiah explained. "That involves roasting meat in a fire pit outside. After the crowd gets pretty loud and raucous, the newlyweds leave for their night's slumber, and things quiet down. But during this deceptive lull, the guests surround the house and all at once start banging on pots and pans and screaming and yelling. They believe this adds to the couple's enjoyment."

"How barbaric!" Sylvie exclaimed.

"Yes, it can be, if they refuse to cease and desist after just an hour or two. But you do need to know what you're in for," Josiah concluded with a smile.

Sylvie could not tell if he was teasing, and she wondered whether anyone would come out to bang pots and pans; it was a Tuesday night, after all.

"Our livelier friends might take it into their minds," Logan warned. "I'm thinking mainly of ranch hands, who don't spend much time in town. They don't see themselves getting married any time soon, so they don't picture any revenge coming their way."

"But surely they're out on the grazing land, way west of here," Sylvie protested.

"We hope so—that's where we like to keep them," Logan said.

"If these *charivari* people show up tonight, are we expected to invite them in for food and drink, like a *bouillon* party?" Sylvie asked.

The guests at the dinner table broke out laughing at her earnestness.

"No, I would not recommend doing that," Logan replied. "It would only encourage them."

"You are absolutely *not* going to do that," Andrew said. "If we ignore them, they'll go away. You'll have other opportunities to show your hospitality to the town."

With the prospect of more convivial evenings to come, the newlyweds rose to leave. After many thanks and best wishes all around, it was pleasant to walk the half dozen blocks to their house, where they would go inside alone together. They walked quietly, enjoying thoughts of the evening, warm with wine and food, with joy and anticipation.

"Are we ever going to quarrel?" Andrew asked, when they turned onto Pecan Street.

"Why ever would we?"

"It seems that people do, when they're married. I remember my father and mother arguing at times. Having the last word is like grabbing a valuable item. Do you put much stock in it?"

"I do rather like it," Sylvie said.

"I can let it go. In any case, when the discussion is done, I'd still do whatever I thought was the right thing."

"Men usually do. Ultimately, they own everything and have the legal rights. So why not let a woman at least have her say?"

"That makes perfect sense. I will just say, 'Thank you for your opinion,' and that will show I've heard you."

"How about, 'Thank you for your opinion, and I will give it considered thought'?"

He repeated it lightly under his breath. "Okay. I can do that."

"And then I will say, 'We may need to speak of this again.' Or, I might say, 'All right, *monsieur*, have it your way,' and bang my cooking pots around."

He laughed, and after a moment she added, "I don't think I'm going to be very good in a quarrel. Do you know about the Pensoneau temper? Have I told you how notorious my father was, for getting angry quickly when he felt he was right?"

"That doesn't bother me, much. Go ahead and show some temper if you see a principle is at stake. That actually can help, around here. It gets people to listen and think for a moment, and then they might not act so rashly and will choose a better course. Plus, they'll think of you as a strong woman."

"Is that what you want, for me to be a strong woman?"

"It's not a case of wanting or preferring. It's what this life requires."

Andrew unfastened the front gate, and they walked silently through the dooryard. In the house, he lit a lamp, and Sylvie felt the sense of belonging leap up with the shadows and light and absorb itself into her skin. They had to step around the final trunk still waiting to be unpacked. She bent to remove her shoes, and Andrew stepped behind her and gently tugged at the ends of her sash, undoing the bow. She stopped as the lavender ribbon came loose and drifted through his fingers, falling to the floor.

"Stockings next?" he said. "Or buttons?"

"Buttons down the back, please. It's hard to reach all of them."

His fingers kept fumbling on the tiny, slippery, rounded buttons. "What are these made of?" he asked.

"They are composed entirely of patience. Everything about them speaks to being patient." After a moment, she added, "I can reach these last few. Will you go get us some fresh water? Fill the jug, so we have some for the washbowl."

"Certainly," he agreed.

In the bedroom, Sylvie had a few minutes to remove layers of undergarments and petticoats and find her new nightgown. To get into their small bedroom, she passed through the larger one, which had a long, horizontal window built high in the wall to accommodate two sets of bunk beds built underneath. She imagined six or eight children could sleep in that room, and she shook her head, wondering at how the two of them could create so many, and at how she would manage their upbringing.

Soon, he joined her in the bedroom. And with no further delay, they fell happily into each other's arms and into their married life.

A brief, ferocious banging and yelling disturbed them later on.

"Pay them no mind," Andrew said, stroking her shoulder as she lay against him.

And soon they were left in peace again.

Sylvie felt that nothing could make her budge out of the warm bed, anyway. Surely, nothing could make her move out of the bedroom until morning sunlight beamed into the kitchen. Surely even then, there would be no need to get up right away. Probably nothing could make her ever leave this home, this place where she truly belonged, at last.

Chapter 28



**Summer 1838**
**Bastrop, Republic of Texas**

SYLVIE WANTED TO SEE THE GRASSLANDS WEST OF TOWN that made up most of Andrew's land claims, and Lucinda Mays—now Vandeveer—also wanted to see the land she and Logan had similarly gained. Their holdings adjoined the Magills' land, and the two women began planning an outing and a picnic for a day that the men judged safe enough for such a venture. Their husbands felt a larger party would provide protection, and they asked Noah Smithwick and Peter Kerr to accompany them.

Noah's claim also lay nearby, and the men tended herds together and covered for one another when any of them needed to be town. Noah had filled in for Andrew fairly often since the wedding, promising Andrew would pay him back in the fall, when he planned to marry.

Peter Kerr had decided to live near Bastrop, and Sylvie was glad he had made his claim close to the others. She enjoyed seeing him again and reminiscing about their ride with the mail years earlier, plus the trek they'd shared as refugees. Peter was now venturing into the cattle business. He refused to ask his family back East to stake him yet again in a new venture and instead was building his herd heifer by heifer, and cow by cow, along with the occasional steer.

On a day when no Comanche had been spotted for several weeks and the weather was fair and mild, the group set off at sunrise. By late morning, all were tired, thirsty, and hungry, and they pulled up in the midst of lightly rolling hills. This far west of Bastrop, they could see no houses or fences, just prairie grass shifting in channels of darker and lighter gold under the breeze, with purple patches of shadow from clouds racing across. Sylvie stretched up in her saddle to sweep her gaze along the horizon and enjoy her happiness and pride.

"Is this my land?" she asked Andrew.

"Yes, ma'am." He pulled off his wide-brimmed felt hat and nodded. He wore a red bandanna at his neck that accented his browned skin. "Our land starts about one hundred miles north of San Antonio, if you draw a straight line. The land I'm managing for Conrad's estate lies over there. Your land is next to mine—or smack dab in the middle of it—wherever you want to say it is."

"All right. I like the looks of this land right here," she said. Among the low hills, a few piñon pine and cottonwood trees grew in the clefts of creek beds, where she could also see cattle clustering in scant shade. Toward the north, rocky ridges stood bare, where rain and wind had worn off topsoil and sculpted the ocher and orange stone into intricate columns.

Sylvie asked whether Andrew owned the cattle that were on her land, adding, "You just might owe me some grazing fees."

"I'll pay your fees if you'll grant me a long-term lease. In what form would you like your payments?" He grinned at her.

"Oh, you're impossible." She mock-scolded and clucked to move her horse away. Over the summer, Andrew had stayed close to home, for neither the army nor the Texas Rangers had called for enlistments. He took advantage of the lull to perform a stint of jury duty in town. Married life was beginning happily; he even came home fairly often to share the midday meal.

Sylvie pulled up next to Lucinda and pointed out a potential picnic spot that offered shade near a small stream. They rode over, dismounted, and started checking for snakes, scorpions, and anthills. Peter joined them and tried to shoo away a heifer that stood nearby, chewing its cud. Sylvie batted flies from its haunch and peered at the inverted small "e" next to a capital H that had extended serifs. This was Andrew's brand; Noah had fashioned their branding irons at his blacksmith shop.

Lucinda spread a red-checked cloth, and Sylvie began unpacking the saddlebags.

"Logan says you are quite effective at bargaining in Spanish when they buy cattle," Lucinda said to Peter.

"A quality of the language does seem to encourage that aspect of my character," he said. "I believe, though, that the results have been beneficial to all of us in the partnership."

"You're bargaining on behalf of our husbands, not just building your own herd?" Sylvie asked.

"Why, yes. My goodness, is it possible that you two do not know of my business arrangement established with your husbands?"

Sylvie and Lucinda exchanged a glance, and both shook their heads.

"Then let me tell you of this most ingenious practice we've devised. Actually, I am not surprised your husbands, being of such estimable character, would themselves fail to mention the generosity and faith they've placed in me as a business partner—"

"In short, Peter, what exactly is your arrangement?" Sylvie asked.

"In short, my dears, when the two of them arrange purchases to increase their herds, they often deal with speakers of Spanish. As neither possesses much skill in that area, they have empowered me to take up negotiations after they have arrived at a price—and have departed the scene.

"Then I begin the bargaining in earnest, using the sellers' own lingo. With luck, I work them down to a lower asking price. Your husbands insist on paying the original, higher price agreed upon, as befits gentlemen keeping to their word. Then, in my role of conveying the money to the sellers, I pay the lower price and pocket the difference as a personal stipend. My earnings allow me to build my herd slowly, but I am content because good things do take time, and I will succeed only in proportion to my skills."

The women had stopped laying things out, and Lucinda stood looking at Peter, her hands on her hips. "Well, that sounds like a workable plan to me."

"Yes," Sylvie agreed. "It's very clever."

Peter went to tend the horses, and the women conferred quietly; neither had heard about the arrangement.

"Peter probably wears them out with all that talk," Lucinda said softly. "They'll agree to anything to be done with it."

Sylvie chuckled. "All three are behaving completely in character, aren't they?" She had put out cornbread and wheat bread, dried turkey and roast chicken, and she gently unwrapped some apricot tarts.

"Do you know why Peter keeps cows on his land near town and lets them roam free?" Sylvie asked. "He was so distressed by seeing hungry children in the colonies that were failing, and in the refugee trains, that he wants anyone in need to take the milk—at no charge."

"Ah, so that's his reason."

"It's truly sad he lost the love of his life. I think he would make a good father of a family."

The men arrived and took positions around the picnic cloth that let them view the landscape and watch one another's backs. They all glanced reflexively toward the hilltops nearby, and then scanned the horizon line. The horses were within sight near the creek, just downstream. Sylvie knew that everyone was thinking about Comanche raiders, even as she began serving and passing food.

After they'd been eating for a few minutes, she asked Noah about the time he'd spent living with a band of Comanche. Noah described daily life on the Great Plains and how he had tried to establish enough trust to run a trading post. Good trade relationships could lead to peace negotiations—or so he'd hoped.

"That sounds like the French," Sylvie said. "It's what my family did for generations, and still do, actually."

"Either I lack their skill or the Comanche aren't ready yet to give up their visions of war and empire-building. The main benefit, after my months of effort, is being able to speak the language a bit."

As they finished the meal, Sylvie went to fill two flasks and returned with cool water dripping pleasantly over her fingers. The others were planning the return trip.

"We might have just enough time to visit Sherrod's Cavern for a quick look," Logan suggested. "I don't know when Lucy and Sylvie will be out this way again, and it's an interesting spot."

The women agreed the stop would help break up the long miles back, and the group repacked and mounted the horses. The caves were not far away, and as they left the grasslands and skirted a tall outcropping, the horses picked carefully among rocks and boulders.

Sylvie did not see the cavern until she was upon it. A natural rock bridge arched above, disguising the large shadowed opening below.

"Wait—don't ride out on that," Noah cautioned. "I don't know how much the arch will hold, and it has holes carved by rainwater over the years. We can walk on it, though, if you want to look down."

Peter held the horses while Sylvie and Lucinda followed Noah. They crept carefully along the arch and peered below, where Andrew had gone down and stood in an open area as high as a house. He gestured toward the dark mouth of the inner cave.

"Wait a minute while I scout the first few rooms and make sure no one is camping in there."

Noah led them back to a narrow path that wound downward. "The cave has tunnels that branch off and small passages that go way back. I don't know if anyone has explored them all. People have camped here for ages, and you'll see some rock drawings and carvings, plus remains of fire pits."

Sylvie held back when they reached the large first room, hoping Andrew would emerge. A cool, musty breeze wafted over them; it felt good on the hot day, even if it smelled stale. The layers of the limestone walls varied from cream to red and brown, and sand was mounded along their base as though someone had left piles from sweeping. The walls were dry, the ceiling blackened by smoke. Rock rings for campfires stood in several places, and Sylvie had an eerie sense of people having recently departed, or remaining hidden and watching them. Logan walked about, peering into dark tunnels.

Andrew had disappeared, and his voice echoed from a passageway, calling, "Hello, hello, is anybody here?" Soon he emerged and assured them it was safe.

"I'll ask around, too," Noah said, "but in Comanche parlance."

He stepped into the passage, and soon they heard his calls, the foreign words garbled and echoing.

Peter squatted and poked at campfire ashes. "Fairly recent, I'd say. But I'm glad there are no bones from cattle, just small game."

"Would it be Indians, camping here?" Sylvie asked.

"Someone stopping to spend the night," he replied. "I'll head back out and keep an eye on the horses."

"We'll hear if you holler or fire shots," Andrew said. "We'll join you in a few minutes."

"Sylvie, come here," he added. "You should see these beautiful rock formations, from water seeping through minerals and dripping down. In some places they've built up on the floor, too. They're magnificent, like crystals. I have a few matches left, so you can take a look."

"All right, just a quick look." As she edged into the passage, Sylvie was revolted by the smell; it was not just musty, but rotten. What could cause that? Their shoes were crunching on what looked like bird guano.

"Bats!" she cried. She ducked as she made out a pattern of black cones thickly carpeting the rock overhead. "They're all over the ceiling!" Still hunched over, she waddled away as fast as she could. "I hate bats! They get tangled in your hair and bite you!"

Lucinda was still in the main room, and she hugged her arms as though shivering. "Sylvie, your screaming is going to wake them up."

"I've seen enough! I'm heading back out." She emerged into bright, dry air gusting with heat and smelling of piñon. Peter was a little ways off, his back turned, his rifle across his chest. Sylvie took deep, grateful gulps of air, and soon the others joined them.

Andrew came to stand behind Sylvie and put his hands lightly on her shoulders. "You seem calmer, and you're safe; everything is just fine. Look out west and then south, and repeat: 'This is my land. I belong here.' Can you say it with conviction, maybe if you say it enough times?"

"I don't feel that quite yet. It's so new to me, and it's so vast. And we're never going to dig in the soil here to grow things. Herds of cattle will move across the entire area. But if we don't get our hands into the earth, how is this land ever going to know us, to tell us apart from anyone else? Or make its claim upon us?"

Andrew let a few moments go by. "You have a different way of looking at things, sometimes. But I like it."


It was wonderful to ride back to the house in Bastrop after her first trip away, and Sylvie felt strongly that she was returning home. The evening sun filtering through pecan trees cast a peach tint on the white house, on ruffles of the window curtains, and on the purple cosmos, white stock, and golden marigolds in the front garden.

Andrew tended to the horses, and she opened the double front doors to catch any breeze off the river. Abigail Mays had looked in to mind the poultry. Mail must have arrived, for she'd left several letters on the kitchen table. One was from Isabelle, addressed to Mrs. Andrew Magill. Sylvie smiled and traced a fingertip along the line; it was the first letter from Cahokia that used her new name.

The cut flowers on the table had wilted, so she went out back to toss them. She stopped at the kitchen garden to find something to add to the omelets she planned to make. She still was amazed at how food grew so plentifully. The sun and heat allowed three growing seasons each year, and the well on the property stayed high and full. Showers had arrived often enough during early summer to sustain the crops Andrew was raising on the labor of land near town. The harvest was so plentiful that Sylvie was working hard already, smoking, drying, and making preserves.

She enjoyed getting her hands in the soil of her *potager*, the kitchen garden. Stooping to pull carrots and onions reminded her of other gardens in other places. It was getting hard to recall the despair she had felt at times in the past. If she had believed then in this future well-being, would it have lightened her worry? The chickens clucked contentedly, even as the rooster squawked to gather them in for the night.

Andrew often was surprised that Sylvie could produce a meal from just a few things on hand. Two handfuls of flour, two eggs, some milk, and a walk through the kitchen garden were enough for a quiche or crepes. She made layered dishes, one with rice called *tian*, and some with cheese, called *gratins*. Dishes with noodles were called *pâtes*. Andrew was learning the terms and adopting a few. Sylvie rarely made cornbread, though. He said that was fine, that he had eaten enough of it—and of beans, bacon, and dried turkey—to last his lifetime. Sylvie's cooking was inexpensive, given her unfortunate tendency to use every scrap of an animal. Occasionally, Andrew fibbed to friends rather than admit that she had served a sauce of fish livers, or that she wanted to pickle chicken's feet and even the hooves of pigs. Andrew did his best to try every dish, even the ones that required some courage.

Back in the house, Sylvie moved the letters to the side to be read after the meal. She took up an envelope addressed to Andrew and puzzled at the handwriting. It looked familiar and feminine, and it had been mailed in Illinois. The paper was wrinkled and grimy. She set it with the others leaning against the sugar bowl, which held honey.

After the meal, Sylvie opened the letter from Isabelle. She watched surreptitiously as Andrew took up the mysterious letter and looked at it, front and back, and then smiled.

"Just as I guessed—it's from you!"

With a jolt, Sylvie recognized her own handwriting. So this was what her letters looked like after many months in the mail. "When is it dated?" She tried to snatch it from his hand. "It must be more than a year old."

"No—it's my letter." He laughed, holding it beyond her reach. "I have to see what you wrote to me, back on, let's see . . . April 13, 1837."

"Oh, I remember that one," she said, though she was not certain and still curious to see it for herself.

"At least it's not one with crucial news," he said after a minute. "Can you imagine if I'd waited all this time to hear whether you were coming back or wanted to marry me?"

"Is it about the newspaper articles being published, or visiting Aunt Peggy in Missouri?"

"Yes, all that and some general news." He read for a few moments. "You sound so pleased with the articles. Have you ever thought about writing more?"

"Yes, I have, now and then. But I get busy and forget about it. Today's trip would make an interesting story, wouldn't it? I could weave in how the land preserves signs of people's past travels. Plus how we're now making land claims, doing surveys, and registering boundaries."

"And how the claims are disputed and people turn to the courts when they can't settle their differences." While serving on juries that summer, Andrew had heard half a dozen civil cases involving disputed property lines and amounts owed from sales transactions. So far, he and his peers had consistently found in favor of the plaintiffs, and Sylvie teased him that she would know true justice was being dispensed when they finally found for a defendant.

Sylvie continued reading her letter from Isabelle.

*May 12, 1838*
*Cahokia, Illinois*
*Dearest Sylvie,*

*I hope this letter finds you well and happy. I was delighted—several of us were—at the news of your wedding, and I wish you and Andrew all possible happiness. I am sure he is a fine man. Your letter of April 1 arrived in only five weeks.*

*Nothing much is new with me, so I'll start with the news around town. The railroad, ever a troubled venture, has been sold. The families were fortunate to find a buyer, I think, given present conditions. It was sold for $20,000, considerably less than it cost to build. Combine that with the operating costs, and each partner is losing about $12,000 to $13,000. As you can imagine, this is a significant blow to our family fortunes. These amounts are not secret—everyone around town talks about it. John Reynolds practically boasts of his losses as if to show off how well he can bear the misfortune. But even for the famed Jarrot family wealth, this is a hard blow.*

*Vital was elected to another term in the state assembly and is working hard on new development projects. He talks about a factory to roll steel, and a newspaper, and other ideas. He still hopes the new town of St. Clair will prosper, though little building is going on.*

*The Mississippi River has changed its course as Lieut. Lee's work projects have taken hold. Crews did dredging and built two dikes, so the channel between Cahokia and Bloody Island has filled in. No more duels there! You can walk straight out for a good view of St. Louis. The river is deeper on that side and ten feet shallower on our side. Vital and others fought this in court, but they lost the cases. Lieut. Lee, on the other hand, has won praise and been promoted to Captain. The work continues, and St. Louis's port is thriving.*

*Narcisse's new town of Athens has collapsed with the country's economic problems. He counted five thousand residents last fall, and has barely a thousand now. He and his partners are sustaining enormous losses on mortgage defaults, but he says he will be all right if he is patient, for he bought the land rather cheaply and is hanging onto it. Apparently, many people were building houses at their own expense. Still, what a lesson in life, to see fortunes rise and fall so rapidly!*

*I am thankful that dear Edward still prefers farming. He and I manage to meet and enjoy some time together, but Maman is ever watchful and disapproving. I so admire your courage to live your life as you wish! Even though you are now legally disowned, you do not have to see those family members around town all the time. If Edward and I were to marry, we would have to witness how they reject us and refuse to speak each time we crossed paths with them. I know I could not withstand that.*

*I smile to think of how your own hopes might be growing and beg you to send another letter full of news and adventures. Just keep safe from Indian attacks. I often see Etienne, which is a pleasure; he is doing very well and asks me to send his regards. He does so much business with the Anglais that he's changed his name to Stephen (or maybe Steven, I'm not sure.) He plans to marry Julie Adeline Belanger this fall, just like in a storybook romance.*

*I remain your loving and affectionate niece,*
*Isabelle*

Sylvie's hand was trembling as she set down the letter. "So I am officially disowned. Isabelle mentions it in passing."

"You did expect that to happen."

"Yes, but I didn't expect to learn in an offhand way, as a side remark in a letter from my niece. I suppose it's common knowledge back there. But shouldn't I receive an official document of some kind? Or a letter from Jeanne or Nicolas?"

"Maybe there is no legal document. Maybe it's only a matter of family feelings or a religious decree, like back when Catholic priests administered French colonies. It doesn't sound like it would stand up these days in a court of law, except in highly traditional areas."

"Like Cahokia and St. Clair County."

"Someday you'll contest it. We'll find the time to get back there and work on unraveling what's happened. But you do know that we don't need them."

"It's still a shock, Andy. And I'll have to wait until courts grant women more property rights, if they ever do." After a moment she added, "We live in a foreign country now, as well. That makes me wonder: as citizens of Texas, do we have standing to bring a legal case inside the United States?"

"I don't know. I can find out more, though. We have a good supply of law books at the courthouse."

"Thank you, but there's even more bad news. The railroad has failed, and they have sold it at enormous losses. That will cut into whatever I stood to inherit."

"So you don't own a railroad anymore?"

"No, alas." She allowed a small smile in response to Andrew's grin. "And the dredging has changed the course of the Mississippi River, the new towns people founded are failing, and Isabelle still can't marry her cousin."

Andrew rubbed his chin, watching her. "My dear wife, are you glad you ended up here? I think you saw all of this coming, from what you said in your letters." He nodded toward the old, stray page on the table.

"Yes, I did see difficult circumstances closing in on even good intentions and efforts. And yes, I am very glad and grateful to be here with you, especially now that I am not only an orphan, but also disowned."

Her eyes brimmed and a few tears crept down her cheeks, dropping to streak her blouse. Andrew came and knelt to take her in his arms. "We are so lucky to have everything we need right here. I am providing very well for us, and they can go to blue blazes."

"Blue blazes?" Sylvie wiped her eyes and took a breath. "Where the hell is that?"


As summer grew late and fall approached, the townspeople dreaded the Comanche attacks that often arrived with autumn's full moons. Reports came that Indians were attacking farther west, raiding settlements along the Guadalupe River. It was time for Sylvie to talk again with Andrew about which forays he would respond to in the future. She knew he felt compelled to step up when the military leaders he trusted—Ed Burleson and Jesse Billingsley—called up a posse.

She had learned gradually of other boundaries he was setting: He was skeptical when individual settlers tried to form their own groups, especially if they seemed motivated by anger and personal revenge. He would hold back and ask about strategy and tactics, and if those were faulty or absent, he would shake his head and advise the men to devise a plan that could succeed before riding off and risking their lives.

Sylvie worried less about Andrew responding too quickly to rumored threats, and he seemed more measured than his younger self who'd boasted how he "rode hard and shot fast." But the overlay of reason fell away when friends and neighbors were attacked or killed. It was difficult then not to lash out in anger, and she felt it herself.

One afternoon, Andrew came home and found Sylvie snapping beans on the back porch. He took a seat and said he had news, patting a letter in his shirt pocket.

"My parents have decided to come to Texas within the year, and my father is winding up his affairs in Kentucky. My younger brother will come too, but my sister will stay in Kentucky with her husband and young child."

"It will be good to have them here, won't it? I like the idea of more family around."

"For the most part. My father is easygoing, though my mother can be strong-willed and a bit direct in her speech. I think you two will get along. My father wants to look at land around here, so they probably won't live with us for very long."

"Live with us, here? Oh."

"We'll show them true Texan hospitality, won't we?"

"Of course." Sylvie began picturing how they would accommodate three more people in the house. If only the second bedroom didn't have those narrow bunks built into two walls. "Wait—what about that settler's house on your labor? You've made some improvements."

A small house had been erected there by an early squatter who later realized he could make no claim to the land and had abandoned it to move farther west. She could imagine three people living in it comfortably, if the inside was fixed up a bit more.

"That's a good idea, and my mother might prefer that to living in town. She likes a house that stands out in the middle of the land."

"Just like an *Anglais*," Sylvie said. "I'm sorry, but I'd never want to live that way, at a distance from friends and neighbors."

"Then we'll all be happy." Andrew pulled out the letter and flicked it with his fingertips, and Sylvie asked if he wanted her to read it.

"No, best not to. I've told you how my father is quite the military man. I get the impression—though he doesn't exactly say it—that he'd welcome the chance to do some fighting here. He thinks it's time my brother saw battle, and then they both could get land grants for their service."

He paused to check Sylvie's expression. "I've made it sound worse than I should have. He has waited until I wrote that it was safe to come here, and he assuredly didn't want to fight the Mexicans. So he is actually being quite reasonable. Maybe he's just showing he's aware of the risks and willing to face them."

"And your mother? She can't be happy about leaving her daughter and the new grandchild."

"He does not report what she has to say. I think I've mentioned she holds hard to her own beliefs, and that they argue at times."

"Oh, Andrew, I hate the thought your father could put pressure on you to join a battle. You'll have to defend your right to decide on your own when to respond to a call-up, and when not to go out."

"I agree with you, and I'll keep my own counsel. Here's what I will tell him—and you, since we're talking about it. One: it has to be good, experienced military leaders who are calling up men. Two: the attack has to be on this town or on people nearby. Three: when an attack is farther away and involves people we don't know, I will wait for men in that area to respond first and then see if I'm still needed."

Sylvie studied him for a moment, surprised he had arrived at such clear stances without discussing them ahead with her. And she had been worrying about how to bring up the subject yet again. "Wonderful, my dear. That should work very well."

Chapter 29


**Spring – Summer 1839**
**Bastrop, Republic of Texas**


FALL CONTINUED PEACEFULLY INTO WINTER, and Sylvie and Andrew traveled to Edna to spend Christmas with the Kerrs. They stayed for a week, which let them get to know Sarah and Jim's new baby boy, named James.

Jim had disconcerting news about settlers near Gonzales who had been attacked recently. Comanche raiders had killed several and kidnapped children, including two daughters in the Lockhart family. Their father had done the land surveys for Andrew, and Sylvie remembered the sisters from when she lived in the town. She was horrified to imagine their fate, especially Matilda, who was a young teenager and most likely would be made a slave, or a secondary wife. Sylvie hoped the younger girl might be adopted to replace a Comanche child who had died, for then she would be accepted and treated well. She recalled how Nancy Brown's husband John had fared with his Waco captors years earlier, and she hoped for the best.

Jim said a ranging party tried to rescue the children, but had returned without finding the band of Comanche involved. He and Andrew discussed the events several times, and as they second-guessed the rangers' strategies and decisions, Sylvie suspected they felt they could have helped, if they had been along.

In February, news reached Bastrop that tested Andrew's sense of when to fight. Comanche had attacked Robert Coleman's home on Webbers Prairie, west of Bastrop. Coleman had been Andrew's first officer when he joined the Bastrop ranging party years earlier, and he had since died by drowning. During the raid, his widow and oldest son were killed, and another child was missing and presumed kidnapped.

Ed Burleson and Jesse Billingsley were calling up rangers, and Andrew trusted both as military leaders. However, Andrew had disagreed with Coleman's leadership, first in June 1835 when he decided to execute captured Indians suspected of robbery, rather than return them for trial, and later when he led the unsuccessful nighttime attack on the Tawakoni village. More recently, Coleman had been in charge of building the new fort southwest of Bastrop, and a number of men under him had deserted or committed suicide.

Andrew hesitated about responding to the call; he stood in the front room and shifted from one foot to the other, as though testing different stances.

"I think your doubt might be a decision in itself," Sylvie said. "If you felt strongly about this, you'd be done packing by now."

Details of the attack were grim. Coleman's widow and twelve-year-old son had fought for some time before being killed, which allowed the other children to escape. Only a five-year old boy was missing. Sylvie barely let herself imagine what it must be like to be a mother in such a plight and to die fighting along with her child. But she pointed out that the home was distant from Bastrop, and men in that area were already volunteering for the ranging party.

Andrew still made no move to pack and finally said, "I guess I've made up my mind, though my conscience isn't happy. This will be the first time I haven't volunteered when Jesse Billingsley or Ed Burleson called us up."

"These decisions may require a little more practice," Sylvie said. "But with time, I'm sure they will seem more natural and right." She hoped she wasn't being purely selfish.


Early in March, Sylvie became certain that a new life had taken root and was growing within her womb. She anticipated telling Andrew, wanting to choose just the right words and just the right moment. She finally shared her news when they were talking about his family arriving soon.

"Think of how delighted they will be to see not only us, but a baby, a grandchild, as well!"

Andrew's eyes widened, and he smiled broadly as he asked when such an event would happen. Sylvie's eyes were brimming, making it hard to say more than simply "about the middle of August."

"Oh, my word. Oh, my dear. Do you need to . . . do anything?"

Sylvie laughed. "No, everything goes along perfectly naturally, and we're fortunate to have a good midwife in town, plus several physicians, if any is needed. Are you truly happy? It's going to change our lives, and this time together has been so pleasant."

"Will it be a boy? Oh, how stupid of me. Of course you don't know."

"I'll let you know if I get a strong feeling one way or the other."

"Come here, Mrs. Magill." He gathered her in his arms. "I am taking care of two of you now."

"Yes, and I've started eating for two. I thought you might have noticed."

"No, but you did finish off the pan of biscuits this morning."

"I did not—you'd already had half a dozen, at least."

It felt good to have Andrew's arms around her, even in the middle of the day in the kitchen. She had vowed not to confide to him her simple, basic terror of childbirth. He dealt with enough dangers, and she had to face this one on her own. She could draw on her growing friendship with Lucinda, who would undergo her own trial before Sylvie did.

As though following her thoughts, Andrew said, "I should put in extra work with the cattle so Logan doesn't mind covering for me later on when I'll want more time in town."

"You will be covering for him, first," Sylvie said. "Haven't you noticed that Lucinda's shape has changed a bit? I thought it was pretty apparent."

"Oh! No, I didn't. Though now that you mention it, she has put on weight. I just thought she was getting older and filling out."

"Yes, she is so very old at sixteen. Do you mean Logan hasn't said anything?"

"No, but then, men don't. Can I mention it to him, about Lucinda—are you sure he knows?"

Sylvie had to sit down while she was laughing, given the unfamiliar pressure in her abdomen. She deferred to Andrew so often, as he was so capable and experienced, that it felt good for once to know more about a part of life than he did. Maybe that was a reason women kept quiet about childbearing; they could preserve mystery and specialized knowledge in their own sphere. It helped to even things out, now and then.


In mid-March, Sylvie was coming in the back door with eggs from the henhouse, thinking about baking a cake to celebrate her birthday and their first wedding anniversary, when she heard two shots fired in quick succession. They were repeated, and more shots echoed. She nearly dropped the eggs onto the counter, her hands were shaking so hard. Pounding came on the front door, and Andrew answered it.

Logan stood on the porch. "Ed Burleson is raising a force, and we have to go, fast."

"Where? Is Lucinda all right, the baby?" Sylvie peered around Andrew, concerned because Lucinda was due to deliver any day.

"She's fine; nothing is new," Logan said. "They're firing shots because a rancher came in and reported a force of about seventy-five men on the march north of here. They camped up in the hills, and he trailed them for a while toward the southwest. They'll pass nearby."

"Comanche?" Andrew asked.

"No, it's other tribes, but the main force is Tejanos who are still loyal to Mexico. They've also pulled in some slaves or indentured servants. Burleson says the leader is Vicente Córdova, the man who's been organizing uprisings near Nacogdoches. We have scouts out, so we'll know more soon. But Burleson wants to head out fast."

"Do they want to get to Mexico, or do they mean to fight us here?"

"Burleson thinks they're heading to Matamoros to join forces with the Mexican army."

Andrew mouthed a silent expletive and looked at Sylvie.

"I know, you have to go," she said.

"I'll get Zeus ready. Will you pack some food? Maybe a couple of days' worth."

It was hard to think of what to pack for Andrew, not knowing how long he'd be gone. She chose ready-made food for the first day or two, and ingredients like cornmeal and bacon for camp cooking after that. If the men stayed out longer, settlers in the area would help to feed them. Andrew was back in the house quickly and started gathering ammunition, a jacket, extra pants, and socks.

"I am so sorry, Sylvie," he said when they paused for a moment. "We made it through our first year of married life, though, without this happening."

"It has been good." Sylvie nodded. Her words implied a finality that felt wrong. She added, "It sounds like a small force, though. At least it's not hundreds of men."

"My guess is they'll pick up more along the way as they move south. Burleson will organize a rear guard, so don't worry. And we'll be back soon if Córdova's group is only seventy-five men."

"You sound hopeful."

"It doesn't hurt when you're heading out. Wish me luck."

"Oh, I do! Much more than luck." Andrew held her hard against him, and Sylvie sensed his energy and excitement pressing against her fear and worry. When she was frightened, she grew angry and then often wept; he grew grim and determined to take action.

Standing in the dooryard, she watched Andrew and Logan merge with the crowd of men gathering near the stockade. They numbered forty or fifty, most on horseback. She watched until the two rode off, dispatched in a cluster of ten men. Andrew did turn to look at her and wave at the last moment.

Sylvie returned to the quiet house, already feeling how long the day would stretch. Everyone had worried in the years following the war that disaffected groups might band together and join Mexican troops at the southern border of the new republic. To the northeast, Córdova had been able to rouse rebel fighters and win promises of support from Mexican officers happy to foment uprisings inside Texas.

In the kitchen, eggs and sugar stood by the mixing bowl, but now Sylvie hardly had a reason to bake the cake. Except that some of the women might like it. She could invite Lucinda and her mother, Abigail, Margaret Wilbarger, and several other friends, for all of them would welcome a gathering to break up the tedium of waiting for news.

On the fourth day the men were gone, Lucinda's labor began. Sylvie was frightened for her and resented the men's absence. How could a husband be away at such a time? She went to be with Lucinda and urged Abigail Mays to send word with a scout that Logan was needed at home. But Abigail said Sylvie was "daft to even think of it" as she left to run errands.

Lucinda did not seem distressed. "I would far rather have my mother and womenfolk at my side than a nervous husband." She had been pacing in her front room while the contractions were mild, and she grasped a chair as she winced. Then she took a deep breath and resumed walking. "They'd send Logan away when I started shrieking, anyway. Husbands get more upset than anyone else at those times."

"Lucy, tell me, are you frightened at all?"

"I am, yes, but I'm more . . . excited, like anticipating something good. Your own time is coming, and my mother and I will be there for you, Sylvie, don't worry. Besides, we have Bess, and she's an excellent midwife."

She stepped over and grasped Sylvie's hand, then began squeezing it in time to an internal rhythm. The Mays women did not seem to share Sylvie's fears, and she tried to dismiss the old curse—which she didn't believe in—any time its shadow dimmed her optimism.

Abigail returned with a gust of spring air, a loaf of fresh bread, and news from Burleson's forces. "Our men have fought a battle, and none of them were killed, just a few lightly wounded."

Sylvie sighed with relief, and Lucinda sat down for her next deep breaths. "Maybe that will finish it and they can come home."

Abigail said that the men had caught up with Córdova's force about six miles east of San Antonio. Sharpshooters fought at first in a wooded area, and then cavalry were able to chase the rebels into the Guadalupe River bottom.

"I'd guess Andrew was part of the cavalry charge," Lucinda said. "Logan was probably one of the sharpshooters. I can see him moving among the trees, all quiet and stealthy."

Sylvie agreed, and Abigail added that when night came, the men had fallen back to a nearby town. There was no word on when they might return.

In the evening the midwife arrived, and Sylvie prepared a meal. After she helped to ready clean sheets, hot water, towels, and medications, Abigail sent her home. In spite of the day's worries, Sylvie slept deeply. She awoke early, rushed through chores, and left as soon as she could to check on Lucinda. To her immense relief and pleasure, she found Lucinda napping peacefully with a baby girl swaddled and tucked by her side.

The men finally returned after almost three weeks. Sylvie was proud that she had managed the house, animals, and garden for that time, with only a short list of tasks that Andrew needed to handle when he got back. Thoroughly weary of solitary days and long evenings, she was grateful she lived in town and could pay visits to friends or stop for a cup of tea while doing errands.

During her times alone, Sylvie worried not just about whether Andrew might be killed or wounded but also about his state of mind when he returned. If he was enduring much fighting, especially hand-to-hand, it would take time for his outlook and spirits to recover.

She tried to recall what she and Rachel had done to help when he was so dazed after the battle at the San Jacinto River. All she could remember was the struggle to survive and their giddy relief at being alive for another day. Now it would be different to return to a home with its quiet domestic routines. Sylvie wondered what news she had to share that would be interesting or that might pull him out of one of his stern and silent stretches. She remembered her half-brother David speaking of the joy and relief he found with his children.

When Andrew did return, lean, sunburned, and unshaven, he did not come directly into the house. She heard a noise outside and looked to see a tall man with a slumped gait leading Zeus back to the stable. After a few minutes spent unsaddling, he came through the back garden and stood at the pump. Then he looked up at her and grinned. It looked a bit forced.

"Welcome back, stranger!" She stood a few feet away, hugging her arms. She still wore her apron from preparing dinner.

"Let me wash, first." He held up his hands to display the grimy palms, then bent to pump water over his hands and face. He took a few swipes at his bearded chin and throat, then tore off his shirt and tossed it on the porch steps. He was splashing water all over his chest and trying to slap it down his back.

Sylvie approached and silently patted palmfuls of water where he couldn't reach. After a few moments, he stopped and straightened. She put her arms around him from behind and stood holding him for a time, the dampness soaking the sleeves of her blouse.

When he finally loosened her arms and turned, he flashed a smile that faded off. "Well, we didn't catch all of them. But the ones we caught are dead, a good two dozen of them, and the rest will have a hard time getting past San Antonio. We left off when other rangers took over farther south."

"I am so glad you're back."

"Not as glad as I am to be here."

It was a threadbare response, something everyone said. She searched his eyes and wondered about damage, wounds that weren't visible. "Let's go inside. You must be hungry and thirsty. Did you hear that Logan has a daughter now?"

He nodded. "Yes, they got the news out to him. And you are doing well? You look fit and healthy."

"Yes," she said, smiling. "I am perfectly well, and even better, now."

Andrew grasped her in his arms and held on tight. He embraced her hungrily, and it felt like clinging. His hands moved down her back and over her hips, and she wormed her way loose.

"What's wrong? No one can see us." He glanced around the fenced garden and outbuildings before following her inside.

The baby was not due for another two months when Sylvie finished the preparations on her list. She wanted to be on good terms with everyone before she went through the ordeal of childbirth, so she wrote fond letters to Louisa, Isabelle, and Etienne, and to her Aunt Peggy and her half-brother David. She also sent notes to Jim, Sarah, and Minny. After writing her letters, she felt as much at peace with everyone in her world as she figured she could be. There was no hope for her relationship with Jeanne until her half-sister altered concepts that girded her life.

Andrew spent days away at a time with the cattle so he could spend longer stretches at home later in the summer. He alternated that work with tending a few crops on the allotment near town and improving the house there for when his parents and brother arrived. Sylvie had little to do beyond minding the gardens, cooking and baking, knitting baby clothes, and visiting friends for tea.

One day in the middle of August, Sylvie sat on the back steps to look over the kitchen garden, which was so full of ripening vegetables that she found it hard to rest. She needed to pick and dry tomatoes, make pickles, and can beans and more tomatoes. The peaches were in danger of falling off the trees before she could get to them. She and Lucinda had teamed up to do canning, and that afternoon, Lucinda made it clear that Sylvie had to take time to rest.

"Stop it! You are not lifting that heavy pot!" Lucinda said crossly. The kitchen was superheated with steam on the hot afternoon, and her brown, wavy hair had flattened into sweaty streaks on her brow. She edged Sylvie away from the pot on the stove where bottles of baby cucumbers in brine stood just under the surface of boiling water.

"*D'accord, d'accord*," Sylvie muttered, dropping into a kitchen chair. "It's too hot to do this work. I want to lie in a hammock and read a book. We both should; we'll need to make some hammocks, first."

Lucinda looked at her closely. "We're almost done here."

"There's still so much to do, and only seven days left, if Bess is right."

"Really? I've seen your list, and almost everything is crossed off."

"Like making up with Jeanne. I never should have let things get this far. We can't stay enemies—my soul will need her prayers and her blessings."

Lucinda frowned and clamped tongs on a bottle to lift it up. "You'll have plenty of time to do that after the baby comes, years and years. Children have a wonderful way of bringing people around."

The women were confiding more in each other as their friendship grew, and Lucinda had some idea of Sylvie's deep fear of childbirth. She had found little to say when Sylvie mentioned, in passing, a curse against the women in her family. But she had firm opinions about Jeanne. "Your sister's attitudes are outside of your control," she said more than once. "There is absolutely nothing left for you to do. She will find it in her heart to act generously, or she will not. You have done nothing that needs forgiveness."

Still, Sylvie sat with a red face and scrunched eyes, propping her cheek with her fist. "You have no idea what it's like to have your family reject you."

"No, I'm happy to say I don't."

"So how am I supposed to bring a new family member into this life? How does that work?"

"You're overtired, my dear, from this heat and from overpreparing. You are building a new family, and once you and the baby look into each other's eyes, you will belong utterly to each other, and all the rest will matter less. At least, that's what I've found."

"What do you mean, saying I'm overpreparing?"

"Sylvie, stop it! I am your friend, and your life isn't going to change that much—let alone end—with this one event, having a child."

"It might. It very well could."

"Look, you have to go into this with more hopefulness. I almost fear that I won't be of any help to you at all."

"I'm sorry. Thank you for putting up with me. Sometimes I become overwhelmed by fear and by a certain loneliness that's hard to describe."

"We'll take care of that." Lucinda started to dry implements and pans, putting the kitchen back into order. "Tell me what you want from the garden for supper, and I'll get it. Then once I see you settled in a chair in the shade, I'll head home."

Sylvie agreed and thanked her again.

Late the next morning, the pains began like distant rumbles of thunder, their spacing indicating it was time for final preparations. The contractions were not really uncomfortable, but just tightenings, as though Sylvie's body was rehearsing. *I can handle this,* she thought. Andrew was out, so Sylvie made the walk to the Mays' house and asked Abigail to get a message to the midwife. Bess arrived at Sylvie's house shortly after, carrying her basket of medical supplies. Soon she had checked Sylvie's abdomen and was timing her contractions, pulse, and respiration.

"Breathe regularly," Bess reminded her, "and as easily and deeply as you can."

Bess estimated the baby would not arrive until the next morning. When Andrew returned for dinner, he ate silently and quickly, his eyebrows up on permanent alert. *This is what he would look like terrified,* Sylvie thought. *Does he look like that just before a battle?*

The pains grew more intense and frequent as the day lengthened into afternoon, and then they quieted with dusk. Bess kept Sylvie walking about the rooms and breathing regularly. Lucinda arrived, announcing her baby, Eliza, was asleep at her parents' house and she could stay for hours. She held Sylvie's arm, and they paced together.

Then the pains began tearing at her body, and Sylvie knew that she was going to die. Finally the women let her rest on the bed. She resigned herself to her fate, except that Bess kept forcing her to breathe and resist the urge to push quite yet. Bess would actually prod Sylvie's head up and urge her to open her eyes and stare into Bess's own eyes to control the intensity of the pain. Sylvie shrieked and cursed her in French. Andrew had long since disappeared.

"It's just that your hips are so small, they don't allow a lot of room for the child. We'll hope it's small as well," Bess said.

Finally, in the early hours of morning, Bess told her to push and push hard. A strange clarity descended upon Sylvie as she floated above and watched herself below on the bed. That Sylvie was very pale and kept her head tipped back and her eyes shut. Bess and Lucinda each grasped an arm and propped her upright. Then Sylvie noticed a young girl, about three years old and dressed in white, watching from across the room with an expression of great calm and affection, her eyes filled with the warmest love.

The Sylvie up by the ceiling came back down and went into her body. She opened her eyes and leaned her weight hard, twisting in the grasp the two women maintained on her upper arms. It was ending; she could see a wet, dark head emerging between her thighs. Another hard push was needed for the shoulders.

"A beautiful girl!" Lucinda exclaimed. "She will be a sister for my girl! Oh, Sylvie, I am so happy for you."

Sylvie lay back, certain she could die in peace now. Her guts were twisting in new, hard contractions, and Bess was massaging the aching places and saying what a fine job she had done.

After a space of blank darkness, Sylvie gradually perceived that she was propped up on pillows with fresh pillowcases. Clean sheets were tucked over her and under her, and her hair was arranged to the sides. Her face felt cool and clean, as though freshly washed.

"Are you laying me out?" Sylvie asked groggily, and Lucinda giggled.

"No, you're not quite ready for that, I assure you."

Sylvie felt a solid bundle against her right side, propped against her arm. Barely moving, she peered at the face emerging from the cotton cloth and light blanket. The baby's eyes were closed, but her tiny mouth made little *moues*, the lips pushing in and out daintily. Her nose was a bit flattened but perfectly shaped and petite, and her eyebrows were dark and arching.

"The shape of her head and face will change over the next day or so and become a bit rounder," Lucinda said. "But of course you already know that."

Bess had changed her apron and washed, and Lucinda looked as pretty and fresh as ever. "We are ready for the father, aren't we?" she asked.

"Yes, I think Andrew should see his child now." Sylvie pushed back an edge of the cloth to check if this girl had inherited her father's ears. Happily, they looked more like her own: half a heart with a lobe shaped just right for earrings.

"And are you ready to have half a dozen more?" Lucinda asked.

"No, not at all," Sylvie said.

"Well, that day will come," Lucinda sighed. "Ready or not."

"I guess it might, since it seems I've lived through this first one."

"You have, and you came through very well!" Lucinda bent over to give her a kiss on the forehead.

"Oh, I was awful. I know I was mean. I remember cursing in French."

Bess smiled and shrugged. "Fortunately, we could not understand a word you were saying."

Andrew rushed in and hovered over Sylvie, kissing her, feeling her face, her hands, her arms, and asking over and over if she was all right. It was only after a few moments of reassurance that he could focus on his new daughter. When he was invited to hold her, he sat stiffly upright on a chair, cradling the bundle and holding his breath.

"Oh, good, all ten fingers," he said, after a time of gazing at her.

"And ten toes," Sylvie said. "Were you worried? Maybe there is something I should know about your family?"

They both laughed. "She is wonderful, just wonderful. Sylvie, I am so proud; you have made me so happy."

"I am so glad."

"She is the first of many more. Do you think we might have a son next time?"

"*Oh, la la,*" Sylvie sighed.

They named the girl Mary Naomi, just as planned. Sylvie wanted Mary as the first name, for every French child had a saint's name, and her own was Marie. Andrew was pleased with Naomi because it was a traditional name in his family.

Bess would continue to check on Sylvie during the coming weeks to help prevent dangerous conditions that could prove fatal to new mothers and their infants. During that time, Sylvie did her best to rest and avoid thinking of the woes that had befallen Jeanne. As her heart swelled at her good fortune, she was better able to imagine the enormity of her sister's grief over losing two babies and a child.

Sylvie held Mary Naomi to her breast and tried to relax as the baby fastened herself with powerful suction. There was nothing wrong with this little one's appetite. It was very pleasant to lean back in bed as the milk began to flow and she could glance about the room, out the window, or at this earnest little being.

Several months after Mary Naomi joined their lives, Sylvie was preparing for the arrival of Andrew's family in Bastrop. She had enlisted Lucinda to help thoroughly clean the house, wash the curtains, and tidy the flowerbeds. She sought her opinion repeatedly on which dishes to prepare for the dinner when she would meet Nancy, Samuel, and Andrew's younger brother, James. Lucinda was anticipating meeting them as well, for Nancy was Logan's aunt, and before now she had met only his brother.

In a recent letter, Samuel had said they would be happy to live in the house on the allotment fronting the river; Nancy much preferred that to living in town. James wanted to continue his studies in law, and Samuel asked Andrew to look into how he might do that. He added that he and James were interested in enlisting for military duties as needed. If they liked the area around Bastrop, such service could help in making land claims.

Sylvie nodded as Andrew reported these plans until he mentioned Samuel wanting to enlist. "He is how old—over fifty?"

"Fifty-five. I haven't seen him for half a dozen years, but he used to be quite fit and able."

As much as Sylvie longed for close family, she felt a bit overwhelmed when the three Magills arrived. They were very pleasant, shaking hands and complimenting the house and gardens. Samuel seemed to fill the room, at more than six feet tall and two hundred pounds. He showed the same restless energy that she often sensed in her husband, and he had bequeathed Andrew his large ears.

Nancy was tall as well, at least to Sylvie. As she took Nancy's hand, she met Andrew's eyes in his mother's face, and they focused with the same shrewd, light-colored gaze. "You'll want to see the baby," Sylvie said, as Nancy's clasp lingered, holding her fingertips.

"Yes, is she sleeping?"

"I'll take you to her." First, though, Sylvie shook hands with James, who ducked his head and tried a few phrases in French. She laughed with delight and responded in kind.

Sylvie led Nancy into the large bedroom, where her mother-in-law stopped abruptly at the sight of the bunk beds. "Good Lord, if you fill those up, you're going to have a lot more children than I have!"

Sylvie blushed hotly and stepped into the small bedroom that she and Andrew shared with the baby in her little cot. Nancy gazed at the sleeping child rapturously, and Sylvie thought how pretty Mary Naomi looked, with her dark hair coming in in fine little waves.

"It just about broke my heart to leave my daughter and our first grandchild back in Kentucky. I hope you won't mind if I regard you in that way. I will try not to let my presence become overbearing."

"I will be most happy to welcome a mother into my life," Sylvie said. Though she had prepared this line, her voice thickened with emotion at the heartfelt wish.

At dinner, Samuel asked about joining a Masons group, and Andrew said a local chapter had formed; he was serving as treasurer. "Sometimes our meetings in the past seemed to overlap with military planning sessions," he said. "It's all the same people. And during peaceful stretches, it's a good place to talk with other men who've been through similar experiences."

"I wonder how you are dealing with the effects of combat," Nancy said. "Men like to pretend it doesn't affect them, but it does. Some get short tempered and want to have control over every little thing in daily life. And they think they're the only ones who can handle major decisions. I'm not speaking about everyone, of course—each man is different—just some patterns I've observed."

Silence fell around the table, and Sylvie looked down at her plate. Then, remembering her role as hostess, she quickly passed serving dishes and offered more food. When she did glance at Nancy, her mother-in-law was looking at her kindly.

"Well, as I was saying . . ." Andrew cleared his throat. "I find that talking with other men, like at the Masonic meetings, is very helpful. I've noticed a few of those tendencies in myself."

Samuel nodded a thin smile at everyone and changed the subject. "You may have heard, France has recognized the Republic of Texas as a new country—the first nation to do that. And they plan to open a consulate in the capital, which will be up here, in the town of Waterloo. It's being renamed for Stephen Austin, and we heard the decision is finally through the state legislature."

"Sylvie, that's great news, isn't it?" James said. "Then you can meet the consul and speak a little French, maybe invite the family over for a genuine French meal. Or would that be a Franco-Texan meal?"

Sylvie laughingly agreed, for the idea was fun to imagine.

Chapter 30


**March – August 1840**
**Bastrop, Republic of Texas**


PEACE ARRIVED LIKE A RUMOR ON THE SPRING WIND. Talks were being set up with a number of Comanche chiefs. Would it happen? Could peace be a real possibility? Sylvie feared putting faith in it, for it would hurt so much if hopes collapsed. No such talks had taken place before. But as a date was set for a parley in San Antonio in March, she caught glimpses in Andrew's eyes, and in the expressions of friends and neighbors, of a furtive hopefulness and vision of life without the fighting and constant fear of attacks. Everyone wanted to believe it was possible yet kept up their guard.

Comanche chiefs would meet Texas negotiators at the Council House, where they would also return women and children they held captive. The Texans settled on the roster of officials and set the date for March 19. When Sylvie heard that her Uncle Jim would attend, she allowed herself more hopefulness because of the treaties he had successfully negotiated in the past. Peace would make a very fine gift for her twenty-third birthday, which fell close to the same time. She couldn't think of anything she wanted more.

Andrew agreed to mind his partners' herds, for both Logan and Peter wanted to go to San Antonio. They would be spectators, but they wanted to be on hand in case the Texans needed backup—or better— if they celebrated later with a big party. Andrew and Noah would stay out and guard the cattle. Both felt uneasy about the large number of Comanche likely to pass nearby on the way to San Antonio.

That left Sylvie and the other wives keeping one another company in town. Sylvie was hoping that the two Lockhart girls, kidnapped eighteen months earlier, would be released to their family. As evening drew late on the day of the talks, townsfolk clustered with neighbors to hear any word, and when it finally arrived via a relay of riders, the news was of a disaster.

The Indians had produced only a few captives, but one of them was Matilda Lockhart. She bore signs of abuse, including scarring from burns, and she said other bands were still holding a dozen captives. The Texans were horrified by her condition and insisted that all captives had to be released for negotiations to continue. The Comanche argued that each chief led only his own band, and that the chiefs gathered at the parley had no control over these other groups.

The talk had rapidly disintegrated into arguments. Shots were fired in anger, inside the Council House. Fighting spilled into the street, and at least half a dozen Texans were dead. Comanche had scattered throughout the town, where Texans hunted them down, killing all they could find—men, women, and children alike.

Sylvie and Lucinda quietly talked over the situation as they walked along Pecan Street on their way back from hearing the news at the courthouse. Their babies were tucked under their shawls against the cool spring night. Both were concerned about Logan and Peter, and no one yet knew the names of the Texans killed.

"There's a rider," Sylvie said, grasping Lucinda's arm. As they peered through the dark, they could see someone dismounting in front of Sylvie's house.

"It's Peter!" Lucinda exclaimed. "But why is he alone?"

Sylvie was frightened by Peter's troubled manner as he tied the reins to the rail without speaking. He had ridden more than a hundred miles in a hurry and must have changed horses several times. They went inside, Sylvie got water for him, and he began telling them how he and Logan had started riding back north as soon as fighting broke out at the Council House. Some miles outside of San Antonio, they saw signs of an attack: a wagon overturned, horses missing, some supplies scattered about, including fabric and notions a woman would buy.

"The tracks leading on showed they kept the horses with them, and probably a captive. We figured they had a young woman because we saw pieces of ribbon along the way, like she was leaving a trail. The

Comanche must have driven the men off on foot, since we didn't find any bodies.

"We decided to split up, and Logan rode on north to keep tracking the raiding party. I headed this way, toward Bastrop, and when I reached some of the places west of here, I started alerting the settlers. I believe they'll raise a party of rangers, but maybe not, with so much else going on."

Just then, Lucinda's mother, Abigail, arrived, breathless and upset. "Some of the King family came into town," she said, without preamble. "They say their daughter Mariel has been kidnapped. They've heard from the men who were with her and were driving the wagon when the Comanche attacked. The men got away, and some other settlers found them. The Comanche took her captive and were heading north."

Abigail looked from Peter to the women. "Where on earth is Logan?"

"Riding north—alone—tracking them." Lucinda spoke in a flat voice, her eyes intense. Sylvie had taken the babies and tucked them into the cot in the bedroom.

"Now, now, let's not jump to unwarranted consternation," Peter said. "Logan will head straight to where we usually camp, and he'll find Andrew and Noah before he does anything else. He has shown time and again that he is not foolhardy."

"I hope he finds Andrew and Noah first, and that the Comanche don't surprise them," Sylvie said.

"And I hope a ranging party gets out there fast so it isn't just the three of them," Peter said.

"Surely they—the three of them alone—wouldn't attack a band of Comanche," Lucinda said. "Would they?"

No one answered; they simply looked at one another. Peter went to wash, and as he ate food Sylvie set before him, he filled in the details that he knew. He assured Sylvie that her Uncle Jim was alive; at least Peter had seen him after the shooting in the Council House ended. He had caught a glimpse of Matilda Lockhart before a woman had taken her home to care for her, and her appearance truly was frightful.

"That caused tempers to flare, to say the least," he said. "Then when it became clear the Texans would have to make separate treaties with a dozen other Comanche chiefs to get the rest of the captives back, there was a lot of shouting about false pretenses and lies and ill will.

"By then, some of the Indians who had gone about town on their own in a friendly fashion were being attacked. That in turn outraged the chiefs, and the shooting erupted quickly. It was dreadful, though, so many people firing inside such a small space. There was enormous confusion. When we left San Antonio, some Texans were chasing small groups that had scattered. I guess that's what we ended up doing, too, though well north of town."

"Even if nothing happens—if Logan finds Andrew and Noah and they don't locate the Comanche—they still have half a day's ride to get back here," Sylvie said.

"That's the quickest they can be back. If they do pick up the trail and chase the band out farther west, or north . . ." Peter shrugged.

There was no way to guess what was happening. And so the waiting wore on. Abigail decided it was time for Lucinda and the baby to get home and try to rest.

"I'll walk with you to your houses," Peter offered. "And then I'll head home, too. I think we're pretty safe in town tonight."

After Sylvie said good night to them, she went to bed, though she doubted she would sleep. As she waited through the long night, her moods and emotions swung wildly with the different scenarios she imagined. Of course Andrew would try to rescue a kidnapped woman, especially when the Comanche seemed to be headed straight north toward his land. At times, she felt angry with Andrew. Why was it so natural to him to rush out and put his life in danger? Did he not owe some thought to her and their child? Yet how would she regard him if he did nothing but keep his own family safe?

In the morning, Andrew's parents came by for any news. Samuel seemed a bit bluff in his confidence, which Sylvie found annoying at first. Rumors were flying around town, but they had made eddying pools around Sylvie and stayed clear of her hearing. Nancy started to pass on what people were saying, but Samuel waved her words away like smoke from his pipe. Who could possibly know anything? It would take riders a long time to reach the area, and then to report back. But after the two left, Sylvie did feel stronger, buoyed by Samuel's faith in his son, or the courage he carried like a shield from his own battles years earlier.

Finally, late in the day, Andrew, Logan, and Noah all returned. Catching sight of them, Sylvie rushed to the front porch. Andrew dismounted and shared a weary wave with the others as they continued toward their homes. He did not look at her, or look up at all, but led Zeus back toward the stable.

From where she stood, Sylvie could see blood on his clothing. She went inside and crossed to the back porch. The wait seemed longer than usual, as though the distance he had to travel to her had grown greater. When he came toward the pump, he pulled off his bloodied shirt and threw it on the midden pile.

Sylvie sighed, a short hard breath. What a price they were paying. She wondered how many men he had killed already, and now this. She had resolved never to ask. She knew Andrew could feel her watching as he primed the pump and stooped to let water gush over his head and shoulders.

"I want to get rid of this before I go into the house," he said, straightening up and letting the water drip from his hair. "The whole feeling of it. The killing, the hunting men down, the fear, and then that triumph. After the moment passes, I don't like that triumph. It is repellent. It smells like blood for days."

"We should draw a full, proper bath for you. It wouldn't take long, and while you're bathing, I'll get a meal ready."

"I want to shed this like a snake sheds its skin and grows a new one."

"Tell me what happened," she said. "Let's talk right here, right now, so you don't have to carry it inside the house."

"Logan and Peter were tracking a Comanche raiding party. You've probably heard about that. Peter split off, and Logan came and found me and Noah at our camp when it was getting dark. He figured from the tracks that it was just half a dozen Indians, probably with a captive.

"So while we could still track them, we followed. Do you know where they went? To Sherrod's Cavern, the cave we went to that day. We caught them by surprise, fortunately."

"But that's a long way for anyone to ride, even Comanche; it's a hundred miles from San Antonio."

"It is. They move incredibly fast. We staked out the cave and waited until it was completely dark. We picked off the sentry first— Noah did that, tricked him by calling out in their language. Then we rushed in. We saw the woman tied up, off to the side, and the Indians gathered around the fire like they had been cooking and were about to eat. We fired at close range. We each had two pistols, so it was over pretty quick."

"Is she all right? Was it Mariel King? Her family came to town and said she'd been taken."

"Yes, that's the name she gave, and she's as well as can be expected. Not tortured or burned or cut, at any rate. We took her to the first settler's house we passed, and they're caring for her."

Sylvie thought over the scenario for a few moments. "If I am right, this is the first time you've gone into a battle on your own without someone like Ed Burleson or Jesse Billingsley giving the orders and making the plans."

"Yeah, that's right."

"So who did the planning, the leading—was it you?"

"Pretty much," Andrew said and sighed. "We settled it among ourselves, first. Actually, Sylvie, there wasn't much to discuss. Noah is smart, and he lived with them for a while, so he had good advice. And Logan trusts me, doesn't rush things. Gets me to slow down."

Sylvie imagined how the fighting had taken place in close quarters, rather than from a distance on horseback. Andrew bent to pick up his jacket, rifle, and saddlebags. He stepped around Sylvie and went inside. She stopped in the kitchen and stared out the window. The white shirt bright with blood lay like a flag on the pile of household refuse. She would go out and burn it as soon as she had the chance.

In spite of what Andrew said, she knew deaths from gunshots often were not quick. They'd had only one shot per Comanche, which left none to spare. In fact, it was highly unlikely all six shots had been lethal. Of course there had been close, bloody fighting. He had simply cleaned his knife and the stock of his rifle long before getting home.

And this had happened on their land, or on her land, the parcel they were calling her own. She could never go there again. It would be impossible to go into the cave without the horror of the killing and that woman's suffering coming foremost to her mind. Her land, sullied by murderous blood, including her husband's blood. She'd seen several long scrapes, cuts that had stopped bleeding, while he washed.

She watched Andrew, now wearing a clean shirt, as he moved between the main room and the bedroom. Mary Naomi was sitting up on a blanket on the floor, and when she banged the tin cup she was playing with, he went over to stroke her head and speak some soft, high-pitched words.

Sylvie leaned on the back of a chair and wondered how much a little child actually understood. Could she sense her father's anguish or how Sylvie now also felt flooded by dismay? Despair made everything dull and washed color from the room. It closed off any enthusiasm she had felt earlier for simple things in her life. It would be a monumental task to care even about getting dinner ready.

Andrew finally looked at her. His face drooped as though he could sense her bleak estrangement. "Come here," he said, and he put his arms around her so they could stand quietly for a few moments. "We'll be all right. We've been through this before."

"After San Jacinto," she agreed.

"So many times, Sylvie, in that summer after the war, while you were away back home. I haven't told you about all of it. You get numb after a while."

"How could that ever be the case?"

"I don't know. I honestly don't. I'm almost afraid to come back and see you, that I won't get down to the good feelings inside, or that they'll be gone or hidden—or worse, burned through. Or if they're there, they'll spill out, and I'll get all weepy. God forbid."

"It might not hurt you if you did cry one day, Andrew."

"Oh, it probably would," he said. "The men always talk about keeping ourselves hard, how you have to be strong and carry on. It's so true."

Sylvie considered his words, wondering when and how his male friends had claimed primacy in the realm of her husband's feelings. Wasn't the emotional life the province of women, the realm where a wife should have the greatest sway?

"We've had some wonderful times in the past couple of years," she said.

"Were they real?" he asked. It was a simple question, and it chilled her. "Or is that all illusion, and what's truly real is life's basic brutality?"

"Here. Now. This moment. This is real. I know this, and I am certain," she said.

He eased from their embrace, and as he let his arms drop, she grasped the fingers of one hand. As he clasped her fingertips in return, she felt a hint of play returning to the gesture.

"We need to get a message to your parents and let them know you are all right," she said, and her voice sounded flat, even to herself.

"I'll go and see them myself after a bite to eat. My father will want to hear all about it, all the details." He grimaced.

Sylvie got food ready for both of them, though he would chomp his meal with determined jaws and without the faintest idea what he was eating.

Mary Naomi was eagerly scooting herself forward and backward, crawling a little. She craned up her neck, her eyes full of delight. She laughed, calling, "Ba, ba, ba!" She crawled over to Andrew, plumped down on her rear, and held up her arms in triumph.

Sylvie watched him melt into smiling; he looked fascinated and thrilled.

"Isn't she wonderful!" he exclaimed. "When did she start doing that?

"Just now," Sylvie said. "A welcome home for her papa." Actually, she had started crawling a day earlier, but she was not going to lessen Andrew's delight.

* * *

Sylvie had found a plain pair of leather moccasins in town, not elegant like the beaded ones Paschal had given her years earlier, but similar in shape, and she enjoyed slipping them on for an occasional walk by the river. Mary Naomi liked going along the shady riverside path, but Sylvie sometimes went there on her own. She typically got the chance on late Sunday afternoons, following supper with Andrew's parents. Nancy enjoyed time alone with her granddaughter in the garden, while the men sat back to talk about cattle or recite war stories.

Sylvie encountered few other townspeople walking at that hour, and the farther north she went from the river ford and its small, busy ferry, the more peaceful it became for gazing over the water or into the lush tangle of trees, vines, and brush on the banks. It was midsummer, and when the Comanche Moons approached in another month or two, she would not walk alone out of sight from the streets.

This afternoon, as she imagined encountering Indians, she conjured friendly ones, like the Delawares who had traded food for her moccasins. She paused to watch turtles sunning on a tree trunk mired in the shallow river; the water was patterned blue and brown, shifting with ripples and the slant of filtered sunlight. She could easily climb down the bank six or seven feet to the water's edge, and she could even throw a stone across the Colorado, if she really tried. Back in Illinois, she'd stood on banks hundreds of feet high to watch the Mississippi River, which ran far too deep and fast for turtles to splash about and laze on logs stuck in just a foot of silty water.

"*Une rivière si petite, mais de telle importance,*" she murmured. Such a small river, yet of such importance. She savored the sound of the French words resonating in the air. She never spoke French anymore, rarely dreamed in it, and had only recently had started to use a few phrases at home so Mary Naomi would learn something of her mother's heritage.

Her children's heritage: what would that be? Sylvie liked to muse, as she walked, that a son of hers could possibly go back to Illinois and right the wrong of her disinheritance. The child she was carrying now, due in November, was a boy; she felt quite sure, though she had not told Andrew this yet. When that son, or another one, was old enough, she would write a document explaining that she had done nothing wrong, not by immigrating nor marrying nor attending Protestant services. She had not defied her guardian but waited until she was of legal age to marry on her own. The days of Jeanne's world, when Cahokia was a colony ruled from Québec, were far in the distant past.

She was blameless, and that lent her ease. However, just as often, Sylvie felt she shared Andrew's anguish following the battles and the killings. Before she had borne Mary Naomi—a whole new being arising from her body—she had never imagined that another person could be so close. Now both the baby and her husband felt like extensions of her own body. She reached out her hand, tanned and faintly lined from aging and housework, and in this still air she could almost feel it brush against their hands, back at the house.

That connection had made the days after the fight at Sherrod's Cavern more difficult and painful than earlier times. For several days, Andrew hadn't looked directly at her, and he had barked only short answers when she spoke to him. She had to ask him questions, for everything had to be elicited that way, when this other person, whose body and soul mingled with hers, was blocked from speaking with a clear mind or an open heart. For his part, he seemed to believe he was acting normally, just as he always did.

Sylvie picked up a stick and brushed gently at some weeds along the edge of the path. She wondered if she was growing to pity Andrew, the tinge of that emotion being more complicated than compassion. She knew well that she could pick up a weapon, or anything that would serve as one, and strike anyone who threatened her home and her child.

But to set about wielding violence in a planned way, to calculate it as a strategy, to justify it with words and ideas that lay coolly on top of the passion—this ability lasted over time after fury and fear were spent. Sylvie believed she would not be able to act violently except in sudden, instinctive self-defense. But, she realized ruefully, Andrew considered it a man's role in life to protect a woman precisely so that she could remain above the chance of that happening. All the men in town talked that way, about protecting women and keeping them pure, whatever that meant.

Sylvie often shook her head when she heard this and silently wondered why the approach felt contrary to the way she'd been raised, or even to the reasons the settlers gave for being here in Texas. What kind of ideal society engaged in war so regularly? True, the Texas government had managed peace treaties with a number of tribes other than the Comanche, who didn't seem to want peace with anyone. But what kind of ideal society allowed slavery? She had been disappointed, though not truly surprised, that the new Republic perpetuated it, a move that was encouraging planters to move in and establish cotton-growing on a large scale, like in the American South.

Sylvie was coming to appreciate her mother-in-law's views and her habit—much like Sarah's—of speaking in favor of social ideals. Nancy would occasionally ask outright, "Why did I have to leave my home, my friends, my daughter and her family—especially at my age—and come out to this wild new country, if not to make it better than the one we just left?"

Sylvie smiled and reached toward a patch of brown-eyed Susans that still held a few dusty blooms in a sheltered, shady spot. The afternoon heat was oppressive, and she hoped to feel a waft of cooler air off the river soon. She picked a flower, twirled it in her fingers, and turned to walk back along the river, rather than take the path uphill toward the north end of town.

As she chose the direction toward home, the question formed in her mind: how and when had her ancestors known it was time to leave, to try a new place? Some had left France because they were Protestants and feared for their lives. Her father had left Montreal to expand his land ownership and build houses and towns. And she had left Cahokia because—she needed to pinpoint this—leaving was the route to finding a broader life where she could thrive, plus a narrower domestic sphere where she could belong and be loved.

"What a conundrum!" Sylvie murmured in English; she liked the sound of the final word's three syllables. For a few moments, when she spied no houses, boats, people, or traffic on the far bank, she could imagine her ancestors standing along other rivers in the heat, or in the cold, watching for animals to trap, for Indians to engage in trade, for good land to grow crops. They had longed for home, for a place to belong—ideally forever, but more likely only for a time. What if her heritage was itself a form of restlessness born from this hopeful belief that a true home could be established in some fresh, new place?

Oh, her poor children if that was the case. How soon would they be moving on again, leaving Texas for the vast, storied Far West? She smiled, and still seeing no one around, she stroked her rounding belly and murmured a few reassuring words in French. She would encourage them, if any wanted to do that, and tell them to try again.


"Look at this, Sylvie—this is going to change the history of Texas!" Andrew laid a large pistol on the kitchen table so she could look it over. "Do you see the difference?"

"Well, yes—here." She touched the metal cylinder, which had chambers shaped to hold cartridges. "It looks like it spins around."

"It does. When you fire a bullet, the cylinder turns so you can fire the next one a moment later. It's called a Colt repeating pistol, after the man who invented it back East. The Texas Navy just bought several shipments. The army has rejected the design, though."

He grasped the handle and raised it. "They think it's too heavy and will get too hot. Jesse got hold of a couple so we can try them out. It allows five shots, all in a row, and fast. Imagine wearing two of these and firing from horseback. Ten shots, without dismounting and taking time to reload."

"It could make a difference in a battle against the Comanche, since they shoot arrows from moving horses."

"Exactly. And that's why they've been almost impossible to defeat, at times, in some terrain. While we have to dismount to reload, a Comanche swoops by on horseback and fires a volley of arrows. We're lucky to get a shot or two from a pistol at close range."

Andrew said he and some others were headed outside of town to practice firing repeated shots, from a moving horse, at a target. "Who knows, maybe something will come up soon, and we can try them in an actual skirmish."

"You probably won't have to wait too long," Sylvie said. In his enthusiasm, he did not notice her resigned tone.


Sylvie began planning a small party to celebrate Mary Naomi's first birthday in the middle of August. She would invite Andrew's family, and they could try making ice cream for a treat. She also wanted to tell them about the new baby on the way, for her bulge was becoming noticeable.

Andrew was working on the farmland near town, and she had spread out some deep pink fabric on the floor to cut a dress pattern, when two warning shots rang out. She held her breath, and two more followed shortly. "*Merde!*" She cursed and sat back on her heels.

It didn't take long for Andrew to cross town and come rushing into the house. "Burleson is raising a hundred men. A big party of Comanche attacked John Linn's warehouses at the port, and they've set Linnville on fire. The whole town is burning. The raiding party is headed back this way."

"Have people been killed? What about John and his family?"

"I think they're all right. A couple of schooners were in port, and they were able to load a lot of townsfolk on boats and get them out to the ships in the harbor. It sounds like John was leading the effort. After the Comanche thoroughly looted the warehouses, they set them on fire. And before, on their way down to Linnville, they rampaged through the Guadalupe River Valley. And here is something: Minny Kerr got word of the Comanche and rode all the way from Victoria on her own to warn Linnville that the Indians were coming."

"Minny! Good for her; I can just picture her doing that. What courage."

"Sylvie, get a couple of days' worth of provisions together as fast as you can. My father and brother are coming, too."

"No—surely not. Both your father and your brother?" Sylvie was certain she had misheard, but Andrew shouted from the bedroom that they were joining up.

"My mother will pack some food for them," he added.

"Your mother will . . ." Sylvie couldn't immediately locate the word for how she expected Nancy to react. She went to the bedroom door and said, "Surely she is arguing against this with your father as we speak!"

"Yes, I'm sure she's having her say."

"Andrew, people don't do this—all the menfolk in a family fighting and risking their lives at one time. Her husband and both of her sons! *Mon dieu*, what will happen to us, if anything—"

"It won't matter much what my mother says. My father is determined that we're going to share this experience, the three of us together." Andrew straightened, shoved a few items into his pack, and closed the flap.

"Does it matter to you what I am saying?" Sylvie's voice rose high and she stopped, pressing her hands over her mouth.

"Yes, I am listening to you," Andrew said quietly.

Sylvie turned and strode from the doorway and into the kitchen, where she fetched flasks, a packet of coffee, and another of dried turkey. She was having trouble seeing what she was doing; her vision was blurring. Her hands kept reaching for things that had passed through John Linn's warehouses. She tried to imagine the vast structures burning, the Comanche loading horses with goods, the townspeople watching from schooners anchored in the bay.

And what had happened in Gonzales when the Indians passed through the Guadalupe River Valley? Had they attacked the town, burned it once again? The Comanche's route would bring them near Bastrop on their way back north, and of course Andrew had to go and fight. But that did not mean that his father and teenage brother had to go as well.

Andrew was assembling weapons, ammunition, a jacket, and his pack when Sylvie handed him the supplies and asked, "Do you know where you're headed now?"

"We'll try to cut them off south of here. Matthew Caldwell was scouting and said the force is large but moving very slowly. They took so much stuff they couldn't get it all on the pack horses. Women and children are walking along, carrying as much as they can. There's only one place where they can ford Plum Creek, loaded up that way. So we'll try to cut them off there. I know the spot—we built a bridge there when we were road building."

Andrew paused and looked at her. "In fact, that's where I first caught sight of you, when you and Minny rode out with the meal."

"Oh, Andrew."

"But we'll see what Ed Burleson says. We'll gather at his place and go from there."

They moved into the front room, and seeing her downcast expression, Andrew gently raised her chin so she would look at him. "Don't worry. We'll be a large force—all the settlers from around here. And Chief Placido's band of Tonkawas are ready to fight with us, I hear. Plus we have our new weapon, the repeating pistols, which have the advantage of being a surprise."

"Andrew, I will say one last time that it is completely wrong for you and your father and your brother all to go into this battle. You could eliminate your family line and leave your mother, your wife, and your children all alone in this world. And for what? Some kind of male pride, or ritual of bonding? But to the death?"

Andrew shrugged. "They're on their way. No stopping them now unless my mother has done something drastic. They're both fit, and they ride and shoot well. Maybe they'll be able to defend me." He grinned faintly.

"Every civilized society allows one son to stay behind for the family."

"Which one of us will that be, Sylvie? It sure as hell isn't going to be me. I'm the one with experience, and speed—and luck."

"Tell your brother, then, that he has to stay and protect his mother, or me and our children—whatever works. He admires you, and he'll listen."

This situation was so hurried, and so ultimately serious, that Andrew considered Sylvie's demeanor for a moment. "You risk making yourself ill. In your condition, you should not become this upset."

"Then don't upset me with this stupidity; this is foolhardiness."

"It's just this one time, Sylvie. Next time, I'll persuade them not to go. But the odds now are in our favor, and if we win a substantial victory, it might stop more battles from happening in the future."

"We've both lived here long enough to know that is not true. Each battle just brings more battles. And as soon as we have a son, you'll be doing this again, won't you? How long before you feel you need to take a boy off and show him how to fight?"

Andrew sighed. "It's a sad fact of life here, and that probably will happen. But it's hardly my fault. Everyone lives this way, and we just hope our children won't have to. Until that time you have to accept this. Now, I have to leave."

Andrew stooped to pick up Mary Naomi, who had started to fuss. He held her and kissed her several times on the forehead. "I'll be back for your birthday, my fine girl," he said, giving her his broadest, most adventurous grin.

"Bye-bye, Papa!" She laughed and grabbed at his ear.

He took his things to the door, and Sylvie tried one more time. "Andrew, I am very, very opposed to this. You are mad. You've gone mad from too much fighting."

"Call it that, then. Aren't you going to kiss me goodbye and wish me luck?"

"*Bonne chance.*" Her face felt rigid and the words, said so low, sounded more like a curse.

He tipped his hat, strode off the porch, and attached his saddlebags and rifle to the saddle on Zeus. He turned to look at Sylvie, who'd followed to the porch. Then she ran down the steps, grasped him, and reached up to kiss him. But he would not lean down; he was already scanning the dooryard and street for any hidden enemy.

"I love you!" she cried.

"I love you, too. And our home. And I do listen to you, I swear."

Then he pushed away to ride off, and this time, he did not turn or wave. Sylvie went into the house, slamming the door behind her. She sat down and held her trembling hands together, tried to even her ragged breaths. They had never had such a bad argument. And certainly not before a battle. What a terrible time for her temper to leap its bounds. She couldn't remember ever directing her anger so fully at him. But no issue had ever been so momentous as the possible destruction of all the men in the family.

Sylvie recognized it was unlikely all three would die. Perhaps there would be a single death, and wounding was even more likely. Yet wounds were disabling: She thought of Josiah Wilbarger surviving the scalping, and of Logan's long recuperation after the battle at San Jacinto. How Sylvie counted on Andrew to stay alive. Her anger cut through something, though, as cleanly as her shears had cut through the cloth still lying on the floor. Mary Naomi had picked up a remnant and was waving it over her head like a rosy banner.

Sylvie began picking up the pieces and folding them away, working calmly as though removed by a great distance from the argument with Andrew. They would now stand on opposite sides of the breach, in a land where they both would speak and act differently. Sylvie had mainly felt anger and shock. And as these feelings passed, no tears welled in her eyes as they usually did. Yet she had always been one to cry so easily as she calmed down. When had that passed and gone away? She tried to remember the last time she'd wept any tears. Maybe it was when she read the letter from Isabelle telling her she was disowned. Oh well, it hardly mattered.

"Let's go for a walk by the river," she said. Mary Naomi smiled and pulled on a chair leg, working her way up to standing. "We'll do something to celebrate your birthday, just you and me."

They moved slowly, crossing the streets of town, for Mary Naomi insisted on walking now and then, clinging to the baby carriage for balance. She loved to stop and look at flower blossoms, intriguing rocks, and insects. Sylvie let her set the pace, and when they finally reached the river, they meandered in sun-dappled shade and watched turtles plopping from a log into the water. Mary Naomi laughed and clapped her hands.

With Sylvie's anger draining away, the landscape was regaining color, sound, scent, and warmth, until she finally could sense its hushed serenity and power. She could almost feel the presence of her ancestors, and of distant family members, surrounding her and her daughter in spirit. It was the river; it had always been the river, the course connecting their lives. Mary Naomi came near, taking her hand and edging into her solitude.

"*Ma petite fille*, it is time for me to tell you an important story. This is about our family, starting with your ancestor Anne Le Ber, a *Fille du Roi*. She was, above all, a brave young woman. She traveled far across the ocean to a new land, and she married a soldier there on the edge of the wilderness."

"Look, Mama!" A shimmering blue dragonfly hovered at her daughter's eye level, a foot away, watching her with the same fascination she was showing toward it.

"I'll write down the story for you when we get home," Sylvie said. And she knew the idea was right. It was time to commit the story to paper, with a copy in French and a second in English. And she might add the stories of several other women, such as her own mother. Given time, and if she lived long enough, she would add her own story. This way, her children would know their traditions and values. With that knowledge, they could fashion new outcomes for their part of the tale, even venturing farther west and trying again if that was what they wanted.

She would warn them to step more gracefully upon the land, to leave slavery behind, and to build good relations with Indians who would tolerate settlers nearby. The land here in Texas was so bloodied and so locked in inequality that . . . Sylvie was shocked by the drift of her thoughts. They could have done it right, here. But was there still time?

She felt certain Andrew would survive this battle and return to her. And then they would have their own peace to make. He had taken her into his heart and helped to create the loving relationship, home, and family where she truly belonged.

As she told Anne Le Ber's story to her daughter, in little pieces that kept pace with their stroll along the river, she realized that Anne's story—as well as Paschal's, and Amy's, her parents', Andrew's, and even her own—were at heart about crossing not just land and water but also the lines of religion, culture, language, and even race in the grand adventure of loving people truly different from oneself.

"Our family's stories can help us live well," she said to Mary Naomi, who nodded solemnly, then broke free to chase another dragonfly. By tomorrow their lives might be very different from today, and this risk was going to continue. She would survive by ensuring her children had a way to live and to leave, to seek new land where they might build a more ideal way of life, and to ensure firm ties of love. Beyond that, they would take the story into themselves and refashion it with their own challenges, risks, attachments, and conclusions.

She could go peacefully back home, now, and await their fate.


Sylvie was out in back for some time, throwing leftovers to the pigs, gathering eggs in the henhouse, and pulling fresh vegetables from the garden. She returned to the kitchen to work, Mary Naomi shadowing her steps, hanging onto her skirt, a table leg, or a chair, as needed.

Somehow, she missed seeing Andrew take Zeus to the back, wash at the pump, and come inside to look for her. She was sorting eggs at the counter, her back turned, when he said, from the doorway, "There you are."

She whirled around, so startled that she gazed at him as if he might be a ghost.

"What's wrong? I'm sorry, I didn't mean to frighten you."

"You're alive. And you're well, and all together?"

"Hardly a scratch." Andrew took a few steps toward her, opening his arms. "And it was a big victory, a major rout. They won't attack again for a long time."

"Your brother and father?" Sylvie remained standing by the counter.

"They are fine, too." He paused for a moment. "My father is clearly past his prime for fighting that kind of battle. I think he saw it, though he might not admit it. But I'll talk to him—and Jesse, to make sure he doesn't ever get signed up again."

Sylvie allowed herself a small smile.

"My brother conducted himself well. He followed orders, kept his head, didn't take too many chances."

"And can he ride fast and shoot well?"

"He can. Probably better than I can, now. It was actually lucky that he guarded my back a few times." Andrew gave a wry smile.

"Thank goodness; then I guess we'll have more time in the future to see what happens, how this plays out."

"Sylvie, I did hear what you were saying—I did listen. But my father's big dream of having us all fight together was too far along for me to stop it. I promise you now, though, my dear wife, that I will never go along with that again."

Mary Naomi, sensing her mother's mood, had stayed by the table, clinging to a chair leg. With Sylvie not coming to him, Andrew squatted and opened his arms to his daughter, who toddled across the floor, her little toes tripping behind her outstretched arms.

"Look at her, walking all alone! When did she start doing that?"

"Just now, to get to you."

"Sylvie, I'm going to hold to the promise I have made to you. It's a solemn vow that I will keep."

"I trust that you will."

"And I may be adding a few more rules to my list about going off again at all."

Andrew straightened, detaching Mary Naomi's arms and letting them wrap around his knees so he could reach toward Sylvie. She approached him, and as their eyes met and held in a current of love and hope, she closed the distance between them.

# Afterword

THIS WORK OF FICTION HAS BEEN INSPIRED by the lives of real people, many of whom appear with their names and accurate accounts of family events such as births, marriages, and deaths, plus historical events such as wartime battles and business ventures. For example, dates and events in James Kerr's life are historically accurate, as these provide a framework for Sylvie's story.

But the key characters are fictional because I had to create so much of their daily lives—dress, habits, appearance, values, and conversations. These include Sylvie's half-siblings Jeanne and David; her husband, Andrew; the servant Amy; and her friends in Texas, notably Rachel Flint; Armand Fulshear, Annette, and members of the Kerr family. Andrew is based on William H. Magill, an early colonist in Bastrop (Mina), and events in his life are accurately represented because they form the basis of Sylvie's marriage and family life.

The fictional Sylvie is my attempt to fill blank stretches in the life of my grandmother five generations back, Marie Rebecca Pensoneau. Records show she was born sometime between 1816 and 1818 into the traditional French community of Cahokia, Illinois. Her parents died before she was four years old, and she next appears on historical accounts when she marries in Bastrop in 1838.

I've long wondered how she got to Texas, and why she chose William Magill, especially when the marriage outside the Catholic Church apparently prompted her relatives in Illinois to disown her. She is included in the *Daughters of the Republic of Texas, Patriot Ancestor Album,* with her family name spelled "Pensana," indicating she probably arrived before the area won independence from Mexico in 1836.

Rebecca died in her early thirties, either in 1848 or 1849. In spite of extensive searching, I've never discovered the cause of death or where she was buried. She gave birth to seven children, and several migrated with their families to the West Coast, becoming pioneers themselves.

These few facts are the basis for the fictional Sylvie Pensoneau, a young woman who comes of age during tumultuous times and finds her way through wars, financial collapse, slavery, colonization, and contested cultural traditions in her struggle to make a place for herself in life, find love, and impart enduring values to her children.

While conducting research that stretched from archives in Québec City to the files of the Historical Society in Bastrop, I found abundant material documenting the men in the real Rebecca's life, particularly her father, Etienne Pensoneau; her husband; her uncle by marriage, James Kerr; and her niece's husband, Vital Jarrot.

Yet the woman herself has remained elusive, like a painting with the background filled in but only an outline where her face would appear. This novel is spun from that collision of abundant information with the basic absence of it, and if its publication prompts more information to appear about Rebecca and the other women who shared her world, it will be a wonderful and welcome outcome.

As Sylvie tells her young niece the story of their ancestor the *Fille du Roi*, she says to remember the details, for men's stories get written down, but women's don't, and it is up to us to remember all the names, places, and dates. *Sylvie's Chance* is my effort to do that.

Readers interested in the family's French Canadian background, and the lives of the Magills in Texas, will find more information and photos at my website, www.CarolynDale.com/familyhistory  A memoir by Ella P. Jordan Dale, *Life on the Farm for the Seven Jordan Sisters, 1890-1919*, tells about Magill descendants settling in early Washington state and is available as an e-book.

# Sources

Several books about the 1830s and 1840s brought the era alive for me by providing essential details of ordinary life, including dress, food, music, games, household implements, chores, social customs, and even popular gossip or stories. One is a family history compiled by Ella P. Jordan Dale and her daughter Barbara Dale Thompson.

For Illinois, key books include Brink, McDonough & Co.'s *History of St. Clair County, Illinois*, Carl Ekberg's *French Roots in the Illinois Country*, and the two memoirs by the governor and US Congressman John Reynolds. Reynolds knew many of the people who appear as characters in this novel.

For Texas, John Holland Jenkins' *Recollections of Early Texas*, and Noah Smithwick's *Evolution of a State* also vividly portray people who are characters in the novel; both lived in the Bastrop area, and Smithwick himself appears as a character in *Sylvie's Chance*.

**Illinois**

Alderfer, William K., Ed. *The Blackhawk War, 1831-1832*. Vol. 1, Illinois Volunteers, Ellen M. Whitney, Ed. Galvorro, Ill. Illinois State Library Collections of Illinois State Historical Society, 1970.

Ambrose, Stephen E., *Undaunted Courage: Meriwether Lewis, Thomas Jefferson, and the Opening of the American West*. New York: Simon & Schuster, 1996.

American State Papers, Public Lands, Vol. 2, Duff Green Edition, (pages 132-4). National Archives. www.archives.gov

Armstrong, Perry A., *Black Hawk War: with Biographical Sketches*. Springfield, Ill.: H.W. Rorker, Printer and Binder, 1887.

Babb, Margaret E., "The Mansion House of Cahokia and its Builder, Nicholas Jarrot," Transactions of the Illinois State Historical Society for the Year 1924.

Baldwin, Carl, *Echoes of their Voices*. St. Louis, Missouri: Hawthorn Publishing Co., Inc., 1978.

Bateman, Newton; Paul Selby; Charles A. Parkridge, Ed.s, "Vital Jarrot," *Historical Encyclopedia of Illinois*, Chicago: Munsell Publishing Co., 1914.

Bond, John W., *The East St. Louis, Illinois, Waterfront: Historical Background*. Office of Archeology and Historic Preservation, National Park Service, 1969.

Brink, McDonough & Co., *History of St. Clair County, Illinois*. Philidelphia: Corresponding Office, Edwardsville, Ill., 1881.

Brink, W.R. & Co., *History of Madison County, Illinois, with Biographical Sketches of Many Prominent Men and Pioneers*. Edwardsville, Ill., 1882.

Christian, Shirley, *Before Lewis and Clark: The story of the Chouteaus, the French Dynasty that Ruled America's Frontier*. New York: Farrar, Straus & Giroux, 2004.

Donnelly, Joseph P., S.J., "The Founding of Holy Family Mission," *In Old Cahokia*, John F. McDermott, Ed. St Louis, Missouri: St. Louis Historical Documents Foundation.

East St. Louis Action Research Project, *Social History Project*. eslarp.uiuc.edu/ibex/archive/

Ekberg, Carl, *French Roots in the Illinois Country: The Mississippi Frontier in Colonial Times*. Urbana and Chicago: University of Illinois Press, 1998.

England, Jerry, Ripples from La Prairie Voyageur Canoes, "Paschal Pinsonneau–Fur-trader, and interpereter with the Kickapoo Indian Nation." laprairie-voyageur-canoes.blogspot.com/2017/12

Freedom Trails 2 Legacies of Hope, "Slavery in Illinois," East St. Louis, Ill.: African-American Tourism Development.

Gray, John S., *Custer's Last Campaign: Mitch Boyer and the Little Bighorn Reconstructed*. Lincoln, Neb: University of Nebraska Press, 1993.

Hirsch, Arnold R. and Joseph Logsdon, Ed.s, *Creole New Orleans: Race and Americanization*. Baton Rouge: Louisiana State University Press, 1992.

"History of French Village Precinct," St. Clair County Genealogical Society, Illinois. stclair-ilgs.org/1881fr.htm

Holy Family Church, Cahokia, Illinois. records: pilot.familysearch.org

Illinois Census for St. Clair County, 1818 and 1820.

Illinois Waymarking, Pensoneau-Caillot Pioneer House. waymarking. com/waymarks

Ingalls, Sheffield, *History of Atchison County*. Lawrence, Kansas: Standard Publishing Company, 1916.

Jackson, Donald, Ed., *Black Hawk Autobiography*. University of Illinois, 1955.

The Jarrot Mansion website, jarrotmansion.org

Jetté, René. *Le Dictionnaire généalogique des Familles du Québec; des origines à 1730*. Montréal: Presses de l' Université de Montréal, 2003.

Johnson, Simone Amadeil, *The French Presence in Kansas 1673-1854*. David Dinneen, Ed.  kuscholarworks.ku.edu

Jones, Velma Loiuse Pensoneau and Donna Flood, "Pensoneau Family." electricscotland.com

"The Lincoln Log, A Daily Chronology of the life of Abraham Lincoln," Lincoln Sesquicentennial Commission and the Abraham Lincoln Association.  Government Printing Office, 1960. thelincolnlog.org

Missouri State Archives, St. Louis Circuit Court Historical Records Project, Freedom Suits Case Files, 1814-1860. stlcourtrecords.wustl.edu

Parrish, Randall, "The Battle against Slavery," *Springhouse Magazine*. accessed April 2010.

Pensoneau, Paschal, Statement to Geroge Remsberg, Secretary of Manuscripts Department, Kansas State Historical Society, 1883.

Quillivic, Bernard; Marguerite Lafontaine, Gérald Ménard, Jocelyne Nicol-Quillivic. *Les Filles du Roy 1663 à 1673*. migrations.fr/700fillesroy.

Reavis, L.U., *Saint Louis: the Future Great City of the World: with Biographical Sketches*. C.R. Barnes, 1876.

Reiss, Tom, *The Black Count: Glory, Revolution, Betrayal, and the Real Count of Monte Cristo*. New York: Crown Publishing, 2012.

Reynolds, John. *My Own Times, Embracing also the History of My Life*. Illinois, 1855; also: *Pioneer History of Illinois*. Belleville, Illinois: N. A. Randall, 1852, 2nd Edition, 1887.

Roell, Craig H., "John J. Linn," Texas State Historical Association Handbook Online.

Schmidt, Elizabeth and Sarah Schmidt, "Descendants of James Wells," *Little Wells*. homepages.rootsweb.ancestry.com

Scott, Franklin William, "Newspapers and periodicals of Illinois, 1814-1879." Thesis for Ph. D., English, Collections of the Illinois State Historical Library, Vol. VI, University of Illinois Library, 1903.

Seuss, Adolph B., *The Romantic Story of Cahokia, Illinois*, May 1, 1943. East St. Louis Area Research Project. eslarp.uiuc.edu/IBEX/archive.

Snyder, John Francis, *Adam W. Snyder and his Period in Illinois History 1817-1842*. Virginia, Ill: E. Needham. Second Edition, 1906.

Stevens, Frank Everett, *The Black Hawk War, including a Review of Black Hawk's Life*. Chicago: Frank E. Stevens, 1903.

Stroughmatt, Dennis, "Old Mines Music," Archaeology Archive interview, June 17, 2004. archive.archaeology.org

Tonguay, Cyprien, unpublished notebooks of Cahokia records, at Le Centre de Référence de l'Amérique Française, translation by the author and archivist Peter Gagné, visit May 25, 2010.

Verney, Jack, *The Good Regiment: the Carignan-Salières Regiment in Canada, 1665-1668*. Montreal; Buffalo: McGill-Queens University Press, 1991.

Voyer, Larry. *Voyer & Bedard Family History and Ancestry*. larryvoyer.com/genealogy

Walton, W. C., "Chapter V. Early American Settlers of St. Clair County," *Centennial History of McKendree College* 1928. www.rootsweb.ancestry.com.

Zochert, Donald, "Illinois Water Mills, 1790-1818," Journal of the Illinois State Historical Society, 65: Summer 1972.

**Texas**

Barr, Alwyn, *Texans in Revolt: The Battle for San Antonio, 1835*. Austin: University of Texas Press, 1990.

Bass, Caroline B., "Calvin Boales," Texas State Historical Association Handbook Online.

Bastrop County Clerk Returns File Number 000001, and File Number 000005; also, "Record of Claims" for William Magill.

Bastrop County Historical Society Museum, Bastrop, Texas. Vertical files: 609 Pecan Street; William Magill; Orgain Mansion. Visit April 16, 2012.

Billingsley, Jesse, article, *Galveston News*, Galveston, Texas: Sept. 19, 1857. Herzstein Library, San Jacinto Museum. www.sanjacinto-museum.org.

Brown, Henry L., *The Indian Wars and Pioneers of Texas*. Austin: L. E. Daniel, 1880. texashistory.unt.edu/ark

*Burnet Bulletin*, "Death of Capt. W. H. Magill," (obituary) Dec. 11, 1878. Doris Ross Johnston, "Our Texas Family," Rootsweb.ancestry.com

Cantrell, Gregg, *Stephen F. Austin, Empresario of Texas*. New Haven: Yale University Press, 1999.

Census of 1850 for Bastrop County, Texas, entry for "McGill" (pages 186 and 187) and for Travis County, entry for "Vandever."

Cox, Mike, *The Texas Rangers: Wearing the Cinco Peso, 1821-1900*. New York: Forge Books, 2008.

Crain, James Kerr, "A Texas Family," Sons of DeWitt Colony Texas, 1957.  tamu.edu/faculty/ccbn/dewitt

Dale, Carolyn, "William H. Magill," Texas State Historical Association Handbook Online, November, 2013.

Debo, Darrell, *Burnet County History: Family Histories, Vol. II*. Burnet, Texas: Eakin, 1979.

Dixon, Sam Houston and Louis Wiltz Kemp, *The Heroes of San Jacinto*. Houston: Anson Jones, 1932.

Fulton, Lora Magill, "Capt. William H. Magill," *Daughters of the Republic of Texas, Patriot Ancestor Album, Vol. 1*. Turner Publishing Co., 1995.

General Land Office "Abstract of Land Claims," entries for Capt. William H. Magill. Galveston: Texas Comptrollers Office, 1852.

Gooch, Fanny Chambers, *Face to Face with the Mexicans*. New York: Fords, Howard & Hulbert, 1887. www.archive.org

Gray, James D. "Robert McAlpine Williamson, 'Three-Legged Willie.'" *Texas Ranger Dispatch Magazine*. texasranger.org/dispatch/backissues

Gwynn, S.C., *Empire of the Summer Moon: Quanah Parker and the Rise and Fall of the Comanches, the Most Powerful Indian Tribe in American History*. New York: Scribner, 2011.

Hardin, Stephen L., "James Kerr," Texas State Historical Association Handbook Online.

Ivey, Darren L., *The Texas Rangers: a Registry and History*. Jefferson, North Carolina: McFarland & Co., Inc., 2010.

Jenkins, John Holmes, III, Ed. *Recollections of Early Texas: The Memoirs of John Holland Jenkins*. Austin: University of Texas Press, 2008.

Jillson, Willard Rouse, *A Chronology of John Magill, Kentucky Pioneer and Historian*. Louisville, Kentucky: Standard Print Co., 1838.

Kemp, Louis Wiltz, "William Harrison Magill," *San Jacinto Sketches*. Herzstein Library, San Jacinto Museum. sanjacinto_museum.org

*Kentucky Gazette*, issues for June 1836, online, kdl.kyvl.org/catalog

Magill, John, *The Pioneer to the Kentucky Immigrant*. Frankfort, Ky.: James B. Marshall, 1832.

Magill, Robert M., *The Family Record*. Richmond, Va.: Magill Publishing Co., 1907.

"Masonic Lodge in Burnet," Ancestry.com/boards for Burnet County, 1878.

McKeehan, Wallace L., Ed., Sons of DeWitt Colony Texas. Biographical entries for Esther Berry, James Kerr, Shade and Anis, and family. www.tamu.edu/ccbn/dewitt

Mitchell, Anita, "Cemetery to receive historical marker," *The Highlander*. Marble Falls, Texas, Oct. 24, 1985. (photocopy)

Mitchell, Anita, "Historical marker given to cemetery," *The Highlander*. Marble Falls, Texas, Oct. 31, 1985. (photocopy)

Moore, Stephen L., *Savage Frontier: Rangers, Riflemen, and Indian Wars in Texas, Vol. I, 1835-37*. Denton: University of North Texas Press, 2002.

Niemeyer, Stephanie P., "Magill, James P.," Texas State Historical Association Handbook Online.

Pioneers Monument, Burnet, Texas, 2006. texashistory.unt.edu

Rogers, Weldon Wayne, *Greener Pastures, from the Tidewater to Texas and Beyond*. Marietta, Georgia: 1996. Family History Archives, tripod.com

Smith, Zachary F., *The Battle of New Orleans*. Louisville: John P. Norton & Co., 1904. Also: *The History of Kentucky*, 1886.

Smithwick, Noah, *Evolution of a State or Recollections of Old Texas Days*. Austin: University of Texas Press, 2003-2010. lsjunction.com/olbooks

Utley, Robert M., *Lone Star Justice: The First Century of the Texas Rangers*. New York: Oxford University Press, 2002.

Yoakum, H., *History of Texas from its first settlement in 1685 to its Annexation to the United States in 1846*. Two volumes, New York: Redfield, 1856.

Zimmerman, June; Lucille S. Craddock, and Ralph Smith, "Logan Vandeveer," Texas State Historical Association Handbook Online.

## About the Author

CAROLYN DALE has worked as a journalist, editor, and university professor and is now writing fiction and essays. *Sylvie's Chance* is her second novel. She lives in Bellingham, Wash., and is emeritus associate professor in the Journalism Department at Western Washington University, where she taught writing and editing courses for nearly thirty years. She enjoys gardening, cooking, traveling, and hiking on nearby Mount Baker.

## Additional Works

Author: *Second Rising, A Novel* (Cairn Shadow Press) 2020.
Co-author, with Tim Pilgrim, *Fearless Editing: Crafting words and images for print, web and public relations* (Taylor & Fancis) 2015.
Editor, *Life on the Farm for the Seven Jordan Sisters, 1890-1919*, A Memoir by Ella P. Jordan Dale (Editing Works) 2018.

www.carolyndale.com • www.cairnshadow.com